The Cornish Gift

By Angela Tibbles

A Little Yarmouth Mystery

COPYRIGHT

ISBN: 978-0-9865830-2-5

To Alan: my editor, webmaster, fiercest critic,
greatest cheerleader and all-round partner in crime.
Love always,
A.

Author's note:

The town of Little Yarmouth is fictional. It is based on the countless small towns across Ontario which share its pioneer history and vibrant spirit. If you are lucky enough to live in one of these communities, you live in Little Yarmouth.

Angela Tibbles was born in London, England and emigrated to Canada in the 1970's with her husband, Alan. They have lived in Bowmanville, Ontario ever since. Over the years, they have shared their century home with many beloved cats and dogs. Angela maintains a lively interest in genealogy, antiques, local heritage initiatives and choral singing.

Your feedback would be greatly appreciated.
You can rate the book at
https://www.amazon.com/review/review-your-purchases#. Or, please visit Angela's website at www.littleyarmouthmysteries.com where you will find information and pictures of Little Yarmouth and details of Rosie's next adventure, "Old Sins".

Contents:

Chapter 1 - The Funeral

June 23, 2000
Little Yarmouth, Ontario

There was no escaping the fact; St. Jude's was the ugliest church in Little Yarmouth. Built in 1957 of grey angel brick, it was the end result of much lengthy and contentious debate among the members of its parish council.

The structure began well enough, with an unremarkable mission style frontage blending neatly into the streetscape, (a style selected on the advice of local builder and council member, Pablo Alvarez). A good choice, they had all agreed. Unfortunately, everything had gone downhill from there.

Mrs. Violet Chumley had stated unequivocally that *'a church is not a church without a spire'* and, as the Chumley family were contributing handsomely to the building fund, a tapering wooden spire was duly hoisted into place above the front entrance.

And what was a church without a bell tower, to ring the Angelus and call the faithful to Sunday Mass, asked council member Luigi Moscone, another reliable contributor to St. Jude's coffers.

His proposal was debated vigorously but, in due course, a square bell tower arose from the rear of the church, and Moscone Paving Services continued its generous support of church finances.

Now it was well known around town that Luigi was a sentimental man, who cherished many happy memories of his boyhood in the Tuscan hills. Consequently, no-one found it remarkable that even a passing glance at the impressive bulk and red campanile roof of "his" tower could always bring him to easy tears.

And he was not alone in this heart-felt response. Quite a number of his fellow parishioners blessed (or cursed) with more tender architectural sensibilities had also been known to shake their heads and shed a tear or two when viewing their parish church.

But on this particular Friday morning, St. Jude's architecture was the last thing on Rosie Rowe's mind as she hurried along Victoria Street toward the looming structure. Glancing at her watch, she picked up the pace and made for a side door. A large, hand written sign advised all-comers that they had reached; *ST. JUDE'S CHURCH OFFICE. 9:30 a.m. to 4:30 p.m. Monday, Wednesday and Friday. Closed 12:00 p.m. to 1:00 p.m.*

It was nine twenty-five. In a few brisk steps Rosie crossed the cramped space, raised the blind and plugged in her coffee-maker. Then opening the adjoining sacristy door, she dipped her fingers into the holy water stoup, blessed herself and went into the church.

As she knelt in the nearest pew, she closed her eyes and tried to concentrate on giving thanks for another day. It was going to be difficult, for sure; the Wesley funeral guaranteed that.

Tony Wesley had died suddenly and, in church parlance, decidedly "unprepared." Rosie was of a generation that remembered the days when a Funeral Mass would have been out of the question, given the late Mr. Wesley's lack of church attendance. But times had changed, and it was now considered more appropriate to assume that every deceased had received the grace of perfect contrition, just before drawing his or her final breath.

As the unfortunate Tony's final breath had been taken at the bottom of his basement stairs, whence he'd fallen drunk and insensible, Rosie had her doubts. But she hoped the Mass would be of some comfort to his family although, knowing several of them as she did, she doubted that as well.

The sacristy door swung open and Rosie opened her eyes to see housekeeper Liz Curtis stride in purposefully, mop and bucket in hand. As usual, Liz's tall, spare frame was buttoned-up in a baby-blue polyester overall, and Rosie wondered how she could work so energetically, wound up in the equivalent of a full torso plastic wrap.

Maybe that's why she stays so thin, her thoughts ran on, rather like those weight-loss body suits advertised on late night T.V.

"Morning, Rosie. Asking for strength are ya? We're gonna need it today for sure! Thought I'd have a quick wipe through before that stuck-up bunch arrives – don't want old Ma Wesley looking down her nose and thinkin' I don't keep things up to scratch."

"Hi Liz, how are you doing?" Rosie murmured. "Yes, I think it's going to be quite a to-do. Just hope everyone stays civil."

She watched Liz attack the altar steps with a vigour that reflected the state of her temper this morning. The Wesley and Curtis families had been at odds since 1964, when Tony Wesley had admitted fathering the unborn child of sixteen year old Lucy Curtis.

Although Tony had done the "decent thing" and walked Lucy down the aisle, neither family had greeted their union with enthusiasm. No sooner had the young couple departed St. Jude's for their reception, than an all-out brawl had started on the church steps.

Depending on which family version you heard, Lucy, virtuous and innocent, had been despoiled by Tony, the town ne'er do well. Or in the Wesley version, Tony, kind-hearted and trusting, had been trapped into marriage by a conniving slut, intent on marrying up.

Well, all water under the bridge now, thought Rosie. Tony and Lucy had stayed together for thirty six years, until death, via the basement stairs, had parted them. They hadn't stayed long in Little Yarmouth as a married couple. Within weeks of the wedding they moved to Sault Ste. Marie, where Tony found work in the steel mills. Quite a come-down for Mike Wesley's only son, heir to the Wesley Mill and General Store.

And for thirty-six years, Tony had steadfastly refused to come back; not even when Mike Wesley's famous temper brought on a fatal stroke. The day after *that* funeral Tony's mother, Clodagh, had moved into her husband's office and taken over operations. Now almost eighty, she still ruled with a will of iron and was universally disliked.

Liz finished her impromptu cleaning and went back into the rectory, the sacristy door closing behind her. Its soft *thump* drew Rosie's attention back to the day's schedule. She hurried back into the office and reviewed her work; a stack of bills to sort through and next week's Sunday Bulletin to finish. Thank goodness she didn't have to sing at the funeral today. With a bit of luck she'd get most of her paperwork done before the mourners started coming with donations or for Mass cards.

Rosie usually sang at funeral Masses, but Clodagh Wesley had asked that her granddaughter, Monica, sing today instead. Recalling Monica's last choral offering in church, Rosie gave a brief shudder. She didn't like *"Amazing Grace"* at the best of times, but sung too slow and off-key it resembled a Latvian dirge! And as that occasion had been a wedding, Monica's rendition had been particularly grating. Hopefully, all the assembled guests had been tone-deaf.

Not for the first time, Rosie wondered why, with such a wealth of beautiful music available, *Amazing Grace* was endlessly trotted out to baptise, marry and bury St. Jude's parishioners. 'If they play it at my funeral, I'll climb out of the casket and run down the aisle,' she said to herself.

The next two hours flew by. It was a surprise to hear the organ begin *Sheep may safely graze* and realise that Tony Wesley's final visit to St. Jude's was imminent. With one eye on the clock Rosie worked hurriedly, her goal of completing the Bulletin in sight.

"I'm just goin' through," Liz's head came around the Sacristy door. "Tony may have been a Wesley, but he stuck by Lucy all these years, and that counts for somethin'." Of course, thought Rosie, Lucy was Liz's cousin by marriage.

"Sorry I can't come with you, but the phone's been busy all morning. Are Steve and the boys coming over?"

"Yeah, he's closed the garage for the morning." Liz sniffed, "Most of the family will turn out. Lucy's pretty cut-up about things, and none of them Wesley's have called her, nor nuthin'." The door closed abruptly.

Oh dear, thought Rosie, I hope there won't be another fight on the church steps. The extended Curtis family was large in number, and its men folk generally large in size. She went back to collating the Bulletin, but curiosity finally trumped concentration.

Switching the phone to voice mail she got up and went through into the sacristy. Turning right, she hurried down the interior corridor to the church vestibule, up a short flight of stairs and into the choir loft. The organist, Loretta O'Halloran, gave a little wave as Rosie crept quietly behind a pillar and looked down into the church. It was almost full; no-one in the parish wanted to antagonise Clodagh Wesley by being noticeably absent. No matter that she never said a kind word about her son for thirty-six years, the proprieties must be observed.

Tony Wesley's coffin sat in front of the altar, on the wheeled trolley Mason's Funeral Home now used in place of pall bearers. Masons were sticklers for tradition but, as Dave Mason had said, after a heavily overweight pall bearer dropped dead half way down the aisle last year, "even funerals need to move with the times."

The general comment in town was that Mason's had done alright, with a second funeral following hard on the heels of the first; the unfortunate pall bearer had been on borrowed time anyway, what with his weight, the cigarettes and the drink. But Dave had felt the whole episode cast the funeral home in a very unprofessional light, and had promptly purchased an "Extensional Church Trolley." Since then, the processional and recessional hymns at every funeral had been accompanied by a discreet descant of metallic squeaks.

Near the front on the left side of the church Rosie could see Liz, her husband Steve and their two strapping sons. She recognised Tony's widow, Lucy, sitting in the left front row with her parents Agnes and Roy Curtis. Next to them were several younger people unfamiliar to her. Clodagh Wesley was sitting in the right front row, with her daughter Carmel, son-in-law Patrick Myles, granddaughter Monica and several others. All the Wesley's were in deepest black. A brief glance across the congregation showed Rosie that the great divide between families had transcended death, and everyone was clearly observing the rules.

The Mass moved along briskly. Father Matthews reached the Offertory Prayer, and Marg O'Halloran played the introduction to *Amazing Grace*. As Monica stepped forward to the side altar and picked up a hand mike, Rosie made for the stairs. *AAAA MAAAZING GRRRRAAACCE* echoed through the building. Good grief, what an appalling racket, she thought, scurrying back to the relative peace of the office. It's enough to wake the dead.

It took another thirty minutes to finish up the Bulletin. Better skip lunch today, Rosie thought regretfully. No point closing up when people will be coming for Mass cards, right after the funeral. As she picked up the phone to dial home, the office door opened and a short, red-headed girl with a toothy grin bounced in.

"Hi, Auntie Ro, who's getting buried? There's cars all round the block."

"Mr. Wesley, you don't know him. I was just going to call to say I'm stuck here, and you should make your own lunch." Rosie smiled at her eleven year old niece. Moira had that effect on everyone, with her cheery voice and naturally sunny disposition.

"Gussie got out, and I had to chase him right down Albert Street, before he stopped to sniff at a lamppost. So, as I was practically here, I thought we'd come all the way and walk back with you." Moira opened the door, to reveal a chubby beagle panting on the step, his leash tied to the adjacent bicycle rack. "Can I bring him in, he's really pooped."

"Alright, but not for long. The funeral's nearly over, and when people start coming through with donations Donny and Seel might show up, too."

Rosie was fond of the rectory cats, Dominic and Cecilia, and enjoyed their frequent visits. But the cats' congeniality evaporated at the mere hint of anything canine, and she could imagine the pandemonium if a beagle and two cats squared off in her tiny office. As Gussie sidled across the room, she took the saucer from beneath her teacup and filled it with water from the bottle on her desk.

"Hi baby, are you thirsty? Did you take off on Moira; what a bad lad." Gussie licked her hand, and looked up adoringly. "Here you go, have a nice drink." She put the saucer on the floor and, straightening up, scrunched the beagle's velvet ear gently in her hand. Gussie drank noisily, then sank down with a sigh and laid his head on his paws.

Moira was riffling her fingers through the stacked Bulletin sheets. "Can I help with anything, Auntie Ro?"

Recognizing the signs of imminent boredom, Rosie said; "Well, you can start typing those envelopes for the bill mail out, if you like." She moved her chair further to one side, leaving space for another chair in front of the typewriter.

Moira pulled up a chair and sat down. "Honestly, when is Father going to get a computer in here? This thing's positively ancient!" She pushed an envelope into the roller. "If you had a computer, you could just print off labels for everything."

"Father doesn't feel the expense is justified," said Rosie, with the merest twinge of conscience. "I manage perfectly well with the Remington."

In truth it was she, not Father Matthews, who was reluctant to update St. Jude's office systems. Last November, the Diocese had organized a two day conference for its priests and parish staff; *Embracing the New Millenium; how technology can further our mission in the parish and the world.*

Rosie was in a complete fog for the entire two days, but Father Matthews had been the quintessential duck taken to water. By Christmas he had a computer in his study and by Easter St. Jude's had its own web-site. Several times, he had offered to show Rosie how she could use the computer for "word processing," but to no avail. So, with his typical kindness, he just continued to give her his letters and homilies to type.

Moira and Rosie worked on, their companionable silence broken only by Gussie's snores and the Remington's friendly "clack, clack." About fifteen more minutes elapsed before the sacristy door opened abruptly, and Rosie caught a snatch of *Lord of the Dance.* So it's all over, she thought. Well, there's nothing like jogging the coffin down the aisle to cheer everyone up. Heaven forbid that anyone should actually *mourn* at a funeral. No, let's all have a really jolly time. What were funerals being called now in more secular settings? A Celebration of Life? For goodness sake, a funeral is meant to be a public expression of grief, and the right music is so important. Try grieving for someone who just disappears, and there was no funeral because they're only dead when the law says so …

"Auntie Ro!" Moira's voice cut into her thoughts. "Mrs. Curtis was asking if you'd like something from downstairs."

"Sorry Liz, I was miles away." Rosie looked up to see the housekeeper standing by the door. "An egg or cheese sandwich would be really nice, thanks for asking."

"It's just close family to the cemetery, so the rest are all goin' downstairs for the 'freshments. And I figured you'd be stuck here, doin' donations." Liz blew her nose loudly. "Poor Lucy, she's just beside herself; at least she don't have to sit in a car with Ma Wesley. Do you know, that old (Liz struggled to find an epithet suitable to the company and location) *madam* sat on the right side of the church and then pushed up to be first for communion, ahead of Lucy and her kids. Father was that embarrassed, he didn't know which way to look." Liz's tight grey curls quivered with indignation; yes, the Curtis/Wesley feud was definitely alive and well. "Do you want somethin' too, Moira?"

"No thanks Mrs. Curtis; I think I'd better take Gussie home. I'm going over to Chelsea's for a swim this afternoon, and I don't want to just shut him in and leave." Moira was very soft-hearted where animals were concerned. Rosie thought that Gussie would probably be glad of a quiet nap, after his uncharacteristic gallop down Albert Street. Although only two years old, he would far rather snooze in the sun than go for the long walks that were needed to keep his weight in check.

"Suit yourself, hon. I'll be back in a few minutes, Ro." The sacristy door closed with its characteristic thump.

Moira picked up Gussie's leash and clipped it to his collar. "I'd better get going, Auntie Ro," she said. "C'mon Gus, wakey, wakey, let's go."

"Be sure you eat something before you head over to Chelsea's" Rosie replied. "You could open a can of soup, or there's salad and cheese in the fridge. Don't go without anything, it's not good to swim on an empty stomach."

Her niece sighed and rolled her eyes. "Yes Auntie Ro." She opened the office door, "Oh my gosh, there's crowds of people out here."

Rosie stood and went to the open door. She could see Mason's hearse pulled up at the side of the church, with Tony Wesley's coffin on the trolley beside it. Out front, two black limousines were parked at the curb. There seemed to be a lot of pushing and shoving on the church steps, and she could hear Clodagh Wesley's imperious voice raised over the hubbub; "Let us through, get out of the way. I said, move out of my way!"

Gussie whined and strained at the leash to get out. Recognizing the signs of a full canine bladder, Rosie weighed the undesirability of a large, yellow puddle on church premises against a possible canine/feline encounter. Deciding, she said "Moira, go through the inside corridor instead. You'll be able to get out the side door and miss all this crowd. Watch out for Donny and Seel though." Another loud whine. "Be quick, I think Gussie needs to go. I've got to drop the Bulletin off for printing on the way home, so I'll see you around five. Thanks for all the help with the envelopes."

"No problemo, Auntie Ro, see you at home." With a quick wave Moira disappeared through the Sacristy door, an eager Gussie tugging on the leash ahead of her.

About ten minutes later Liz came back with two sandwiches and a glass of lemonade.

"What was all that going on outside?" Rosie asked.

"Oh well, a few of the boys were just havin' a smoke and a bit of a chat on the steps, ya know, after Lucy and the kids got into the limo."

"Oh, yes." said Rosie "And I don't suppose that keeping Clodagh Wesley out of the first limo had anything to do with the length of their chat, do you?"

"Now Rosie, how could ya think they'd be doin' such a thing?" Liz smiled and winked. "Well, I've gotta get on; Father's visitin' the old folks at the Lodge this afternoon, so I'm gonna make a start on his study. It's just covered in dust and cat hair." Liz wasn't a fan of Dominic or Cecilia who, with typical feline contrariness, were forever weaving around her legs, purring loudly.

The afternoon passed quickly, with a steady stream of parishioners and locals coming in for Mass cards or to make donations to Bibles for Lepers, the family's designated charity. The choice surprised Rosie, who couldn't imagine Tony Wesley caring about either bibles or lepers, but maybe it was important to Lucy or her parents.

At four twenty-five, she gathered up the draft Bulletin sheets and outgoing mail, covered her typewriter and put her waste basket and chair up on the desk, ready for Liz to come in and vacuum.

When Rosie started as church secretary six years earlier she had offered to keep the office dusted and vacuumed, thinking to lighten the housekeeper's load. But Liz had seemed miffed at the offer, and she heard later that Steve's auto body shop was struggling, making every hour's work at the rectory an economic necessity for Liz. So, although Steve's finances had long since improved, she still left the dust bunnies to Liz.

There's another week done, she thought as she closed and locked the office door. The sun was warm on her back, and she could smell the cherry blossom from the trees lining the church path. Spring had come late this year and, although it was almost the end of June, the trees were still a mass of pink. Fallen petals on the path made her think of confetti; such a lovely tradition, banned now, like so many others in the name of efficiency. No doubt the kill-joys on the parish council would ban cherry blossom too, if they could.

Rosie loved to walk, and drove her elderly Buick as little as possible. In good weather she walked the three blocks from her home on Cedar Street to the church, four times a day on workdays; there and back, plus a round trip home at lunchtime to take Gussie out. There was also a round trip on Saturday and Sunday to sing at Mass. Like Gussie, she needed to walk to keep her weight in check, although lately she seemed to be losing the battle. Not every pair of pants she put on could have shrunk in the wash!

She turned right and headed up Victoria Street. It would take about fifteen minutes to get to King Street and drop off the Bulletin sheets at the *Little Yarmouth Clarion*. The Clarion was a local institution. First published in 1860 it remained a fierce independent, still in the hands of its founding family, the Robertsons.

Everyone in town subscribed to the weekly, which had survived into the new millennium by catering to local pride and nostalgia, while efficiently diversifying into large scale printing. Every birth, marriage and death in Rosie's family had been reported in the Clarion, starting with the death of her great-great-great grandmother Ann Louise Cornish in 1870.

Nathaniel and Ann Louise Cornish had emigrated from Norfolk, England in 1850. Accompanied by their four children and Nathaniel's unmarried sister Charity, they were among a larger group of emigrants to come to Canada under the settlement campaign of John Galt's Canada Company. Rosie and many other present day inhabitants of Little Yarmouth could proudly trace their ancestry to Canada Company pioneers, hardy folk who'd braved the bitter winters and fierce storms of Huron County to carve out a better life for themselves and their children.

Victoria Street was a tree-lined, eclectic mix of old and new buildings, its only jarring note being the squat, brick bulk of Memorial Hospital. 'How many times have I walked up this street?' Rosie thought, as she dropped her bundle of envelopes into the mailbox on the corner. Other than four years spent in New York at Juilliard and the years of her ill-starred marriage, she'd lived her whole life in Little Yarmouth. Twice she'd left home for good, once for a shining career and once for the promise of love, and both times fate had brought her back.

Deep in thought, she was almost surprised to reach the double wooden doors of the Clarion office. She entered to a familiar *jangle*; the shop bell that had announced every visitor to the paper since 1860. And the office would have looked much the same to visitors then, as it did to Rosie now. The original hardwood flooring, long oak counter, wooden shelving and brass light fittings were all still in place. The Robertsons were not big on change for changes' sake. Even the tin ceiling and pot-bellied stove were still in evidence, although she knew the stove's function had long since been replaced by central heating.

But a step through the door marked *private* at the rear of the office showed the operation in an entirely different light. Although the printing press (installed in 1949) was only the second in the paper's history, the rest of the room was given over to a large commercial Xerox machine and three desk-top computers, each with its state-of-the-art printer. No luddites at the Clarion!

"Well, hello there, Miz Cornish; got the Bulletin sheets for me, have you?" A short, bespectacled figure with thinning grey hair got up from a desk behind the counter. "Oh there I go again, its Mrs. Rowe now, isn't it? I'm sorry, getting real forgetful in my old age."

"That's alright, Mr. Robertson. Just call me Rosie, nearly everyone does, you know." Even as she said it, Rosie knew that Willie Robertson, the Clarion's proprietor, editor and sales manager for the past fifty-four years, would never call her by a diminutive. He was of the generation that believed any female over the age of sixteen must always be addressed by the proper honorific. "How are you keeping?"

"Doing fine, all things considered. It's been a busy week. I'll be glad when Sunday comes and I can get into the garden." Willie was always a strong contender in the vegetable competition at Little Yarmouth's Fall Fair. "Bulletins'll be ready as usual on Wednesday. Do you want to pick them up, or shall I send the lad round with them on Thursday?"

"No, please don't put Joe to any trouble." Joe Mackie, the Clarion's delivery "lad" was asthmatic, thin as a rail and at least fifty and Rosie lived in dread that one day he'd collapse in her office. "I'll come by around lunchtime on Friday; the bulletins aren't needed until Saturday."

Willie took a pen out of the pocket of his shapeless green cardigan and jotted down *customer to call noon Friday* on her order form. "Big funeral up at the church, today."

"Yes, Tony Wesley, Clodagh and Mike Wesley's son. Did you know him?"

Willie straightened up, removed his glasses and rubbed the bridge of his nose. "So that's who it was. Yes, I knew him alright. Damn fool broke his neck, didn't he? Can't say I was surprised, or sorry for that matter. He had a lot coming to him, that one." His tone sent an unexpected shiver down Rosie's spine.

For a moment she couldn't think of anything to say, and just stood looking at the old man. That Willie, usually so proper and non-committal, should not only speak vehemently ill of the dead, but also use the word "damn" in female company, was so out of character that words momentarily failed her. The silence was filled by loud ticking from an old Regulator wall clock; she'd never noticed before just how loudly that clock ticked. Finally, she managed to blurt out, "Yes, well, I'd better be going.

Moira's at home and she'll be wondering where I've got to."

Willie put his glasses back on and smiled at her. "Little lass still with you, then? When do her mom and dad get back?"

Feeling an absurd sense of relief that the strange moment had passed, Rosie said "A week Sunday. John had to go to New York for a medical conference, so they decided to make a holiday of it and tour around upstate for a few days." Why am I gabbling, she wondered, and paused for breath. "He really needed a good break; the practice just gets busier and busier. And it was their wedding anniversary while they were away. Poor Elspeth rarely gets to celebrate anything with John; he's always getting called out, so it's been a real treat for them both."

"You know what they say, like father like son. Your pa was just the same. Call him and he'd come, no matter how late or whatever the weather. Came out to my dear mother once, through a snowstorm. His loss was a great tragedy for this town." Willie took his glasses off again and wiped his eyes. "Funny we should be talking about that, the day Tony Wesley gets buried."

Rosie couldn't think what he meant, and she certainly wasn't going to ask him. She had no time or inclination for a trip down that particular memory lane; she just hoped Willie wasn't beginning to lose his grip. He was pushing eighty, after all.

"I really must be going, Mr. Robertson. I'll call for the Bulletins on Friday. Have a good day in the garden on Sunday; weather's going to be perfect." And with that she was out the door and hurrying home.

Chapter 2 – A Sleepless Night

It was ten past five when Rosie finally turned onto Cedar Street. Belying its name, the street was lined with sycamore and maple trees all casting their soft, dappled light onto the sidewalk.

The large houses at the Victoria Street end had been built late in the nineteenth century and featured lacy gingerbread, gothic windows and every style of fanciful cupola and turret. At age seven she had become convinced that the one with the largest turret was home to Rapunzel, and for a whole summer had crept out every evening after supper, hoping to see a handsome Prince climbing the maiden's long golden braid.

A glance down Cedar Street was a look at the development of Little Yarmouth's architectural and social history. After the imposing Victorian villas, with their large lots and sweeping lawns, came the more restrained Arts and Crafts houses of the early twentieth century. And beyond these, across Albert Street, were modest brick bungalows built in the thirties and forties, designed for the families of working men and returning veterans, all new to home ownership.

Rosie's family home was on the corner of Cedar and Albert. Constructed in 1925 the three storey brick house had been built for her grandfather, Dr. William Cornish, and had a low pitched roof, mock-Tudor gables and overhanging eaves. The porch was supported by sturdy brick pillars and surrounded by wooden railings. On the Albert Street side there was a separate entrance that had once led to the Doctor's waiting and consulting rooms, but now opened into a small self-contained apartment. Dr. Cornish and his wife Minette had raised five sons and two daughters in this solid home, and 64 Cedar Street had seen its share of joy and tragedy.

As she hurried up the path, Rosie noticed that Moira's bicycle was exactly where it had been at ten past nine this morning. Surely she hadn't *walked* all the way to Chelsea's house, right over on the far side of town?

Her first step onto the porch was greeted with joyous barking from inside the house. This was followed by the skittering of doggy claws on hardwood culminating in a loud *thump*, as Gussie's wild slide ended in his inevitable hard contact with the front door. As she put her key into the lock, the beagle's open mouthed face went up and down like a jack-in-the-box, ears flying, as he jumped in ecstatic welcome behind the door's etched glass panels.

"Hang on Gus, mom's coming" Rosie said as she struggled with the door handle. The door wouldn't open, and after a moment of frustrated rattling she saw that instead of unlocking it, she'd locked it again. The door was already unlocked. Now decidedly uneasy, she turned the key again, opened the door and braced herself for Gussie's onslaught.

Despite several courses of obedience training, Rosie had never been able to cure Gussie of the exuberant welcome he lavished on her, whenever she came through the front door. It made no difference whether she was gone four minutes or four hours, Gussie would hurl himself at her every time. At the back of her mind, she knew that her lack of success was because she secretly enjoyed these rapturous greetings. Who cared about scratched hardwood and torn pantyhose, when you could rely on a welcome like that?

"Alright, steady now, good boy." Rosie bent down to Gussie as she had been taught in obedience class, rubbing his neck and ears, and applying light pressure to his back. "Sit, there's a good boy; sit for mom." Gussie continued to dance around her; well at least he was getting some exercise. "Moira", Rosie called, "are you home?"

As if in answer to her question, Gussie turned and headed up the stairs. Rosie noticed his leash was lying on the floor just below the first step. "Moira, are you alright?" she called again, anxious now, as she hurried up behind the panting and rapidly slowing beagle. The guest bedroom door was ajar. Gussie pushed it open and, with one last herculean effort, heaved himself up onto the bed.

"Oh, hi Auntie Ro, I'm sorry, I didn't hear you come in. What time is it? It can't be five already." Moira sat up and swung her legs off the bed. She looked pale and exhausted, as if recovering from a nasty bout of the flu.

"Sweetie, whatever's the matter? Did you get sick at Chelsea's?"

"No, I never went over. I just felt really bad coming home and thought I'd lie down for a bit. I must have fallen asleep."

Rosie put her hand to Moira's forehead. The girl wasn't feverish, but she certainly didn't look well. "Have you got a headache or been sick? Does your tummy hurt, or anything?"

"No, none of that. It was...." Moira hesitated, "Oh, I feel really stupid; I just don't know how to explain things."

Rosie could see just by looking at her that Moira was genuinely upset. What could possibly have happened since lunchtime? She sat down on the bed and took Moira's hand. "You know you can tell me anything. It'll be alright, just begin at the beginning." Gussie moved over on the bed until he was sitting on Moira's other side and, from a combination of affection and exhaustion, leaned heavily against her.

Taking a deep breath Moira said, "Well, when we headed home I took Gussie out the side door, like you said, and Mason's hearse was right there. They were putting the coffin in the back and Gussie wanted to stop and pee, but I didn't want him to go there, it seemed wrong somehow, with the coffin and all. So, I was trying to pull him along by the side of the church, when all of a sudden I started to feel really weird. Like a big, black cloud had dropped over me and I'd never be happy again. And I thought I could hear someone whispering somewhere."

"Why on earth didn't you come back to the office?" Rosie asked.

"Gussie started to howl; it was awful, I've never heard him do that before. He was really pulling on the leash, and people were looking at us and before I knew it we were running down the road. I don't remember getting home; I just wanted to get indoors. I sat on the stairs to take off his leash and he was shaking all over. And then I realised I was shaking all over, too. I thought I'd feel better if I had a lie down, so we both went upstairs and I guess I fell asleep until you came home." Moira looked at her aunt, "Auntie Ro, I was so scared."

While she'd been listening to Moira's story, Rosie's memory had turned back to her twelfth summer, almost forty years earlier;

She'd been struggling to deal with the overwhelming grief of losing her beloved father and grandparents in a terrible fire the previous fall. So, when she began having vivid dreams about a small child trapped in a dark place her mother at first comforted her, assuming the dreams were part of a necessary grieving process. But the dreams persisted and began to invade her waking hours. She often heard a sad little voice, singing over and over 'Ding, dong bell, ding dong bell' and once, a whisper; 'It's me, Kitty, I want to be with my mommy...'" Weeks went by and Rosie's school work suffered. Her marks dropped, and she and her mother grew increasingly frustrated with each other; Rosie, because no-one would believe what she was saying and her mother, because she was angry at Rosie for "acting up," misbehaving just to draw attention to herself.

Finally, she stopped talking about the dreams and strange whisperings, deciding to ignore everything in the hope that life would go back to normal. But the dreams only intensified, she lost her appetite and became increasingly withdrawn and unhappy.

And then her Aunt Margaret came to Little Yarmouth for her first visit since the previous year's funerals. Her mother and aunt sat down for coffee in the kitchen, and Rosie was banished upstairs to do homework. But she'd lingered in the hallway, intent on hearing Margaret's reaction to her mother's complaints of how difficult Rosie had become, constantly making up stories about strange dreams and voices whispering to her. She was amazed to hear her aunt laugh.

"Mary, whatever's the matter with you? She's almost twelve; she's not making anything up, it's just the Gift. Surely Gerard explained about girls in the Cornish family, and their er… odd abilities?"

"When Rosie was born, he did say something about one girl in every generation having some kind of psychic talent. I just dismissed it as ridiculous superstition; we actually had quite a fight about it, I recall. Don't tell me you believe in all that rubbish?"

There was a long silence, and then her aunt replied; "Well, I rather have to, I'm afraid. You see, I'm the lucky recipient in my generation."

Rosie had heard her mother cough and splutter as her coffee went down the wrong way. Her aunt's chair scraped the floor as she got up to help, and Rosie had run upstairs as quietly as she could. She never knew how the rest of the conversation went, but a short time later her aunt had come upstairs and gently told her that a soul in distress was reaching out and needed her help.

Far from being frightened, Rosie had been relieved that the dreams and whisperings had a logical explanation. Her aunt advised her that when she next woke up from the dream, she focus all her concentration on the little girl and ask her what she wanted.

It took several days, but Rosie was finally led to a long abandoned homestead nearby. She and her mother found the broken well cover, hidden by years of undergrowth. They cleared it as best they could and, pulling one half aside, they looked

down to see the gleam of a small skull and tiny white bones in
their flashlight's beam.

Local police forensics determined that the remains were
over fifty years old, and by a process of elimination identified
them as Katherine Marie Micheals, aged six, who had
disappeared in 1910. There had been a travelling carnival in
town when she vanished and it was assumed she'd been
abducted by a carnival worker. But no trace had ever been found,
and her parents had lived in hope that one day she'd come home.
By 1960 Katherine's father was long dead, and her mother was
close to death in Yarmouth Lodge Home for the Aged. She died
the day after she was told that Katherine had been found. Mother
and daughter were buried together, re-united at last.

So Rosie had a good idea of what had happened
to her niece. But it was not her place to tell Moira about
their family peculiarity, at least not before she had
discussed it with John and Elspeth. And maybe it was all
nothing, just nerves at being near a hearse and Gussie
being impatient to be fed. Even if things were as she
suspected, Moira might never have another such
encounter. Then an unpleasant thought struck her; if
Moira's experience was genuine, then Tony Wesley was
definitely not resting in peace.

Still holding Moira's hand she smiled
reassuringly; "I promise you, there's no need to be scared.
I'm here and Gussie's fine and, whatever happened,
everything's alright now. You've probably just picked up
a little bug, that's all. And I bet you haven't had anything
to eat since breakfast, have you?" Moira shook her head.
"How about you come downstairs and I'll make you a
bowl of chicken soup? That cures anything, you know."

"No thanks, Auntie Ro, I'm not really hungry."

Rosie persisted, "You must eat something, what
about some ice-cream? I've got strawberry, that's Gussie's
favourite, and if you have some you can give him a little
bit, too. He's had lots of exercise today, so a treat won't
hurt." Yes, there's my philosophy on dieting, she thought,

and anyone looking at me and the hound can see just how well it works!

But the thought of giving Gussie a forbidden treat worked like a charm. Moira smiled and stood up; "O.K, but I think I should give him his kibble first. He must be absolutely *starving,* I forgot all about feeding him, you know, when we got home." A shadow passed across her face. But Gussie had heard the magic word *kibble*, and was already off the bed and trundling purposefully toward the stairs. "Oh Gus, you're such a piggy," Moira called and laughing, clattered down the stairs after him.

Rosie took a few minutes to straighten the bedspread, and then headed down to the kitchen where Gussie was already crunching enthusiastically. He must be really hungry, thought Rosie, to be eating that diet kibble without complaint. Looking at her niece, she was relieved to see colour back in Moira's cheeks and marvelled at the therapeutic power of caring for a beloved animal.

The rest of the evening passed happily. Moira called Chelsea to apologise for missing their swim and to catch up, at length, on all the latest pre-teen gossip. Then Rosie, Moira and Gussie each had their ice-cream and walked four blocks, to try and undo some of the caloric damage. But walking that far gave them all big appetites so, throwing good nutrition to the wind, Rosie ordered a six-topping pizza, half veggie and half meat-lovers. Between the three of them, they finished off every morsel while watching one of the CD's Moira had brought with her for her two week stay.

Rosie tried not to think what Moira's mother and Gussie's vet would say about the evening's bacchanal. Elspeth and Dr. Katz were delightful people, but both were firm believers in the deadly properties of refined sugar and processed food, substances to be ruthlessly eliminated from human and canine diets. Both had given her stern instructions about the proper feeding of children and dogs respectively and now, standing as she did *in loco parentis*, Rosie felt decidedly guilty about her nutritional lapses.

As they tidied the living room before going up to bed, she said; "When you spoke to Chelsea, did you remember your dad said he'd call us tomorrow morning?"

"Yes, I'm not going over until after lunch, she's got to go shopping with her mom in the morning. It'll be great to talk to dad; and mom too, of course." (There speaks daddy's little girl, thought Rosie). "I hope they're having a good time. Do you think they've been able to talk to Bobbie, or will he still be stuck in the woods somewhere?" Moira's twin brother Robert was at a Wilderness Adventure Camp and phone calls were difficult.

Rosie heard the wistfulness in Moira's voice and knew she was missing her brother, although wild horses would never have dragged the admission from her. The two were fraternal, not identical twins, a distinction that was very apparent in both their appearance and personality. Where Moira was stocky, with the white skin and freckles that accompany red hair, Robert was tall for his age, with black hair and an almost olive complexion; he was definitely destined for heartbreaker status in five or six years' time. In personality too, they were entirely different. Moira was good natured, outgoing and inclined to over-optimism, but Robert was an introvert, given to moodiness and sulking. They were truly yin and yang, and a more perfect example of one egg splitting to create two opposite, but complementary, halves would be hard to imagine. Over the years, she'd often thought how both twins would have benefitted from a smidgen of each other's looks and personalities; just a little leavening out might have made the future a lot easier for them both to navigate.

"I'm sure they'll have spoken to him by now," Rosie answered. "Your mom told me that the camp sets up special times for parents to call during the two weeks. I bet

Bobbie's having loads of fun; probably hasn't washed for days."

"I can't think why anyone would want to live in a tent, with bugs and no hot water, or proper *toilet* or anything. I s'pose it's different if you're a boy. I'm just glad I didn't have to go, it's much nicer here with you and Gussie." Moira looked at the sleeping dog spread eagled across the couch, his head hanging over the edge. "Do you think he ought to go outside before we go to bed?"

"Yes for sure, or we'll be up in the middle of the night. Just open the back door; he'll wake up as soon as he hears the latch." But as she finished speaking the beagle's eyes opened, he rolled off the couch and trotted into the kitchen. Mind reading again, she thought, as they both followed and Moira let him out into the warm, scented night.

Crossing to the old fashioned porcelain sink, Rosie ran water into a glass; "Here's your water, sweetie. Go on up to bed, I'll wait for him, he's never very long, last thing. And don't forget to clean your teeth after all that pizza and ice-cream. I don't want your mom blaming me if you get cavities." She gave her niece a kiss; "God bless, sleep tight", and Moira answered as she went back through the kitchen into the hall;

"And don't let the bed bugs bite. 'Night, Auntie Ro."

Rosie sat down at the pine kitchen table; it was already old when her grandparents brought it with them to their new house in 1925. She had eaten countless meals on its battered surface, sat here with her crayons, her homework, and later with a bottomless coffee pot, cramming for high school exams.

Watching the moths and June bugs batting at the screen door, she remembered her relief when John told her that Robert had decided to try wilderness camping, in preference to spending two weeks with his sister and aunt. She loved her nephew and was proud of his musical talent (he was a gifted pianist), but she would have had no clue how to keep him entertained for two weeks. And she had little patience with his moods; his mother might excuse his temper as being "highly strung," but Rosie thought he was just self-absorbed and rude. I bet camp life's come as quite a shock, she thought and grinned to herself.

Gussie was soon scratching at the screen door to be let in. "Quick Gus, don't let the bugs in" she said, as he dawdled on the threshold; "come on, time for bed." And boy, will I be glad to see my bed tonight, she thought. This whole day has been a bit *off*, somehow. The funeral, Willie Robertson, Moira; everyone's behaviour has been out of kilter. The only person who ran true to form was Clodagh Wesley, just as miserable and selfish as ever. All that money and no joy in anything; couldn't even be kind to her daughter-in-law on the day she buried her husband.

She turned off all the lights, checked the locks on the front door and climbed wearily up the stairs. Moira's door was closed and no light showed beneath; good, she's gone straight to sleep, no lingering shadows from this afternoon keeping her awake. By the morning the whole episode might be forgotten; maybe she wouldn't even bother telling John about it.

Rosie's bedroom window was open, and a soft breeze was blowing through the screen, billowing the curtains out like little sails. Gussie jumped up on the bed, and a with a deep sigh stretched himself full length along the bottom. " Well, I guess you've had another tough day" she said, stroking his head and wilfully ignoring Dr. Katz's admonition that dogs must *never* be allowed on the bed, it was bad for discipline.

She fell asleep immediately and soon drifted into a dream so familiar that it was almost as real as her waking life: *She was standing on a jetty looking up-river, waiting for David. The evening was drawing in, and she could hear loons calling across the water. Why was he so late coming home, surely he's just around that bend in the river? The sun had almost set now and she was cold. Where are you David? He must be coming now, it's nearly dark, and he never stays on the river after dark.........*

"Auntie Ro, Auntie Ro, please wake up," someone was shaking her. "Auntie Ro, there's something in my room."

Rosie struggled to open her eyes and, still disorientated, tried to concentrate. She sat up and reached for the light over the bed. In its sudden illumination she saw her niece standing next to her, shivering despite the warm night and with tears on her cheeks. "Moira, whatever's the matter? What time is it?" Answering her own question she looked at the little bedside clock; 3:00 a.m. Why do nightmares always wake us at 3:00 a.m.?

"There's something in my room, Auntie Ro. I don't want to go back in there; can I stay here with you?"

"Well, of course you can sweetie, but what's in your room? Is it a mouse or a spider or something? I can easily catch it and put it outside." Rosie didn't believe in killing things just because they looked ugly or scary. Even flies were never swatted or sprayed, just shooed out through a door or window.

"No, it's not bugs or anything. I woke up freezing cold so I got out of bed to get a blanket from the closet. But when I opened the closet door I could see behind me in the mirror, and there was something misty moving in the corner of my room. And I could hear that *whispering* again. I started to feel the way I did this afternoon outside the church, really down and sad. Then Gussie started scratching at the bedroom door. It sort of woke me up, so I just opened the door and ran in here to you."

So, Rosie thought, this afternoon was a genuine experience after all and Moira's brought a little friend home with her. Time for some damage control, and then, tomorrow, a long talk with John and Elspeth.

"Well, there you are then. You said you woke up, so you were just having a bad dream. Too much pizza and ice cream, I expect. Tell you what, you get into my bed, and stay here with Gussie while I go along to your room and make sure there's nothing there. Alright?"

"But you're coming back here again, aren't you?" Moira asked anxiously as Rosie tucked her into the big double bed.

"Yes, of course I am. I'll be right back, sweetheart. You just stay here and take care of Gus."

Closing the bedroom door behind her, Rosie went along the corridor to the guest room. The door was open, and as she switched on the light she could see her breath hanging in the air. She went inside and closed the door firmly. The room felt deathly cold and it was hard to breathe, as if all the air had been sucked dry. In the far corner there was a faint, smoky outline and she went towards it.

"Tony Wesley, is that you? I want you to leave the child alone, she can't do anything; she's too young and doesn't understand yet. I know you need help, and I promise to do whatever I can. But you must leave Moira alone; if you frighten her like this she won't ever want to help anyone later on. Do you understand?"

The smoky outline intensified and seemed to grow taller and more menacing. "It's no good trying to scare me, Tony. If you want my help, you must do as I say. Leave Moira alone, and I'll start looking into things tomorrow."

A faint whisper came to her and then died away. "Not my fault, not my fault, not my fau ..." The room was warm again.

Chapter 3 – Family History

Rosie woke to bright sunlight and the sound of birdsong coming through her window. She looked at the bedside clock and was surprised to see how early she had wakened; it was only six fifteen. Moira was still fast asleep, as was Gussie, lying sprawled in his usual spot at the foot of the bed. Everything looked so normal that she was hard pressed to believe in the strange happenings of this morning's wee small hours, events which had culminated in her "conversation" with the recently deceased Tony Wesley.

Communicating with the restless dead was not a new experience for Rosie, and she was no longer disturbed by a spirit's ability to pop up where it was least expected. What did concern her this morning was how to deal with Moira's inevitable questions, and then how to determine what exactly was causing Tony Wesley to remain earthbound.

Taking care not to wake the sleepers, Rosie got out of bed, crept across the room and along the passageway to the guest room. She opened the door quietly and, going inside, could tell immediately that Tony's unwelcome presence was long gone.

The room had been her mother's and still reflected Mary's taste for pink roses, ecru lace frills and scatter cushions. The bedroom furniture was hers also, the mahogany tallboy and kidney shaped dressing table still standing exactly where she placed them forty years earlier.

In 1960, two weeks after Rosie's father Gerard died so tragically, Mary vacated the third floor bedroom she had shared with him, and turned it into a playroom for Rosie's younger siblings, Josephine and John. Then she moved into this room and occupied it until her death four years ago.

Although everything about the room was decidedly shabby, Rosie couldn't bring herself to redecorate. Left as it was, she could sometimes make-believe that her mother was just away briefly on a visit somewhere and would soon return, to be her daughter's comfort and mainstay once again.

Automatically, she began making the bed and generally tidying the room. She was pushing on the window to try and get it open when a sound behind her made her turn. Moira was standing in the doorway, looking in apprehensively.

"Morning, Auntie Ro."

"Morning, sweetie. Come on in, there's no bogeymen in here. Plenty of dust bunnies, though; maybe you could have a bit of a clean up this morning."

The window finally gave and a fresh, sweet breeze filled the room. Moira stepped inside, and looked behind the door anxiously.

Handing Moira her robe Rosie continued; "Here, put this on, we can't be eating breakfast in our pyjamas. Did you sleep okay? You and Gussie were dead to the world when I got up. I didn't want to wake either of you so I left my robe in the closet." Moira was still looking around the room and Rosie half expected her to get down on the floor, and look under the bed. "Come on, sweetie. You just had a bad dream and now its morning. Run and get my robe for me and we'll get breakfast started; Gussie's probably rattling his bowl already."

Finally satisfied that nothing sinister was lurking in her room, Moira put on her robe and went out the door. Returning with Rosie's robe she asked; "Can we make pancakes this morning?"

Ah, the resilience of youth, thought Rosie. She smiled; "Well, alright, but you've got to do the dishes." She put her arm around her niece and together they went down to the kitchen.

By the time the phone rang at ten o'clock, breakfast was over and they were both showered and dressed. Moira, her night-time fright forgotten, was out in the garden with Gussie and, as Rosie picked up the phone, she was still undecided how to broach Moira's experiences to her brother. "Hello?"

"Hi Rose, how's everything up there in God's back pocket?"

"Well, just fine thank you very much. And how are you enjoying the idle life? Where are you, exactly?"

"Somewhere in the Catskills. I think we've hit every antique shop and country craft emporium between here and New York City. You know how El loves that stuff."

"How was the conference?"

"Really great; I ran into two guys from my graduating class. Both specialists now, not like me, just a lowly country doctor." John laughed; they both knew how much he loved family practice. "And Fifth Avenue is still reeling from El's assault. You don't know the meaning of shop till you drop, until you've seen her in action!"

"Lot of pent-up demand John, El hasn't had a good shopping trip in years. Have you spoken to Bobbie? How's he enjoying camp?"

"Let's just say it's been a learning experience, and he'll be really glad to get home." They both chuckled. "Seriously, I think it's been good to shake him up a bit. El coddles him too much. We all know he's talented, but sometimes he's way too far off the ground, if you know what I mean. How's my girl doing?"

"Really well, we're having a great time. And she's loving being around Gussie…" Rosie hesitated.

"But? What's wrong, Rose?"

Rosie never could hide anything from her brother. She took a deep breath and told him about the funeral, Moira's fright outside the church and being terrified in the night by what she saw in her room. When she finished, she waited for John to say something. There was a long silence. Finally, he said; "Just what are you trying to tell me, Rose?"

"You know what I'm telling you, John. She's eleven years old, and she's the only girl in her generation of the family. Did you think she'd never experience anything like that, or were you hoping the Gift was going to skip a generation?"

"You're not far wrong. I guess I had my fingers crossed that it would show up on some other branch of the family tree this time. It's certainly complicated your life, and got you into some nasty situations. And it's been bad enough worrying about my sister chasing spooks, without starting to lose sleep over my daughter as well."

Rosie sighed; "Well, I've downplayed everything with Moira so far; do you want to leave it that way for now? What does Elspeth think? When Moira was born, you and El must have discussed the possibility that this would happen at some time."

There was another long silence.

"John, you have told Elspeth about the Gift, haven't you?"

"No, I haven't." John sounded defensive. "It was never the right time to bring it up. I mean, you fall in love with a girl and you ask her to marry you and then you say casually; *Oh, by the way, our family is descended from an eighteenth century witch, and in every generation one girl can talk to the dead.* I'm sure that would guarantee a fast trip somewhere, but it wouldn't be to the altar!"

"Don't exaggerate, Prudence Arnstruther wasn't a witch. She was a gifted healer with psychic abilities, and that's no different to having a talent for music or gardening or anything else."

"I think having visions, or talking to the dead is a bit different to growing prize marrows, Rose." John was starting to sound officious.

Rosie could feel her temper rising; "This isn't getting us anywhere. You're Moira's parents; it's up to you to decide what she should be told. But I think you should tell her soon; she was really scared yesterday and knowing the truth is always the best way to deal with any kind of fear."

John dropped his voice; "Yes, I know that. And, as you say, we're her parents, so just leave it with me to deal with at the proper time."

"Elspeth's there now, isn't she? Well, I know just how you're going to deal with it; you're going to duck the issue until it happens again."

"Rose, please, you have to trust my judgment on this." John took a deep breath; "Who was it came calling last night, by the way?"

"The recently deceased Tony Wesley. I warned him off; told him if he didn't leave Moira alone I wouldn't help with his problem. I don't think he'll bother her again. Do you know anything about him?"

"Name rings a bell." There was a pause, then; "No, I didn't know him; think I was in grade two at Holy Angels when he got married. The only reason I remember *that* is because I was a server at his wedding, along with Frankie O'Halloran. We had a great time watching the punch-up on St. Jude's steps, until old Father Carlisle came out to read the riot act. Frankie might have known Tony Wesley though; he's quite a bit older than me."

"Well, I have to make a start somewhere. I don't want Tony rattling around the church parking lot, or anywhere else Moira might run across him again. Anyway, I'll call her in; she's been dying to talk to you. By the way, you did remember she's going up to Aunt Margaret's cottage next week?" Rosie went to the back door and called; "Moira, your dad's on the phone."

"Yes, that's fine; she'll have a great time with all the cousins. Rose, I'm not sure where we'll be for the next few days, but you've got my cell number and we'll be back in New York next Friday, then flying to Toronto on Saturday. Should be home late Sunday night. Oh, and we've got tickets for *Phantom of the Opera* on Friday night. I'll see if I can get you a few pointers."

"Hah-de-hah-hah, very funny. Don't think I'm letting you off the hook on this, John. Take care of yourselves, here's Moira. Love to Elspeth," and she handed the phone to Moira.

"Hi, daddy, are you enjoying your trip……."

Moira's excited chatter followed Rosie as she went out onto the terrace, where Gussie lay stretched out panting, a soggy tennis ball between his paws. His tail wagged feebly, but he didn't get up. Rosie sat down next to him on the warm flagstones; "Poor old fellow, has Moira been giving you a workout?" Another feeble wag. She stroked him absently, her mind on possible causes for Tony's earthbound state. It was always unfinished business that held spirits fast, usually guilt over something left unsaid, or more often, left undone.

She remembered he had said *not my fault;* what was not his fault? Falling down the stairs? Perhaps the best place to start would be a visit to his widow, Lucy. She'd bake some muffins and make a condolence call after four thirty Mass today. She and Lucy had been in the same class all through school so, even though they hadn't been particular friends, her visit wouldn't seem out of place.

Her niece's voice came from the kitchen. "Daddy says bye." "Say bye for me" Rosie called back, as she stood up and crossed to the stairs at the edge of the terrace. Sitting down on the top step she leant back against the wall, and was soon lulled into drowsiness by the sounds of the garden busy all around her. The drone of bees in a flowerbed, the throaty cooing of two mourning doves, a gentle rustle of leaves; her head nodded, and she struggled to keep her eyes open.

It was night; the sky was bright with stars. She could smell burning… what was burning? Voices calling, shouting, flames crackling….

Rosie opened her eyes with a start to see Gussie pawing at her lap and whining. "Did I nod off, Gus? Not enough sleep last night, I guess. Are you getting hungry?" Gussie wagged his tail hopefully. "Come on then, time for kibble." Hearing his favourite word, the beagle turned and trotted toward the screen door. As she followed him into the kitchen, the words to an old nursery rhyme kept running through Rosie's head; *Have you seen the muffin man, the muffin man, the muffin man, Have you seen the muffin man that lives on Drury Lane?* I'd better make a start on those muffins, she thought, and then get lunch on the go.

Moira was talking excitedly on her little pink cell phone. She waved at Rosie, and putting her hand over the mouthpiece said; "Can I sleep over at Chelsea's tonight? Her mom says it's okay."

Rosie measured kibble into Gussie's bowl. "Is her mom there now?" she asked.

"Chels, can you put your mom on the phone? Yes, I *know* (the eyes rolled), but they're *always* like that. See you later. Oh hi, Mrs. Simons, my aunt wants to make sure it's alright for me to sleep over. She's right here," Moira passed the phone to Rosie.

"Hi Tracey, are you sure it's no trouble for Moira to stay over? Well, that's really nice of you; what time's good? Around two? Okay, I'll bring her over at two and pick her up tomorrow morning about ten thirty. Thanks so much; bye now." She handed the phone back to Moira who was pouring more kibble into Gussie's bowl. "Moira, he's had all he's supposed to have for lunch. Dr. Katz will give me another lecture on dog obesity if Gus hasn't lost a bit of weight by our next appointment."

"But he's *starving*, Auntie Ro."

"He's always starving." It was too late. The dog bowl was already empty, and Gussie was gazing up mournfully. When no more kibble materialized, he put his paw into the empty bowl and rattled it.

'I must get on with those muffins,' she said to herself. "How about you take him for a quick walk," she suggested to her niece; "get his mind off food, for a while. We'll have lunch when you get back.."

"Okay" Moira sighed, and trailed into the hall for the leash. "C'mon Gus, time to walk off some baby fat." Always ready to go anywhere with Moira, Gussie trotted happily after her. "Bye" she called and Rosie heard the front door close behind them.

Peace at last she thought, as she turned on the oven and gathered her ingredients. She enjoyed baking, and slipped effortlessly into the routine of measuring, mixing and filling the muffin pans. Why do Cornish men have such a hard time explaining the Gift to the women in their lives, she wondered? Her own father had raised it just once with her mother, on the day Rosie was born, and now she'd found out that John has never discussed it with Elspeth at all. And to make matters worse, he was intent on burying his head so far in the sand, that he was probably counting kangaroos!

As she worked on with the muffins, her mind turned to the events of forty years earlier, and to poor little Kitty Micheals, finally connecting with someone who could reunite her with her mother. Aunt Margaret had told her what to do then, and had later given her a dog eared copy of their family history, complete with a genealogical chart. She had been fascinated by the story and its explanation of how some of the Cornish women came by their strange talents.

In the Year of our Lord 1685, Sir Crispin Wyndham Cornish embarked from the family plantation on the Caribbean isle of St. Kitts, to take up his inheritance – the baronetcy and manor of St. Marsham Major in Norfolk, England.

He was accompanied by his lady, Elizabeth, and their five children.

Over the next nine years, the Lord blessed Sir Crispin and Lady Elizabeth with five more children, their family numbering three sons and seven daughters. As custom decreed that the entire estate must pass to his firstborn son, Crispian, provision was made that the second born, Guy, enter upon a military career and that the third born, Edmund, take up Holy Orders.

Edmund duly went to Oxford where he obtained his Master of Divinity and, in 1720, was ordained an Anglican priest. He returned to Norfolk, to the living of St. Beotulphs, which being the parish church of St. Marsham Major was in his father's gift.

He first laid eyes on Prudence Arnstruther at his second Sunday Communion Service. The church was as full as on the previous Sunday, all the village still being desirous of viewing their new Rector, the previous incumbent having been stooped and aged. Of a certainty, the unmarried, twenty-five year-old Edmund had set many female hearts a-flutter.

When he climbed into the pulpit to deliver the second sermon of his career, his glance fell upon one of the occupants of the third row of box pews. She was small, with the black hair, dark eyes and olive complexion of her Welsh ancestry. Unbeknownst to Edmund she was only thirteen years old. He was instantly smitten, to the point that he could barely remember the fine theological treatise he had planned to bestow on the assembled congregation.

During the following week, he began to make what he, foolishly, thought were discreet enquiries. He soon learnt that Prudence was the only daughter of Martin Arnstruther, a local yeoman with a small landed estate, and that she had three brothers. Much to the scorn of the villagers, Martin had married "away", his wife Mfanwy being Welsh, having been born on the Isle of Anglesey. He noted a strange reluctance among his parishioners to speak of Mfanwy, marked by dropped voices and furtive glances backward; as if afeard she might materialize behind them.

The following Sunday, after services, his father had accosted him in the vestry and instructed him that his interest in the Arnstruther girl was causing scandal in the village. "God's blood, sirrah" Sir Crispin had thundered, "Can you not find a decent wench to take your fancy?"

Bewildered, Edmund could only say that the Arnstruther family had owned land in Marsham for generations. What fault could his father find with them?

"Nought, until that witch Mfanwy charmed Martin Arnstruther into marriage" was his father's astonishing answer. "They're all devils' spawn and you'll not be pursuing that girl unless your ambition is to be a curate in the Marches. What's mine to give is mine to take away, so if you're desirous of remaining Rector of St. Beotulphs cast your eyes elsewhere for a wife!"

Edmund considered himself a child of the Enlightenment and, as such, gave no credence to the idea of witchcraft. But he was also his father's son and accustomed to obey. The living of St. Beotulphs was a rich one; rents and Great Tithes provided a generous income for the Rector and, with only 250 souls in his care, his responsibilities were not onerous. So, he heeded his father's words and tried to put the beguiling Prudence out of his mind.

Within the year, he had taken a suitable bride. Blanche Montgomerie had impeccable breeding and was of a gentle nature. So, if his eyes strayed to Prudence Arnstruther in church on Sunday, or followed her progress along the village street, he reminded himself that man's natural inclination is to sin and that all stand in need of redemption.

A year passed, during which he oft had occasion to recall his father's words about Mfanwy. She was never attendant at church with her family, and it was well known that she and Prudence were abroad on moonlit nights in the fields and forest gathering herbs. For all their fear, the villagers went to her with their ailments, and for love potions and charms to ward off evil. It was also said that she could foretell the future, and increasingly Edmund found himself reluctant to pass her in the street.

Then, after two years of marriage, Blanche was brought to bed of a child. After a day and night labouring in agony she delivered their son, Arthur, who lived only long enough to be baptized. Blanche took the infant in her arms, closed her eyes and died.

Edmund's grief was deep, but its true cause was the guilt he felt in that he had never loved Blanche. He vowed never to re-marry, a vow he kept for eight years.

In 1730 his father died, and the baronetcy passed to Edmund's oldest brother. On the morn after their father's burial, Crispian rode to the parsonage and told his brother that, should he ever wish to quit his celibate state, he was content to allow him the bride of his choice.

Edmund lost no time in petitioning Martin Arnstruther for his daughter's hand. The banns were announced at St. Beotulph's on three consecutive Sundays (each time to a ripple of murmured disapproval from the congregation) and on a fair May morning in 1730, Edmund Cornish and Prudence Arnstruther were finally wed.

When their few guests had left the parsonage, Prudence looked at him with her great, dark eyes and said; "I knew on that Lord's Day ten years past that we would be married. Mother had seen it. She says we will be happy, but not for long."

For five years, Mfanwy's prophecy held true. Edmund and Prudence were indeed happy – they were blessed with three children; Eleonor, Arthur and Giles. The villagers came to love Prudence for her healing touch and gentle counsel, and they loved Edmund for her sake. And if, betimes, she had strange knowledge that a bad storm was coming, or that a child's birth was imminent, or   a sick villager would live or die, nothing was made of it. Her mysterious gifts were used only for good, and to the benefit of all.

In the summer of 1735, there was no rain for three months. Crops failed and a goodly number of the villagers fell ill with the sweating sickness. Prudence and Mfanwy gave of themselves unstintingly, but were soon overwhelmed by the multitude of sick and dying. By September when rain finally came and the sickness had run its course, Prudence had poured out her spirit until there was nothing left to keep her soul anchored to the earth. Frail and weak, she took to her bed and no amount of loving care from Edmund and Mfanwy could save her.

In the dawn light, with the gentle sound of rain falling outside the window, Edmund held her hand and wept. "What shall we do without you, my love" he whispered.

Prudence smiled, "Be comforted dearest, for I shall never be far away, and all will be well in Marsham, which will have a healer in its midst for three generations." Then she asked for Eleonor to be brought to her bedside. Putting her hand on the little girl's shoulder she said; "And I promise to be present in every generation of our daughters. This is my gift to our descendants and to the family of my beloved Edmund." Then her spirit fled.

Chapter 4 – Lucy's Story

The muffins turned out well and were cooling on the counter when Moira and Gussie came in from their walk. Gussie made a bee-line for his water bowl and drank noisily, lapping more water onto the floor than into his mouth. Before he could trail wet paw prints across the kitchen Moira tore off some paper towel and wiped the floor, then plunked herself onto a chair; "It's so hot outside that Gus didn't want to go far. We just sat by the creek for a bit and then he went in after a duck. No chance of course, I think the ducks were all laughing at him. Wow, it's gonna be *spectacular* swimming at Chelsea's this afternoon."

Rosie looked up from washing greens for the salad; "I bet. What would you like in your sandwich, hon? Chicken or cheese?"

Moira picked up a muffin and started nibbling at the edges. "These are really good. Cheese sandwich please, Auntie Ro. I'm thinking of going vegetarian, like you."

Oh great, thought Rosie, I can just imagine John and Elspeth's comments about that. For all her sister-in-law's commitment to healthy eating, she had no qualms about sinking her teeth into large chunks of red meat, or expressing her negative opinion of Rosie's views on eating dead animals. First the Gift, now vegetarianism; they'd probably never let Moira stay over again.

Smiling at her niece she replied; "That's a great idea, sweetie. But you might want to wait until you're a bit older, you know. Right now your bones and muscles and everything are still growing, so you need lots more protein than I do. Remember, I didn't become vegetarian until I was in my thirties." Definitely time for a quick change of subject. "Do you think you ought to run upstairs before we eat and get some things together for the sleep over?"

After lunch, she drove Moira across town to Chelsea Simons' house, which was on the same street as Moira's home. The girls had known each other since kindergarten, and had been best friends all through Holy Angels Elementary. This fall they were starting at St. Michaels together, an event both were anticipating with a mixture of excitement and dread.

It had been a struggle getting Moira organised for the sleepover; *did she have her pyjamas? Yes, clean undies? Yes, toothbrush? No, something tidy to wear for Mass tomorrow morning? No.* Rosie wondered how parents managed to keep ahead of everything and felt a new respect for Elspeth who had not one, but two, eleven year olds to keep on track, day-in and day-out. No wonder she needed a rest.

When Rosie finally pulled up outside the Simon's house Chelsea was waiting for them, and the two girls greeted each other with loud shrieks and hugs, as if they'd been parted for a year, rather than a week.

Arrangements were made for Rosie's pick-up time on Sunday morning then, with a quick kiss, Moira disappeared into the house. Rosie drove to the I.G.A for groceries, (it was incredible how much food they were getting through) then hurried home. She needed to be at St. Jude's by four to review the music she was singing at Mass today.

She rather dreaded the four-thirty Mass on the last Saturday of each month; it was a Folk Mass, so the music was more suited to singing around a camp fire, than singing in church.

For some reason, the diocese thought that music of the sixties and seventies was irresistible to younger members of the parish. So, once a month, Father Matthews put on his home-spun vestments, took out a wooden chalice and paten, and swayed along to *Michael, row the boat ashore* with the rest of his congregation.

Despite her dislike of popular music in church, Rosie always made an effort to sing enthusiastically at the Folk Mass. This was mainly to encourage Kevin and Star Bright, a teenage brother and sister who came to play the guitar and tambourine accompaniment. Kevin and Star were both at St. Michaels, Kevin in grade eleven and Star in grade ten. They were really nice kids, and Rosie hoped their commitment to playing at the Folk Mass would spark an interest in more challenging sacred music.

At 4:00 p.m. Rosie parked her car in the lot at St. Jude's, and went toward the side entrance of the church. She wanted to check for any sign that Tony Wesley was still lingering at the spot where he and Moira had connected yesterday, and was relieved to sense nothing untoward. Spirits were frequently unreasonable in their expectations of how quickly she could move them on, and being unreasonable often translated into being angry.

She had come to understand that the dimension in which they were trapped existed outside normal linear time, so hours, days, even years made no impact on their consciousness. As far as Tony Wesley knew, it could have been fourteen years, rather than fourteen hours since he had communicated with Rosie in her guest room. The thought of desperately unhappy souls being held fast in this timeless limbo always struck her as immensely sad.

There were not many at Mass, but it was usual for Saturday attendance to drop off in the summer with parishioners away at family cottages or busy in their gardens. Kevin and Star were their lively selves, strumming and rattling energetically through *Like a Sunflower, It's a Brand New Day* and *You are My Friends,* while Rosie and the congregation struggled to keep up with Kevin's arbitrary changes in tempo.

The duo struck gold, however, with the recessional hymn. As soon as Kevin played the first bars of

We Shall Overcome (workers of the world unite, Rosie thought acidly) the congregation, relieved at last to hear a tune they recognised, rose eagerly and joined in with enthusiasm. Flushed with success and exertion, Kevin and Star played all six verses and choruses, stopping only when they realised the church was completely empty except for their mother, waiting patiently to drive them home.

At five forty-five Rosie went out through the side door, her ears still ringing from proximity to Star's tambourine. 'I know I'm a dinosaur' she said to herself as she got into the car, 'but really, there should be a law against tambourines in church. And *We Shall Overcome?* What's next – *Look for the Union Label?'* Consoling herself with the thought that the Folk Mass was only once a month, she pushed *Opera Gold* into the CD player and set about soothing her musical spirit.

Nessun dorma, nessun dorma… Placido Domingo serenaded her as the Buick bumped along Victoria Street toward King. No matter how many times she heard that beautiful aria, the music always brought tears to her eyes and an irresistible urge to sing along. Rosie often accompanied legends of the operatic world as she drove, a habit which brought curious glances from other drivers who could see, but not hear, her enthusiastic vocalising. Today it was Clodagh Wesley's daughter, Carmel Myles, who pulled up beside Rosie at the King Street lights where she was waiting for green, in full operatic mode. Carmel shot her a withering glance and pulled away with a squeal of tyres. "Oh grow up!" Rosie said aloud, and then demonstrated her own maturity by putting her tongue out at the rapidly disappearing Lexus.

Veteran's Avenue was a long terrace of small brick houses, six blocks north of King. Built in 1919 to house soldiers returning from the Great War the two-up, two-down properties were almost exclusively rentals, a fact reflected in their unkempt appearance.

Number 26 was one of the few exceptions. The tiny front lawn was neatly trimmed, red geraniums bloomed in a flowerbed beneath the window and the front door had been recently painted royal blue. A red mat proclaiming *Mi Casa es Su Casa* covered most of the cracked concrete step.

As there was already a car in the driveway, Rosie parked on the street. She got out, balancing her purse and the plate of muffins precariously, and walked briskly up the short driveway. She couldn't see a bell, but there was a small brass doorknocker shaped like a horseshoe so, lifting it, she rapped twice on the door. A few minutes passed, and she was just about to knock again when Lucy Wesley opened the door.

"Yes?" Lucy's voice was barely a whisper, her eyes puffy and bloodshot, and she was hugging a heavy blue sweater tightly round her body. Rosie knew wrenching grief when she saw it.

"Hi, Lucy. I don't know if you remember me; I'm Rosie Rowe, Rosie Cornish that was. We were at school together. I spoke to your mom this morning about stopping by." When Rosie called Lucy's number before lunch Agnes Curtis had picked up the phone, and after a brief word with her daughter, had said she would be glad to see Rosie later. But now, looking at Lucy, Rosie wondered if her visit was premature. "I'm really sorry to have disturbed you. Would you rather I came back another day?"

Lucy pulled a tissue from her pocket and wiped her eyes. Struggling to be polite she said, "No, please come in; I could do with some company. The kids left this morning, and my mom had to get caught up at home, so the house seems really empty." She looked back into the hall sadly.

Rosie handed her the plate of muffins; "I thought these might come in useful for visitors. It's a really good recipe, the muffins stay moist for ages and they freeze well, too. I made two dozen but my niece, Moira, got into them; she's got a sweet tooth, like me." I'm babbling, she thought as she followed Lucy into the chilly living room.

Lucy took the plate from her; "My kids were just the same; I couldn't keep baked goods in the house. Tone loved anything sweet, too..." her voice broke. She swallowed and, with an effort, continued; "Please, sit down. Can I get you a tea or coffee?"

Rosie sat down on a leatherette loveseat. "Whatever you're having" she replied; "can I help, at all?"

"No, the coffee pot's been on all day. I'll be right back."

Rosie looked around. The room was stuffed with furniture, not good quality but immaculately clean. A huge T.V filled one corner, with a leather recliner, EZ slide rocker and the loveseat grouped in front of it. There was a small fireplace with a two bar electric fire on the hearth. Rosie was very tempted to switch it on, (the room was frigid), but good manners prevailed. Instead she went over to the mantelpiece to see if she recognised anyone among the family photographs displayed there. She was looking at the picture of a young man in uniform when Lucy came back in, carrying a tray.

"That's our Dean" Lucy said; "he's in the Forces, a Search and Rescue tech. His dad was so proud of him when he qualified, although I worry about some of them dangerous places he gets into." She put the tray down on an outsized marble topped coffee table. "Cream and sugar's right here; will you have one of your muffins?"

"Only if you do," Rosie replied, remembering how grief shrivelled the appetite, and then lack of food made depression and exhaustion worse.

Lucy sat down next to her on the loveseat and reached for one of the coffee mugs. Wrapping her fingers around it she said; "I'm sorry, I just can't seem to get warm. It seems crazy this time of year, but would you mind if I turn the fire on?"

"Of course not" Rosie answered; "it is chilly in here."

"You feel it too, then? I thought it was just me." Lucy got up, went over to the fireplace and switched on the fire. Immediately, both bars began to glow red.

Rosie opened her mouth to answer, but felt her breath literally sucked away. Right behind Lucy, and towering over her, was a wavering grey outline, completely obscuring everything behind it. A pall of grief and sadness enveloped Rosie, and it took all her strength to focus the thought, '*Be patient, Tony. I haven't forgotten you.*'

The air seemed to clear and Rosie heard Lucy's voice coming from a distance. She said "Sorry, Lucy, what was that?"

"I was just saying, this house has been freezing for days. There, it seems warmer already. Amazing the heat these little fires can put out."

"Yes, it's really amazing. You mentioned your kids. How many do you have?"

"Just the two. There's Linda, she's the oldest. Only married a year; she's got her own hair salon back in the Soo. And then there's Dean of course, down in Trenton with the Air Force. He's not married yet, does have a lovely girlfriend, though. We told them both to get a move on with the grandchildren; Tone really wanted to be a grandpa." Lucy stopped abruptly and reached into her pocket for another tissue.

"I'm so sorry." Rosie was beginning to think that Lucy was too fragile for this conversation. Maybe she should leave and come back in a few days.

But Lucy wiped her eyes and carried on: "Well, it wasn't to be. And Linda's only twenty-eight, there's plenty of time for babies."

"Twenty-eight? But I thought..." Rosie spoke before she had time to think. Dear God, don't say they lost a child and I've opened up that wound, as well.

But Lucy was smiling, and Rosie caught a glimpse of the girl who had stolen Tony Wesley's heart: "Oh, you mean the shotgun wedding? Well, I'm afraid Tone and me weren't entirely honest about our, er...situation, back then." She paused to take a bite of muffin and drain her coffee mug.

Putting the mug down she continued; "We were crazy about each other, but my dad said I was too young to go steady, and Tone's parents thought us Curtis's were all beneath them. To break us up they enrolled him in one of those private colleges down in the States, so me and Tone decided to say I was pregnant. Lord, I'd never seen my dad so angry. First, he said he was going to kill Tony. Then he went storming up to the Wesley place and threatened to have the police on Tony for rape. Well, Mr. and Mrs. High and Mighty didn't like the sound of that one little bit, so they agreed a quick wedding was the best thing all round. And that's how we came to get married. Had to leave town pretty fast afterwards, though. Tony was barely twenty and the Wesley's would have had everything annulled, no problem, if they'd figured things out."

Rosie was speechless. One of Little Yarmouth's most enduring cautionary tales had just disintegrated in front of her, and she couldn't think of a word to say.

Remembering the subterfuge seemed to lift Lucy's spirits. She giggled and continued; "Me and Tone laughed about it for years; his mum and dad looking like thunder at the wedding, old Father Carlisle treating me like a fallen woman and then the fight outside the church. I did feel bad about lying to my mom, though. After we went up to the Soo I used to phone her every week, and she'd ask if I was okay, and was I taking my vitamins and when was the baby due. It was just awful. In the end I had to tell her the truth, and she was so upset that she wouldn't speak to me when I called home after that. It was ages before we made up."

Rosie at last found her voice; "But why didn't you come back when Tony turned twenty–one? Maybe the Wesley's would have come around; he was their only son, after all."

"I always thought we were coming back," Lucy answered. "We had a hard time up there at first, neither of us had any skills or work experience. Tony drove truck for a while and then it was just one minimum wage job after another. That's why we were so careful not to start a family for real; we both had to work just to pay the rent. After he was twenty-one, I'd ask him on and off about coming home, but there was always some excuse why we couldn't. And then finally he said he was never going to set foot in Little Yarmouth again, and that was the end of it. I don't know why, but by then he'd got the job at Algoma Steel, so life was easier moneywise. But he was always hung-up about Little Yarmouth, as if he was trying to shake something off. I used to think it was romantic; that it was all about how his parents had treated me, but as I got older I saw it was nothing to do with that. There was something back here he didn't want to be reminded of."

Lucy suddenly seemed drained, and her voice choked up; "Not that any of that matters now. You know, he was my one and only love, there'll never be anyone else....," and the tears started to run down her face. As Rosie reached to take her hands, Lucy leaned into her and started to cry, with sobs so deep that her whole body shook.

They sat together on the loveseat for a while, with Rosie's arms around Lucy, until her tears subsided and she began fumbling in her pocket for more tissues.

"Whatever must you think of me, Rosie?" she said, "This keeps happening over and over. I think I'm getting some control, and then it's like a switch turns on, and I start screaming and crying. I tried to keep it in while mom and dad were here, and the kids, but when I'm on my own I just howl at the walls."

Rosie understood only too well. Seeing Lucy's grief reminded her of the losses in her own life, and of months spent in a haze of tranquillisers, sleepless nights and exhausting bouts of tears and rage. But she also knew the house was full of Tony's negative energy, which was both fuelling Lucy's natural grief and feeding from it.

"Don't be silly; it's all part of coming to terms with such a dreadful loss. Anyone who loves you will understand why you need to cry." Rosie took her arms from Lucy and stood up. "Let me get you a glass of water, or perhaps another coffee, something to warm you up." She put the coffee mugs back on the tray and lifted it.

Lucy got up unsteadily; "Maybe a coffee would help. I'll get it, the kitchens in the back," and she made her way slowly into the hall, taking careful steps like an invalid afraid of falling.

Despite bright sunlight streaming through the door transom, the short hallway was dark and very cold. As she followed Lucy toward the kitchen, Rosie's glance fell on a doorway under the stairs. The door was closed, but it seemed to waver and tremble as she passed by and she felt a shock of misery, icy and dank as the tomb. 26 Veterans Avenue was not a good place for Lucy to be alone.

The kitchen was old, with shabby cabinets and a stained sink, but the walls had been freshly painted in soft primrose and blue floral curtains brightened the cracked windows. A wide table and four chairs dominated the room, too big in the small space.

Lucy had already filled two more mugs with coffee, so Rosie put the tray down, took the empty mugs over to the sink and sat at the table.

"I hate this house," Lucy said as she pulled out the opposite chair. "We tried to make it nice, but everything's falling apart and the rental agency doesn't care. Those windows were cracked when we moved in last year, but do you think they'll come and fix anything? Tony was always calling them, but he might as well have saved his breath." She took a long draught from her mug.

"What do you think changed his mind, about coming back here after all those years?" Rosie asked.

"An old friend offered him a job" Lucy replied. "Tony's lungs got really bad and the plant laid him off in ninety-five. He was just a year short of getting his full pension, so they paid him sick benefits until the year was up, and we thought we'd be alright. Then the company doctor said his breathing problems were caused by smoking, not work-related so he wasn't eligible for full pay-out. We applied to Workers Comp. but they turned us down as well, for the same reason. And who knows, maybe it was the cigarettes. I was working in a call centre then, so between my pay cheque and his little bit of pension we struggled on, but we were just getting deeper into the hole all the time. And then the call centre went off shore and my job went with it. We lost the house and were just about broke, when he said Dougie Ferguson at the bakery here had a job for a delivery driver and Tony could have it. So, we packed up and came back home."

Through all of her conversation with Lucy, Rosie had been listening carefully for any clue about what was keeping Tony earthbound. It seemed likely that he was carrying guilt for something that had happened before he and Lucy were married. Something that had prevented him from coming home for years. Finishing off her second muffin she said; "I bet your mom and dad were glad you came back to town. What about Clodagh Wesley? Was she happy to see Tony?"

Lucy sighed: "As far as I know, she never spoke to him. I made him phone when we first got into town, but she never called back. Pretty quick to take over the funeral, though, and pay for it all. I had no money to bury him so I can't complain; *he who pays the piper* and all that.

No offence Rosie, I know you're very involved at St. Judes, but me and Tone weren't much for church going. I'd much rather have buried him quietly from Mason's parlour, but I didn't have much say in anything."

That's Clodagh, Rosie thought. Wouldn't speak to the son who'd been away for a life-time, but quite ready to buy a fancy funeral, dress up in black and play the bereaved mother.

Lucy took another muffin and bit into it; "You're right, Rosie, these are really moist. Maybe I'll get the recipe and make some for ..." she paused, and a tear dropped onto her plate as she realised there was no-one to bake for anymore.

She blew her nose and continued; "Now, my mom and dad were just thrilled we came home. I'd missed them so much, and they never had a chance to see the kids growing up, just at Christmas or summer holidays. And dad's not well now, so it's good that I'm on hand to help out."

She paused to finish off her coffee; "It's so unfair. Things were looking up, Dougie was paying Tone such a good wage, that we finally had a bit of money left after the bills were paid. He'd even talked about us moving to a nicer place, and then, just like that, he's gone and everything's over. Tony was such a great guy, it's just not fair…" and she put her face into her hands and began to cry again.

Rosie came round the table and leant over her. "Lucy, I don't think it's a good idea for you to stay here by yourself. What about going over to your mom's? I could drive you."

Lucy raised her head; "Maybe you're right. I can't stand being in this place; it feels bad, somehow. Mom asked me to go and stay with them, but I thought if I had some time on my own, I could get things straight in my head." She blew her nose. "But now I don't want to be here when it gets dark, and it's so cold, I just can't get the place warmed up..." She lifted her head and brushed the hair out of her eyes. "You're right; I'll just put a few things in a bag and go over to my moms. Thanks for offering Rosie, but I don't need a lift, the car's right outside."

"Well, if you're sure I can't drive you, I should be getting home. My dog's been shut in for hours, and he's probably sitting by the door with his legs crossed by now."

Lucy laughed shakily as she got up and walked with Rosie to the front door.

Opening the door she said; "Thanks so much for coming over, Rosie. It's been great to see you, and I feel so much better for talking everything out. Sorry for bending your ear, though."

As she returned Lucy's hug, Rosie looked over her shoulder and down the hallway. A white vapour was gathering near the kitchen and, as she watched, its shape intensified enough that she could see a hand pointing to the door under the stairs. Then the image dissolved into nothingness.

"It was lovely to see you too, Lucy. I'm just sorry we didn't get together sooner, before all this happened, you know. Give me a call when you feel like company; maybe you could come over for supper one night next week? Now, promise that you're going straight over to your moms."

"Yes Rosie, I promise." Lucy smiled and gave Rosie another quick hug. She hesitated, then said slowly; "You're the only person I've said this to, but I've started wondering if there wasn't something funny about Tony's accident."

Here it comes, thought Rosie. "What do you mean, *funny*?"

"Everyone said he was drunk and fell down the basement stairs. Well, I found him when I came in from bingo, and yes, there was a smashed bottle of rye next to him. But Tony hadn't had a drink in twenty eight years, not since he got drunk on the job and nearly caused an accident. He went to AA after that, and never took another drink. And we don't keep liquor in the house, so I don't know where that bottle came from."

"But surely the autopsy showed whether he'd been drinking or not?"

"There wasn't an autopsy. I didn't think about it for days, I was so out of things, but my dad asked Dave Mason, and he said all he knew was that the doctor in the emergency room had signed off on accidental death. I wish now I'd insisted, because everyone's going to remember Tony as a drunk." Lucy's eyes filled up again with tears.

Rosie was becoming more certain by the minute that there was a lot more to this death than a simple accident.

"Would you like me to talk to my brother John about it?" she asked. Lucy looked puzzled. "Oh, you wouldn't know; John's a family doctor here in town. He was getting ready to leave for New York when Tony died, so he wasn't on call that night. But he knows all the staff at the hospital mortuary, so maybe he can get some information for you. He's away right now, but when he gets back I'm sure he'll do anything he can to set your mind at rest."

"Rosie, I'd be so grateful if he could. I know Tony wouldn't have been drinking; he was really cheerful when I left. Maybe someone came over unexpectedly and brought the bottle with them, not knowing that Tone didn't drink. And afterwards it got left behind and he decided to put it in the basement out of sight, and just missed his footing." Lucy looked at her hopefully.

The first part of that scenario is probably spot-on, thought Rosie, but I'm not so sure about the second. Trying to sound confident she replied, "That's sounds possible. If someone did come over, they'd know that Tony was sober when they left." She didn't add that, despite the Clarion's front page coverage of Tony's death, no-one had admitted to being with him that night

"Yes, you're right. We could put an ad in the paper, or maybe Clodagh would offer a reward for information...."

Shoot, publicity is the last thing we need right now, thought Rosie. She interrupted Lucy mid-flow; "She might, although I don't think it's very likely, do you? Look, why don't you let things settle for now? Wait until John gets back and we can see what he finds out."

Lucy was suddenly deflated. "Sorry Rosie, I'm really tired and I'm just not thinking straight. If there had been someone with Tony that night, they would have come forward by now, wouldn't they?" The unspoken thought hung between them, *unless that person had something to hide.*

Rosie took her hand. "I've got to go, and you need to get to your moms and have a good night's sleep. Be sure and call me next week." Lucy's eyes were bright with tears and she held tight to Rosie's hand. "Lucy, I know how hard it is to get through the days right now. And I'm not going to say it'll get better soon, because it won't. But I promise you, you will survive this and you will be happy again. Hang in there, sweetie."

"Thanks Rosie, I'll try." Lucy smiled through her tears, stepped back into the hall and shut the door.

Rosie put the key in the ignition and the old Buick coughed into life. She glanced at the clock on the dash; 7:30 already, she hadn't realised she'd been talking so long with Lucy. Other than a growing conviction that Tony hadn't fallen down the stairs because he was drunk, the visit had raised more questions than it had answered

She pulled away from the curb and drove along Veterans Avenue. If Lucy was to be believed and there was no liquor kept in the house, then someone had called on Tony and brought that bottle of rye with them. And in all probability, that person knew of Tony's youthful reputation as a heavy drinker, but didn't know that he was now a reformed alcoholic. So, had the bottle been brought innocently, or with the intent of staging an alcohol-fuelled accident? And if the accident had been staged, who wanted Tony Wesley dead and why?

As she drove slowly along Victoria Street, Rosie reviewed three possible reasons for Tony's inability to break free of his mortal life. *Distress that he had caused his own death by drunkenness;* depending on what John could discover at the mortuary, this cause might be easily remedied. *Anger, that someone had deliberately, or accidentally caused his death;* more difficult to fix, as someone would have to confess to their actions. *Guilt, related to a youthful secret so heinous that it had kept Tony away from Little Yarmouth for thirty-six years.* Considering this last reason, Rosie felt a familiar lurch in the pit of her stomach. Looking for long buried secrets was like turning over rocks in a garden – both activities always brought lots of unpleasant things crawling into the light of day.

It was a relief to turn onto Cedar Street and see her haven, number 64, standing solidly four-square on the Albert Street corner, its windows ablaze from the rays of the setting sun.

Since her mother's death in 1996 she had occasionally thought of selling up and moving to a smaller, more modern house. These thoughts usually surfaced in the winter, after several weeks of shovelling heavy snowfalls. But although she knew the house was far too big for one person, Rosie couldn't bring herself to let it go. It still represented all she knew of family and security and, as she'd said to John on more than one occasion; 'I'll probably be here until I'm carried out in a pine box.'

She turned into the driveway, and through her open window heard Gussie's familiar welcome, literally hitting full stride as he careened into the front door. It was impossible to disguise her arrival when she drove, but sometimes when she walked home she would creep round to the back door, hoping to save Gussie's nose from yet another collision.

Time was getting on, and she needed to call Tracey Simons and make sure all was well with the sleepover. She locked the car door (the Buick wasn't worth stealing, but she would hate to lose her CD's) and started up the steps to the porch. The front door rattled, as Gussie scratched at it excitedly.

Ten minutes later, he was in the garden and she was sitting on the sofa, an empty wineglass in one hand and the phone in the other. Tracey reported that Moira and Chelsea had been in the pool all afternoon, only getting out when the pizza was delivered, (Oh Lord, more pizza, thought Rosie. I must remind Moira not to mention that to her mom). They were down in the family room now, watching a "chick-flick." And, as the Simons' family were going to 11 a.m. Mass tomorrow morning, they would bring Moira, so there was no need for Rosie to drive across town to pick her up. Rosie thanked Tracey again for her kindness, and hung up.

She would never have admitted it, but Rosie was rather glad to have the evening to herself. Having lived alone since her mother died, she was surprised to find how tiring it could be to have another person constantly in the house. Although Moira was the dearest girl, Rosie wasn't used to children, or to planning activities and meals. With a sigh, she realised she was getting older and rather set in her ways. 'Now, if Gussie were a cat instead of a dog, I could almost qualify as an old biddy,' she said to herself.

How different life would have been if either of her great plans had been realised. The operatic career that vanished away before it ever started, and the marriage that ended in unresolved loss were both broken dreams that sent her home to Little Yarmouth.

Following her unexpected return from Juilliard her music teacher, Sister Mary Bernadette, had told her the

Lord must have other plans for her. She had thought those other plans were marriage to David, but events had proved this to be just another illusion. So now here she was, a part-time church secretary and cantor, living alone in her family's old house in rural Ontario. It seems the Lord didn't have very big plans for her, after all.

An insistent scratching at the back door announced that the old biddy's beagle wanted in. Rosie gave herself a mental shake; she really should know better. Thoughts of David always depressed her, and drinking on an empty stomach only made matters worse. Time to smarten up. She walked briskly into the kitchen, opened the door to an indignant Gussie and set about feeding them both.

*   *   *   *

Roy Curtis peered over the top of his newspaper as his wife came back into the room.

"That was Lucy on the phone. She's decided to stay with us, after all. Said she'd be over in about half an hour."

Roy gave a sniff of disapproval; "Finally showing a bit of sense. Why she wanted to stay in that house all alone I've no idea." His head disappeared back behind the sports section.

Agnes navigated her way through the toys and balloons littering her living room floor and sat down heavily on the sofa. I'd better start cleaning this up, she thought, feeling guilty about having a birthday party the day after her son-in-law's funeral. But it had hardly been a huge celebration, just the two of us with Amber, Todd and the twins, and it was the only time we could have it. Todd was going back to work on the rig in Nova Scotia tomorrow.

"She said she wanted to be quiet, try to get her thoughts in order." Agnes picked up a scruffy teddy bear and hugged it to herself. "I know what's preying on her mind, Roy. She thinks something's not right with this whole accident thing."

Her husband reappeared from behind his paper. "What's to think about? That stupid arse got drunk and fell down the stairs; the only thing not right about it is that it didn't happen years ago."

"Oh, don't say that, hon. He stayed off the booze for years, and did his best to be a good husband and father." Agnes sat the bear next to her on the sofa and reached for a glass of wine sitting on the end table. She sipped it thoughtfully; "Dean and Linda turned out just great, anyone would be proud of them."

Roy's expression softened at the mention of his grandchildren. "Yes, well, that's as maybe. But I'd be willing to bet their raising was more down to Lucy than him. No, once a drunk, always a drunk I say. And what do we know of her life with him? We only saw them once a year, if that." Dropping his paper on the floor he got up, and walked stiffly to an old fashioned cocktail cabinet set against the wall.

His wife handed him her empty glass; "Here, top this up for me," she said half rising from the sofa; "Your trouble is you never liked him, not from the get-go."

"Darn right I didn't." Roy picked up an open bottle of sparkling wine, poured some into Agnes' glass and passed it back to her. Leaning over the coffee table, he cut a generous chunk from the remains of a large birthday cake and balanced it on a paper napkin.

He walked over to the window, and stood silently forking cake into his mouth. How much longer will I be able to work out there, he wondered, looking out over his immaculate lawn and tidy flowerbeds. After a moment he went on; "She was only fifteen when he took up with her, Aggie. Fifteen! What the hell was he thinking about? She was just a child, for God's sake."

"I wasn't much older than that when I met you remember, and I pretty much knew my own mind right from the start."

He turned around and smiled at her; "That was different, hon, that was wartime; we all grew up a lot quicker then. Besides, I never went sneaking around behind your dad's back. He knew we were dating, gave me the lecture too, what he'd do to me if I took any liberties." Roy stopped short and leant against the window ledge for support, as his breath started coming in laboured gasps.

When he could finally speak, Roy continued as if there'd been no interruption. "But not the crown prince, oh no. We didn't know a thing about the carryings on, till that night I saw them necking in his car." He started coughing as a crumb of birthday cake went down the wrong way.

His wife looked up in concern; "For heaven's sake, come and sit down." She picked up a plate from the coffee table and waved it at him, "Here, take this. You're dropping crumbs all over the floor."

Roy crossed the room, took the plate and sat down in his chair. For a few minutes neither spoke, as he concentrated on eating and Agnes sipped her wine.

Then she shrugged; "There's absolutely no point in rehashing the past. He's dead and gone, and we've got to help Lucy through all this. Apart from anything else, he's left her with nothing; no house, no life insurance, not even a decent car. We'd even have had to pay for the funeral, if his mother hadn't stepped in."

"Yes, and that's the least she could do, in the circumstances," her husband snapped back. "If she and the almighty Mike Wesley had raised their son properly, he wouldn't have raped a fifteen year old girl!"

Agnes sighed and mentally counted to ten. How many times had she listened to this worn out record? "For goodness sake Roy, you know full well he didn't rape her.

She told us she was willing because she was in love with him."

"That doesn't mean a thing. She was under age and he took advantage of her. What did she know about sex? He took advantage of her innocence, and in my book that counts as rape. And then to start their marriage that way; lying to everyone, pretending she was pregnant." Roy stopped abruptly, trying to catch his breath again.

"Stop working yourself up over it. Lucy told us why they said that. The Wesleys were going to send him away to some college, and Tony didn't want to be parted from her."

Her husband looked at her in exasperation. "Oh, come on. You never bought into that fairy tale!"

Guilty as charged, Agnes thought. She reddened and picked up the teddy bear again. Retying the frayed ribbon round its neck, she said in a low voice; "Lucy believed it, and that's all that counts."

But Roy's temper was in full flood; "Could you really see Mike Wesley sending his son and heir away to the States just to break up a romance? Not a chance. All through high school that little bastard had a string of *unsuitable* girlfriends, and a bunch more the year he worked at the mill with his dad. And suddenly, they're going to send him away because of Lucy? No, he had to leave town for some reason, and Lucy was gullible enough to believe whatever tale he told her."

Agnes was by nature a gentle soul, and she rarely raised her voice in anger. But now, she came close to shouting at her husband; "Don't you *ever* say anything like that to Lucy. She believes her husband gave up everything for her, and now that's all she's got left. And anyway, if he had to skip town, why bother with her? He could have just packed up and left one night, and nobody any the wiser."

Sensing he'd gone too far, Roy dropped his hectoring tone and tried a softer approach. "Maybe he couldn't just leave. Maybe he needed some excuse, or when he told her he was leaving she made up the story about being pregnant, to try and keep him. Then he figured if he married her, that'd put him on the outs with his parents and give him an excuse to go."

"Maybe this, maybe that. What does any of it matter anymore?" Agnes got up from the sofa and began collecting toys, tossing them into a brightly coloured box next to her husband's chair. Then she stopped abruptly and shot him a triumphant look; "So now you're agreeing he did the right thing by Lucy, are you?" And, as if to emphasise her point, she picked up a dessert fork and started popping the balloons.

Rapidly running out of enthusiasm for the argument Roy made a weak effort to counter his wife's logic: "Well" *pop, pop* "only if she" *pop* " lied to him about" *pop, pop,* "being pregnant" he finished with a rush. Glaring at Agnes, he leant down and retrieved his paper. "Stop doing that for a minute and listen." His wife mischievously popped the last balloon, then turned to look at him wide-eyed. He stifled a laugh. "Be serious now, you know neither of us liked him. I don't think he ever looked me straight in the eye; not from the first time I met him at their wedding, to the last time I saw him alive, here last Friday, when he dropped Lucy off."

Agnes threw the last of the toys into the box. She straightened up and sighed; "Oh, give over, won't you? What difference does it make now?"

"No difference at all. But we both know she'd have been happier if she'd never got mixed up with him. She could have gone to university or college, or married a nice local boy, and stayed close to home. Instead of being dragged off to Sault St. Marie, living hand to mouth…." Roy's thin body was shaken by a sudden paroxysm of coughing.

Agnes looked at her watch. "I'll get your pills; it's nearly time. Just sit quiet, luv, you're going to have another bad turn if you keep on like this."

She hurried out to the kitchen, as much to get away from her husband's arguing as to fetch his medication. The phrase "married a nice local boy" was rolling around in her memory, and she heard her mother's voice saying almost the same words to her father, back home in Sussex, in 1944.

"Mark my words, Jim, if she takes up with this Roy, when the war's over she'll be gone to Canada, and we'll never see her again. No, best put a stop to it now. You'll see, once our boys come home she'll find someone nice and local to marry. She'll soon forget all about this character."

The first part of her mother's prediction proved all too true. Agnes and Roy married and, in 1946, with baby Barbara in tow, Agnes had crossed the Atlantic to be reunited with her husband and start their life together in Canada. And sadly, her parents had never seen her again. Both had died, by the time she and Roy could afford a trip back to England.

So when Lucy and Tony married and left Little Yarmouth, Agnes found it easy to understand her daughter's eagerness to abandon everything she knew for a brand new life with the man she loved. And she had comforted herself with the thought that there wasn't an ocean dividing them, just the eight hours of road between Little Yarmouth and Sault St. Marie. She also thought they would soon be back, once Mike Wesley's temper had cooled and Tony had experienced life without the buffer of his father's money.

But things hadn't turned out that way. For all she saw of her daughter and grandchildren in the Soo, they might just as well have been across an ocean. Far from returning home, Tony refused to even visit Little Yarmouth and it was always up to them to make the long trip north. And their infrequent visits were so uncomfortable, as Roy's resentment of their son-in-law simmered away below his surface bonhomie.

Not even death could bring Tony back to Little Yarmouth. There was real surprise in town when he missed his father's funeral in 1985, although that quickly evaporated when the details of Mike Wesley's will became known. The rift in the Wesley family was obviously permanent for, not only was Tony disinherited, but Mike Wesley had pointedly ignored his two grandchildren, Linda and Dean.

He also refused to come two years ago, when Lucy's sister, Barbara, died of leukaemia. It was Dean who drove his mother and sister to Little Yarmouth for the funeral, Tony being supposedly too ill to travel. Another strike against him, as far as Roy was concerned.

And then last November, out of the blue, Lucy called to say they were coming back to town. Dougie Ferguson had offered Tony a job at the bakery, so they were packing up and finally heading home.

Roy's taciturn comment; "Bit late in the day, isn't it?" had summed up their reaction. They knew about Tony's illness, and had figured the only way they'd see Lucy back in Little Yarmouth was as a widow. But then Linda got married and Lucy had the possibility of grandchildren, so they finally gave up any hope that their daughter would come back home.

Of course, once the initial awkwardness of their reunion was over, Roy and Agnes were overjoyed to have Lucy so close again. And, if seeing Tony on a regular basis was the price they had to pay, well, so be it.

Agnes sighed, and picked up Roy's pills from the kitchen window ledge. As her fingers closed around the vial, her eyes prickled with unexpected tears and she leant against the countertop, resting her forehead on a kitchen cabinet. The last two years had been so hard, so full of grief.

First her beautiful Barbara, getting sick and dying by inches, then Roy's diagnosis of heart disease. And now this business with Tony. Not that she grieved for him. Roy

63

was right, she never liked her son-in-law, but it broke her heart to see Lucy so devastated. Her daughter had loved that selfish sod from the first day she laid eyes on him, and would probably go on loving him until she took her last breath. Agnes shook her head. Whoever said *love is blind* was right, for sure.

"Aggie, what about my pills?" Roy's shout from the living room broke into her thoughts. "Coming, luv," she answered, but no sooner had she gone into the hall than the doorbell chimed. Opening the front door, she threw her arms around her daughter and drew her into the house.

Chapter 5 – A Rainy Day

Although Rosie's dreams were again filled with anguished cries and the crackle of flames, she woke only once during the night, and soon fell back to sleep. Experience had taught her that an unquiet spirit would use every opportunity to creep into her subconscious, and this had long since ceased to frighten her. Her Aunt Margaret once told her that it was the living she should fear, not the dead, because the departed could only use illusion to get her attention, whereas the living could hurt her in reality.

Sunday passed uneventfully. After Mass, she cut the grass and tidied some flowerbeds while Moira made two attempts at using the barbeque. Her first batch of hamburgers and veggie burgers were rather charred, so she surreptitiously donated them to the starving Gussie, who could hardly believe his luck.

On Monday morning, Rosie opened her eyes to black clouds and the sound of thunder in the distance. It was a workday, so she hurried along the hallway to get into the bathroom before Moira who, although only eleven, could easily spend an hour basking in the tub and primping before the mirror.

When the house had been built in 1925 two bathrooms, one each on the first and second floor, had been considered the height of modernity. For the following twenty years, nine people had lived at 64 Cedar Street and managed quite well with only two bathrooms. But nowadays, as Rosie had once been informed by a condescending realtor, two bathrooms in a house this size were considered wholly inadequate.

Rosie knew her home was in dire need of updating. The last major renovations had been done in 1955, the year her father left the military to come home and join his father's practice in Little Yarmouth. Rosie had been seven when she moved there with her parents, five year old sister Josephine and baby brother, John. Her six aunts and uncles had all left Cedar Street years before, so Grand Mere Minette had been thrilled to have children in the house again. Grandpa William, on the other hand, had become used to quiet surroundings and took rather longer to adjust.

The guest room door was half open, and a glance was enough to reassure her that Moira was still asleep, curled up with Gussie at her feet. Remembering Friday night, the girl been hesitant to go up to bed until Rosie suggested leaving the hall light on and the bedroom door ajar. And unusually, Gussie had gone straight into Moira's room with her, and sat upright at the end of the bed as if on guard duty. With these safeguards in place, Moira had soon drifted off peacefully to sleep.

Rosie went into the bathroom, slipped off her robe and got into the shower with a shiver. Even on the hottest day this room stayed cool – the result of being in the shadow of a century old maple tree, and also of being entirely covered in white and green marble tiles.

As she soaped and lathered, Rosie considered her next steps in solving the Tony Wesley mystery. During Sunday Mass she had looked down from the choir loft, and been surprised to see Lucy in church with her parents, half leaning against her mom. She looked completely drained, with barely enough energy to get up and down through the various parts of the Mass. Rosie had made a mental note to call her early in the week to ask her over for supper, and to make sure she was staying away from the house on Veterans Avenue.

Talking to Lucy again might help her discover more about Tony's childhood and teenage years. Who else could she ask? Like all the Catholic kids in town, he would have gone to Holy Angels, so maybe Sister Mary Bernadette could fill in some blanks. Although Sister was closing in on ninety, she still taught a junior music class, and her memory of past pupils was encyclopaedic. 'I'll pop over to the convent sometime this week' Rosie said to herself. One thing about elderly nuns – you always knew where to find them.

Towelling off, she put her robe back on and crossed to the sink. The mirror was fogged with steam and, as she lifted her hand to clear it, the word *sorry* slowly took shape in front of her. Then the room seemed to dim, and her whole body began to shake as the temperature plummeted. An invisible finger continued to trace the word *sorry* over and over again on the mirror, until the words were indecipherable. She felt rooted to the spot, conscious only of the freezing cold and a rising tide of panic as her mind filled with the thought *I can't get out of here*. From somewhere she heard barking, then the door was pushed open and Gussie was jumping up at her.

The cold vanished as she half stumbled, half knelt next to her canine guardian angel. Putting her arms round him, she buried her face in his warm fur and held on tight. "Thanks Gus," she whispered, "From now on, you can come in the bathroom whenever you like. And I'll never tell you off for drinking out of the toilet again." She got up shakily, soaped a facecloth and began to wash off Gussie's welcome, but smelly, face licks. He stayed sitting at her feet while she cleaned her teeth and then a sound caught his attention, his head swivelled and with ears pricked he disappeared back into the hallway. Moira must be up, thought Rosie.

Feeling decidedly fragile, she made her way back toward her bedroom. Through the open guest room door she could see Moira in her pyjamas, playing tug with the beagle. "C'mon Moira," she called, "time's getting on. Don't hang about in the shower; breakfast will be ready in fifteen minutes." Gussie had dropped the tug rope, and was looking at her expectantly. "Yes Gus, time for kibble," she said as she carried on down the hall and in a heartbeat, he was out the door and down the stairs ahead of her. He can certainly move when there's food on offer, she thought.

As she laid the breakfast table, Rosie found herself listening for any unusual sounds from upstairs. She was almost certain that Tony wouldn't bother Moira again, but if he did, she was resolved to sit down with the child and explain about the Gift. John and Elspeth would just have to get over her interference. Apart from any other consideration, Moira would get it into her head that her aunt's house was haunted (which it was, but hopefully not for long) and be afraid to ever visit again.

But her fears were groundless. Twenty minutes later she heard her niece run down the stairs, jumping the last two – just like I did at her age she thought, and probably my dad and his brothers and sisters, too. She felt a sudden connection to all her family, both the living and the dead, and knew with comforting certainty that, despite this morning's unnerving visitation, she was protected in this house.

There was a huge crack of thunder and rain began to pour down in torrents. Rosie reached across the table and switched on the radio; much as she disliked hearing about the world's troubles first thing in the morning, she did need to know the weather forecast.

"Morning, Auntie Ro." Moira sat down at the table and poured herself a glass of orange juice.

"Morning, sweetie. Do you want toast or eggs, or just cereal this morning?"

Moira picked up the cornflakes. "I think I'll have cornflakes and then some toast, please. Do you think it's going to rain all day?"

"I'm just waiting on the weather forecast. What do you have planned for the morning? Anything outside?"

"No – I need to sort out what to take to Gams. Could you show me how to use the washer before you go to work?"

Rosie had forgotten she was taking Moira to her Great Aunt Margaret's cottage on Tuesday – *going to Gams* was a summer tradition in the family, not just for Moira and Robert, but for a whole crowd of other Cornish cousins.

"Sure, it's almost the same as your mimms. Be careful with the dryer, though – it's so fierce it shrinks anything with cotton in it. You can hang that stuff in the basement, or out on the line if it stops raining."

"Okay." Moira finished her cornflakes and took a slice of toast. Buttering it, she continued; "After lunch a bunch of us thought we'd go over to Strattens. I could bike it, or maybe you could take me if the rain keeps up."

Little Yarmouth was unique in many ways, but one of its oddest claims to fame was the survival of Strattens Roller Rink. To Rosie's knowledge, there were only a handful of Roller Rinks left in Ontario, and Strattens in Little Yarmouth was probably the oldest. In continuous operation since its bright blue and orange doors first opened in 1920, the faded sign over those doors still cheerfully promised *Family Fun at Family Prices*. And despite its decidedly old fashioned atmosphere, it remained as much a gathering place for millennial teenagers as it had been for their parents, grandparents and great grandparents.

"Hold on a minute, hon." Rosie held up her hand as the weather forecast started. After a two minute monologue featuring lows, highs and troughs the final verdict was *rain all day*. Turning off the radio she asked; "And who exactly is in this bunch?"

"Oh, you know, just kids from school. Chels of course, and Marta, Francesca Litton, Dena Marshall, her brother Ryan, his friend ….."

Rosie interrupted; "Ryan? You're going to the rink with *boys?*"

"Come on, Auntie Ro. There are boys at Holy Angels, you know. And it's just the Roller Rink, not a rock concert."

Rosie looked at her niece; "Does Chelsea's mom know there are boys going this afternoon?"

"Yes, Chelsea asked her on Sunday morning, and she said it was okay as long as we stayed at the rink and didn't go anywhere else."

Rosie felt out of her depth. She had no idea whether John or Elspeth allowed Moira to go out in mixed groups, and her first instinct was call Tracey Simons and make sure her permission had really been given. But that would be the same as telling Moira she didn't trust her so, relying on the girl's usual truthfulness, she decided to take her at her word and give permission.

"Well alright, but you know if I drive you, you'll have to stay there until I finish work. That'll be close to four hours – are you sure you won't get bored?"

"No, there's loads to do. They've got the arcade now and a snack bar – it's changed lots since you used to go, I bet."

Yes, I bet it has, thought Rosie. The last time she went roller skating was in 1986, two days before her wedding. There was a hen party at her maid of honours apartment and, after several bottles of wine, someone suggested a trip to the rink. They all piled into two cars, and descended on Strattens with the abandon found only among inexperienced drinkers intent on having "a good time." She remembered trying to tie her rented skates, giggling helplessly all the while, then skating round and round the rink wearing someone's First Communion veil. Her friends had followed behind in a parody of the bridal procession, shrieking with laughter and singing a very unorthodox version of *Here Comes the Bride*. The next morning she'd woken with a throbbing headache, a mouth like a dustpan and memories of friendship that still warmed her heart.

"Good grief, is that the time?" The hall clock was chiming nine and she still had her hair and makeup to finish. "Sweetie, put the dishes in the dishwasher for me, when you're done." As she stood up, Rosie spotted Gussie chewing. "And don't give him any more crusts!" At the sound of her voice, the beagle looked up innocently. I swear that dog's smiling at me, she thought. Gussie knew a soft touch when he saw one, and Moira was about the easiest he'd ever come across. No wonder he stuck to her like glue.

Rosie fixed her face and hair, gave Moira a crash course on using the washer and then spent a fruitless ten minutes looking for her umbrella. She finally pulled into the church parking lot at nine-forty, with the rain still bucketing down. In the few minutes it took her to run to the office door and unlock it, her pant hems were soaked and her shoes filled with water. Not a good start to the week.

She squelched inside and hung her jacket behind the door. Crossing the room to raise the blind and plug in the coffee maker she spotted her umbrella, laying neatly furled on top of the filing cabinet. 'Wouldn't you know it' she said aloud. There must be some kind of Murphy's Law ensuring umbrellas were always somewhere other than where they were needed. Feeling decidedly bad-tempered Rosie pulled out her chair, whisked the cover off the Remington and sat down.

She began to tackle the paperwork from Tony Wesley's funeral. There were twenty seven donations to Bibles for Lepers for receipting and forty two Mass offerings, which had to be scheduled as Memorials in upcoming Bulletins. Rosie pulled out her calendar chart, and began writing the memorials into vacant days – this was going to be a long job. Father Matthews said that any kind of scheduling was easier on the computer, using something called a *spreadsheet,* and as she flipped back and forth through the calendar chart she began to wonder if it wasn't time to get serious about having a computer in the office.

About an hour went by, and then the office door opened suddenly to admit a tall man, entirely bald and with the physique of a football quarterback. Rather surprisingly, he was dressed in a formal black jacket and pin striped trousers.

"Morning Rosie," Dave Mason boomed; "How's everything with you this lovely wet morning?" He shook the rain from his umbrella and propped it on the boot tray. "More donations from last Friday's funeral" he said, dropping a damp envelope marked *Offerings, St. Jude's* onto her desk.

"Thanks Dave. Got time for a coffee?" The big man nodded. "Still raining, is it?" She went over to the coffee maker and filled two mugs.

"Yup. Coming down cats and dogs, and set for the day by all accounts. We're gonna get pretty wet up at Union Cemetery this afternoon, if it keeps up." Dave sat down opposite Rosie and poured cream and sugar into his mug.

"Anyone I know?"

"No, not someone anyone knows, at least, not so far. It's that John Doe the CN guys found last year under the railway bridge – town's finally burying him."

"Yes, I remember that. The police couldn't figure whether he'd fallen, jumped or been pushed. They were trying to find his next of kin."

"Well no luck there, I'm afraid. And we can't keep him on ice indefinitely, not like a big city morgue. The cops have got DNA samples and his clothes, so if anyone ever comes looking he'll be identified. Not likely, though. Probably just a wino; got drunk and fell off the bridge."

Rosie kept her eyes down as she added cream to her coffee; "There seems to be a lot of that about, just now."

Dave rubbed his hand across the back of his neck. "You mean Tony Wesley? That whole business was way off base, if you ask me. But then, with Clodagh Wesley calling the shots, what can you expect?" He picked up the offerings envelope and turned it round and round in his hands. "We'd no sooner done the hospital run to pick him up than she was in the office, telling us what we were gonna do, and how we were gonna do it."

Rosie reached for an old metal tin marked *Crackers*. "Cookie?" Dave shook his head. She gave the lid a twist and took out a giant oatmeal cookie. "They're sugar free. The bakery's getting into healthy alternatives. You know Dougie, always keeping up with the trends." She broke a piece off and chewed it slowly. "Not bad, I suppose. Rather have the real thing, though." Swallowing, she continued; "I was round to see Lucy on Saturday. She's in a pretty bad way over Tony being labelled a drunk. Apparently, he'd been on the wagon for years – they never even kept liquor in the house. And she can't understand why there wasn't an autopsy."

Dave sipped his coffee thoughtfully. "Not many people knew he was off the booze, me included. As for an autopsy, all I know is we got a call from Memorial on the Saturday morning, paperwork done up, no mention of an autopsy, required or requested. Cause of death was *fracture cervical spinal column-* that's broken neck to you and me – *due to a catastrophic fall.* As I said, old Mrs. Wesley was in my office before lunch, wanting to see caskets and set up visitation hours."

"But surely, that was for Lucy to decide."

"That's what I told her and she left in a fine temper. I called Lucy right after the old bat had gone, but her mom said the doctor had given her pills and she was sleeping. Finally, they all came in on Monday morning, and Lucy signed off on whatever Mrs. Wesley wanted. Even then, I don't think she knew the half of what was going on. It was pathetic to see her." Dave drained his mug and got to his feet. "I'd better get going, thanks for the coffee."

He stood for a moment, looking into the middle distance. "You know, I always had a bit of a crush on Lucy. We went together for a while at high school until Tony spotted her, and then it was game over for me. He had a car, lots of money and the "bad boy" reputation. Why do girls find that so irresistible? God, he didn't deserve her – it was a new girl every week with him, and Lucy just waiting around for his call. But there was no-one else for her, and now he's left her for good; poor kid's gonna have a hard time getting over that bastard." He walked to the door and picked up his umbrella. "Sorry about the language Rosie, but that's what he was. And leopards don't change their spots."

Well, well, someone else who didn't like Tony Wesley, Rosie thought. "What time will you be burying Mr. Doe?"

"We'll be at Union around two. Why?"

"I'll go into the church and light a candle for him. No-one should be buried without a prayer."

Dave smiled. "That's real nice, Rosie. See you tonight at the meeting?" She nodded. He opened the door and, putting up his enormous black umbrella, said "You take care now," and ducked back out into the teeming rain.

Rosie went over to the window and watched him run down the path to his car. He's such a nice man, she thought, shame he's on his own. And then she wondered; could he still have feelings for Lucy after all these years? And what about the resentment towards Tony for stealing his girl – had it re-surfaced when they came back to town? Was it enough to inspire murder?

She spent the rest of the morning trying to finish the memorial schedule, but it was a day for interruptions. First it was Liz, keen to recount the various insults traded back and forth between the Curtis and Wesley families at the funeral reception. Not much Christian sentiment at that gathering, Rosie thought. Then it was Father Matthews, in a flap because he was late for a meeting at the bank, and couldn't find St. Jude's quarterly financial statements. And when Rosie got back to her office after locating the errant paperwork it was to find Donny and Seel curled up together, fast asleep on her desk.

She looked at the clock. It was 11.50, and everything seemed to be conspiring against her efforts to finish the memorial schedule. 'Oh phooey, I'm going home' she said to the cats, who responded by burrowing their noses even deeper into their fur, showing their complete disdain for human conversation. She could hear Liz up the hall, cleaning the Rectory kitchen. "Liz, I'm taking an early lunch" she called and, without waiting for a reply, switched the phone to voice mail, put on her jacket and headed out into the rain.

Before Rosie got home Moira had finished her laundry, and had even managed to drag a reluctant Gussie around the block. "Honestly, Auntie Ro, you'd never think he was a *hound, the* way he hates going out in the rain!" she complained, rubbing his back vigorously with an old towel. In dog heaven, Gussie closed his eyes and sank to the floor.

Surrounded by the aroma of wet dog, they ate a quick lunch of mushroom omelette with grilled tomatoes, and by 12:40 Rosie was turning onto Donlevy Street and into Stratten's parking lot. She could see Chelsea and two other girls sheltering under the front awning and, almost before the car had stopped, Moira had her seat belt off and was opening the passenger door.

Rosie caught her arm; "Moira you are not, under any circumstances, to leave here without calling me first, understand?"

Moira sighed "Yes, Auntie Ro."

"Have you got your phone?" Silly question, Moira was never parted from her little pink companion, even sleeping with it under her pillow.

"Yes, Auntie Ro." Two green eyes rolled at the idiocy of adults.

"The office number is on your speed dial if you want me," Rosie continued, "and I'll pick you up about twenty to five, so be ready at the door. You know I've got the school reunion meeting tonight, so supper will be a bit of a rush, okay?" Moira was halfway out of the car. "Go on then, have fun. See you later." She waited until the girls disappeared inside, and then pulled out into the street.

She drove the short distance back down Donlevy and sat at the intersection for several minutes, waiting for an opportunity to turn onto Victoria. Now, in addition to the heavy rain, a strong wind was getting up and sodden litter was blowing all along the road. It took a few minutes for her to realise that nothing was moving in either direction, so she reluctantly turned off the engine, got out and walked to the corner.

As she struggled with her windswept umbrella, Rosie could hear sirens wailing and see the red flashing lights of emergency vehicles. There must be an accident somewhere between her and St. Jude's, and it was snarling traffic the entire length of Victoria Street. 'For goodness' sake, why can't people learn to drive in the rain?' she said aloud, and then immediately felt guilty. Who knew how many lives might have changed forever, this rainy afternoon? Chastened, she said a quick prayer to St. Jude, Patron of desperate cases and lost causes, asking him to intercede for anyone needing help today.

With every passing moment, the rain was getting heavier. Rosie ran back to the Buick and in the few minutes it took to open the car door, get inside, and wrestle down her saturated umbrella, her shoes and pant legs were soaked again and rain was running down her face and into the neck of her blouse. There was nothing for it, but to drive back along Donlevy, go around the block and try to cut across Victoria further north. Then she could go west across town, turn down Albert Street and get to the rear of the church.

Trying to ignore how cold she was, Rosie started the car and drove the length of Donlevy Street. It wasn't long before warm air started to come from the heater and her wet face and hands began to dry. On the bright side, she thought, there was no way Moira and her friends would be tempted to leave Strattens in this horrible weather. There wasn't an umbrella between them, and none of the girls would stoop to wear that most reviled article of clothing, a rain jacket. And it was ever thus she thought, remembering anguished arguments at age eleven with her own mother, adamant that Rosie continue wearing woolly underwear to school. In common with mothers of every time and place hers was convinced that, left to her own devices, Rosie would succumb to pneumonia long before reaching adulthood.

She turned north and drove up Murdoch Street, past Campbell, Burns and then Alistair, the corner dominated by Knox Presbyterian Church. In the 1880's, these four blocks had been the exclusive home of Little Yarmouth's Scottish community, and many of their descendants still lived here, in tidy houses named *Caledonia, Loch Lomond, Bonnie Doone* and other sentimental remembrances of a distant time and place.

I should be up far enough now, she thought and watched for the next turning on her right. As she made the turn Rosie realised she was on Veterans Avenue, and with her progress slowed by driving wind and rain, she found herself looking for number 26. Under a grey sky the row houses looked even drearier, as she counted off the numbers; *thirty two, thirty, twenty eight.*

It was lucky there was no-one driving behind her. She had reflexively stepped on the brake at the sight of Lucy's front door swinging wildly in the wind. Even from the road, she could see rain beating into the hall. There was no car in the driveway but Lucy could still be in there, if her mom or dad had dropped her off for some reason.

Rosie knew she couldn't just drive past and call someone when she got to St. Judes. Suppose Lucy was in the house, and something had happened to her? Suppose she had become ill, and had managed to open the door, but got no further. Suppose….darker possibilities began crowding into Rosie's mind, together with the thought that this was a time when a cell phone would have been really useful. Fear made her attention wander; maybe I should look into getting a cell phone she thought, I wonder how much it would cost…..? With an effort, she re-focused her mind on the problem at hand.

She turned into the driveway and with the engine running, sounded her horn. Minutes passed and nothing happened. She sounded the horn again. Still nothing. Taking her courage in both hands Rosie turned off the ignition, and ran up the short pathway to the front step. Soaked again!

"Lucy, are you there? It's Rosie. Are you alright?" She listened intently for any response, but the house was wrapped in silence. No clock ticked or floor creaked, the stillness of the house a testament to its abandoned state. Rosie stepped across the puddle collecting at the threshold, lifted the horseshoe door knocker and rapped loudly. "Lucy, is everything okay? It's Rosie, I'm coming in."

Leaving the front door open, she walked softly along the passageway and into the living room. It was as cold as on her previous visit, but whether the frigid temperature was the result of Tony's presence, or simply caused by wind and rain blowing into the hall, she couldn't tell. A quick glance around the room showed everything in order and the kitchen just the same. Nervously, she opened the basement door, switched on the light and ventured down a few steps, but she saw and felt nothing. The cramped space was empty, except for the washer, dryer and a few cartons stacked against the far wall.

She went back along the hall and called up the stairs; "Hello, is anyone there? Lucy, its Rosie." As she started up the stairs her hand was clammy on the baluster, and her heart thumped wildly with each ascending step. Aunt Margaret's warning, that it was the living she should fear not the dead, popped back into her mind. 'Oh, perfect! Why did I have to think of that right now?' she said to herself. But there was no-one upstairs. The two small bedrooms and bathroom were undisturbed, as neat as Lucy had left them two days earlier.

Relieved, Rosie swallowed, took a deep breath and started back downstairs. Strange, how we hold our breath when we're scared, she thought. But there was no great mystery here, just a faulty latch and a strong wind blowing the front door open. Lucy had said everything in the house was in poor repair. I'll wipe up the water, close the door firmly when I leave and call Lucy at her mom's. Maybe her dad can put a better lock on the door - keep things safe while the house is empty.

With these thoughts running through her head, Rosie went into the kitchen and picked up a roll of paper towel from the counter. She had just started back along the hallway when the front door slammed shut, with such force that all the panes in the transom rattled. The phrase *jumped out of her skin* had always seemed inane to Rosie, but today she understood what it meant. She screamed, started with fright and dropped the paper towel. It rolled along the floor before finally coming to rest against the basement door.

Completely unnerved, Rosie ran to the front door and frantically turned the door handle back and forth in a panicky effort to get out. But despite all her turning and pulling, the door wouldn't budge. After a few seconds her fright began to subside; nobody had deliberately slammed the door, it had just blown shut, and now the latch was probably jammed. There was a phone in the kitchen - she'd call Lucy, and get her to send her dad over with a tool kit. Wait, what was the Curtis's number? Maybe there was a directory in the kitchen with the phone.

She turned around, and saw the roll of paper towel being pushed slowly across the floor as the basement door swung open. A heavy mist was filling the far end of the hall, and Rosie finally understood that it hadn't been the wind, or human hands, that had swung wide the entrance to 26 Veterans Avenue as she drove by. Tony Wesley wanted to draw her into the house.

For 99 percent of humanity, finding themselves trapped in a locked house with a ghost would have caused abject terror. For Rosie, it was just the opposite. Lost souls were no problem, it was human beings that sometimes scared her witless. She recalled the spectral hand she'd seen pointing to the basement, when she hugged Lucy goodbye on Saturday. There must be something down there that Tony needed her to see.

"Okay, Tony I get the message," she said aloud and walked toward the basement door, her breath becoming visible in the icy atmosphere. As she switched on the basement light, the mist at the end of the hall began to lighten and disperse. Ghosts are really quite predictable she thought, once you clue in to what they're trying to tell you.

Rosie walked down the wood frame stairs, and took a quick look around. The basement ceiling was low; she stood five foot four, and there was very little headroom above her. The space was about ten foot by twelve, with limestone walls and a cracked concrete floor. She gave an involuntary shudder at the sight of a dark stain about three feet from the bottom step. Against the far left wall stood a fairly new washer and dryer, with a grubby laundry tub next to the washer. There was no furnace; heating on Veterans Avenue had originally been fireplaces, two up and one down, but now relied on electricity, either freestanding heaters or baseboards. Over the years, Rosie had often heard people complain about the cost of heating these small houses, with their poor insulation and ill-fitting doors and windows. But landlords are rarely interested in energy conservation, when it's tenants who pay the hydro bills.

The only other items in the basement were an old trunk and three cardboard boxes set against the back wall. The trunk was locked, but Rosie was able to rummage carefully through the boxes. To her disappointment, all she found were wire coat hangers, mismatched glasses and Christmas decorations; just household effects still unpacked from the move, none of which seemed likely to be relevant to Tony's death.

'But there must be something' she said to herself, 'he went to so much effort to get me down here.' She walked slowly around the room, even looking inside the washer, dryer and laundry tub. Still nothing. There was hardly any dust either; despite her dislike of the house Lucy was a conscientious housekeeper.

Rosie glanced at her watch and was horrified to see it was already 1:20. She imagined lines of parishioners waiting at the locked office door, and a myriad calls piling up on the voicemail. Tony, what is it I have to find?

As if in answer to this unspoken plea, a light mist began to form at the base of the stairs. She knelt down and began to crawl hesitantly across the floor, running her hands in circles ahead of her and looking from left to right. She soon found herself kneeling directly on the stained patch of concrete, and gagged with nausea as she breathed in a heady smell of whiskey combined with something more metallic. 'Don't think about that,' she said to herself sternly, and went on with her careful explorations.

Now something was making her light-headed, the grey stone of the wall ahead was becoming indistinct and she couldn't focus her eyes properly. There was a scraping noise above her and, looking up, she saw a huge shadow at the top of the stairs. As she watched, the shadow seemed to come apart and a heavy black mass came tumbling silently down toward her.

Rosie knelt motionless as the shadow at the top of the stairs descended a few steps. Just a little further and she'd see a face. But it stopped halfway down and, to her horror, she heard a low giggle as the shadow gently tossed a bottle into the basement. Involuntarily she ducked, but there was no sound of breaking glass. She felt nausea rising in her throat, and a sensation as if an icy hand had gripped her heart. And smoke – she could smell smoke...

The room swam around her, she felt dizzy and then, as if coming up from underwater, she opened her eyes and gasped for breath. I've just witnessed a murder, she thought, not that I could ever tell anyone about it. "Yes, Officer, I definitely saw Tony Wesley murdered. Where was I when it happened? Well, I was in my house across town, but ten days later I went and sat in his basement and watched it all then. I talk to the dead, you know." Oh yes, cue the men in white coats.

She got up and walked to the stairs, but her head was still spinning and she sat down abruptly on the bottom step. Visions of past events were a rare occurrence for Rosie, and the experience always left her disorientated as her consciousness readjusted to her own time and place. She bowed her head and concentrated on taking deep, calming breaths - in, out, in, out. Her heart began to slow to its normal rate, as more mundane thoughts began crowding into her mind. 'I must get going, I'm so late for work' she said aloud and started to get up.

As she turned to put her foot on the bottom step, a metallic glint caught her eye. There was something on the floor between the wall and the side frame of the wooden staircase. The gap was too small for Rosie's fingers, she needed something long and thin, a stick or a skewer - something to push down between the stair frame and the wall. Even without looking, she knew there was nothing lying around in the basement that would work. But surely she'd seen something down here? Yes! A quick rummage in the top storage box and she had her implement; a wire coat hanger.

It took only a few minutes of reaching and scraping before she was able to snag the intriguing little item. She picked it up and laid it across the palm of her hand. Her prize was a small piece of silvery metal, about two inches long and less than a quarter inch wide. At one end, the object culminated in a curved and flattened end, and at the other was a tiny ball. The centre was depressed slightly, as if it had been compressed by a thumb or finger. Rosie turned it over and over in her hand, but although it seemed vaguely familiar, its purpose eluded her. The silvering was bright so, whatever it was, it hadn't lain against the basement wall for long.

It was not until she reached the top of the stairs, that Rosie realised she'd probably compromised an important piece of evidence. Not only had she removed it from its original site, her fingerprints were all over it, effectively obscuring others that might have been relevant to the murder. And now this evidence was lying in her jacket pocket along with accumulated lint, a dog biscuit and two balled up tissues.

'Well, no use crying over spilled milk,' she said to herself. As far as the police were concerned Tony's death was accidental, and she had no viable reason to ask them to review this official position. Visions and ghosts didn't count. The only spirits which interested their local O.P.P. detachment were of the bottled variety, routinely smuggled off reserve by pick-up trucks headed for Sarnia and Goderich on moonless nights.

Confident that she had seen everything there was to see, Rosie picked up the roll of paper towel and hurried along the hallway to the front door. She mopped up the puddle under the threshold and put the paper towel back on the kitchen counter. Then she went to the front door and gave the handle a tentative turn. To her relief it opened easily, and in minutes she was driving across town toward Albert Street.

She pulled into St. Jude's rear parking lot at 1:55. It was still blustering and raining hard, and Rosie could barely keep her umbrella from blowing inside out as she scrambled for the back entrance. Getting around in this kind of weather was like fighting an elemental; a helpless struggle against an entity which took perverse pleasure in splashing, soaking and blowing unfortunate humans into submission.

She unlocked the door, and stepped into the dim church. Despite its architectural shortcomings St. Judes was still a place of devotion and, for over forty decades, prayer had seeped like spiritual incense into its ugly grey walls. Whenever she came into the church Rosie was instantly aware of its unique quiet stillness, as if her spiritual antennae were tuning into the vibrations of this sacred space.

It was nearly 2:00 p.m. She walked quickly down the centre aisle, genuflected before the tabernacle and turned into the side chapel dedicated to the Blessed Virgin. This was her favourite place in the church. The beautiful statue of Mary holding the Christ Child was one of the few things saved from the 1956 fire which destroyed old St. Judes. Like most of the original church furnishings the Virgin had been carved by Quebec craftsmen, and her serene smile had gazed down on St. Jude's parishioners for over a hundred and twenty years.

There were several candles glowing in blue holders on the votive stand. Always blue for Our Lady, thought Rosie, and red for the Sacred Heart. She pushed a five dollar bill into the collection tin, and taking a taper from the sand tray, caught a flame from one of the burning candles. She lit two votives – one for John Doe, and one for Lucy. "Eternal rest grant unto him, O Lord, and let perpetual light shine upon him. May he rest in peace" she said, closing her eyes and thinking of the unknown man being buried in a lonely grave, far from anyone who may have loved him. Then she murmured a brief prayer that Lucy would be comforted in her grief, and find strength to face whatever lay ahead. And, as an afterthought, she asked her own guardian angel to stay close as she tried to help Tony Wesley reach the next stage of his journey.

She stood quietly for a few minutes watching the candles flicker. Then her thoughts were interrupted by loud footsteps.

"Hi there Rosie, did ya get stuck in all that mess along Victoria?" Liz Curtis came striding down the aisle, water droplets flying left and right off her black rain slicker.

"Yes, I had to go all round town, in the end," Rosie replied. "Moira wanted to go to Strattens for the afternoon, and when I came back down Donlevy both sides of Victoria were at a standstill. Do you know what happened?"

"Oh, just two idiots, as usual. Van coming southbound tried to beat the lights at King, and hit a car trying to beat the lights on a left turn. They knocked each other into both sides of the intersection, so between that, and all them fire trucks and ambulances nothing could move." Liz paused for dramatic effect. "And you'll never guess which idiot was making the left turn." Rosie shook her head and, before she could speak, Liz announced triumphantly, "Old lady Wesley! Tried to get her own way once too often I guess, and you know what they say, *what goes around, comes around.* I sure won't be shedding any tears over her comeuppance."

"You mean she's dead?" Rosie was shocked.

"No, worse luck. That Merc she drives is built like a tank. No, just hauled off to Memorial – probably making everyone's life a misery in emerg right now. Let's hope she gets her license yanked; shouldn't be driving at her age, anyway. *And* she'll probably be charged with something. Let's see her wriggle out of this one. You know them Wesleys – think none of the rules apply to them. I remember one time, Carmel..."

Sensing the start of a full scale anti-Wesley tirade, Rosie interrupted quickly; "You know, I must get the office opened up. The phone's been on voicemail for hours, and I've got to get that memorial schedule finished." She started to walk towards the sacristy door then, struck by a sudden thought, turned around. "By the way, what happened to the van driver?"

"Nothing much. Pat said he walked into emerg, didn't even need a stretcher. The van's a write-off, though." Liz saw Rosie's puzzled look. "Steve's sister Pat's on reception in emerg."

I should have known, thought Rosie. Nothing of note ever happened in Little Yarmouth without at least one Curtis bearing witness to it, then passing it along the family bush telegraph. Followed by Liz, she went through the door and towards the church office. "Well, back to the salt mines."

"Yup, see ya later, girl," Liz replied as she headed into the rectory.

The cats were still curled together on her desk, noses buried deep and eyes tight shut. Rosie crossed the room; "Sorry guys, I need my desk back now" she said, as she reached over and gently scratched behind Seel's ear. One amber eye opened and regarded her impassively for a moment, then the calico got up, gave an impatient shake and jumped off the desk. With tail erect, she stalked from the room, every inch of her neat little frame expressing annoyance. Only two humans held any significance for Seel; Father Matthews, whom she adored slavishly, and Liz who dispensed her cat food.

Donny watched his sister's performance with admiration, but remained lounging comfortably across Rosie's paperwork. "Come on, Donny" Rosie cajoled, scratching his neck and being rewarded with a deep throaty purr.

Dominic and Cecelia were two of four kitten siblings, left in a box outside the church office three years earlier. One pair had been taken by Loretta O'Halloran, and promptly named Wayne and Gretzky by her three hockey mad boys. The names stuck, despite Dr. Katz's' later pronouncement that Wayne was a female. The other two were adopted by Father Matthews, but not before he had indulged in some lengthy soul-searching over the appropriateness of animals in a Rectory.

Of course, anyone who had seen him playing with the kittens when they were first discovered knew there was no way those four fluffy charmers were going to the Humane Society. Liz, not a cat lover, had later confided she was deathly afraid he was going to keep them all!

And presumably whoever had left them at the church had the same idea, it being well known in the parish that, where animals were concerned, their pastor was an easy mark. Not being a sports fan, he predictably chose names more in keeping with the kittens' ecclesiastical accommodation. *Cecelia*, because the calico had "a very musical meow," and *Dominic* because the boy kitten was a tuxedo, and this put him in mind of the Dominican black cowl and white habit.

Rosie had always thought that Cecelia, with her dainty manners and patrician elegance, was well named after the Patron Saint of Music. But Dominic? Unless that great monastic reformer had been clumsy, rambunctious and, as Liz said *two bricks short of a load*, Rosie doubted the name was anywhere near appropriate for Cecelia's big lug of a brother.

Although he was still purring, Donny's eyes had closed again, and he obviously had no intention of going anywhere under his own steam. With an effort, Rosie picked him up and laid him gently on the spare office chair where he remained motionless, except for that universal sign of feline displeasure, a slightly twitching tail.

At last able to sit down at her desk, Rosie was relieved to see there were no message lights blinking, so the phone had been quiet during her extended lunch break. And, for sure, no-one would have been to the door in all that rain, so her worries about frustrated parishioners had been groundless. She made a mental note to work an extra hour on Wednesday to make up for the time taken today. With Moira at Aunt Margaret's cottage, there wouldn't be the same urgency to get home.

She worked steadily and, unlike the morning, without interruption. Even the phone was silent and, to her surprise, at 4:25 she lay down her pen to review a completed memorial schedule. Amazing what you can do, when you're left alone to do it, she thought. It was too late to start any receipts, so she tidied her desk, unplugged the coffee maker and covered the trusty Remington.

Donny was still sleeping on the office chair, stretched out now, with head and front paws hanging over one side and his tail and back legs hanging over the other. Rosie looked at him affectionately; yes, definitely dumb as a bag of hammers.

She crossed the room, ran her hand gently over his silky fur, and immediately heard the rumble of a friendly purr. "See you Wednesday, Donny" she said as she put on her jacket and, picking up her umbrella, opened the office door and went out into the rain.

Traffic on Victoria Street was moving normally again, and apart from some broken glass scattered across the King Street intersection, there was no sign of the earlier accident. Moira was waiting for her under the awning at Strattens, and they were soon back home, getting organised for the evening.

Chapter 6 – The Reunion Committee

Rosie held the hood of her rain jacket closed tight, as she hurried across the high school parking lot. It had almost stopped raining, but the wind was still gusting around and she wanted to stay reasonably tidy for the meeting. After today's various excursions, her hair had frizzed out in every direction and it had taken a good thirty minutes to blow dry, tong and tease it back into shape. This was nothing new. Her mother had despaired of Rosie's unruly mop of curls, which needed only a few minutes exposure to wind or rain to give her the look of a demented hedgehog. Over the years her family and friends had learnt never to say, *you're so lucky to have naturally curly hair.*

The High School had been built in 1950 to replace its much smaller predecessor, when that Victorian pile fell victim to provincial road widening. Typical of its era, John Galt was a three storey brick rectangle, with parking lot to the front and playing fields at the back, its utilitarian appearance softened by several stands of magnificent maple trees around the perimeter. Over a century old, these had once shaded an 1845 pioneer homestead, its clapboard house, barn and outbuildings lost to "progress" when the property was sold to the school board in 1949.

Rosie pushed one of the entrance doors open, and made her way down the big central hallway. Nothing seemed to change in the school from year to year, and it still looked much the same as when she started in 1960.

There was no Catholic high school in Little Yarmouth until St. Michaels was built in 1990. Before then everyone either went to John Galt or, for girls, the residential St. Gabriel's Academy in Goderich. Rosie had been enrolled at St. Gabriel's in September 1960, but transferred back to John Galt two months later, after her father and grandparents died in the Memorial Hospital fire. It was no great sacrifice - her mother needed her at home, and Rosie was glad to come back. She knew it would have been too hard to grieve privately in a dormitory with twenty other girls.

She hurried past the office, then the cafeteria and reached the Staff Room only a few minutes late. Five other committee members were already sitting at a big oval table, enjoying coffee and doughnuts – the latter courtesy of Dougie Ferguson's Wee Scottish Bakery. One of the advantages of having Dougie on any committee was the generous supply of cookies and doughnuts that he brought to every meeting.

Rosie hung up her jacket. "Hi, folks, sorry I'm a bit late" she said to no-one in particular. Sitting down at the table, she pulled her reunion binder from the depths of a battered leather hold-all. The hold-all was actually a music bag, a gift from her mother when Rosie left for Juilliard in 1966. Since then, it had been used almost every day and was now definitely showing its age. These days, the bag was used more for weekending and shopping, than for carrying music to recitals.

"Ahem," came Peter Anderson's reedy voice; "Mrs. Rowe makes a quorum, so let's get started. We seem a bit thin on the ground this evening – any regrets, Ms. Fish?"

Ellen Fish looked briefly startled, as if the Chair's question related to the direction of her personal life, rather than her role as committee secretary. Flustered, she recovered herself and answered breathlessly; "Yes, Chair. Sharon, sorry, Mrs. Lewis, can't make it tonight and Mr. Carscadden will be a bit late. I don't know about the rest."

"Well, note the absences down, Ms. Fish. This really isn't good enough at this stage of the game."

Rosie listened to this exchange with amusement. Peter Anderson was a lawyer and more pedantic than most. His predilection for Robert's Rules of Order wasn't surprising, given his profession, but she thought his insistence on formality during meetings was ridiculous. Most of these people had grown up together – how could anyone keep a straight face while calling the rotund and affable Dougie, *Mr. Ferguson,* or glamour queen Carol, *Mrs. Hunter*? Oh well, it wasn't for much longer. The Reunion Weekend to celebrate fifty glorious years of education at John Galt High School was only seven weeks away – three more meetings and she'd be done.

There was a brief interruption as Dave Mason arrived, then the minutes of the previous meeting were proposed and accepted, and discussion moved on to Business Arising. First up was Harvey Schnurr, member of the committee by virtue of being current school Principal.

Harvey came from Toronto and had only been Principal for a year, so he had embraced the Reunion as an opportunity to cement relations with "the local rubes" (as he privately called the residents of Little Yarmouth.) Convinced that nobody in town had the intelligence or expertise to create a website, he had volunteered the services of the school computer lab to set up and run an appropriate Reunion site.

Now using his laptop, he projected the website onto the wall and proceeded to "walk" the committee through its various pages, all the while speaking very slowly and spelling out every technical word as if those present were deaf, mentally challenged or a combination of both disabilities. He concluded by reporting that the site had been operational for two weeks, and was receiving numerous "hits" daily.

Laying down his laser pointer, he smiled beatifically around the table and asked if everyone were now "au fait" with the website, or whether any member was still having "conceptual struggles." Dave Mason, whose struggles were not "conceptual" but sprang from an overwhelming desire to shake Harvey until his teeth rattled, said; "Yes. Could Mr. Schnurr please spell *hits,* and explain what the word means?" The room exploded in laughter and Rosie didn't dare look at Dave, afraid she would lose her struggle to keep a straight face.

Peter Anderson, who had no sense of humour, coughed and said; "Please direct your questions through the Chair, Mr. Mason," but Harvey, his face flushed beet red, had already got to his feet and, muttering about another meeting, was preparing to leave. "Yes, well, thank you very much Mr. Schnurr – I'm sure the website will be a great asset to our activities……." Peter Anderson called after the principal, who'd left in a flurry of indignation, letting the Staff Room door slam behind him.

Momentarily confused, the Chair cleared his throat and said; "Well, moving on…." His glance fell on a slender young woman, whose long nose and darting glances always put Rosie in mind of a weasel. "Can we have your report on catering and decorating for the dance, Ms. DeGroot?"

Within half an hour everyone but Sharon Lewis was sitting around the table. Each late arrival had been treated to a glare from Peter Anderson and the same chilly comment; "Note time of arrival, Ms. Fish." Carol Hunter was last to arrive and, never one to take criticism to heart, had answered pertly; "Oh, dear – will you want me to stay after class, Mr. Anderson?" a remark that was greeted with sniggers around the table.

Everyone in town knew that Carol and Peter had a torrid affair the previous year, which ended abruptly when his wife, Marcia, found out and threatened to "take him for all he was worth, and then some." As her father was senior partner at Peter's law firm, (Tortress, Tortress, Benchley and Anderson) he knew this was no idle threat. Carol was unceremoniously jettisoned from both the relationship and her job as Peter's legal secretary.

Now the Chair blushed deeply, being sufficiently disconcerted to knock over his cup and spray coffee dregs across the table. Carol smiled sweetly and, with a shimmy that set her numerous chains and bangles jingling, sat down next to Rosie enveloping them both in a cloud of heady perfume.

The meeting wore on. Dave and Dougie, co-chairs of promotions and publicity, presented samples of the assorted buttons, pennants, coasters and pens they were proposing for swag bags, and reported that the Clarion would print posters and tickets at cost. Willie Robertson was also giving the committee a great deal on paid advertising, and was amenable to printing press releases every week for three weeks ahead of the event. Dave moved adoption of their report, and a spirited discussion followed on the pros and cons of the various promotional items presented.

Why are people always so eager to get bogged down over nickel and dime items, Rosie wondered, recalling numerous other town committees on which she'd served. It's as if they're afraid to deal with the major issues, so just retreat into thrashing out the cost of paperclips, toilet paper or, in this case, buttons and pens. Dougie was going on at length about the merits of buttons versus coasters and, despite her best efforts to pay attention, she was finding it increasingly difficult to keep her eyes open. The voices around her began to recede, the room darkened and … was that smoke she could smell?

"Are you voting, Mrs. Rowe?" Peter Anderson's voice broke into her consciousness and she saw everyone looking at her. "Are you in favour of purchasing two hundred Astoria Click Action Pens and one hundred plastic coasters for a hundred and nineteen dollars, plus tax and shipping?"

"Yes, sorry. Yes, that sounds fine to me" Rosie stammered, embarrassed that she had no idea what had just been discussed.

"Fine. That's carried then. Can we have a seconder for the promotion and publicity report? Thank you, Mr Carscadden. All in favour? Carried. Kudos to Mr. Mason and Mr. Ferguson for their efforts. And now, since some of us seem to be having difficulty staying awake," Peter Anderson paused and looked at Rosie, "I think a fifteen minute comfort break is in order."

Chairs were pushed back, and a buzz of conversation started around the table. Carol turned to Rosie and said loudly, "What a dipstick! Only Pete Anderson could say *comfort break* with a straight face. Well, I need to pee, so I guess I'd better hustle on down to the *comfort station* and get *comfortable* before our fifteen minutes are up. Get me a coffee, would you Rose," and she flounced out the door.

Rosie strolled over to the coffee maker and waited behind Dougie Ferguson as he poured himself a coffee.

"Oh, hi Rosie" he said, as he turned around. "Here, you take this – I'll get another."

"No, that's alright Dougie. I need to get one for Carol too, so you go ahead." She stepped up to the machine. "I quite like those sugar free cookies, by the way."

Dougie beamed. "Well, thanks Rose, that's really great to hear. I've been working on the recipe for quite a while now. The challenge was to keep the taste and texture the same, while reducing fat and sugar, and I think I've finally pulled it off." He paused to bite into a large doughnut then, brushing powdered sugar from his shirtfront, continued; "Healthy goodies are definitely the way of the future you know, and folks are happy to pay extra to feel good about what they're eating."

Rosie smiled, and cast around for an escape. Dougie was the only person she'd ever met who got excited talking about baked goods and, once started, he could go on interminably. Carol was back, but she was across the room in deep conversation with Alan Price, the school's tanned and athletic phys.ed. teacher.

Rescue came limping slowly towards her in the form of a tall, distinguished man with a shock of white hair. He was nattily turned out in cream linen jacket, red tie with matching handkerchief in the breast pocket and navy trousers with a knife edge crease.

"Hello, Mr. Carscadden, it's good to see you. How have you been keeping?" Rosie had to stop herself from addressing Ross Carscadden as *Sir*, the form of address she'd used throughout the years he'd been her school Principal. In fact, he'd been Principal to everyone in the room, having held that position from the school's opening day in 1950 until his 1983 retirement. His role on the committee was very much that of *Principal Emeritus.*

"Tolerably well, thank you Rose. My arthritic hip gets no better, but one must expect some aches and pains at my age."

"Here you go, sir." Dougie handed him a coffee and stepped back respectfully.

"Ah, thank you, Douglas. And how are things with you? I hear you've been having some transportation difficulties?" Both Dougie and Rose looked puzzled. "Your delivery van was towed into my son-in-law's service station this afternoon, while I was filling the Chrysler. I believe I heard him say the van was beyond repair."

Dougie's cheerful expression disappeared and his voice hardened. "Yes, it is. Hired this new delivery guy just last week and the stupid fuc....," Dougie stopped himself just in time, old habits died hard and Mr. Carscadden had never tolerated profanity, "stupid fool didn't know enough to stop on red. Now I'll have to use the SUV for deliveries, until the insurance comes through."

Rosie saw an opportunity; "That was your van in the accident with Clodagh Wesley this afternoon? I'm really sorry to hear that, Dougie. But at least your driver wasn't badly hurt. He was Tony Wesley's replacement, I guess? Lucy told me how good you'd been to them, helping Tony out with a job so they could come back home. That was so kind of you."

Dougie smiled sheepishly. "I was glad to do it – the driving job was only minimum wage but better than nothing, and he couldn't manage much with his lungs the way they were." He took another bite of his doughnut, and chewed reflectively.

Rosie waited for him to continue, but as his silence lengthened she prompted; "Were you friends for a long time?"

"Oh, yeah, we went back a long way; in the same class here for four years. Lost touch when I joined the military, but then he called out of the blue a couple of year's back, after he got the push from Algoma. That was a raw deal, but I guess he wasn't the only one." Dougie reached across the table and took another doughnut. "Just sorry I couldn't do more."

Ross Carscadden had been listening to their conversation and now he shook his head. "Sad waste of a life, I call it. That boy had so much promise – bright, good family, money – he could have done anything." He handed his empty cup to Rosie.

"Can I get you another, sir?" she said. The "sir" slipped out before she knew it.

"No, thank you Rose. You know, I never understood why Tony Wesley went off the rails, he started out so well. That first year he was an "A" student, on the football team, in science club, everything. Then he seemed to fall apart. And to end up dead in a basement on Veterans Avenue. The demon drink, indeed" and he shook his head again. A devout Methodist and lifelong teetotaller, the old man believed firmly that the road to Hell was paved with bottle caps.

"Actually, Mr. Carscadden…" but Rosie was interrupted in her attempt to salvage Tony's reputation by Peter Anderson's call to order.

As everyone took their seats Carol leaned towards Rosie. "Don't you think he's gorgeous?" she whispered, gazing winsomely at Alan Price, who smiled back at her across the table.

"Yes, very attractive," Rosie whispered back; "but isn't he a bit young for you?" Carol had been two years ahead of her all through high school and wouldn't see fifty four again, despite her short skirts and high heels.

Carol giggled; "Oh come on Rosie, age is just a state of mind, and my mind states that I'm twenty-eight. Haven't you heard that sex is the best exercise, and you know how important it is to keep fit at our age?" Rosie could feel her colour rising – Carol always enjoyed teasing her about sex – and now Peter Anderson was glaring at them. "Shhh," she whispered ineffectually but, for Carol, the Chair's disapproval was like a red rag to a bull.

"I guess I'd better shut up, or we'll be getting detention with ass-hole up there." She raised her voice; "He should be so lucky!" But her temper seemed to evaporate and she turned her attention to shredding the edge of a paper coffee cup.

"Mr. Price – your report on the planned sports events, please" the Chair intoned, and the "gorgeous" teacher stood obediently.

Rosie felt a quick wave of sympathy for Carol. She knew what it was like to be abandoned by someone you loved and trusted, and unfortunately Carol had believed everything Pete Anderson had told her about his miserable life with Marcia, and their impending divorce. But she had misjudged him badly, and was devastated when he dumped her immediately their liaison came to his wife's ears.

She hadn't been much use on the Reunion Committee either, and Rosie suspected she'd only volunteered to have the opportunity of needling Pete Anderson at every meeting. It had fallen on Rosie to complete virtually all the work on their joint project – a

Fifties/Sixties Room – but she didn't really mind. She'd enjoyed hanging out with Carol again, tracking down old photos and yearbooks and sharing lots of "remember when" stories. Now, as if on cue, she heard the squeaky summons; "Can we have the report on your Room project please, Mrs. Rowe and Mrs. Hunter," and got to her feet.

It was nine forty-five when the meeting wrapped up and, as Rosie gathered her papers together, she had a sudden impulse to find out what Carol remembered about Tony Wesley. "Carol, I'm starving. Do you fancy a milk shake? The Creamery will still be open."

Carol was putting on a tight denim jacket. "Don't you have to get home for Moira?" she asked.

"No, Ruth Anderson's girl, Shannon is sitting with her. She's saving to take a beautician's course, so she won't mind getting paid for an extra half-hour." Moira had been incensed at the idea of having a baby-sitter, but settled down once she knew it was Shannon coming over. Despite their age difference the girls got on well together, and Rosie knew Moira would be sporting nail polish and probably a new hairstyle by the time she got home. Shannon was always on the lookout for a willing guinea pig.

The Nice'n'Creamery was just a few minutes away from school and Carol and Rosie were soon sitting in a booth, sucking up their guilty pleasures. Rosie remembered being told, in a weight loss class, that there were more than a thousand calories in a Creamery milkshake. But just think of all the extra calcium I'm getting, she told herself as she finished the last delicious dregs, and anyway, I haven't eaten much today. I'll start dieting again tomorrow.

They chatted happily for a while, reviewing everything that had gone on that evening, and making plans to find more items for their joint Room project. Then, as the conversation lulled, Rosie thought the time was right for a change of subject.

"I was over to see Lucy Wesley on Saturday" she said, by way of an opening gambit. "You remember, Lucy Curtis that was. She was in my class until she dropped out to marry Tony Wesley."

Carol pushed her half-finished milkshake to one side. "That's enough for me. Why do they make these things so huge?"

And that's why she's thin as a rail and I'm......not, thought Rosie. She tried again; "She's having a hard time coming to terms with Tony's death. That was a terrible thing to happen; she found him, you know."

"Yes, I heard all about it. But don't expect me to feel sorry for that conniving little slut." Carol pulled a lip gloss palette out of her purse and slowly reapplied colour to her lips. She closed the palette with a crisp "snap" and went on in a tight little voice; "They both got what they deserved – what goes around, comes around for sure. I'm just glad it happened here so I could see it first-hand."

Rosie was shocked by the bitterness in Carol's voice. "My God, Carol, what did they ever do to you, that you'd be happy to hear of a tragedy like that?"

"Oh, only ruined my life, that's all." Carol looked up, her eyes suspiciously bright. She blinked and brushed a hand across them impatiently. "Everything would have been different if little Miss Smarmy hadn't started showing up everywhere we went. All smiles and blushes and *Oh Tony, this* and *Oh Tony, that* – she made me sick!" Carol pulled a tissue out of her purse and blew her nose. "He was *my* boyfriend and he ditched me a week before his Graduation Prom to take little Goody Two Shoes instead. She was still wearing ankle socks for God's sake!"

Rosie looked at Carol, aghast at the fury in her voice. How could anyone still care so much about a school prom all those years in the past? She spoke gently; "Carol that happened a lifetime ago, and surely missing a prom didn't ruin your life..." but Carol was getting to her feet.

"Yes, well you don't know the half of it, do you? I was a laughing stock all round town." She picked up her purse. "I've got to go. I've got more important things to do than waste my time being sorry for Tony Wesley, or that bitch he married. I'm just really glad she's miserable, and I hope she's lonely and sad and suffers for years." And with that she turned and walked away.

Rosie drove slowly home, her mind in turmoil as she searched for answers to Carol's extraordinary reaction to her questions. She knew there must be much more to the story than just a missed prom and some hurt teenage pride. But she was beginning to understand why Tony Wesley hadn't wanted to come back to Little Yarmouth – everyone she'd spoken to, except his wife, had hated him.

And time hadn't mellowed those feelings; Willie Robertson, Dave Mason and Carol Hunter were all glad he was dead. Then there was Lucy's view of Tony; loving husband, caring father, good provider – had she been deluding herself all these years? Had the real Tony Wesley stayed hidden, even from Lucy? No wonder he couldn't rest in peace. And the list of actions for which he might be sorry was growing longer by the day.

*   *   *   *

Carol got out of the car, dropped her cigarette butt on the garage floor and ground it viciously underfoot. She rested her purse on top of a metal bin festooned with happy faces and cheery messages (*let's keep our butts out of everyone's face, get your butt in here, litter is butt ugly*) and pulled out an unopened pack of Lavinia Slims.

Her hands were shaking so much that she could barely pull off the cellophane wrapper but she managed and then, with a flourish, threw it down to the ground. She smiled. Somehow that act of childish defiance had made her feel better. And judging by the amount of smoking related litter surrounding the butt bin, a good number of her fellow tenants felt the same way.

Carol lit her cigarette and pulled the smoke deep into her lungs. God, why must people interfere in other people's lives? "If I want to smoke, that's my business," she said aloud, as she locked her car and stalked angrily to the elevator. *Thank you for not smoking,* smirked another happy face, this one stuck on the elevator doors. She blew smoke onto the sign and jabbed "3" as the doors closed behind her.

"C'mon, c'mon," she muttered irritably as the elevator made its slow and creaky ascent. She just wanted to get into her apartment, sit down and try to pull herself together. Work had been hellish today, and then that god-awful, miserable meeting. Why had she ever thought that joining the reunion committee would make her feel better about Pete Anderson? God, how she hated that prick! Sitting there, looking down his nose at everyone – all she'd wanted to do tonight was go over and knock that smug look off his face. And then to top it all off, Rosie had started on about Tony Wesley. That had been the last straw.

After she fled the Creamery, she barely managed to pull into an adjacent parking lot before the dam burst. She had cried noisy tears of anger, frustration and heartbreak until, exhausted, she re-started the car and made her way home.

The elevator doors opened and Carol drew deeply on her cigarette, before stubbing it out on the floor, right under the happy face exhorting everyone to *Keep our Building Clean.* As she walked along the hallway to her apartment she noticed how grubby the carpet and walls looked. She toyed with the idea of complaining to the management company. The building would certainly be a lot cleaner if Lionel spent less time putting up posters and more time vacuuming and washing paintwork. But what was the point? The little turd would find out about her complaint, and then he'd never come when something needed fixing. No, let someone else stick their neck out; she had enough useless battles to fight.

She let herself in and dropped down on the loveseat without bothering to take off her jacket or shoes. After the crying jag her stomach was churning, and she felt as if a lump of lead was sitting in her chest. "So much for letting it all out," she said to the empty room; "fucking stupid psychology!"

Damn Tony Wesley! She understood Rosie's reaction – yes, it was all a lifetime ago - but he really had ruined everything. All the hurt had come flooding back that day last December, when she'd seen him strolling down King Street with Lucy. He'd taken his wife's hand as they crossed the road and Carol had watched, holding her breath, praying to see them both flattened by a truck.

Afterwards she was briefly ashamed of this reaction, but her better nature was short-lived. Seeing their happiness had torn open all her old wounds, and years of suppressed rage had boiled up inside her. She realised she still hated them.

"I need a drink" she muttered, and headed into the little galley kitchen. Taking down a half empty bottle of rye, she filled a tumbler and topped it off with a dash of water from the tap. The message light was blinking on her phone.

"Hi mom, sorry I missed you," her son's voice broke the silence. "Just calling to say hi. Hope you're fine. We're all good here; Nancy and Daisy send their love."

I bet, thought Carol. "Love" was the last thing her daughter-in-law would be sending, and Daisy could hardly love a grandmother she'd seen only twice in all her little life.

"Look, mom," Ian's voice hesitated. "About us coming for the high school reunion. We're not going to be able to make it, after all. Nan…, I mean we, think it's just too far to bring Daisy, a seven hour flight and then the drive up from Toronto. Maybe next year – or maybe you can come out to us sometime? Anyway, give me a call. Love ya. Bye."

Just before Ian hung up, Carol heard Nancy's voice in the background; "For God's sake Ian, you didn't invite her here, did you?"

"No need to worry about your undesirable mother-in-law dropping by, dearie," Carol said to the handset. "I haven't got any money for trips out West." That bitch had no idea what it was like to have to watch every penny. No, she'd gone straight from daddy's bank account to Ian's six figure income. All those years of scrimping and saving to send him to university, and then getting loans to help him set up as a chiropractor. And for what? So he could move as far away from her as possible.

She swallowed her drink and refilled the glass. There was nowhere to sit in the little kitchen so she stood at the sink, staring out at the blackness.

If Tony had taken her to the prom, she wouldn't have tried to make him jealous by going with Chris Hunter. And she wouldn't have got drunk, or ended up pregnant. No, she'd have gone to college – her grades were good enough – and everything would have been different. But, because of *them*, she had to marry Chris Hunter and then struggle on as a single mother when he ran off before Ian's first birthday. Yes, her life had been ruined the night of the prom, but she'd got back at them alright. She'd made sure the happy couple paid for all the misery they'd caused her. And she didn't feel sorry at all.

Chapter 7 – Visiting Gams

It was a lovely sunny morning, the only trace of Monday's storm a scattering of leaves blowing gently across Cedar Street's neat lawns and driveways. The townships on this eastern shore of Lake Huron were famous for their changeable weather, and the locals had long ago adopted a phrase more commonly used in England; *if you don't like the weather, wait half an hour.*

Rosie and Moira were both up early. Rosie, because she'd slept only fitfully, her mind endlessly going around Carol's surprising reaction to Tony Wesley's death. And Moira, because she couldn't wait to get started on the trip to her great-aunt Margaret's cottage.

After breakfast, Rosie loaded Moira's bag into the car, and waited while she said a tearful goodbye to Gussie. "Come on, Moira! He'll still be here when you get back on Sunday. I told Gam to expect us for lunch, not dinner!"

"Are you sure we can't take him with us in the car?" Moira wheedled. "Look, he's so sad; he knows we're going somewhere nice without him."

Rosie thought Gussie's hang-dog expression was more likely due to seeing his treat dispenser disappear, than to any great desire for a car trip.

"He doesn't like the car; he'll just think he's going to the vet, and get all upset. And I'm only staying at Gams for lunch, then I'm coming straight home. He'll have all that long drive just to turn around and come all the way back again."

Moira pouted. "But he *loves* the cottage."

Rosie sighed and searched for a compromise; "Tell you what. If Gam has a spare bed for Saturday night, I'll come Saturday instead of Sunday, and bring Gussie up with me then. He can chase chipmunks all Saturday night and Sunday morning. Okay? Now, can we please get going?"

Mollified, Moira gave Gussie a final hug, led him back into the house and closed the front door. "Bye, Gus" she called through the letterbox, "See you Saturday," and ran down the driveway to the car. They were finally underway.

Rosie turned onto Highway 21 and headed north. It took about 45 minutes to reach Kincardine, then she turned east and drove along a long series of concession roads. If you were unlucky enough to get behind a farm vehicle or a camper, this leg of the journey could be very slow. Today was no exception, and it was close to midday when she finally reached the gravelled track leading down to the cottage. She drove carefully – the Buick might be old, but its bodywork was still in good shape and she didn't want it all scratched up by the densely growing trees and brush.

Moira, who'd been quiet through most of the trip, let out a squeal of delight as she spotted her great-aunt waiting for them at the end of the track. She grabbed Rosie's arm; "Look, Auntie Ro, there's Gam!" and, regardless of the branches whipping past, she wound down her window, stuck out her arm and yelled "Hi Gam!"

"Yes, alright Moira, I can see her" Rosie answered waspishly. It's a good thing I was driving slowly, she thought, or Moira's excitement would have had us wrapped round a tree. As the car drew to a stop Moira jumped out and ran down the pathway to the short, grey haired figure walking towards them.

"Hello, Moira – it's *so* good to see you, my pet. And how tall you've grown since Christmas!" Margaret swept Moira into a bear hug, then held her at arm's length. "And what interesting colours streaked through your hair. Did you do that yourself?"

"No, my friend Shannon did it. She does babysitting because she's saving up to go to *Aesthetic Artistes* in Goderich. She's ever so clever at hair and she does nails, too. Look..." and Moira stretched out her hands to show off Shannon's expertise. Her nails on one hand were painted deep purple and a brilliant orange on the other.

"My goodness, your nails match your hair perfectly. I don't think I've ever seen quite that combination before," and Margaret glanced across at Rosie, who raised her eyebrows and shrugged.

Rosie opened the trunk and pulled out Moira's bag; "Sweetie, take your stuff inside and get unpacked, while I give Gammy a hand with lunch."

"Which room, Gam?" Moira called over her shoulder, as she hauled her bag toward the cottage.

"Woodpecker, hon. You're in with Susie; she's been talking about you coming for days." Susan was the eldest of Margaret's great grandchildren and, at ten, the nearest in age to Moira.

As Moira disappeared into the cottage, Margaret turned to Rosie and said with a smile; "The hair? You know Elspeth will have a *fit* when she sees it."

"No worries, Auntie Marg. It's only spray on colour – couple of dips in the lake and it'll all disappear. She was so worried this morning that it would wash off before we got here that she borrowed my shower cap and was all finished in ten minutes. I've never known her out of the bathroom in less than half an hour before." Rosie took her aunts arm, and chuckling together they strolled companionably down the path and into the cottage.

The wooden screen door slammed behind them as they went into the kitchen. Built in 1929, this was the oldest part of the cottage, originally a fishing cabin for Rosie's grandfather, Doctor William Cornish. For the first few years, the cabin was little more than a shack where William and his two eldest sons, Joseph and Gerard, could go to fish and escape the restrictions of life in Little Yarmouth.

But as the family grew Minette (William's wife and Rosie's grandmother) insisted that the cabin be extended and improved enough for the whole family to enjoy. By 1936 summer at the cabin, or *cottage* as it was now more properly known, had become an established tradition. Minette, William and their seven children, with ages spanning fourteen years between the eldest and the youngest, would spend all July and August at Heron Lake, with William coming and going as his busy practice allowed.

The log cottage was a long, single storey building, made of timber cut from the Cornish's surrounding five acres of bush. Over the years, ongoing alterations and improvements had given it the approximate shape of a letter E. The original cabin made up one end, with a great room added on to the west side and two later additions extending to the back, one half way along the great room and one at the far end. On the lake side, a screened porch ran the length of the building and, at water's edge there was a flat roofed boathouse. Dotted around the property were a bunkhouse, three woodsheds, a workshop, generator shed and a brick bathhouse. To general relief, the venerable outhouse had been retired six years earlier, and replaced by two indoor chemical toilets.

"Who's staying right now?" Rosie asked her aunt, as they set about making sandwiches and washing fruit for lunch.

"Steve and Kath are here with their three until Saturday morning, and Sharon's up with Wayne and Winona, but they're going home Friday. She'll be sorry to have missed you; broke a tooth yesterday, and had to go into Kincardine this morning, to the dentist."

Rosie shuddered. She had never grown out of her childhood fear of dentists, despite the gentle treatment dispensed by Dr. Morley, Little Yarmouth's kindly practitioner.

"Oh, that's a shame; hope she doesn't have a bad time." With a shiver, she banished the image of needles, drills and shiny metal instruments assaulting Sharon's defenceless mouth. "So, you must have had your hands full this week; five kids and now Moira."

"It has been a bit loud," Margaret admitted with a smile. "But Steve's pretty good at keeping order. And they're all much of an age, so no-one gets left out of anything." Steve, Margaret's grandson, had grown up spending his summers at the cottage and knew every mood of the lake and every inch of the woods.

"Have you got room for me and a dog on Saturday night? Moira thinks Gussie needs a break from his hectic schedule."

Her aunt laughed. "Poor thing. I'm sure he's just worn to a shadow! Yes, I'd love you to stay over Saturday, and Sunday too, if you like. There'll be no-one else here by then, just me and Moira, so we can have nice quiet evenings toasting marshmallows and listening for the loons. Just like old times." She looked up from buttering bread and gave Rosie a keen look. "And how are you doing? You look a bit washed out. Is everything okay?"

Rosie cut a stack of bologna sandwiches in half then laid down her knife. "Not really, Auntie Marg. I've got a bit of a problem, and it's turning out to be more complicated than I expected."

"What kind of problem?" Margaret caught Rosie's eye. "Oh, you mean *that* kind of problem. Anything I can help with?"

"Maybe. I'd like to talk it over with you, see what you think." She paused, then went on hesitantly; "And I'm not sleeping well, either. I've started dreaming about the fire again."

Margaret came around the table and put her arms round Rosie. "Do you think...?", but whatever she was going to say was lost, as the screen door banged open and two small boys burst in.

"Gammie, can we have something to eat? It's gotta be lunchtime, by now," the taller of the two shouted as he barrelled into the room.

"Chris, quietly please. Say hello to your cousin Rose, then get those hands washed. And Wayne, take your shoes back outside – they're covered in mud. Where on earth have you been this morning?"

The next hour was filled with the noisy chatter and clatter of a family meal. There were few rules at the cottage, but one thing Margaret insisted upon was that everyone sit down to lunch and dinner together.

In ones and twos the family assembled until there were four adults and six children sharing sandwiches, salad and fruit around the kitchen table. Rosie chatted happily with her cousin Steve and his wife Kath, glad of the opportunity to catch up on their busy lives. From time to time she glanced across the table at Moira, who was demonstrating her prized cell phone to Susan, Steve's eldest girl. She wondered how long it would be before the inevitable question came and then; "Dad, when can I have a cell-phone?"

That was fast, Rosie thought, as Steve was drawn into the inevitable debate on the pros and cons of cell phones for pre-teens. Having never been a parent, Rosie was the first to admit that she didn't know much about raising kids, but she did know that this was one argument Steve was doomed to lose.

The noise around the table began to diminish, as one by one the kids finished eating and disappeared outside. Steve and Kath said their goodbyes and hurriedly followed the shouts and whoops towards the lake. They both had full afternoons ahead; Steve taking the two boys canoeing and Kath supervising the girls swimming off the dock.

It seemed very quiet in the kitchen as Rosie and her aunt tackled the pile of dishes waiting by the sink. Her hands busy in soapy water, Margaret said casually;

"So, do you want to tell me about this problem?"

It didn't take Rosie long to cover all the details of Tony Wesley's death, funeral and subsequent visitations to Moira and herself. Her aunt listened intently, her head inclined to one side, interrupting only once when Rosie described John's reaction to Moira's experience.

"Isn't that just typical" she said, crossly. "Just like your father, and probably every other Cornish male whose daughter had the Gift, all the way back to Edmund!"

"I know. He's just hoping it'll never happen again, but if our lives are anything to go by, Moira's headed for a steep learning curve. At least these days none of us are in danger of being burned at the stake." Aunt and niece looked at each other and smiled.

"Well, as I see it, you've made great strides over the past few days. You know for sure that Tony was murdered, and you've got three potential suspects: Dave Mason, Willie Robertson and Carol Hunter."

"Yes, but do you really think Dave or Carol would kill someone over a high school romance? And I don't even know what's at the bottom of Willie's antagonism. Maybe he just didn't like Tony because he was a spoiled rich kid. That's no motive for cold-blooded murder."

Margaret stacked the last of the dishes on the draining board and picked up a tea towel. "But was it cold-blooded? Maybe it was just an argument that got out of hand."

"I don't think so. Remember, I saw Tony *thrown* down the stairs, and I didn't see anyone making a frantic dash into the basement to try and help him. In fact, it was quite the opposite. Whoever did that had absolutely no remorse. And then there's the bottle of rye. No, it was planned, alright."

The conversation paused for a moment as they dried and stacked, each silently coming to terms with the fact that peaceful Little Yarmouth was probably home to a vicious killer.

Margaret stopped mid-dry, her hands full of cutlery. "Rosie, did you just say Tony Wesley was *thrown* into the basement? You didn't see a struggle of any kind, at the top of the stairs?"

"No, the two figures seemed to be just standing together by the basement door. As if one person were holding the other upright..." Rosie's voice tailed off as she realised the implication of what she was saying. Why hadn't she thought of it before?

Her aunt put Rosie's thoughts into words: "Well, don't you see? That means Tony's neck was likely broken before he was pitched down the stairs. If he was still alive, there would have been a struggle. And if you can get a pathologist to prove that, then the police will have to investigate, and you can take a back seat." Margaret put her hand on Rosie's arm. "Because my dear, you've got to be very careful – this is a murderer you're dealing with and if he or she figures out what you're doing....." Margaret let the rest of her fears remain unsaid.

"I know, Auntie Marg." Rosie's legs felt suddenly weak and she sat down at the kitchen table. "This isn't like the other times I've dealt with murder. Most of those deaths were crimes of passion; something that happened in the heat of the moment, or almost by accident. There wasn't deep malice involved, just a lot of guilt and grief. But this is different. I felt a real sense of evil, of malevolent satisfaction in that basement. And that awful giggle – almost as if killing Tony was fun." Rosie shivered, despite the warm sunshine streaming in through the kitchen window.

Her aunt took the kettle over to the tap and turned on the water. "Let's have a cup of tea, calm those nerves" she said briskly. "*The cup that cheers*, and all that." She set the kettle on the stove, and the propane popped alight.

Sitting down again she went on; "You said Tony's widow isn't happy with the accident theory?"

"That's right. Lucy can't understand where the bottle of rye came from, because he'd been on the wagon for years. And it's bothering her that there wasn't an autopsy. Must say, that seems pretty strange to me as well. Anyway, I told her I'd get John to speak to the pathologist when he gets back next week. He'll get to the bottom of it."

Their gloomy conversation was interrupted by the kettle's cheerful whistle, and Margaret busied herself making tea the old-fashioned way. She warmed the brown betty teapot with hot water, emptied it out then put in a spoonful of tea for each cup. After adding one for the pot, she filled the pot with water just off the boil, and crowned it with a bright yellow knitted tea-cosy.

Watching her aunt bustle about, Rosie was struck by the dichotomy of their lives; lives which, to a casual observer, were no different to thousands of others, just a mundane round of daily routines and responsibilities. And that same observer, looking in through the cottage window, could never have imagined that the two women quietly chatting together were discussing murder most foul and wanderers from beyond the grave.

"What about you, Auntie Marg? Have you ever run into anything this nasty before?"

Margaret looked up from pouring the tea. "No, I haven't" she replied. "But as you know, my Gift is a bit different than yours, just as Moira's will probably be different to both of us. It's not unusual for the Gift to vary somewhat with each girl's personality. Mine has always been more about the future than the past, and if I see the dead it's always someone I knew well. Last time was Rob Murdoch." She paused; "Are you off sugar again?"

"Yes. But I'll have a splash of milk, please. I remember reading about Mr. Murdoch – it was front page news in the Clarion last year. Farmer who shot himself when his wife left him?"

"That's what the inquest found, but turns out it wasn't suicide, it was an accident. He'd been shooting rabbits and left the safety off the shotgun. Climbing over a fence he dropped the gun and it went off. Stupid thing to do, but he hadn't been on the ball since Lindsay took off. So, because he'd been depressed, everyone just assumed it was suicide." Margaret picked up the two cups of tea, put one in front of Rosie and sat down. "Anyway, he couldn't rest because he knew the insurance company wouldn't pay out for suicide and the kids needed that money to keep the farm going. Luckily, I was able to persuade the powers that be to look again, more thoroughly this time."

Rosie smiled and sipped her tea. Her aunt's powers of persuasion were legendary and it didn't hurt that, after thirty years as a Justice of the Peace, she was on first name terms with most of the local judiciary. And although she'd gracefully accepted her mandatory retirement seven years earlier at age seventy, she was still very much involved in the municipal and judicial affairs of Huron County.

"Do you really think an autopsy would show if Tony was killed before he went down the stairs? And how do we go about getting one?"

"I know several good pathologists, and any one of them will find the evidence, if it's there. But first things first. Tony will have to be exhumed, and unless you can come up with some compelling evidence of foul play, I can guarantee the police won't apply for an order." Margaret paused to add more milk to her tea; "No, the family will have to convince a coroner that there are sufficient grounds, then he'll order both the exhumation and an autopsy. I think its old Doc Caduggan in your neck of the woods. He shouldn't be too hard to convince. If the widow wants to go that route, I'll have a quiet word with him next bridge night."

Rosie shifted in her seat uneasily. "He won't think we're taking advantage somehow, will he? You know, friends in high places, and all that."

"Hardly, my dear" her aunt replied sharply. Her years on the bench had left her sensitive to any suggestion of cronyism. "He owes me more favours than he's had hot dinners." She tasted her tea and added more sugar. "No, *we* know there's been a murder, but unfortunately we can't tell anyone *how* we know. So there's absolutely nothing wrong with using the tools we have to hand. And if that includes offering to partner a hopeless bridge player, then so be it. I'm willing to make the sacrifice." Margaret cast her eyes heavenward and assumed a look of saintly resignation.

They began to laugh, and for a few minutes just sat together, happy to enjoy Margaret's excellent tea and to briefly put aside their knowledge of troubled spirits and violent death.

As if to break the tension, conversation turned to family matters; Margaret's three children had all married young, as had several of *their* children and her descendants now numbered in double digits. To Rosie, their triumphs and trials were like a soap opera, and she was endlessly fascinated by the domestic dramas which surrounded her aunt at every turn.

Finally, she looked at her watch. "I'm sorry Auntie Marg, but I'd better get on the road," she said. "Gussie's been shut in since ten, and he's only got a six hour bladder. If I get stuck behind a trailer I won't make it home until five, and there'll be a puddle in the hall, for sure." She took her cup over to the sink and began rinsing it.

Margaret chuckled. "Yes, they do keep us on a short leash, don't they? Henry used to sit on the stairs and tear off strips of wall-paper, if I was gone too long." Her aunt's adored, but exceedingly bad-tempered, corgi had died the previous fall at the ripe old age of seventeen. "I do miss him, you know. He was such a love." And she fumbled in her pocket for a tissue.

Rosie leant her saucer against the cup already on the draining board and looked out to where Henry's marker stood, on the edge of the woods. *I could come up with a lot of descriptions for Henry, but such a love wouldn't be one of them,* she thought. The corgi had been a dedicated ankle-biter, and anyone who had ever visited Margaret at home, or the cottage, had felt his sharp little teeth. When he died several family members, including Rosie, had come to the cottage for his interment; to support Aunt Margaret, who was grief-stricken, but mainly (as Steve had said privately), *to make sure the little bastard was really dead.*

Gathered around the deep hole Steve had dug across from the cottage, they all managed to look suitably funereal, until the first *thud* of dirt had landed on Henry's cardboard coffin. Then, Rosie had lifted her head and taken a quick look around. Predictably, her aunt was in tears, but there were secret smiles on every other face. "Yes, none of us will ever forget him, that's for sure," she answered guiltily, as she turned back around from the window.

Her aunt was wiping her eyes. "That's the trouble with pets" she said, her voice husky with emotion, "there's always the sad parting, unless of course, one gets a parrot." She laughed shakily. "Oh well, life goes on – and, of course, I do still see him around the place. I think he's waiting for me before he passes over, you know."

Rosie looked down nervously, half expecting to see a spectral Henry circling her ankles. "Sorry to rush, Auntie Marg, but I do have to make tracks." She leant down and gave her aunt a quick peck on the cheek. "Thanks for listening – it always helps to talk things out with you."

But her aunt didn't move or reply. Her eyes were closed and her skin colour had drained away, leaving her faces a frightening ashy grey. For one awful moment Rosie thought she was having a stroke. Then, realising what was happening, she sat down at the table and waited quietly.

It was a few minutes before Margaret's eyes opened and, seeing Rosie sitting opposite, she said in surprise; "Oh, you're still here. I thought you'd gone home."

"No, auntie, I'm still here. Are you feeling alright? Would you like a glass of water, or maybe tea? There's still some in the pot."

"Yes, another tea would be lovely." She glanced up at Rosie's anxious face. "Don't worry dear, I'm fine. I just need to sit and gather my thoughts," and she closed her eyes again.

Rosie poured the tea, set the cup in front of her aunt and sat down again, feeling decidedly uneasy.

After a few moments Margaret's eyes opened, she took a deep breath and reached over for Rosie's hands. "I've felt all afternoon that something's been trying to come through. Rosie, I don't want to frighten you, but you must promise me that you'll be very cautious who you trust from now on. I couldn't see much that will help you, but I do know we're dealing with something very bad, and certainly more than one death. This business with Tony Wesley is just the tip of the iceberg, and part of it comes very close to you. You'll need every bit of your strength, spiritual as well as physical, to get through this."

Rosie swallowed hard, and tried to ignore the lead weight that seemed to have settled in her stomach. Despite the old adage *forewarned is forearmed,* she knew she'd have been much happier investigating Tony's death, if she'd remained ignorant of these wider implications. Then, common sense prevailed, and she found her voice; "So you mean someone *I* know killed Tony, and this person has probably done other bad stuff, too?"

"Yes, it certainly looks that way. And at the moment, he or she is feeling very pleased, very calm about everything. There are no concerns about the murder, just supreme self-confidence and satisfaction." Margaret drained her teacup. She still looked exhausted, but her colour was improving and, gathering her strength, she continued; "The good news is that our killer has no suspicion that Tony's death is being questioned. So, for your own safety, you must keep a low profile until you can get the police involved. Make no mistake, if this person suspects you are on their trail, your life will be in danger."

Rosie's nerves began to get the better of her. Unable to sit still any longer, she stood up and carried her aunt's cup and saucer to the sink. "Don't worry, Auntie Marg, I'll be super careful" she said, rinsing the cup over and over again. "Apart from you, only John knows that Tony's death wasn't accidental and I don't plan on telling anyone else. Lucy knows something's wrong, but I hardly think she's our killer; why would she mention her suspicions at all, if that's the case?" Her hands were shaking as she put the cup on the draining board.

"No, I don't think this is anything to do with Lucy. But it does go back a very long way, I'm sure of that." Margaret got up from the table and hugged Rosie tightly. "Go on, now," she said, releasing her; "get on home and let that poor dog out. I'll keep focused on you and Tony, and if anything else comes through I'll borrow Steve's phone and call right away."

The screen door slammed behind them, as they walked silently up the path to Rosie's car. Both felt an odd sense of constraint, as if the normal banter of farewell was somehow inappropriate after Margaret's trance and frightening insights.

Rosie got into the Buick and wound down her window. "Tell Moira I said goodbye and I'll see her

Saturday. Keep a close eye on her, Auntie Marg. I don't think anything will touch her here, but just the same...."

"She'll be fine, my dear, don't worry. I know what to watch out for. Now, what about this autopsy?"

"I'll be seeing Lucy sometime this week, but I don't think I'll mention autopsies or exhumations to her just yet. I want to see what John finds out at the hospital mortuary first."

"That seems a sensible approach dear, but do impress on him the need for discretion. Remember, someone thinks they've got away with murder, and they're going to be furious at the prospect of an autopsy. So, have you got any idea what to do next?"

That's the million dollar question, Rosie thought as she put her key in the ignition. Aloud, she said; "I thought I'd have a word with Sister Mary Bernadette. It's amazing what she remembers about all of us at Holy Angels, so I might get a bit of insight into what Tony was like as a little boy."

"Yes, I've always thought she was very intuitive, almost as if she had the second sight. I don't suppose her ancestors hailed from our part of Norfolk, did they?"

"No - they all came from Ireland. But she did tell me once that her grandfather was the seventh son of a seventh son."

"Really? Well, I was just joking, but who knows, maybe our good Sister does have a touch of the Celtic vision." Her aunt leaned into the car. "Just one more thing, Rose. When you see Sister Mary B, make sure you ask her to keep us all in her prayers for a while. We're going to need all the help we can get."

Chapter 8 - Reflections

It was a slow ride home. Rosie found it difficult to focus on driving after Aunt Marg's revelations, and was almost grateful to find herself trapped behind a lumbering R.V all the way into Kincardine. Even after the camper turned off she stayed below the limit, unwilling to trust her concentration at faster speeds. Gussie would just have to keep his legs crossed!

Her mind was stuck on an incomprehensible fact; someone she knew was a murderer. Not an accidental killer either, but an individual capable of planning and executing a cold blooded crime, with complete disregard for the victim or anyone who knew him. Unfortunately, saying the killer was someone she knew didn't narrow the field by much. If this was a crime with deep roots, then he or she were probably in the same general age bracket as herself. And, after a lifetime in Little Yarmouth, she was on nodding terms with almost everyone in town over forty.

Despite barely driving at the speed limit, Rosie was soon sitting behind another R.V. She slowed even further, content to troll along in its wake as she made a mental list of potentially homicidal Little Yarmouth residents.

Now, Jackson Haynes at the Post Office had always struck her as a volcano waiting to blow. He had been her mailman for years and was famous for his bad temper. Even the yappiest dogs kept quiet when Jackson came up their path. The slightest infraction of delivery etiquette (*mailbox too low/high/springy, driveway too leafy/wet/snowy*) would result in non-delivery, leaving the unfortunate homeowner no option but to collect their mail from the post office, until the offence was remedied to Jackson's satisfaction.

Matters had come to a head the previous fall when Giles Mackie, who lived three doors up from Rosie, had replaced his standard mailbox with a faux Victorian model. This sported a lift up lid, rather than a pull down door and, as soon as she laid eyes on it, Rosie knew there would be postal trouble.

The first Monday following this installation Giles spotted Jackson leaving with undelivered mail, and had hurried out to demand that the irascible mailman hand over his letters "toot sweet." Jackson refused on the grounds that "mail must be deposited in an appropriate receptacle and cannot be handed to individuals on the street" (no matter that Giles was standing in his pyjamas on his own doorstep). Their verbal exchange, regarding the *appropriateness* of the receptacle in question, rapidly escalated to pushing and shoving as Giles tried to wrench his mail from Jackson's determined grip. After a few moments of ineffectual struggling, Jackson threw all the Mackie mail into their ornamental bird bath, and told Giles he could "go fish for it."

The next morning, Rosie's mail was delivered by a fresh-faced youngster in a brand new Canada Post uniform. After several weeks of "sick leave," Jackson had returned to the post office in his new position of counter clerk, a role which now placed him in a position to bully every unfortunate soul who wanted to buy stamps or mail a parcel. Yes, the ex-postie was certainly vindictive enough to harbour a bitter grudge, (Giles Mackie's mail seemed to go astray with alarming frequency) and Rosie made a mental note to do some research on Jackson Haynes, particularly his years at John Galt High.

The miles rolled by and Rosie's list continued to grow. There was Bill Gifford of Gifford's Fine Autos, suspected by everyone of trying to drown his drunken wife in their pool one hot summer night. And LeAnne Webb, barmaid and town virago, whose boyfriend disappeared mysteriously after they had a violent fight.

Then there was mild mannered Vic Watson, groundskeeper at Harbour Lights Country Club for thirty forelock-tugging years. One beautiful spring morning his veneer of polite deference had finally cracked, when he chased the Club President's foursome off the golf course for not replacing divots. In itself this was not a serious offence. Unfortunately, Victor had been carrying a large scythe at the time and, while in hot pursuit of the golfing miscreants, had vigorously indicated that any member not moving fast enough would soon have no place to put his HLCC Panama hat. After receiving a twelve month sentence for aggravated assault he was conditionally released to a half-way house, where he was still dutifully observing his parole conditions; that he stay away from recreational facilities and large farm implements.

By the time she reached home, Rosie was weary of speculation. She pulled into her driveway musing on the murky undercurrents that flowed beneath Little Yarmouth's tranquil exterior.

To the outsider, life in a small town or village could appear idyllic, peopled with nursery rhyme characters; *the butcher, the baker, the candlestick maker;* all living in perfect harmony and greeting each day with a smile. In reality, life in rural communities was much the same as anywhere else, differing in only one respect; that passions ran all the fiercer for being concealed beneath a cloak of home spun charm.

As she locked the Buick, she could hear Gussie's wild yelps of joy and the familiar *thud* as he slid into the front door. 'Oh Lord, I hope he hasn't been galloping about in a puddle' she said to herself, hurrying up the path. She fumbled her key in the lock, and finally swung the door open. "Hi baby – I'm so sorry I'm late. Who's my good boy, then?" A brown and white blur jumped up at her briefly, then disappeared down the porch steps onto the front lawn. Rosie could almost hear the canine sigh of relief, as Gussie lifted his leg against the nearest bush.

Crossing the hall, she flung her purse over the newel post at the bottom of the stairs and headed into the kitchen. Everything looked fine; no suspicious puddles or wet paw prints anywhere in view. Poor Gussie, he'd really been stretched to his limit today she thought, giggling at her unintended mental pun.

A familiar *skitter scatter* of claws announced the beagle's return, and he galloped into the kitchen intent on completing his boisterous welcome routine. Rosie bent down and put her arms round the wriggling body; "You've been *such* a good dog Gus, I think you deserve a treat."

Opening the fridge door she took out a hunk of cheese, unwrapped it and cut off a few small pieces. The instant she opened the packet Gussie, who loved cheese, began drooling and whimpering. At least Dr. Katz hadn't forbidden Gussie his cheese, Rosie thought, quelling a little voice inside that reminded her she'd never raised the subject with him. She dropped the pieces in front of Gussie who inhaled them, then looked up at her expectantly.

"No, all gone, boy" she said. "Just kibble now, I'm afraid. We can't have treats all the time." She took out the kibble, filled his bowl and set it on the floor. Gussie sniffed it, and looked up at her in disgust. "Yes, and Moira's not here, so that's all you're going to get," Rosie said firmly. Hearing her determined tone, Gussie put his head down and grudgingly began to eat. Just like dealing with a toddler, she thought. Now, what to have for supper?

Opening the fridge again her eye fell on the open bottle of white wine. She reached towards it, then stopped. No, not a good idea. Wine made her maudlin, and she had a lot to think about tonight. And besides, we can't have treats all the time.

After the two of them had eaten their respective meals and the dishes had been cleared away, she took a notepad and pen from her hold-all and sat down next to Gussie on the living room couch. She wrote *Potential*

Murder Suspects at the top of the first page, underlined it and then scratched it out again. It occurred to her the heading might be hard to explain, should anyone catch a glimpse of the familiar names listed beneath it.

From the possibles she'd reviewed on the drive home she soon selected twelve names, and was reluctantly adding Dave Mason and Carol Hunter to the list when the phone rang. Unwilling to be distracted, her first inclination was to let it go to voice mail, but then she remembered Aunt Marg had promised to call if she came up with any more information, and made a belated dash into the hall.

Of course, the handset wasn't in the hall and by the time she found it - *in the powder room, what was I thinking?* – a disembodied voice was already speaking.

"Hi Rosie," Lucy sounded tired. "It's me, Lucy. Sorry I missed you. I'll call again tomorrow…"

Rosie grabbed up the phone; "Hello? Lucy? Sorry, I couldn't find the phone. It's really good to hear from you. How are you doing?"

"Pretty good. I wanted to say thanks so much for coming over last Saturday, it really helped. And you were right; I'm much better staying with mum and dad than at Veterans. That house is such a downer…." Lucy's voice trailed off.

"So you're still with your mum? Have you been back to the house at all since Saturday?"

"No, I just can't face it. My dad went over yesterday afternoon and picked up the rest of my clothes and things. Took him all night to warm up; he said he'd never been in such a cold, damp house."

"Yes, I found it a bit chilly on Saturday too," Rosie said, actually thinking of Monday's rain-swept hall and Tony's icy presence hovering by the basement stairs. "Are you sleeping any better?"

"A bit. I'm trying to get off the sleeping pills Doctor Drucker gave me after ….. after the accident, you know. But if I don't take one, I only drop off for an hour or two then I'm wide awake again."

"I know. Those things really mess up your sleeping pattern. It took me nearly a year to get back to sleeping naturally after David…" Rosie hesitated, "died."

There was a silence at the end of the phone. Then Lucy said softly, "I'm sorry Rosie, I'd forgotten you lost your husband, too."

Yes, *lost* is the right word, Rosie thought. She tried to sound upbeat; "Not to worry, Lucy. It was years ago, and now I just try to concentrate on the good memories, not how it ended." And although most of that brave statement wasn't true, it seemed the right thing to say to a new widow, still coming to terms with her sudden loss.

"Look, why don't you come over for supper tomorrow night?" she went on. "Moira, that's my niece, is away at our cottage until the weekend, and the house seems really empty without her."

"I'd love to come over, Rosie, but not for supper. Mom's babysitting Amber's twins all day tomorrow and won't be home until eight at least, so I'm cooking for dad. I could come round after, though."

"Sounds great. Just come when you're ready. We'll have a glass of wine, and maybe I can pick your brains about the old times at John Galt. You know I'm on the Fiftieth Reunion Committee?"

"No, I didn't know," Lucy sounded hesitant about revisiting old school memories.

Shoot, that was a stupid thing to say, Rosie thought. She hurried on; "Yes, it's been quite an education. You remember Pete Anderson? Well, he's chairing it, so we all have to be on our best parliamentary behaviour." She was relieved to hear laughter from the other end of the phone.

"Yes, he always was a tight-ass," Lucy said. "It was just the same when he was on Student Council," and soon they were both laughing at Pete Anderson's youthful idiosyncrasies. The conversation quickly morphed into *remember-when's*, and Lucy sounded far more cheerful by the time she said goodbye, promising to see Rosie "around eight thirty tomorrow night."

Rosie went back to the living room and sat down again on the couch. She picked up her notepad but, as usual, any mention of David had unsettled her and her concentration was gone. She sat for a while with her hand resting on Gussie's head, listening to his contented snores and letting her mind wander back through the seven years of her marriage. What had she said to Lucy? *I just try to concentrate on the good memories, not how it ended.* Well yes, there had been good memories, but how the marriage ended had overshadowed them almost to vanishing point.

Was David really dead? And if he was, why had he never come to her? Surely he must feel some guilt for the mess he left behind, some need to explain the lies that destroyed her illusion of happiness. If he had loved her at all, he couldn't have rested until he came back for forgiveness. No, Rosie knew she would never convince herself that David was dead.

Over the past years she'd begun to hope for proof of his death, because that was preferable to knowing he had deliberately abandoned her, had methodically planned his escape, leaving her to deal with the appalling fall-out of his double life. Her mind went round and round the same question; if he loved me, how could he do this to me? And, as always, she came back to the same answer; because he didn't love you.

A tear slid down her cheek. Oh God, if he'd only been in a car accident or dropped dead from a heart attack, I'd have been over it by now. More tears began to fall and she brushed them away angrily. That bastard! Will I have to grieve over his cruelty for the rest of my life?

The hall clock chimed ten and Gussie stirred; a creature of habit, it was nearly time for his last trip round the garden. Rosie wiped her eyes. "C'mon boy," she said as she stood up and went towards the kitchen; "let's get some fresh air." Yawning, the beagle opened his eyes, stretched lazily and slid off the couch with a bump.

Rosie flipped on the kitchen light, opened the screen door and stepped out onto the patio. She watched Gussie disappear into the darkness, nose down, tail wagging as he followed some elusive scent. She envied him his uncomplicated life.

The sounds of a summer night were all around. The high pitched whine of courting insects, a distant croak from the pond at the end of the garden, the gentle batting of a moth drawn to the light behind the screen door. Above her the sky was clear, illuminated by a crescent moon shining brightly among masses of stars.

Rosie's Grand Mere Minette had told her once that the stars were tiny holes in a curtain that separated heaven from earth; little tears that permitted celestial light to shine down onto the world below. She'd always found that idea comforting, so much more appealing than the thought of billion year old rocks hurtling through silent space on pre-ordained pathways.

But then she'd always preferred fairy tales to real life, always wanted to believe in "happily ever after." Perhaps that's why it had been so easy for David to hide his lies – she hadn't wanted to know the truth. "No, I'm not doing that," she said out loud, "I'm not taking the blame for what he did to me."

Walking to the edge of the patio, her attention was caught by scuffling noises in the dark. Yes, she could definitely hear something close by, rooting through a flowerbed. Was it Gussie or, heaven forbid, a skunk? With her head full of washtubs and gallons of tomato juice, she called urgently; "Bed-time Gussie, c'mon in now."

A minute later he appeared on the patio beside her, panting, tongue lolling, his coat scattered with bits of leaves and grass. "Well, I hope you've tired yourself out" she said, brushing the garden debris off his back. Gussie looked up at her happily; all was right with his world.

*   *   *   *

"In here" Liz shouted, in answer to Rosie's call from the passageway. She sat back on her heels and looked critically at the inside of the oven. "Dammit, it's gonna have to be a scouring pad," she muttered as she wiped off the last of the oven cleaner, ineffectual as ever against carbonized cheese.

Rosie stuck her head around the rectory kitchen door. "Sorry, what did you say, Liz?"

"I said this oven cleaner's useless," Liz threw her cleaning cloth into a nearby bucket of water in disgust. "Father's bin heatin' up frozen pizzas again without a cookie sheet to catch the drips, and the cheese is all burnt on the bottom of the oven." She fished the cloth out of the bucket and wrung it viciously. "And if Doc Drucker has told him once, he's told him a dozen times to stay off the fats. Well don't blame me, I say, if Father's cholesterol goes sky high again. I cook him good healthy meals all week, and then he's into pizza and fried chicken, every weekend. He'll be the death of me."

"Yes," was all Rosie could think to say, although tempted to point out that Father Matthews' love of junk food put him in greater danger of imminent demise than his lean and energetic housekeeper. But it was never wise to interrupt Liz when she was off on a hobby horse, and Father's disregard for good nutrition was a favourite theme of hers. "Actually, I wanted a quick word with him, but he doesn't seem to be around. Did he get called out?"

Liz was getting to her feet. "And that's another thing. Old lady Wesley phoned while you were at the Post Office. He'd just sat down to his lunch – I'd made a lovely fresh salad with tuna - but off he goes at her beck and call. Left it all on the table and went straight out the door. He'll be into the coffee shop for doughnuts on his way back, just mark my words."

"So Mrs. Wesley's home from the hospital, then."

"Yeah, discharged this morning. Pat said the nurses on her floor were at breaking point. Treated the place like a hotel, she did. *Fetch me this,* and *fetch me that* all day and all night it was. And now Father's got to go running up to the house to hear her confession. Never comes down to the church like the rest of us, oh no." Liz paused for breath.

"Maybe she's not well enough to come out," Rosie ventured.

"He'll be there for hours," Liz continued as if Rosie hadn't spoken. "Goes on and on, she does. Don't make her any better person though, does it?"

Rosie wondered how Liz knew so much about Mrs. Wesley's confessions, then remembered her sister-in-law, Stella, worked as a cleaner at the house. Apparently the seal of confession was no protection against the Curtis bush telegraph.

She began to edge out of the kitchen. "Well, I'll catch him later. I'm working an extra hour today, so I expect he'll be back before I go."

Liz was rummaging under the sink for a scouring pad. "I wouldn't bet on it. A-ha got ya!" She waved a battered pack of Scour A Way pads at Rosie. "Did you say you were working later tonight? Getting a bit behind with things in the office, then?"

Rosie smiled. Although they got on well together, she knew Liz was always watchful for any employment opportunity that might be filled by a family member.

"No, I just have to make up my time for that long lunch on Monday," she answered. "And it's nearly month end too, so I want to finish up entering all the receipts into parish accounts today."

Liz picked up her bucket and emptied it into the sink. "Those nuns up at the school sure did a number on you, Rosie" she said, turning on the tap to refill the bucket with fresh water.

"Whatever do you mean?" Rosie was genuinely puzzled.

"Catholic guilt, girl. That pouring rain on Monday wasn't your fault, nor the accident or the traffic jam. But you were late back, so you feel guilty anyways and have to make up for it. Catholic guilt – nuns specialise in it, ya know."

"Well, there may be something to that. But it wasn't just the weather or the traffic that made me so late on Monday – I'd been ..." Rosie paused, searching for an appropriate description of her impromptu search in Lucy's basement: "trying to find something for a friend, and lost track of time."

Liz shook her head. "Father Matthews wouldn't be expecting ya to work late, not after all the hours you put in singing at Mass every weekend. I'd say that more than balances out the occasional long lunch." She knelt down in front of the oven again. "Sweet Jesus, I'll be scrubbing this mess for hours! I'll be givin' Father a piece of my mind when he comes in...."

Rosie had reached the kitchen door; "I'd better be getting back to those figures, Liz" she called over her shoulder as she hurried back along the passage to her office.

Liz's comments about school reminded Rosie that she planned to see Sister Mary Bernadette after work. It had been quite a while since she'd last seen her music teacher, and she feltwas rather guilty that there was an ulterior motive behind this belated visit. Yes Liz, she thought, more Catholic guilt, but this time very well-deserved. Now over eighty, Sister wouldn't be around for many more years, and one of her greatest pleasures was visiting with old pupils. Rosie resolved to turn over a new leaf; she really had no excuse for not going to the convent more often.

The afternoon sped by in a haze of ledger entries and columns of figures. She heard Liz leave at five, and a few minutes later Father Matthews' shiny Ford Escort went past the office window and into the rear parking lot. 'Almost as if he'd been waiting for Liz to leave,' she mused. She wouldn't be surprised – Father probably knew he was in his housekeeper's bad books, for abandoning his "lovely fresh salad with tuna."

About ten minutes later the office door swung open, to reveal the reverend gentleman himself standing in the doorway.

"Oh Rosie, still here? I thought you'd gone home and left the office window open." Everyone at the Rectory was paranoid about closing ground floor windows after last year's break-in.

"Just working on the month end figures, Father." Rosie looked up from her desk at the dapper figure of her parish priest. As usual, Father Matthews was immaculate; neatly pressed black suit, spotless Roman collar, shiny black shoes, even the top of his bald head looked buffed to perfection. The only thing amiss was a tiny trace of powdered sugar on his lapel. Liz's guess about Father's last stop on his way home had been spot on!

Quite a change from his predecessor, Father (call me Dave) Lewis, who had always seemed ill at ease in clerical garb, and spent most of his time in baggy sweat pants and a T-shirt. He also had some very progressive ideas about liturgy and worship. Sacred Dance ceremonies, Buddhist celebrations, an Aboriginal smoke cleansing ritual; St. Jude had played host to them all during "Dave's" short stint as pastor. Then, shortly after a Wiccan Harvest Festival was held in the church hall, Father Lewis was re-assigned to Kenora and, to no-ones great surprise, later left the priesthood for a career in anthropology.

"You know there's no need to stay late for that, Rosie. And if you'd let me set you up with a computer, the whole thing would be a snap." The priest's eyes gleamed with all the fervour of a recent convert to technology. "Delivery wouldn't take long, you know. I could order it tomorrow and we'd probably have everything in by next week."

Rosie dropped her gaze and prevaricated; "Mmm, I'll give it some thought Father." Part of her knew she couldn't stave off the inevitable forever, and that she would have to learn how to use a computer eventually. But not right now, she thought, I've got too much to deal with at the moment.

She began to tidy her desk, stacking papers in neat piles and dropping paperclips into a chipped glass votive holder. "I did want a quick word with you, though. About next Sunday. Moira's up at the family cottage and I'm going to stay overnight Saturday and bring her home sometime Sunday. So I won't be here to sing at eleven o'clock Mass, I'm afraid."

"No problem, Rosie. Do you want to give Saturday a miss as well? We can manage with congregational singing and just saying the responses for once. It's about time you had a weekend off, you know."

"Thanks Father, but I wasn't planning to drive up until Saturday evening, so I'm okay to sing at four-thirty."

"Well, that's fine then. I'll ask Mrs. O'Halloran to choose old favourites for Sunday, and I'm sure everyone will join in quite happily. Those old tunes are really easy to sing, you know; *Faith of our Fathers, Immaculate Mary,* maybe we'll have *Amazing Grace,* everyone knows that."

They may know it, but they don't get to sing it when I'm in the choir loft, Rosie thought. She stood up; "Well, thanks again Father. I'm going to head out now, unless there's anything else?"

"No, no, I've got to work on my homily for this week-end. Usually finish it up on Wednesdays, but I've been out all afternoon, so times getting short."

"Liz said you were visiting Mrs. Wesley. How is she?"

"She's not too well right now. I think the accident took more out of her than she realised; you don't walk away unscathed from something like that at her age." Father Matthews glanced down and brushed the trace of sugar from his lapel. "We said a rosary together and she seemed comforted, but it's always a shock to come face to face with one's own mortality."

Particularly if you were Clodagh Wesley and figured you could make even the Grim Reaper dance to your tune, Rosie thought. "And then, of course, losing her son like that..." she looked inquiringly at the priest.

A slight change passed across Father Matthews' face, almost like a door closing. "Yes, a tragedy, and many regrets all around, I'm sure. We never know when our time will come." He turned toward the doorway. "I mustn't keep you from your evening, Rosie. My homily awaits and, no doubt, one of Mrs. Curtis' very nutritious suppers." He paused for a moment then added, "You won't forget to close the window, will you?" As he headed into the rectory Rosie heard his wistful murmur; "Maybe tonight there'll be meat."

Chapter 9 - Back to School

It took Rosie fifteen minutes to drive from the church to Holy Angels convent and, despite herself, she began thinking about Father Matthews' reaction to her mention of Tony's death. His comments had been appropriate enough, but somehow she felt he was uncomfortable, even uneasy, with the topic. But why should that be? As far as Father Matthews knew, this death was an accident, plain and simple. He'd never even known Tony, who was still in Sault St. Marie when Father came to St. Judes three years back. Maybe it was merely that Clodagh had discussed her loss with him and, bound by confidentiality, he'd had to choose his words carefully. Yes, that was it. She gave herself a mental slap; "Stop over-thinking everything" she said aloud, as she turned into the convent's winding driveway.

Holy Angel's convent was a limestone mansion, built in the 1890's by local salt baron, Hamish MacIntyre. He'd named it *Castle Abbotsford* in honour of Sir Walter Scott, and it could easily have been a backdrop to one of that great novelist's gothic tales.

Intended to stand as the visible symbol of a poor immigrant's rise to money and power, the huge house was awash in gargoyles, crenelated battlements, turrets and lancet windows. At the front, an imposing granite stairway swept up to the entrance portico, where two massive oak doors were flanked by heraldic beasts.

Sadly, Hamish wasn't king of his castle for very long, dying of apoplexy only two years after its completion. His childless widow lived there in solitary splendour for twenty years and then, in a move which rocked Little Yarmouth's Scottish Presbyterian community, she converted to Catholicism. In those sectarian times, for a Presbyterian to *go over to Rome* had the same shock value that might occur today if the

Archbishop of Canterbury announced his intention to embrace Satanism.

One shock followed another. When she died in 1920 the residents of Little Yarmouth were stunned to learn that the entire MacIntyre estate (properties, stocks, bonds and a controlling interest in the Goderich Salt Corporation) had been bequeathed to a Roman Catholic order of nuns, the School Sisters of St. Finnian and St. Columba.

In 1892, a few sisters from this Irish Congregation had been invited to Goderich to open a free school for the children of poor immigrants. By the time Deidre MacIntyre left her millions to them, both the numbers of children needing education and sisters willing to teach them had increased dramatically.

The only stipulation to Deidre's bequest was that the mansion in Little Yarmouth become a convent, and remain so in perpetuity. So a few of the sisters left their modest school and convent in Goderich for the magnificent chilliness of *Castle Abbotsford.* When they recovered from the shock of seeing the house for the first time, they promptly placed it under the protection of Our Lady and the Holy Angels, and set about modifying it to its new, and higher, purpose.

A few years after Rosie left Holy Angels, the elementary school was moved out of the convent proper and into a new building on the grounds. In the space left vacant by this re-location the sisters opened a Diocesan Retreat Centre and Book Store and, for a convent, Holy Angels was always a very busy place.

Rosie parked her car and walked down the sloping path toward a small basement door, its well-rubbed brass nameplate proclaiming *Holy Angels Convent.* She was better acquainted with the identical entrance on the opposite side of the building which had once led into the Elementary School, now the Retreat Centre.

In the mansion's glory days, both entrances had been for servants; left for men, right for women, in keeping with Hamish MacIntyre's stern Presbyterian scruples. When the sisters inherited the house, they chose a servants entrance for the convent, considering that more fitting for Religious vowed to poverty than the imposing front portico with its massive oak doors. These were only opened when the Bishop came to call!

She tugged at an old fashioned bell pull and almost immediately the door was opened by a diminutive figure, swathed in the Congregations distinctive grey habit and long black veil. Rosie raised her voice; "Hello, Sister Albertine, how are you?" Sister Albertine had been portress for as long as Rosie could remember and, with age, was becoming increasingly deaf.

The tiny nun squinted up at her. "My goodness, is that Rose? I'm fit as a fiddle my dear, praise be to God. It's been a while since we've seen you. How are you, and John, and his lovely family?

"Everyone's doing really well, thank you Sister. John and Elspeth are away on a little vacation and Moira's been staying with me. I expect you know she and Bobbie are going to St. Michael's this September."

"Bless me, yes, and it seems like only yesterday they were starting Kindergarten. Bobbie screamed that whole first day, I remember. I hope he's better behaved his first day at St. Michael's; now Moira, she was never any trouble, such a little angel…." Sister Albertine seemed to be drifting off.

"Sister, I was hoping to have a word with Sister Mary Bernadette. Do you know if she's available?"

Sister Albertine pulled an old fashioned pocket watch from beneath her scapula and looked at it intently. "Yes, I should think so. We've forty minutes before Vespers. I'll call her bell."

Rosie followed the portress into a cubby hole beside the front door. Pinned on the wall above an old-fashioned PBX telephone system was a faded list of names, the papers' edge curled and browned with age. Beside every name was a series of dots and spaces, each representing the individual "bell" of every sister in the house.

Sister Albertine had no need to consult this list, her many years as portress had engrained every sister's "bell" on her memory. She pressed a large brass button on the wall below the list three times, waited, then pressed three times again. Rosie knew the bell would sound in every corridor and room of the convent, except the Chapel. The Portress would wait ten minutes, and if the summoned sister did not appear, she'd *call her bell* again. If there was still no response, it was assumed the sister in question was in chapel or at prayer somewhere else in the house and could not be disturbed.

"Well now Rose, I'm sure Sister will be along directly. Why don't you go down to the Parlour; you know where it is?"

"I think so, Sister. Will I see you on my way out?"

"Of course. Just go straight down here and left at the end. God bless you." The doorbell rang again and Sister Albertine turned in response to another summons from the outside world.

Rosie walked slowly along the dim corridor trying to be as quiet as possible. Despite her tip-toeing efforts, the echo of her heels on the tiled floor made her feel large and clumsy. The convent always had this effect on her, and she suddenly realised this was why she had always preferred meeting Sister Mary Bernadette at the school. And as her music teacher's time there had decreased, so had their visits together.

She pushed open the door to the Visitor's Parlour, went in and sat down. In Mrs. MacIntyre's day, this entire part of the house had been the servant's domain; butler's pantry, housekeeper's office, servant's hall. Rosie's mind began to wander, imagining what it had been like in its heyday, bustling with gossip and intrigue. Certainly a lot noisier and livelier than it was now.

Painted brown and cream, the Visitors Parlour was largely unchanged since the sisters furnished it in 1920. An oblong mahogany table dominated the centre of the room, with a crucifix on a crochet doily in the middle, and four upright chairs placed one at each side. Against the back wall stood a large bookcase filled with devotional material and, in the far corner, a prie-dieu was placed ready for any visitor suddenly overcome by a desire to throw themselves on their knees. The walls were decorated with pious Victorian prints; St. Michael casting Satan down to Hell, Gabriel announcing the Incarnation to a startled Virgin, and a particularly grim portrait of Mother Mary Dimbleby, Foundress of the Congregation. The only cheery picture hung over the mantelpiece; Pope John Paul the second in glorious colour, smiling and waving benignly.

As she sat looking around the room, Rosie became aware that the silence had become so intense that she was finding it oppressive. Even her breathing felt laboured. She was just getting up to go out into the hallway when the parlour door opened, and Sister Mary Bernadette came into the room. Like all the sisters she moved almost soundlessly, with only the clicking of an oversized wooden rosary hanging from her belt announcing her approach.

"Rosie, my dear girl, how lovely to see you. I'd begun to wonder if anything was wrong. Is everyone in the family keeping well? How is your dear Aunt Margaret?" The elderly nun regarded Rosie with concern.

Rosie stood up, came around the table and gave her mentor an affectionate hug. She caught the sharp, clean scent of soap and starch from the nun's snowy coif, and remembered her mother's laughter when, as a seven year old, she'd asked if this was the "odour of sanctity."

"Everyone's just fine, Sister. I took Moira up to the cottage yesterday and had a nice visit with Auntie Marg. She asked to be remembered to you." Slow down, you're gabbling, she thought. Taking a deep breath she went on; "I'm really sorry I haven't been to see you for so long. Time just slips away, you know."

Sister Mary took her hand; "Come and sit down, and tell me all you've been up to. How is the voice? You are keeping up with your vocal exercises, I hope."

"Sometimes, Sister." No, there really was no point in stretching the truth when those bright blue eyes were boring straight through you. "Well, not very often, actually. I don't seem to have the same interest anymore."

"Rosie, your voice is an instrument, and like any instrument it needs to be tuned regularly. You may not be singing at the Metropolitan Opera, but you are singing for the glory of God, and I think that's just as important, don't you?"

Rosie sighed inwardly. "Yes Sister," she said obediently. She loved her old teacher dearly, but Liz's comments about Catholic guilt had somehow struck a chord, and she found herself wishing that Sister Mary B. wasn't quite so adept at spotting her many failings.

"And how is Josephine doing in New York?"

More guilt. Rosie hadn't spoken to her sister in months, but that was nothing new. The sad fact was, they had nothing to say to each other. The life of an investment banker in the Big Apple, and a part-time church secretary in rural Ontario had very little in common.

"Busy, as usual, Sister. She's always flying off somewhere glamorous; last time we spoke she was just leaving for Rome."

Sister Mary's eyes glowed; "How wonderful" she enthused. "I expect she went to Mass at St. Peters, and saw our dear Holy Father. And then the opportunity to visit all those historical sites; the Catacombs, the Coliseum. Oh, how lucky she is to see all those places. "

Rosie hadn't the heart to say that her sister hadn't set foot in a church for years, having no interest in religion in general, and Catholicism in particular. She'd probably spent her free time in Rome shopping along the Via Condotti, or relaxing in the spa at her five star hotel. And that's if she'd had any free time. Josie, or Jay as she was known to her New York friends and colleagues, was a workaholic who could sit on the most beautiful beach in the world, and never lift her eyes from her laptop.

Their conversation moved on to generalities and finally got to Moira and Bobbie. Although John's twins were leaving Holy Angels in September, Bobbie would be continuing his piano lessons with Sister Mary B.

"He's a real talent, Rosie," she said. "I haven't had such a gifted student for years; well, not since you, really. He'll have no trouble getting a place anywhere after high school, even Juilliard. There's a great future for him in music, I'm sure."

Rosie didn't answer and looked down at her lap. Déjà vu, she was thinking. Does Sister remember saying the same thing about me? Well, I sure hope Bobbie has better luck than I did. She looked up to see Sister Mary watching her sympathetically.

"You had no choice, Rosie. After your mother's accident, you had to come home from New York. There was no-one else to take care of her and John."

Yes, Rosie thought. No one else; Josie made that quite plain. She could hear her now, whining down the phone from Montreal; "You can't ask me, Rose. I'm no good at that sort of thing, and anyway I've just got my first promotion. You can always go back to your singing later."

She looked up and tried to smile. "I know. But in the end John and Josie both got their careers, and I lost mine. The price of being the eldest, I suppose."

"We never know what sacrifices God will ask of us. And you could have gone back."

"Not really, Sister. By the time John was through high school and mom was completely well again, I was twenty-seven. A bit late to start an operatic career. No, it wasn't meant to be, and I just have to be content with those amazing years at Juilliard."

Sister Mary leant over and squeezed her hand. "You did the right thing, Rose. For whatever reason, God wants you to use your gifts here, in Little Yarmouth. And I'm sure everyone at St. Judes is uplifted whenever they hear your beautiful voice at Mass. I'm sure you do more good than you know."

The mention of "gifts" reminded Rosie of the main reason for her visit.

"I hope so, Sister." Surprised to find her eyes filling with tears, Rosie pulled out a tissue and blew her nose. "My life didn't turn out the way I hoped it would, but I try every day to stay positive and count my blessings. And I do have a lot to be grateful for." She paused, trying to think how best to introduce the subject of Tony Wesley's death.

Sister Mary sat silently, watching her. Suddenly she said; "Does this room make you uncomfortable?"

Taken aback by the unexpected comment, Rosie had no time to consider her answer. She blurted out; "Yes, it does. I think it's a very unhappy place. Why do you ask?"

"Because it has that effect on me, and on some of the other sisters. Most of them take their visitors out into the garden, rather than stay in here." The old nun placed her hand onto the wooden rosary and lifted it into her lap. As she spoke she ran the beads through her fingers. "I think some sad things happened in this house, before we came. And that's why Mrs. MacIntyre left it to us, and wanted it to be a convent; she hoped that our prayers would help, somehow."

The Chapel bells began tolling and Sister Mary stood up slowly. "There's the first bell for Vespers. I'd better get started; I'm getting so stiff these days it takes me longer and longer to get to Chapel." She gave Rosie a quick hug. "It's been lovely to see you, my dear." When Rosie didn't answer, she gave her an enquiring glance; "Is there something I can help you with, Rose?"

"Yes, actually there is Sister. I was over to see Lucy Wesley last Saturday; she was Lucy Curtis before she married Tony Wesley."

"Ah yes, poor girl. His death must be a great sadness for her. As it happens, I've been thinking about him all this past week." Sister Mary took Rosie's arm. "Let's walk on up to Chapel while we talk." She smiled; "We'll multitask; isn't that what everyone says these days?"

Side by side they started down the corridor, their unhurried pace accompanied by the sound of Rosie's heels tapping, and the gentle click of Sister Mary's wooden rosary beads swinging together.

For a minute the old nun said nothing, seemingly lost in thought. Then she went on; "His mother called to ask for prayers the day after he died, and the whole community was very affected by her news. It was surprising how many sisters remembered him from school. So sad, to think of him dying alone like that."

Rosie knew that all the sisters would have spent many hours on their knees, praying for Tony's soul. "Storming Heaven" they called it; praying for someone long outside the Church, but still a lost lamb that might be saved by enough prayers rising up to the Judgment seat.

"What was he like at school?"

"Just an ordinary little boy, mischievous sometimes, but a good little soul. Quite bright, too and the apple of his father's eye." Sister Mary stopped talking, as they reached the flight of stairs leading up to the Chapel on the ground floor.

"Michael Wesley was a hard man, though," she went on, when they reached the top. "Tony often came to school with bruises on his arms and legs. If we saw a child like that now, we'd call Children's Aid. But it was different back then; most parents believed in *spare the rod and spoil the child.*"

After climbing the steep stairs, Rosie was more out of breath than her octogenarian teacher. *I've got to start exercising,* she thought, as she pulled her way toward a pair of double doors which had once opened into the mansion's elegant ballroom. The room's lofty ceiling and beautiful proportions had made it the obvious choice for conversion to a chapel, and now only the ornate plaster ceiling gave clues to its original purpose.

During her years at Holy Angels school, Rosie had often gazed up at the multitude of lutes, lyres, violas and trumpets which, together with voluptuous swags of fruit and flowers, covered almost every inch of the ceiling. Truth be told, she'd spent more time in Chapel daydreaming about beautiful ladies in crinoline ball gowns, than focusing on more devout meditations.

Sister Mary drew Rosie to one side of the doors, acknowledging several other sisters with a smile as they made their way past. The bells had stopped tolling, and Rosie knew Vespers would soon begin. Time to cut to the chase.

"Sister, Lucy is really uneasy about the way Tony died, and she's asked me to help. Can you think of any reason why someone might have wished him harm?"

Two bright blue eyes regarded her steadily. "Would I be right in thinking you have some personal insight into this death, my dear?" Rosie nodded quickly. Although she had never discussed the Gift with anyone outside her family, she knew her teacher understood something of her unusual talents.

Sister Mary closed her eyes and bowed her head briefly before answering. "I've always felt that something went badly wrong for Tony at high school. I can't tell you what it was, but he seemed to change out of all recognition. When he was with us, all the sisters thought him a very nice boy, cheerful, helpful; always one to be asking questions. And he did really well that first year at John Galt." She paused as a chapel bell began its slow, single chime, signalling five minutes before the start of Vespers.

"I used to see Mrs. Wesley quite often then. There were five years between Tony and his sister, so Carmel was with us for some time after he left. And you know how it is; when Mrs. Wesley came to pick her up we'd chat, and I'd ask how Tony was doing. Both his parents were very pleased with him that first year; straight A's, on the football team, everything just fine." Sister Mary's hand went to her rosary, a reflex conditioned by years of drawing strength from that ancient prayer.

She went on; "The next academic year started just as well, but then he seemed to lose interest in everything. She said his grades were slipping and they weren't sure what to do for the best. There was talk of sending him to some kind of military academy in America." The old nun sighed. "Frankly, I was surprised by her candour."

Rosie said grimly; "She probably had no one else to talk to."

"I don't know about that, my dear. But later I wondered if she'd regretted telling me so much, because the housekeeper started coming for Carmel. It was several years before I spoke with Mrs. Wesley again. Carmel had a solo in our Christmas concert and she came over to thank me for the extra tutoring. I asked after Tony and she told me Mr. Wesley was furious about some scrape he'd got into just before the holidays. What she said really stuck in my mind; *His father took the strap to him, and Tony couldn't go to school for a week.*"

Sister Mary looked straight at Rosie and, with conviction in her voice, said; "Something happened to Tony that second year that changed him from a good student to a full time troublemaker. Later on, when I heard some of the things he'd done, I couldn't believe it was the same boy we'd taught. And then, there was that dreadful accident out on the tracks." She shook her head sadly, and crossed herself.

Rosie could hardly contain her excitement. Was this the answer she'd been looking for?

"Sorry, Sister. What accident was that?"

"You'd have been too young to remember much about it, I expect. It was 1959, late in the year. A boy in Tony's class was killed on the CN tracks just outside town. I can't recall his name, he wasn't a Holy Angels child, but nothing was ever resolved properly. The inquest ended with an "undetermined" verdict and, for months, the town was full of all kinds of talk and finger pointing; most of it directed at Tony Wesley."

Catching the look of surprise on Rosie's face, Sister Mary gave a little chuckle. "We may be enclosed nuns my dear, but everything filters through these walls eventually." She took a deep breath and continued; "You asked if anyone might have wished him harm. Well, some people said Tony pushed that boy in front of a train, and if the child's family is still here, still in Little Yarmouth….." the old nun's voice faded and she shook her head again. "You know I wouldn't repeat any of this, if I thought it just malicious gossip. But now Tony's dead, and whether he died by accident or by someone's hand, his passing was violent. When I heard how he died I remembered that old tragedy, and wondered whether past sins hadn't come back to haunt him."

It's not just old sins that are haunting us, Rosie thought. And despite the tragic nature of Sister Mary's information, she couldn't help but feel elated. Finally, something concrete to go on. If Tony had caused his classmate's death, then it might be guilt for that act that was keeping his spirit earthbound. Of more importance, the tragedy gave someone a compelling motive for murder. If the dead boy still had family in town, then

Tony's return could have stirred a long buried desire for revenge.

Then a sudden, chilling thought struck her. "But he would only have been fifteen years old then, practically a child. Sister, you don't really think Tony could have committed murder at that age?"

Sister Mary looked at her sadly. "Only God knows the truth of it now. But conscience isn't fully formed until we're adults, and so much depends on how a child is raised. Children are easily moulded, for good or bad, and Tony grew up with a father who used violence to impose his will; it wasn't just Tony who came to school with bruises, you know. So what might an impressionable young boy learn from that kind of cruelty?" The chapel bell stopped chiming, and she turned toward the double doors. "I'll be praying that you can help Lucy and …" she paused, "anyone else who's in distress. And now I must go. God keep you safe, my dear."

Rosie gave her a quick hug. "Thanks, Sister. I won't be so long visiting again, I promise." Sister Mary smiled, went into the Chapel and closed the door quietly behind her.

Rosie went back down the stairs, and hurried along the corridor to the entrance. Sister Albertine was sitting in her cubby hole, reading the Office her sisters were chanting in Chapel. She smiled and nodded as Rosie let herself out.

While Rosie was driving home, Sister Mary Bernadette was standing in her Choir stall, trying to concentrate on the Vesper responses passing back and forth across the chancel. But, despite her best efforts, her mind kept turning to Rosie, and the exceptional talent they both knew she possessed, but neither had openly acknowledged.

The Church taught that, after death, a soul was judged and consigned to Heaven, Purgatory or Hell. Its age-old wisdom made no allowance for anywhere in between. This had always been problematic for Sister Mary, who was deeply orthodox in her adherence to the tenets of her faith. Problematic, because she knew, from personal experience, that some souls became trapped after death; held somewhere between this earthly existence and their next appointed destination. She also knew that there were people who could help these souls, because she'd met two of them. One was her grandfather and the other was Rosie.

All those years ago, when little Kitty Micheals' insistent cries for help had caused Rosie to lose all interest in schoolwork and music, Sister Mary had sat her down and gently questioned her about why she was so troubled. Hesitantly, Rosie had recounted the voices and dreams, and to her surprise, Sister Mary had responded by sharing some of her own family history. Most particularly about her grandfather, who had been the seventh son of a seventh son.

"We children used to joke about him, you know, *Oh, grandda knows who's next for the bone yard,* that kind of thing. But it was all bravado, because we were so scared of what he knew and what he could see." Rosie had looked at her, wide-eyed.

"As usual, Shakespeare summed it up very nicely" Sister Mary had continued. "*There are more things in heaven and earth than are dreamt of in your philosophy.* But one thing I did learn from my grandda. There's no need to be afraid of strange happenings as long as you're saying your prayers and going to Confession and Communion. You'll always be well protected."

And with that, she'd gone to the piano, played the first phrase of a vocal exercise and started their music lesson. Rosie had told her later that their conversation had left her puzzled, but somehow comforted. And that when she got home, she'd overheard a conversation between her mother and Aunt Margaret, and everything was fine again now.

Two days after Rosie and her mother found Kitty's remains, there was another music lesson. Sister Mary had said casually; "What a blessing that poor little child has been found at last, and just in time to ease her mother's passing. In such an out of the way place, too. Almost as if someone knew she was there."

Rosie had kept her head down, sorting through the music in her school bag; "Yes Sister, so lucky that we happened to be there."

"And with a flashlight, too."

"Yes Sister, the police said the same thing. But as I told them, we'd been walking our dog earlier and he'd lost his ball around there."

"Oh, I see. Well, the Lord moves in mysterious ways."

"Yes Sister." And no more was ever said about little Kitty Micheals.

During the years that followed, she realised that lost souls frequently came calling on Rosie. The youngster was her star pupil and, with vocal lessons three times a week, they soon developed a close, personal rapport. A cheerful child, Rosie enjoyed her music and, given the least opportunity, would happily prattle on about home and school.

But on occasion, she became quiet and withdrawn, her singing just a mechanical exercise devoid of any spirit or passion. And when this happened, her conversation would turn to questions about the nature of life and death, the afterlife, judgment and esoteric matters never mentioned in the Baltimore Catechism. Once, she'd asked Sister Mary directly if she believed in ghosts.

A different teacher might have been forgiven for thinking Rosie emotionally troubled. But Sister Mary's Irish childhood and family background had given her a healthy respect for things unseen. She also had a talent for discernment, although if asked, she would have simply said she was blessed with good intuition. Others, more involved with the spirit world, would have described her as a natural sensitive.

So, through those early years, she answered Rosie's questions as best she could, and tried to cover her with a blanket of prayer whenever she thought the child was helping a troubled spirit. As Rosie grew older the questioning stopped, and Sister Mary knew that her young charge had come to terms with her abilities, and accepted that some questions could never be fully answered this side of the grave.

Vespers ended, and her attention returned to the present where, two by two, the nuns were filing out of their places, bowing to the altar and returning to their final tasks of the day. But Sister Mary stayed kneeling in the candle lit chapel, keeping Rosie close, praying that heaven's holy angels would protect her from the darkness she feared was gathering.

Chapter 10 – The Year Book

To her annoyance, Rosie had slipped into a post-supper doze the instant she sat down on the living room couch. Now she was jolted awake, as Gussie responded to the doorbell with his usual frenzied barking and wild scramble along the hallway.

She stood up, feeling muzzy and light-headed; her mind barely registering the hall clock chiming nine, its sonorous *bongs* adding bass notes to Gussie's escalating yaps. "Oh God, is that the time?" she said aloud, then shouted to make her voice heard above the canine racket; "Gussie, quieten down, I'm coming."

As usual her call fell on cute but deaf ears, and the beagle barked on, his *woof, woof, woofs* in tandem now with jack-in-the-box leaps up and down at the front door. Rosie made a grab for his collar; "Gussie, enough!" She dragged him back from the door and, holding his collar, managed to turn the door handle. Still bent double, she looked up at her visitor.

"Hi Lucy, come on in. You're not scared of dogs are you? I can shut him in the kitchen..." then she lost her grip on the struggling dog's collar and he threw himself at Lucy's legs in a transport of welcome.

Laughing, Lucy bent down to stroke him. "No problem, Rosie. You're a cute little guy, aren't you?" and Gussie responded by jumping round and round in circles, wagging his tail furiously and panting with his efforts to ingratiate himself with the visitor.

"Sorry to come at this time," she went on. "Dad was a bit shaky so I didn't want to leave him alone, and then Mom was late getting home. I thought about not coming, but I really needed to get out of the house. I feel as if I've been stuck indoors for days."

Rosie picked up the wriggling Gussie and pushed the front door shut with her foot. Ushering Lucy into the living room she said; "Not to worry, I had no clue that it was past eight thirty. I sat down after supper and just nodded right off." She put the dog on the floor, only to see him immediately jump onto the couch next to Lucy. "Gussie, get down." He ignored her and, laying his front paws in Lucy's lap, looked up beseechingly. "Gussie, off!" The beagle responded by putting his head down on his front paws and closing his eyes. "I'm sorry; he's not very well trained. We both flunked obedience class, I'm afraid."

Lucy ran her hand over the dog's head. "I don't mind a bit, Rosie. I always wanted a dog, but mom wasn't keen on animals. And Tone didn't like dogs at all"... her voice cracked. Then, taking a deep breath, she went on; "Anyway, I think this little guy's adorable," and swallowed hard.

Rosie sighed; "That's not how I usually describe him, but he is wonderful company. How about that glass of wine now? Red or white?"

"White please. And make it a large one, would you?"

As she went into the kitchen, Rosie called over her shoulder; "So how are your mom and dad?"

"Mom's alright, she's always on the go. But Dad's not well at all; it's some kind of heart trouble, I think. I don't know exactly what; neither of them will say much. But he seems to have gone downhill a lot in the last few months. He's always so short of breath."

Rosie came back with cheese, crackers, a bottle of wine and two large glasses on a tray. Setting everything down on the coffee table, she filled both glasses and handed one to Lucy. "The wine's nicely chilled, but if you'd like some ice......?

"No, it's just fine like that, Rosie. Thanks." Lucy took a deep swallow, and set her glass back on the table. "I feel so bad about adding to their troubles, you know.

They've got enough to deal with, and now here I am, wandering around the house, crying at the least little thing." And, as if on cue, tears sprang to her eyes. Picking up a paper napkin, she wiped her eyes, and made a feeble attempt at blowing her nose. Gussie whined softly and looked up at her, tail thumping gently in sympathy. "You know, I promised myself I'd make it through this evening without crying. Fat chance; I've only been here five minutes, and your poor dog's getting soaked."

Rosie, her own mother's death from heart disease brought unexpectedly to mind, felt a lump rising in her throat. Wordlessly, she picked up a box of tissues and passed it across the coffee table.

Pulling out a handful, Lucy gave two vigorous blows. "That's the end of the waterworks," she said, in a surprisingly strong voice. "There'll be no more tears tonight," and with that, she picked up her wine glass and downed the contents in one gulp.

"I brought these," she said, rummaging through a shabby mock-croc satchel. "Sorry, I've got so much stuff in here…," she hauled out a scarf, makeup bag, wallet, paperback and a mini umbrella, piling them up on the couch next to Gussie. "They're right on the bottom. I put them in yesterday night to make sure I didn't forget them; ah, here they are," and she laid a stack of John Galt High School Year Books on the table. "They're Tony's. I thought they might be useful for the Reunion. Some of them are for the years he was there before us."

Rosie picked up the one marked *1955-1956* and began leafing through it. "Oh wow, these will be a real help" she gushed, feeling only a tad guilty at her deception. The committee already had hundreds of old Year Books, all packed haphazardly in boxes stacked in a musty storeroom below the gym. She, on the other hand, definitely needed to know who Tony's classmates were in those first years at John Galt, when his personality had changed so dramatically. Lucy's gift would save her hours of dusty rummaging.

"I'm surprised Tony held on to these" she went on, looking at the page where school clubs were listed. Yes, there was his name, entered under Science Club and also under Chess Club. Now that's a pursuit I'd never have ascribed to Tony, she thought. A few pages further on she found his name again; reserve player for the Screaming Eagles football team. He'd certainly been enthusiastic about High School, at least in his freshman year.

"I asked him for them, just before we got married" Lucy answered, her voice breaking. She reached over for the bottle of wine, and refilled her glass. "He was so desperate to leave town, he'd have gone with just the clothes on his back." She lifted her glass, and sipped absently. "But I thought our kids might like to have them someday, and I'd kept all mine." She picked up *1957-1958* and turned to Tony's class photo; "Look at them all, with their crew cuts and plaid jackets. There's Dave Mason – he hasn't changed much, except for the hair, of course."

Rosie flipped back to Tony's class photo in her book. Yes, she recognized Dave Mason and quite a few others who featured on her list of potential murder suspects. Jackson Haynes, scowling at the camera, and Vic Watson, obviously a martyr to acne in his early years. Oh, and there was Pete Anderson, looking surprisingly cheerful.

Lucy flipped to another page and turned her book around. She pointed to an earnest looking teen in horn rimmed glasses; "That's Carl, my brother-in-law." Rosie looked blank. "You know, Carl Wheelan that married my sister Barbara; Amber's dad."

"Oh, right." Rosie glanced at the page. "Sorry, I never knew him."

"He's getting married again. Mom and dad are quite upset about it, but what can you do? It's been two years since Babs died, and life must go on, I suppose." Lucy's voice thickened and she swallowed hard. She picked up the last book and turned to the freshman class photo. "There's Babs; second from the end, top row."

Rosie reached over for the open book. Barbara Curtis smiled up at her, the epitome of 1950's wholesomeness, complete with Doris Day hairstyle and demure Peter Pan collar. Next to her Rosie recognized Carol Hunter (or Bradley as she was then), trying hard to channel Annette Funicello.

On impulse Rosie laid three books out in front of her, each open at Tony's class picture. She looked closely; was it her imagination, or did he really appear so different from one year to the next? No, she wasn't wrong. His smiling freshman picture seemed full of eagerness and enthusiasm, with an openness of expression that wasn't just juvenile naiveté. By year two, the smile had disappeared and by year three, he was matching Jackson Haynes scowl for scowl. In contrast, most of his classmates were barely changed, almost to the point that they could have re-used their first year photo in both succeeding year books, and no-one would have noticed.

Rosie leaned forward to pick up her glass, and inadvertently placed her hand over the *1959-1960* book. Instantly, a surge of misery flooded through her, so strong that her hand jerked back as if she'd touched a live wire. She opened the book up at Tony's class picture and peered at it closely. Tony wasn't just scowling, everything about him; hooded eyes, thin, compressed lips fairly oozed menace.

Lucy's voice broke into her thoughts. "What're you looking at, Rosie?" She reached over and Rosie reluctantly handed the book to her.

"Nothing, really. Just surprised at how much we've all changed, I suppose."

Lucy was smiling down at the book in her hands. "That's a nice picture of Tone," she said. "I always thought he looked a bit like Elvis." She handed it back to Rosie.

Rosie looked at her incredulously. Tony's grade eleven picture exuded evil; what could Lucy see that was "nice" about it? She lifted the book again. Tony beamed out at her, all pearly teeth and smiling eyes. Only his newly slicked back hairstyle foreshadowed the "bad boy" reputation to come.

'Wow, that's a first' she muttered, picking up her glass and draining its contents. She'd heard of psychometry; the ability to read the energy field of an object, and draw specific associations from it. But she'd never before experienced the phenomenon.

Lucy was pouring the last of the wine into their glasses.

"I'll get another bottle" Rosie said, glad of the opportunity to get up and hide her shaking hands. She weaved unsteadily toward the fridge. Lord, she shouldn't have downed that wine so fast, not after having a glass with supper.

By ten thirty, there wasn't much left in the second bottle, and their shared memories of high school had descended from the hilarious to the maudlin. Lucy was dabbing away tears, brought on by reminiscing about the only Prom she'd attended with Tony. "It was his Graduation night, and when they played *You are my Special Angel* he said that was me…" She muffled her sobs with a ball of tissue.

Gussie had been let out into the garden for his bedtime constitutional and now, having satisfied himself that his territory remained secure, was barking loudly to come in.

Rosie stood up with an effort. "Hold that thought, Luce. I've got to get Lussly .. I've got to let Gussly in…" Tottering toward the kitchen, she realised they were both on their way to being well and truly drunk.

Gussie burst in, bounded into the living room and leapt onto the couch next to Lucy, who had slipped sideways and was resting her head on the end cushion.

Rosie shook her gently. "Luce, why don't you stay over tonight? I don't think you should drive, do you?"

Lucy sat up abruptly, and threw her arms round the startled beagle. "What a darling doggie. What's your name, then?"

Rosie went back into the kitchen, opened the phone book and began looking for the Curtis' number. It took her quite some time to fumble through the pages but, finally, she found the listing. With considerable effort she focused on the key pad, punching in the numbers slowly and with great deliberation.

"Hi, Mish. Curtis, its Rosie. Look, I'm sorry to call this late....... no, everything's fine. It's just that we've had a few glasses of wine, so Lucy's going to stay over tonight. ..... yesh, I mean *yes,* I thought you'd feel that way. No, its asbulutely... aspulut... it's no trouble, at all. Give my best to Mr. Curtis. Bye now." She heard muffled laughter as she replaced the receiver.

The next morning, it was well past ten before they were at the breakfast table, watching plates of untouched toast cool in front of them. Even Gussie was subdued, a late night feast of stolen crackers and cheese churning away in his stomach.

His mistress had slept badly, disturbed by spirits that were definitely not supernatural. Rosie's sleep pattern was always the same when she drank too much wine. Initially, she'd fall into a deep sleep, only to wake suddenly after a few hours, and then spend the rest of the night dozing fitfully. Around 4 a.m. she'd gone along the hall to the guest room, and listened outside. But Lucy was sleeping peacefully.

Rosie had wondered if Tony might put in an appearance because of Lucy's presence in the house, but the night passed uneventfully. Whatever was troubling him, it had nothing to do with Lucy.

"More coffee, Luce?"

"Oh, yes please Rosie." Lucy held out her mug. "I'm so sorry about last night. You must think I'm a real lush."

"No, I don't. There were two of us working our way through those bottles, remember." Rosie picked up a piece of toast and took a tentative bite. Swallowing with difficulty, she put it back on the plate and pushed it away. "It's not often I turn down food. Maybe a bottle of wine every night is the answer to my weight problem."

Lucy laughed. "Well, I certainly slept the best I have for weeks. Now I have to go home and face the music. What did my mom say when you phoned?"

"She was a bit worried at first, because it was so late. But she was fine after I explained. I don't know why, but I think she was laughing when she hung up."

"Maybe I'll give her a quick call, if that's okay. Let her know I'll be home soon."

"Fine. I think I left the phone over by the sink."

While Lucy made her call, Rosie sat at the table nursing her coffee mug. She was feeling decidedly fragile. The aspirin she'd taken first thing hadn't done much to relieve her pounding head, and now all she wanted to do was go back to bed. Thank goodness she didn't have to go into work today. Liz's sharp eyes would have spotted her hang-over instantly, and the tale would have been all round town by suppertime.

Lucy came back to the table. "You can never tell with mothers," she said. "Here I was thinking I'd get a lecture about drinking, but all she said was she was glad I'd had a nice evening out."

Rosie smiled; "I enjoyed having some company, too. It's funny, I thought I was used to being alone in the house, but since my niece Moira's been staying the place seems really empty when she's not around."

"I know what you mean. That house on Veterans was a crummy little hole, but I never felt lonely there, even with Tone out so much of the time. And then, when I knew he was gone forever…," Lucy's eyes began to fill. She brushed her hand across them, then picked up a piece of toast and bit into it half-heartedly.

Rosie was instantly intrigued. How much time did it take to do a few bakery delivery runs? "Dougie really cracked the whip, then?"

"I think Tone was helping out in the bakery, as well as doing deliveries. He was usually out all day, and some evenings as well." Lucy checked her watch. "I guess I'd better be heading home." She picked up her satchel; "Do you think I'm sober enough to drive?"

Laughing together, they got up from the table and headed into the hall, with Gussie trailing behind. At the front door, Rosie put her arms around her friend. "Thanks so much for the Year Books, Luce. They'll be a real help. And I'll get them back to you, safe and sound; just as soon as I…we've finished with them."

"I know you will," Lucy said, stepping back from Rosie's embrace.

Rosie opened the door, then remembered she hadn't told Lucy about her visit to Holy Angels; "Lucy, I hope you don't mind but when I was up to see Sister Mary Bernadette yesterday, I asked her what she remembered about Tony."

Closing the door again, Lucy stood with her hand on the handle. "No, of course I don't mind. What did she say?"

"That he was a nice, ordinary little boy when he was at Holy Angels. And that he changed a lot once he went to high school." Rosie paused, not sure if she should be sharing Sister Mary's concerns with anyone, least of all Tony's widow. "Lucy, did Tony ever mention a boy in his class being killed on the CN tracks?"

Lucy shook her head. "No, he never talked about school, even when we were first dating. But I remember it, because we had a big family upset right after. Mom wanted Babs to transfer to St Gabriels. She didn't want to go to Goderich and threw a real tantrum, and then dad said there were too many bad things going on at John Galt, and they didn't want her there."

"Too many bad things?" Rosie echoed. "What else had happened?"

"There'd been a fire, or something. I don't remember all the details. Anyway Babs didn't transfer, and I started there later, so mom must have got over whatever was bothering her." Lucy looked down at her watch again. "Got to go, Rosie. Thanks again for putting up with me. I think I needed to get a bit drunk." She opened the door and started across the porch.

Rosie followed her out. "Bye, Lucy. I'll give you a call after I've talked to John. He's back on Sunday night and I'll get him to ask around at the hospital mortuary." Lucy looked confused. "You wanted to find out why there wasn't an autopsy, remember?"

"Oh, yeah, I'd forgotten. Oh God, my head's always such a jumble these days. Most of the time the accident, the funeral, none of it seems real. I guess I'll get it all sorted out eventually," and with a forlorn wave Lucy got into her car and backed out of the driveway.

Rosie waved her off and turned back into the house. She gazed at the shambles in her living room. I must have been really drunk to leave all that food on the coffee table, she thought. "Well, it won't clean itself up" she said aloud and, opening the hall closet, she pulled out a brush and dustpan, followed by the vacuum cleaner and a garbage bag.

The coffee table was littered with paper napkins, broken crackers, some half-chewed Edam (Gussie wasn't a fan of red rind) scattered pickles (not to his taste, either), glasses and two empty wine bottles. Two suspiciously clean plates were lying on the rug and the wicker cheese tray had been dragged halfway across the room. There were crumbs everywhere.

Gussie sat in the doorway watching her as she worked. "It's alright boy," Rosie said. "I'm not cross. It's my own fault for drinking too much. If I'd stopped at two glasses, we'd both be feeling a whole lot better this morning." The beagle whined softly, and slunk across the room toward her, his tail between his legs. "Okay, don't lay it on too thick" she said, giving him a quick hug, before getting back to the cleaning. Secure in her forgiveness, Gussie jumped onto the couch and began his own cleaning routine, starting with his front paws and then moving on to more personal ablutions.

The living room set to rights Rosie went back to the kitchen and poured herself another mug of coffee. Who would know the name of that boy killed on the tracks? Mr. Carscadden for sure, but how to explain her interest in such an old tragedy? Maybe the best idea was to look through some back issues of the *Clarion*; yes, definitely the best way to go.

Her day filled with domestic catch-up, it wasn't until after supper that Rosie was back in the living room, finishing her coffee and leafing through a favourite mail-order catalogue. She rarely bought anything, (life in Little Yarmouth didn't demand an elegant wardrobe) but she enjoyed the pretence that silk blouses and cashmere sweaters were an important part of her regular attire.

The usual post-supper drowsiness began to creep over her, and she leant forward to put her mug on the coffee table next to Lucy's neatly stacked Year Books. But before she could set the mug down, the topmost book suddenly shot from its place and landed, open and face down, almost in the hearth.

Rosie leapt to her feet, heart pounding, dregs of coffee splashing everywhere. She looked around wildly, with no idea of what she expected to see. Her first crazy thought, 'earthquake,' was dismissed instantly. Nothing else in the room had fallen, moved or been disturbed in any way. A visit from Tony, then. Recovering herself she turned around, searching for the shadowy figure hovering in a corner, or drifting through the doorway. Nothing appeared, but she was soon shivering as his unseen presence began spreading its familiar blood-freezing chill.

All sleepiness forgotten, Rosie crossed to the fallen book. "What now, Tony?" she said aloud. He was certainly using everything in his ghostly tool kit to get her attention. Picking the book up, she turned it over and saw that it lay open to the third page; the *Principals Address.* Mr. Carscadden's bespectacled face looked out at her sternly; school principals in the 1950's were disciplinarians, not cheer leaders.

She carried the book into the kitchen, glancing at the cover as she went. *1959 – 1960,* Tony's fifth year. She scanned the first paragraph; thanks to students, teachers, parents for support etc., etc. The next several paragraphs were devoted to the usual congratulatory comments; fundraising events, scholarships, school club results and so on.

Then, in his final paragraphs, the Principal's tone became sombre. "Sadly, this school year has also brought unexpected challenges and losses," Rosie read. "I would be remiss if I failed to acknowledge the serious setback experienced by our sports faculty and football team during this scholastic year. Due to the total destruction of the team's equipment in last fall's gymnasium fire, the Screaming Eagles were unable to defend their title as SWOHSFL Champions. This unfortunate event was followed within weeks by a much greater loss, the tragic death of Grade Eleven student Martin Robertson. His untimely passing has been the cause of deep sadness and regret among the entire school community. Now, as the 1959/60 school year draws to a close, it is my fervent hope that these unhappy events have brought us all to a greater understanding......."

Rosie stopped reading. Martin Robertson? This must be the boy killed on the tracks, but who was he? Robertson, Robertson; wait, could this be Willie Robertson's eldest son? She'd forgotten Willie had *two* sons; Gordon, who still worked with his father at the Clarion, and an older boy, who died! Willie's voice came back to her, the words he'd spoken on the day of Tony Wesley's funeral taking on a new, and sinister, meaning. "He had a lot coming to him, that one". Had she solved the mystery? Did Willie Robertson kill Tony Wesley?

Chapter 11 – A Clarion call

The next morning Rosie was hard pressed to concentrate on her work. For the past two days the temperature had been creeping up, and now Little Yarmouth was in the grip of a full-fledged heat wave, complete with thirty two degree temperatures and what felt like one hundred percent humidity. But it wasn't her hot and sticky office that was the distraction; it was that long-ago tragedy on the CN tracks.

Her promise to pick up the church bulletins from the Clarion today, around noon, provided the perfect opportunity for a quick word with Willie Robertson. But how to casually mention young Martin's death?   She could hardly say; "Thanks so much for the bulletins, Mr. Robertson. Oh, and by the way, do you think Tony Wesley killed your boy, Martin?" Just mentally hearing that invented conversation made her toes curl with embarrassment.

The hours dragged by. Today was June 30th, and the parish accounts had to be ready for Father Matthews to review, before his monthly finance meeting at the Diocesan Office on Monday. So if she didn't want to be working Saturday, she had to knuckle down and get everything finished.

But, try as she might, the columns refused to balance. The office echoed to the *clack, clack* of her old Monroe adding machine, as she feverishly pounded the keys and pulled the handle. At least, I'm burning off some calories, she thought, and pounded even harder. Moments later, she threw down her pen in disgust after spotting an empty spool where the machine tape should have been. Intent on her task she had missed the tape running out, and now she had no record of her listings to check against the Account Book. And she still didn't balance!

Rosie breathed deeply and mentally counted to ten. The urge to scream, or throw something was almost irresistible but instead she took a long draught from her water bottle, and counted to ten again. Every month, the parish accounts seemed to get more frustrating and time-consuming. Maybe Father was right and everything should be on computer, and month-end would become "a snap" just as he promised.

No, her problem today wasn't her accounting system, it was her concentration. She had to get some answers about Martin Robertson and then she'd be able to balance the books "in a snap" the old-fashioned way. Who needed a computer? Everything was fine, just the way it was. With a glance at the mounds of paper covering her desk, she decided to cut her losses and head out to the Clarion early.

Outside Rosie's office, Liz was vacuuming the hall carpet runner to within an inch of its threadbare life. The noise grew louder and louder as Liz pursued every errant piece of fluff until, finally, she reached the end of the passage and the ancient machine fell abruptly silent. Half-opening Rosie's door she called, "Fresh baked cookies in the kitchen, girl," and disappeared back along the passage.

Rosie followed the familiar grey curls and blue overall into the kitchen. "None for me thanks, Liz. I'm going for the bulletins, and I might not make it back before twelve. Could you listen for the phone until noon and then switch it to voice-mail?"

Liz looked up pointedly at the wall clock, showing 11:15 a.m. "Are ya walkin' in all this heat, then?" It only took five minutes to drive to the Clarion office and they could both see Rosie's car through the kitchen window.

Rosie resisted the impulse to snap, knowing from early experience that Liz was a stickler for "everyone doin' their own job, and stayin' out of everyone else's." She discovered that the hard way when, at the end of her first week, she had innocently taken a duster and vacuum round the office, intent on making a good impression. Days of offended silence had followed, and it had taken all her tact to re-establish good relations with the prickly housekeeper.

"No, but Friday's the last day for putting ads in the paper, and there can be quite a line-up with only Willie on the counter." Why do I have to justify myself, she thought irritably. For heaven's sake, what's the big deal in picking up the phone if it rings? A glance at Liz's face told Rosie this wasn't the right answer. She capitulated. "If you'd rather, I can switch it to voice-mail before I go. I don't expect there'll be calls anyway; with this heat, half the town is already on its way to the lake."

Mollified, Liz gave a tight little smile. "Maybe that's for the best. I've got my hands full making a new recipe for Father's lunch; low cal. fish pie. Fish is brain food, ya know."

Rosie felt a brief wave of sympathy for Father Matthews. Liz was single-minded in her determination to reduce his cholesterol level and, with the phone switched to voice-mail, no "urgent call" would come in today to save him from his healthy lunch. Oh well, maybe he'd see the fish-pie as penitential she thought, remembering her childhood when the entire Catholic world ate fish on Friday as a penance. She'd never understood the connection between fish and penance; to her, it was just another odd part of being Catholic.

Leaving Liz chopping cod and potatoes with her usual gusto, Rosie went back to her office, switched the phone to voice mail and headed out. The heat hit her like a blast furnace and the inside of the car was even hotter. She opened all the windows and drove off. No point in cranking the air, it would barely start working before she parked the car again.

There was very little traffic on Victoria Street, and King Street was much the same. It seemed that all Little Yarmouth's residents had retreated into whatever air-conditioned comfort they could find, and the usually bustling downtown had an old-fashioned Sunday feel.

"Well, there's a bonus," Rosie muttered to herself as she spotted a parking space right in front of the Clarion, and eased the Buick into it. She could feel the heat from the sidewalk coming up through her shoes, as she hurried toward the newspaper's double wooden doors. The old shop bell jangled merrily and, with a sigh of relief, she stepped into a welcome coolness. The Clarion's air-conditioning was working overtime today.

A subdued hum of conversation filled the room. There were five customers waiting at the counter, and Rosie reluctantly got in line behind one of her least-favourite people; Bill Gifford, sole proprietor of Gifford's Fine Autos, President of the Lions Club and all round obnoxious loudmouth. They exchanged smiles and nods, then Bill went back to lecturing his neighbour on the shortcomings of foreign cars. A moment later the shop bell jangled again and Rosie heard a low voice at her elbow.

"Hi Rosie, how are you?"

She turned to see Dougie Ferguson's moon face smiling at her genially, and her heart sank.

"Just fine Dougie, and you?" She sent up a silent plea; *Please don't let him get started on baked goods.* "What brings you here, today?"

He waved a large manila envelope. "Just ordering the reunion posters and promotional stuff. The art-work's really good; here, take a look." And grasping the sample poster, he gave it a sharp tug.

A shower of coasters, pens and buttons flew out with the art work and clattered noisily to the floor. The room fell silent as all eyes turned in their direction. In keeping with his reputation, Bill Gifford broke the silence with "Nice one, Doug," followed by a braying guffaw.

Scarlet faced, Dougie squatted down and began collecting the scattered bits and pieces. As she bent to help him, Rosie wondered how someone that ham-fisted could be renowned throughout Huron County for the delicacy of his cake decorating. After a few minutes of groping around the floor, everything was safely retrieved. They both straightened up, and Rosie laid her small heap of pens and buttons on the counter.

"Thanks Rose. I'd forgotten all that stuff was in the envelope too," Dougie mumbled, his eyes downcast and ears glowing red.

The two of them stood in an uneasy silence for a moment, and Rosie cast about in her mind for something to break the tension. Finally, she remembered the bakery van's accident. "How's your driver doing?" she asked brightly. "I was glad to hear he wasn't too badly hurt, last Monday."

"Dunno." Dougie laid the poster artwork on the counter and began dropping pens, coasters and buttons back into the manila envelope. "I think he's alright. Haven't seen him since Tuesday, when I paid him off."

"Oh, did he quit?"

"No, had to let him go. Don't have a van, so I don't need a driver. I'm using the SUV for deliveries and can't risk him smashing that up too." He frowned and pursed his lips. "Guess it's true what they say. Pay peanuts, get monkeys."

"Well yes, I suppose so." Rosie reflected that Dougie seemed to be having a run of bad luck with his drivers. It was on the tip of her tongue to say so, until she remembered that Tony hadn't just been Dougie's employee, he'd also been an old friend. Presumably his death had been more than just an inconvenience.

Bill Gifford was tapping his fingers impatiently on the counter and looking ostentatiously at his equally ostentatious watch. "How we coming along, then?" he called along the counter. To Rosie's surprise, a female voice answered. And whoever the mystery woman was, she sounded very annoyed.

"I'm doing the best I can, Bill. These folks have all been waiting too, so I'll just ask you to be patient."

Rosie peered around Bill Gifford's bulk, and understood why everything was taking so much longer than usual. Willie Robertson was nowhere to be seen, and his seat behind the counter was occupied by a large woman with a mass of brassy curls piled high on her head.

"I wonder where Willie is today?" she whispered to Dougie. "Hope he's not sick or anything."

"Well, he is getting up there, you know," Dougie answered. He glanced along the counter. "Who's that, anyway?"

"Willie's daughter-in-law, Marilyn. Married to Gordon." Dougie looked blank. "Don't you remember her? She was Marilyn Coker; I think she was in your grade at high school."

"Oh, right." He took another look. "Are you sure? Marilyn Coker was really thin, and she had long black hair." He coloured slightly. "I remember, 'cause I had a bit of a thing for her."

Rosie shrugged. "Well, that's her for sure. I'm afraid we've all changed a lot since high school, Doug."

The shop bell jangled again as two customers opened the door and left, allowing a wave of heat into the store. Everyone shuffled along the counter, slowly moving closer to Marilyn and the conclusion of their business.

It looks as if my excuse for leaving the office early wasn't so far wrong, Rosie thought, as she checked her watch. 11:40 a.m., and still three people waiting ahead of her in line. Beside her, Bill Gifford was still droning on to his unfortunate neighbour.

Suddenly, the man turned to him and said harshly; "Bill, just shut up, will you? I'm sick of you and your *great deals*. Last car I bought from you spent more time in the shop than on the road." Now it was Gifford's turn to look embarrassed. Warming to his subject, his ex-customer's voice was getting louder; "I meant what I said.

I've bought my last car from you, so you can take your special promotion, and stick it up your fat ass!"

The final words of this tirade were shouted into a shocked silence. The door to the back office swung open, and Gord Robertson appeared, his normally placid features creased into a scowl; "Who's doing all the shouting out here?" Nobody spoke. He looked at the red-faced Bill Gifford and the man standing next to him with fists clenched. "I said, who's yelling out here?" Finally his wife broke the silence.

"Mr. Cousins was having a business disagreement with Bill," Marilyn said, with a sniff of disapproval. "And I must say, I don't appreciate his language."

Gord looked from one to the other. He was a big, heavy-set man with hands the size of dinner-plates; definitely not someone to tangle with lightly. He growled; "Well, I'll thank both of you to keep your arguments out of *my* place of business."

Now it was Pete Cousins turn to look shamefaced. "Sorry Gord. Lost my temper. Must be the heat." He picked up his briefcase and started toward the door. "This printing can wait. I'll come back later." He glanced at Marilyn, bristling with indignation at the end of the counter. "Sorry, Mrs. Robertson – sorry, all." The door jangled, and he was gone.

"Gord, I could do with some help out here, you know," Marilyn snapped. "They've been lined up six deep for the past hour."

"Alright, alright. Man can't even have a coffee break, without all hell breaking loose." Gord turned his attention to Bill Gifford; "Those the brochures you want done?" Bill nodded, still flushed with embarrassment. "What stock are we using?" Bill murmured his reply and normality returned.

Rosie was uncertain where to look. To her chagrin, she realised she had rather enjoyed the whole episode; it was rare to see someone get their just desserts so spectacularly.

Dougie leaned toward her, smirking; "Oh boy, that was sweet." Then, as the door opened and closed behind Marilyn's customer; "She's waving at you, you're up."

Sure enough, Marilyn was beckoning to her. Rosie scooted down to the end of the counter. "Hi, Marilyn. It's nice to see you. Mr. Robertson having a day off?"

"No, he's been a bit poorly since last weekend. And this heat doesn't help him any, either." Marilyn fanned herself with a sheet of paper. "I swear the air's not working right." The door jangled again as another customer entered. "God, every time that door opens it gets hotter in here. Now, what can I help you with?"

Rosie had to agree with her. The initial coolness of coming inside had worn off, and a trickle of sweat was running down her back. Even air-conditioning can't cope with this kind of heat, she thought. No wonder we're all so quarrelsome.

"I'm picking up St. Jude's bulletins," she said.

"Yup, they're ready. Give me a minute," and Marilyn disappeared into the back office.

Rosie glanced at the line-up behind her. Bill Gifford was deep in conversation with Gord, and Dougie was waiting patiently next to him. "I won't be long, Doug. Just picking up bulletins."

Dougie lounged against the counter: "Take your time Rose; I'm not in any hurry. It's a darn sight cooler in here than in the bakery today, that's for sure."

Two more customers had come in, and were standing behind him. Rosie recognised Liz's husband Steve, but not the other man. No wonder Marilyn's stressed out, Rosie thought, if her whole morning's been this busy.

Marilyn reappeared, and heaved two bulky packages onto the counter; "Do you want to look them over?" she asked, handing Rosie the invoice.

"Lord, no." Rosie picked up one of the bundles; "I'm sorry to hear that Mr. Robertson's not well. Hope it's nothing serious."

"No, I don't think so; he's a tough old bird. He just got all upset over that Wesley funeral, coming like it did just ahead of this week, you know."

"Sorry? What's special about this week?"

Marilyn leant across the counter and dropped her voice. "His oldest boy's birthday and the anniversary of his wife's death both fall on the same date, June 27th. This week." She glanced surreptitiously at Gord, but he was absorbed in Bill Gifford's print order. "Gord doesn't like talking about Marty; that was his brother."

Rosie could not believe her luck; Marilyn was obviously ready to gossip, and the subject was just what Rosie wanted to pursue. "Oh, I didn't know. That's really sad. But why should Tony Wesley's funeral upset him?"

Marilyn's voice was a whisper; "He blames Tony Wesley for both their deaths."

"No, really? But wasn't Martin in some sort of accident?" Marilyn looked at Rosie in surprise. Oops, I'm not supposed to know anything about that, Rosie thought. She hurried to repair the damage. "I was looking through some old Year Books for the reunion committee, and Martin's death was mentioned."

Marilyn looked round again at Gord, but he was still in the throes of pricing Bill Gifford's order. She whispered; "Poor kid got hit by a train. *Undetermined death,* the Coroner said, but the family always believed Tony Wesley pushed him."

"Why on earth would Tony Wesley kill Gord's brother?" Rosie hoped her surprise sounded genuine enough to support her feigned ignorance.

"It was all about that fire at the high school……"

The room became dim, and Marilyn's voice started to fade, until it was lost completely beneath the crackle and roar of flames. Rosie's eyes were stinging, she could smell smoke, feel intense heat burning her face, she couldn't breathe; "fire, it's always about fire...."

"Sorry, what did you say?"

Rosie was horrified; she had spoken her thoughts aloud. "I said yes, I read about it; the fire at the school. That was in the Year Book, too."

Marilyn took no notice; her reminiscing was in full flood. "My dad started with the Fire Department in 1949, and he used to say that there was a fire bug in town in the fifties. They were always being called out; far more than any other department in the County."

"A firebug? You mean someone who starts fires deliberately? But why would anyone do that?"

"Because they're crazy, that's why. No-one normal does something like that." Marilyn stopped abruptly, suddenly conscious that Gord was watching her. She raised her voice; "So, will you be paying for those today, Rose? Or shall we send the bill?"

"I'm paying now. It's month end, so I've brought the cheque for all of June." She dug into her purse. "May as well save the stamp, eh?"

Marilyn made a great show of writing *paid* on the invoice and handing it back. But she couldn't resist finishing her story. She leant over the counter and whispered; "My dad said there were four big fires in town, and he reckoned the same person started them all." She checked them off on her fingers; "The elementary school, old St. Judes, the high school gym and...," then she paused and dropped her gaze. "Sorry Rose, I clean forgot."

"That's okay Marilyn. I guess the fourth fire was at the hospital, right?"

*   *   *   *

Gord Robertson slammed the heavy back door behind him, then rattled the handle to make sure it was securely locked.

"For God's sake Gord, come on. I'm dyin' of the heat, here!" Marilyn's face was shiny with perspiration and her yellow curls hung limply, the last hairpin having shaken loose mid-afternoon. She turned on the ignition as her husband climbed into the van. "And why we had to use this old bone-shaker today is beyond me" she went on, winding down her window. "It must be a hundred degrees in here."

Gord didn't answer; he was, as usual, tuning out his wife's complaints. "We'd better stop at dads, make sure he's okay," he muttered absently. "Do you think he'll come home with us for supper? What're we having, anyway?"

"I'm just making a salad; it's too hot to be cooking."

"Well, he won't like that. Can't you do something else?"

Marilyn let out an exasperated snort. "No, I can't. That's all I've got, and I'm just wore out with working all week. I've had no time to shop, or anything." They drove on in silence for a few minutes, and then she said; "I suppose I could make him an omelette, or scrambled egg. Would he eat that, do ya think?"

Gord looked across and gave her a quick smile. "That'll probably do him. Look Mar, I'm sorry you've had to come in all week, but he just wasn't up to it. I'm really worried; it's not like the old guy to be away from the business for so long."

"He's seventy-nine, for God's sake." Marilyn raised her voice over the traffic noise coming in through the open window. "How much longer do you think he can work six days a week?" Gord sat silently, looking down at his print stained fingers. His wife glanced across at him and sighed in frustration; "Gord, you've got to hire someone; don't think I'm gonna keep taking up the slack. Half the time I don't know what the hell I'm doing with orders and stuff."

"You'll get the hang of it."

"I don't want to get the hang of it. I've got my own business to look after, remember."

Now it was Gord's turn to sound exasperated: "Oh yeah, that's really important! Dragging bags of make-up round to groups of silly women." He raised his bushy eyebrows almost to his hairline, and said in falsetto: "Ooo, Marilyn, do you think I'm a Winter or a Spring?"

"I don't expect you to understand, but it's a nice little money earner, and I enjoy it," Marilyn bridled. "So get it through your head; I'm not gonna be an unpaid drudge at the Clarion."

Gord leaned back sulkily in his seat, looking out of the window as the old van bounced and rattled along the road. Apparently absorbed in the passing scene, it was a while before he spoke again. "What was the big discussion with Rose Cornish about, then? Sure took her long enough to pick up those bulletins."

Marilyn coloured guiltily. "She was just asking after your dad, that's all."

"Oh yeah? And where did Marty figure in that interesting conversation?"

Not surprised to find that Gord had, after all, been eavesdropping on her conversation, Marilyn went on the offensive. She answered sharply; "So I told her about June 27th. What's the big deal, anyway? It's all ancient history."

"Because it's no-one's business but ours, and dad still gets real cut-up about it." He went back to gazing out of the window. "I'll never forget that day, either. That bastard Tony Wesley killed mom sure as if he'd taken a gun and shot her." He brushed a hand across his eyes.

"C'mon Gord; she'd had heart problems for years. It was just bad luck she saw him that particular day."

"It wasn't bad luck that he started yelling at her."

Marilyn spoke gently. "He was with a bunch of other kids; you know what boys are like, going round together. Your mom called him a killer; if he'd been on his own, he'd probably have just taken off."

Gordon pulled a grubby handkerchief out of his pocket and blew his nose loudly. "She walked through our front door, hung up her coat and dropped dead. Me and dad were in the kitchen, and I shouted out I was gonna be late for baseball practice, and then we heard the thud." He gave a deep sigh. "I was only twelve; you never forget something like that." He stuffed the handkerchief back in his pocket. "If I'd have been older, I'd have killed Tony Wesley. Scum like that don't deserve to live."

Chapter 12 – Up at the Cottage

"Hush, Gussie; it's alright. We're going somewhere nice, you'll see." Whatever possessed me to promise Moira I'd bring the dog up, Rosie thought, trying to ignore the piteous sounds coming from her back seat. Despite a half open rear window, she was engulfed in the hot, musty fugg that only a panting dog can create.

"Poor old boy," she said over her shoulder. "I know, you think we're going to the vet. But we're not – we're going to the cottage to see Moira – you like the cottage, don't you?" The whimpering from the crate on the back seat grew louder, edging toward a full howl.

Rosie leant forward and turned up the volume on her CD player. But Maria Callas was no match for Gussie, and she was soon driving down the road listening to a discordant duet between Madama Butterfly and a howling beagle.

White-knuckled, she focused on the road ahead. At least there wasn't much traffic. Most of the weekenders and tourists had left town yesterday or early this morning. She'd easily reach the cottage before dark, and was looking forward to a good night's sleep; she always slept well at Heron Lake.

After her conversation with Marilyn, Rosie had felt by turns elated and depressed. Elated, because she was confident she'd solved Tony Wesley's murder, and he'd soon be free of the guilt that kept him earthbound. Depressed, because it was almost certain that he was responsible for the fire which had taken the lives of her father and grandparents. Remembering that awful time still made her profoundly sad and, knowing she'd have to forgive Tony to free him made her sadder still. She didn't know if she'd have the strength to do so, when the time came.

She was sure that either Willie or Gord Robertson had killed Tony. Of the two, her money was on Gordon; Willie was too frail to overpower Tony, and throw him down a flight of stairs. Then there was the little matter of convincing Gordon to confess and give himself up to the police. In the past, that had always been the trickiest part of her murder investigations; how to convince a guilty party that she knew what she knew, because a ghost had told her. No, she wasn't ready to tackle Gordon with that just yet.

And on top of everything, she couldn't shake the nagging feeling that, somewhere along the way, she'd missed something important. She'd lain awake half the previous night going over where she'd been and who she'd spoken to over the last few days, trying to pin down what was missing. It was so logical that Gordon had killed Tony – he was a big man, like the shadow she'd seen in her vision, and he certainly had more than enough motive. So why this niggling doubt?

Absorbed in her thoughts, Rosie barely noticed the miles flying by and was surprised to find herself at the turn onto Concession 7. It was finally quiet in the car as both Maria Callas and Gussie had fallen silent; the one because her CD had ended, and the other because, resigned to his fate, he'd given up and gone to sleep.

Ten minutes later Rosie navigated her way down the narrow track leading to the lake, and the cottage came in view. Across the lake the sun was going down in a blaze of red and, as she turned off the engine, she caught the sound of a loon out on the water. Winding down her window, she sat quietly in the car for a brief moment, drinking in the peace and tranquillity. This was such a magical place....

"Auntie Ro!" The screen door flew open, and Moira came hurtling up the path, followed by Aunt Margaret, waving her more restrained welcome.

"Auntie Ro!" Moira threw herself at Rosie, then, catching sight of the back seat, "Oh, wow, you *did* bring Gussie." At the sound of her voice, Gussie started bounding about in the crate, barking excitedly, as he literally rattled his cage.

"Hi, sweetie, have you had a good time?" Rosie gave her niece a hug. "No - wait, don't open the crate until I've got his leash ready…" but too late. Moira had flung the car door open and released the crate lock in a matter of seconds. A moment later both girl and dog were rolling on the ground.

Rosie grabbed the excited beagle by his collar, and clicked on the leash. "Moira dear, get up, you'll be filthy. Here"… she handed over the leash, "take him for a quick walk round, he must need to go by now."

"Okay, Auntie Ro. C'mon Gus, let's catch a fish," and Moira started running toward the lake, the panting beagle well in tow.

"And don't let him off-leash," Rosie called after them. "He'll disappear, and we'll be up all night looking for him." Smiling, she turned to her aunt; "You haven't tired her out, I see."

"No chance of that. I'm starting to think I'm getting too old to keep up with this younger generation," Margaret answered, with a rueful grin.

Rosie gave her a peck on the cheek; "You? Never!" She pulled her old music bag off the seat, grabbed Gussie's blanket out of the crate and picked up his container of kibble. "How'd the week go?"

"I think they all had a good time – but I'm ready for a rest. How was the drive up?"

"Not much traffic, but the sound effects were bone-chilling." Her aunt looked at her questioningly. "Travelling any distance with Gus in the car is enough to make a grown man cry."

Her aunt chuckled and took the kibble container from her. In the fading light they strolled down the path together, listening to Moira's laughter and Gussie's ecstatic barks echoing from the water's edge.

The screen door slapped shut behind them, and Rosie walked through the kitchen into the great room. She dropped her bag to the floor. "It always feels so good to be here," she said. "Nothing ever changes." And as if to underline that fact, she crossed the room and sat down on a small wooden rocker, drawn up to the window. "I remember sitting on grandmere's lap, in this chair. I must have been about eight, and she said I was getting too big to be cuddled *comme un bébé*." She closed her eyes and rocked gently back and forth.

"Yes, this place is full of memories," her aunt replied, her voice low. "The first time I brought Patsy here she was about six months old, and really fretful. I was new to the whole motherhood thing, and completely exhausted from all the sleepless nights." Her smile was tinged with the sadness that often follows happy memories. "Maman just took her from me, sat down in that chair and rocked her away to dreamland. I caught up on six months sleep while I was here for those two weeks." She went over and sat down on a battered wicker loveseat opposite Rosie. Everything was quiet, except for the sound of grandmere's old chair, rocking back and forth.

After a few minutes, Margaret said briskly; "Are you hungry, my dear? I could make you a sandwich – or how about a piece of pie? Moira and I spent the afternoon baking, not the perfect occupation for a heat-wave. But she was so set on making a pie for you, she even chopped all the apples herself."

Never one to pass up home-made pie, Rosie happily waved another diet goodbye - after all, she couldn't hurt Moira's feelings. She got up and followed her aunt into the kitchen. "Pie sounds great, auntie. But it's almost dark, so I'd better be getting those two in first.

And I expect Moira will be wanting to sample the pie, too."

"Yes, good idea. But before she comes in, tell me – how's your special problem shaping up?"

Rosie allowed herself a self-satisfied smile, as she began, "Well...."

"You've solved it!" her aunt interrupted. "I thought you looked like the cat that got the cream, as soon as I saw you get out of the car."

"I'm pretty sure I know who did what. And you were right, it does come very close to me. It looks like Tony Wesley started the hospital fire."

"My Lord!" Her aunt sat down abruptly on a kitchen stool. "And someone killed him because of that?"

"No, there's much more to it, just as you said. He was a firebug and....."

A sudden blast of wind rattled all the doors and windows, the lights flickered and the room went suddenly dark. Before they could react, the lights came on again.

Margaret went to the window, and looked out anxiously. "I'll have to wait to hear the rest of your news – looks like there's a storm blowing up. You get Moira and the dog in, and I'll check the generator. Can't think why it's cutting out, though. It's just been overhauled."

Rosie hurried out through the screened porch but, to her surprise, there were no storm clouds gathering over the lake. Above her the first stars were twinkling in a clear sky and, in the dim light, she could see Moira walking up from the dock, with Gussie trotting behind. The air was still and warm.

"I was just coming to call you, sweetie. Auntie Marg thought there might be a storm brewing."

"It was fine down by the water." Moira said, then stopped just inside the porch. "I think I'd better dry Gus off out here. He rolled in something dead, and even though I made him go all the way into the water, he still smells pretty bad."

That's a record, Rosie thought. We've been here less than an hour, and the beagle's already *canis non grata*.

Margaret appeared from the far side of the house. "Well, I don't know what just blew through, but the sky's clear and the generator's fine." Glancing around, she wrinkled her nose. "Dear Lord, what is that terrible smell?"

"I'm really sorry, but Gussie's running true to breed and found a dead fish to roll in. Moira's gone for old towels to rub him down, but it'll take a couple of days to wear off completely, I'm afraid."

Her aunt laughed. "Not to worry, that's the advantage of having an old-style cottage rather than something out of *House Beautiful.* The furniture's quite used to smelly dogs – come on in, boy." She opened the inside door and Gussie strolled in behind her. Really, he couldn't understand what all the fuss was about.

Rosie had no opportunity that night to share any of her news. After a supper of apple pie with a side of old cheddar, she helped Moira work on the 2,000 piece jigsaw that every visitor to the cottage had struggled with for the past fifty years, and then went into the porch to inspect the "museum" the cousins had been busy creating all week.

"Wayne took his stuff home; he was being really childish about it. But then he is only nine, so I s'pose that's why" Moira said. She picked up an odd shaped piece of grey stone. "Look, Chris says this is an Indian arrowhead. And this…" she handed Rosie a small white object, "…is a rat's skull. It's only a brown rat, though. Chris said it would be really something to find a black rat skull, they're very rare in Ontario."

Repressing a shudder, Rosie replaced the bony exhibit next to its handwritten label; *Skull of Norway Rat. Found by MC June 27 2000.* "Will you be taking your finds home, too?" Rosie asked, imagining her sister-in-law's reaction to these grubby trophies laid out on a window ledge or shelf in her picture perfect home.

"No, I've decided to leave them here, for the rest of the family to enjoy through the summer. And anyway, Bobbie and I are coming again in August, so I'll probably be adding more." She paused. "It was so fun hunting for stuff in the woods, and then reading it all up in Gams books."

Rosie reflected that the absence of T.V and the Internet could sometimes be a very good thing. For sure, Moira and her cousins didn't seem to have missed them this past week.

Much as she wanted to talk to her aunt, by ten thirty all Rosie could think of was her bed. Moira was still up, still chatting on about her adventures with the cousins. "Uncle Steve let Chris and Wayne sleep in the bunkhouse one night, and they saw an owl. Do you think Daddy will let me and Bobbie sleep in there next time?"

Margaret looked at the clock. "I think it's about time for bed, missy." She put down her book. "What about putting that skull and other bits of bones into the porch cupboard? Gus has gone to sleep out there – its cooler I guess – and we don't want him snacking on anything overnight." She didn't say what both she and Rosie were thinking; that it was a mercy he'd chosen to sleep on the porch, saving someone from enduring his fishy stench all night.

Moira stood up reluctantly. "Okay, Gam. But you're not going to lock him out there, are you?"

"No, my little softie. I'll leave the dog flap open, so he can get in later, if he wants."

Rosie's head was starting to nod, until she finally couldn't stifle her yawns any longer. "Sorry, Aunt Marg, I'll have to fill you in on everything tomorrow. I didn't sleep much last night, and now I can't stay awake."

"Well, it'll keep, for sure. Although I must admit, I'm dying to hear all the details."

Rosie picked up the old music bag which doubled as her weekender and started toward the door at the far end of the room. "I'm off to bed, then. Where am I, Auntie?"

"I thought you'd like to be in Blue Jay, this time. There's fresh towels on the blanket rack, next to the tallboy."

"And I changed the bed this afternoon," Moira piped up, her return heralded by a whiff of Gussie's unmistakable aroma.

"Then I'm sure to sleep especially well," Rosie answered, going into the hallway. "See you in the morning - sleep tight." Now barely able keep her eyes open she heard Moira's stock reply; "Don't let the bed bugs bite" as, with a sigh of relief, she closed Blue Jay's door behind her.

"Come on young lady, into your pyjamas" Margaret said, as she locked the porch door and bent to open the dog flap. A slight draft rustled the stack of magazines piled next to her old recliner. "Looks like there's a bit of breeze getting up. Maybe tomorrow will be cooler." She pulled the faded cotton drapes together at one end of the picture window. "Moira, just get those drapes closed at the far end, will you? Thanks, dear. Come on now, it's time we were both in bed."

As Moira headed reluctantly toward her room, Margaret reached into the hall cupboard and took out an old afghan. "Here, put this across the bottom of your bed" she said, handing it to her. "I don't think for one minute Gussie will stay in the porch all night, and it's your room he'll come looking for. And I don't want him smelling-up the spread." She gave Moira a quick kiss. "Don't forget to clean your teeth, now. See you in the morning."

Since her very first summer at Heron Lake in 1936, Margaret had slept in the little room called Chickadee. There was just enough space for two single beds, with a nightstand between them, a washstand with three drawers, and the sink. A rag rug lay on the floor between the beds, and the clothes closet was a row of iron hooks on the wall next to the door. Like everything in the cottage, the bedspreads and drapes were faded, and the furniture battered. But Margaret wouldn't have changed a thing. Every piece of fabric and stick of furniture held precious memories of dear ones, loved and lost.

She was twelve that first year, the only girl in a family with five boys. Then little Rose Elizabeth had been born, and after a few years they were roommates in Chickadee every summer. She still heard her sister's girlish laughter occasionally and sixty years would dissolve away in an instant, and she would be back in the time when they were all so young and happy.

Only three of her siblings remained; Peter, Michael and Sebastian and, of the three, it was only Peter that she saw regularly. Although well past retirement age, he was still a parish priest for the London diocese. Michael, long retired from teaching, lived with his family on the West Coast and Sebastian was also far removed, both by distance and vocation. In 1960, he had entered the Trappist monastery of Gethsemani in Kentucky, another life-changing result of the hospital fire.

Her eldest brother Joe had been shot down over Italy in 1943, and then in 1948, Rose Elizabeth had been lost to them too, a victim of the polio epidemic that had swept through Ontario that summer. Not long after her death, Gerard and Mary had their first child – a daughter they named Rose Elizabeth, in memory of the little aunt she would never know. Small wonder that Rosie had always been Margaret's favourite niece.

Despite her weariness, Margaret was unable to rest. She wished there had been an opportunity to talk things over with Rosie, and began rehashing what she knew, and what she had experienced in her trance state earlier that week. 'Rosie seems so confident that she's got it right' she thought. 'So what is it that's making me uneasy?'

Eventually her eyes closed, but only an hour later she woke suddenly, convinced that something was terribly wrong. She was consumed by a deep melancholy, and wasn't surprised to find her cheeks wet with tears. Her mind was a jumble of confused images; swirling leaves, a familiar building with bright lights shining through big double doors. And a figure silhouetted against the light; small, with dark hair, dressed all in white. The sense of impending disaster persisted and became so strong, that she finally got up and went out into the hall.

But there was nothing amiss. After a reassuring look around the hall, great room and kitchen, she came back to Chickadee and sat on the bed. Taking a deep breath, she closed her eyes and concentrated. The building (she recognized it now as Little Yarmouth hospital) came back into focus. Another figure came hurrying up the steps to join the one in white, and the two went inside together. As the image dissolved, Margaret heard her mother's voice, as clearly as if she'd been standing next to her. "Be careful, mon petite. Things are not as they seem."

With all hope of sleep gone, Margaret got into bed, snapped on the bedside lamp and picked up her book from the nightstand. She hoped Rosie would not be too disappointed tomorrow, when she heard that her aunt was not convinced that Tony Wesley's murder had been solved.

Rosie had experienced no such difficulties. As expected, she fell into a deep sleep as soon as her head touched the pillow. She slept peacefully, undisturbed by the night sounds of woods and lake, or by any importunate spirit restlessly demanding her attention.

When she opened her eyes, the morning light lay in barred stripes across her bed, shining through the stand of birch trees which grew close outside the window.

She stretched luxuriously, and looked around the room. Blue Jay was the nicest of the cottage's six bedrooms and the only one with a full sized double bed. Situated at the end of the cottage, it had two windows – one on the forest side, and one facing out to the lake. It had been her grandparent's bedroom, and all their original furniture was still in place; cannonball bed, heavy bow fronted chest with matching tallboy, and a dressing mirror on the washstand. Other than holding hand towels, the washstand was purposeless. Its jug and bowl had been supplanted a few years earlier, when pedestal sinks were finally installed in all the bedrooms.

Despite having no air conditioning, the cottage was comfortably cool, a result of heavy tree cover and breezes from the lake. "Nature's air conditioning" David had said, on the one occasion he had spent time here with her.

'Now, where did that come from?' she thought, and felt the familiar pang of anger and loss that always followed David's intrusion into her consciousness. It was enough to get her up out of bed and across to the little sink.

Ten minutes later, washed and dressed, she followed the delicious aroma of fresh brewed coffee into the kitchen.

Her aunt looked up from the table, neatly set for breakfast. "Morning, my dear. How did Moira's bed-making hold up? Did you sleep okay, or did all your sheets fall off in the night?"

"Slept like a baby. But then I always do, when I'm here." Rosie looked round. "Is she still in bed?"

"Lord, no. She's already eaten and gone down to the lake with the dog – wanted to try to wash off his interesting fragrance." Margaret stood up with an effort. "What are we having for breakfast?"

Rosie looked at her aunt with concern. "Are you alright, Auntie Marg?"

"Just a bit stiff, dear. *Tempus fugit* and all that, you know." She walked across to the stove. "I had a rather restless night, as it happens. Now, how about some French toast?" and she reached for the frying pan.

"Let me get the breakfast, you look all in."

"No, it's better if I move around. And I know where everything is, so by the time I've told you where to look, I may as well have done it myself." Then, seeing Rosie's uncertain expression, she added; "But I will let you wash the dishes, as a special treat."

Rosie laughed. "Alright, it's a deal."

Although they were both eager to discuss Rosie's "special problem," they seemed to have an unspoken agreement to leave the topic until after breakfast. So, as they worked their way through fresh fruit and French toast, their conversation centred on family matters and Little Yarmouth gossip.

Finally, when all the dishes had been washed and stacked, Margaret said: "Let's take our coffee down to the dock. We can have a good long chat, and keep an eye on Moira and Gussie at the same time."

They walked across springy rock grass to the dock, and were soon settled comfortably in a pair of Muskoka chairs. Although it was only mid-morning the sun was already hot, and Rosie could see Moira splashing along the shore in her swimsuit. Gussie was jumping up and down excitedly as she threw sticks into the water.

Margaret lent back in her chair and sighed; "This is what cottage life is all about." She put her legs up on a handy bait box, and looked at her niece. "Come on, Rosie - when are you going to give me all the details? The suspense is killing me, you know."

Rosie laughed; "It's seems like such an age since Monday, so much has happened." She sipped on her coffee. "After what you told me, I started making a list of all the potential murderers in Little Yarmouth. And that was a pretty scary exercise, I can tell you."

She was interrupted by Moira, waving and calling enthusiastically. "Come on down to the water, Auntie Ro!"

"Later sweetie," Rosie called back, putting her mug down beside her. "Once I started thinking about it, I realised what a strange cast of characters we have in town. Do you know, I ended up with *fourteen* names on my list – that's fourteen people I grew up with, who I seriously considered capable of cold-blooded murder." She shivered involuntarily.

"And when you finally decided who it was, was that name on your list?"

"Sort of" Rosie answered. "I'd better start at the beginning. Lucy called me Tuesday evening, and I asked her to come over on Wednesday night. But before that, I went up to the convent to see Sister Mary B...." Slowly and carefully Rosie recounted everything she had learned from her old teacher, Lucy's year books and finally from Marilyn Robertson. "So, I knew it was all to do with the school fire and Martin Robertson's death. And Tony starting all those fires; that fitted right in with what you said. That there'd been more than one death and that it all came very close to me."

Her aunt looked thoughtful; "So why did Tony kill Martin Robertson?"

Rosie leant forward eagerly in her seat; "He must have seen Tony setting fire to the gym, and was going to tell some-one. Even what I saw in my vision fits; Gord Robertson is a really big guy, who could easily have broken Tony's neck and thrown him down the stairs." She took a deep breath and relaxed back in her seat again. "I'm almost sure I've got it right – Gord Robertson killed Tony Wesley in revenge for his brother's death. And Tony Wesley was responsible for killing my dad, grandpa and grandmere." The words were unexpectedly hard to say, and Rosie's voice dropped, as she felt her throat tighten and the prickle of tears beginning behind her eyes. She struggled for composure, until she was finally able to blurt out; "I don't know if I can let it all go, Auntie Marg. Not enough to release him, anyway."

A dark cloud passed in front of the sun, and a cold wind seemed to whip up from nowhere. Her aunt reached across and gently took her hand. "Yes, you will, my dear. You know better than most that you have to let bitterness go, if you want to finally heal."

The moment passed. It was very calming to sit there in the sunshine, listening to the slap of water against the dock and the rat-a-tat of a woodpecker in the trees behind them. But not for Rosie. Thinking of the hospital fire had set her emotions in turmoil.

After a few minutes, Margaret looked across at her. "What's bothering you, my dear?"

Rosie swallowed hard and spoke with an effort; "Auntie Marg, will you tell me what actually happened the night of the fire?" She hesitated, trying to find the courage to finally hear all the details of their family tragedy. "I know everyone died of course, but I was away at school in Goderich when it happened, and only came back the day before the funerals. And afterwards, mom never spoke of it, and I could never bring myself to ask her any questions."

Margaret looked at her sadly. "I know, Rose. But you have to understand that none of us could bring ourselves to even think of that night for years. And later, when the pain did become bearable, it seemed pointlessly cruel to dredge everything up again." She looked at her niece. "But yes, I think it's really important now that you know as much as possible."

They were interrupted by the sight of Moira and Gussie running along the dock toward them. "Gammie, Auntie Ro, when are you coming down to the lake? It's so warm, it's like bath water. And I think I've got rid of Gussie's smell. I rubbed him all over with oatmeal flakes."

The beagle flopped down between their chairs, tired out from an hour of unaccustomed running and jumping. Rosie ran her hand along his back; he was soaking wet and seemed to be suffering from giant dandruff. She avoided making eye contact with her aunt, who was trying not to laugh.

"He does smell a whole lot better," Margaret conceded. "Where ever did you get the idea for the oatmeal?"

"It was in one of your books, Gammie. There was a recipe for natural shampoo, but the only ingredient we had in the kitchen was oatmeal." She gave a look of mock disgust and pinched her nose. "You were right - he did come in my room last night, and the smell woke me up, so I had to do something. I know we mustn't put detergent in the lake, so I couldn't use our shampoo, either."

"Well, using the oatmeal was very resourceful, sweetie." Rosie said. "But it might be good to take him up to the cottage now, and give him a thorough rinsing with nice warm water and then a good drying. Otherwise, he'll get itchy and we don't want him scratching all the way home."

"Okay – I was going in for a drink, anyway. But you've got to promise to come down to the beach with me when I come back."

"Alright, I promise. But I can't go in swimming, I forgot my suit." This wasn't strictly true - Rosie had deliberately left her swimsuit behind, uncomfortably aware that her increasing girth was stretching the Lycra to perilous lengths.

Moira started to run up the slope. "Won't be long, then" she called, then "c'mon Gus," and the dog reluctantly got to his feet and panted after her.

"Do you remember what it was like, to go everywhere at a run?" Margaret asked. "I swear, that child is never still." She leant back in her chair and closed her eyes. No, it was no good prevaricating – she had to deal with Rosie's questions. After a minute, she said; "It was Halloween. My three were all too old for trick or treating, so they'd gone to a dance with some other kids. I'd just finished handing out the last of the candy, when the phone rang." She stopped speaking, as pictures of that awful night began to crowd in on her, the reality as vivid now as it had been more than forty years earlier.

"When I picked up it was Father Carlisle, phoning from your house. The police had called him and asked him to go over there, but your mom was out, so he'd waited on the porch till she got home. She'd taken Jo and John trick or treating. All he said when he phoned was that there'd been an accident at the hospital, and could I come. Then he said I should get in touch with Peter at St. Augustine's, and ask him to come as well." She picked up her mug and tipped the dregs out onto the grass beside her. "I knew things were really bad, then. He'd never have asked me to leave the kids and drive all the way to Little Yarmouth, or call Peter away from the rectory at ten o'clock at night, unless something truly awful had happened."

Rosie tried to imagine what it had been like, getting that frightening phone call when you were alone. She knew her aunt was accustomed to being on her own – Bernard, her husband, had been killed in the war and she'd been a widow far longer than she had been a wife. Even so, it always helped to have someone with you, at a time like that.

"Did you call Uncle Peter?"

"Yes, he left right away. I picked the kids up from the dance, and then headed straight out to Little Yarmouth. I remember thinking *at least I don't have to find a sitter,* because Patsy was eighteen."

"Why didn't Father Carlisle explain what had happened? He must have known, if the police had asked him to go over to our house." Rosie was finding all this much harder to hear than she had expected.

"Probably thought that kind of news shouldn't be given over the phone – and it's good thing he didn't tell me all the details. As it was, my head was spinning the whole way over, wondering what had happened. But if I'd known they were all dead, I could never have made the drive safely."

There was a little sail boat bobbing up and down on the lake, and Margaret watched it for a few minutes, trying to distance her emotions and focus her memory, before she carried on.

"That was the worst night of my life. Worse even than getting the telegrams about Joe or Bernie, or waiting through the night when little Rose was dying. Sometimes I wonder if the Gift doesn't bring a curse with it. So much suffering for one family...." Margaret's voice cracked as she struggled to swallow the lump in her throat.

Distressed that her questions were causing so much grief, Rosie got up from her chair and went over to the old bait box. She perched on the edge, next to her aunt's feet. "Don't go on, auntie. You can tell me the rest some other time." She looked at Margaret with concern. "I'm sorry – I was selfish, I had no idea that remembering would be so painful."

The ghost of a smile passed across Margaret's face. "No, my dear, it's my fault. You should have known all this years ago. And now, with this business of Tony Wesley, you absolutely have to have all the facts."

It didn't take long for the rest of the story to be told. Haltingly, Margaret described her disbelief and shock when she understood the enormity of her loss. Her parents and brother were dead – the centre of her family gone forever. Rosie and her siblings were fatherless and their mother a widow.

At the inquest, everything was pieced together. On the night of October 31st, Dr. William Cornish had been on call at the hospital's emergency department. A teenage girl had come in with severe abdominal pain, and he diagnosed an ectopic pregnancy requiring immediate surgery. Little Yarmouth was too small to have a resident anestheologist, (one came in from Goderich Hospital when needed) but that night there was no one available. So Dr. William called his son, Dr. Gerard, to stand in.

After the surgery, the patient had been taken upstairs from the ground floor operating room. Less than five minutes later, smoke and flames were seen coming from the single storey addition which housed the surgical unit. Before any help could arrive, a huge explosion levelled the entire structure. It was later determined that a fire had been started next to the area used for storage of medical gases.

"But why was grandmere there?" Rosie asked, as Margaret paused to catch her breath.

"She was helping a friend. Memorial was a very small hospital in 1960 – just a cottage hospital, really. It only had one surgical nurse, Berta Fish, but your grandmere had worked in the O.R at Hotel Dieu in Montreal, so she took the occasional shift. That night, Berta wanted to take her little girl trick or treating, so she asked your grandmere to fill in." Margaret couldn't hold the tears back any longer. They ran silently under her glasses and down her cheeks. "I always found that the hardest part of the whole sorry tale. Maman shouldn't have been there – she was just being kind, as she always was. Only this time it cost her her life."

For a few minutes, the only sounds were the rustle of leaves overhead and a rhythmic *thump thump* from their old rowboat bumping against the dock. Thankful for any distraction, Margaret wiped her eyes and said; "Look at the state of that boat. I really must get Steve to paint it next time he comes." Then she looked across at Rosie, watching intently, waiting patiently to hear the last of the story. She was grateful to be almost done.

Taking her feet off the bait box, she sat up straight and breathed deeply. "The fire department knew it was arson right from the start. There were even witnesses - a few parents still out trick or treating with their kids. And the most important thing they saw was two figures running from the back of the hospital and down Albert Street, just before the explosion." She paused, then went on quickly. "*Two* figures, Rosie. You know what that means."

Rosie stood up and walked to the edge of the dock. Looking out across the water, she answered; "If Tony is our firebug, then it looks as if he had an accomplice."

Her aunt came and stood beside her. "Yes. And if that accomplice still lives in Little Yarmouth, he might have wanted Tony silenced – permanently."

Chapter 13 – Home Again

Although there was no particular urgency to leave the cottage early (Monday was Canada Day and a holiday) Rosie had planned to be on the road by mid-afternoon. But it was well past 6 p.m. when she finally waved goodbye to her aunt, negotiated the bumpy track up to the road and turned onto Concession 7.

To be fair, Moira and Gussie were only partly to blame for the delay. Yes, it had taken much longer than expected to get Moira packed up, and yes, Gussie had taken it into his head to jump off the dock just as they were loading the car, but Rosie knew the late start was mostly her own fault. She and Margaret had been so immersed in their examination of Tony Wesley's life and death, that preparations for the trip home had been all but forgotten.

She had arrived at Heron Lake yesterday happily convinced that Tony Wesley's murder was solved. Now she was returning home with her neatly constructed solution in shreds, and a sinking feeling that she was almost back to square one.

She had made a 180 degree turn in her view of Gord Robertson as the killer. Yes, he was hefty enough, and certainly possessed of a quick temper. But she couldn't imagine him *giggling* at the sight of his victim, lying dead at the bottom of the stairs. If anything, he would have been more likely to go down and give the body a few swift kicks. No, this murder wasn't the result of an angry outburst – it had been carefully planned by a stone cold killer.

Rosie and Margaret's dock-side conversation had ended with Moira's return, and her insistence that they all go down to the beach; "You did promise, Auntie Ro!"

So it wasn't until after lunch, when she'd been dispatched to walk Gussie in readiness for the drive home, that aunt and niece had returned to the vexing question of Little Yarmouth's firebug.

"I'm going to play Devil's Advocate, my dear", Margaret had said, dropping spoons into a tray and closing the cutlery drawer with a thud. "Just bear with me. What real evidence is there to prove that Tony Wesley started all those fires?"

Rosie had racked her brains, and then said regretfully; "None at all, I'm afraid. I rather jumped to that conclusion, based on what Marilyn Robertson said." She hung her wet tea towel across the oven handle. "But I do know that fire is a huge part of all of this. Ever since the night of the funeral, I've been having dreams and visions of fire. And remember, you said that it all comes very close to me."

"I also said that Tony Wesley's murder was just the tip of an iceberg," her aunt had replied. "Tell me, what do you know about your chief suspect, Gord Robertson?"

By this time, they'd gone through into the great room, and were sitting side by side on the wicker loveseat.

"Not much. We were in the same class at John Galt. He was more into football than anything else – a real tough guy."

"Would you say he had a bad temper?"

"Yes, he had a pretty short fuse - still does." Rosie had given her back cushion a punch, then shifted position, trying to get more comfortable on the lumpy seat. "And yes, I could see him breaking Tony Wesley's neck, if he thought he'd killed Martin."

"But what about killing in cold blood? Would he kill again, if he thought someone knew what he'd done?"

"I don't know, Auntie Marg." Rosie tried to picture Gord Robertson, plotting murder in the Clarion's back office. "No, I think if he killed someone, it would have to be in anger. He never struck me as much of a planner; usually seems quite disorganised, actually." She had given up trying to beat the cushions into submission. "Next time I come up, I'm bringing new cushions for this loveseat" she complained, and her aunt had burst out laughing.

"Well, what can you expect? It's older than you are!"

"Well, it's lumpier than I am, that's for sure," Rosie shot back, joining in the laughter. She had thought for a moment, then said slowly; "The more I puzzle on this murder, the more unlikely Gord looks as the killer. That horrible giggle I heard in the basement - it just doesn't fit with him, at all."

"No, and my impression was of a remorseless and calculating killer – one who's very pleased with himself right now. This is a really bad person Rosie, I'm sure Tony Wesley isn't his first victim." Margaret had gone over to her mother's old rocking chair and swung it gently back and forth. "I saw maman last night, waiting outside the hospital for your dad to come. They went in together, and then she told me to be careful; that things are not as they seem."

Rosie wasn't surprised. She always felt the warmth of her grandmere's presence in the cottage; it was one of the reasons she loved coming to Heron Lake. "What do you think she meant?"

"Take your pick. Gord Robertson's not the murderer; Tony Wesley's not the firebug. Or both."

Why are messages from the other side always so vague, Rosie wondered? If it's so all-fired important for the living to fix something, why don't the dead just tell us what the problem is? But no – all we get are huge puzzles with most of the pieces missing. She sighed in frustration.

Her aunt sat down in the chair, and rocked gently back and forth. "Has Tony Wesley actually *said* anything to you, or has it just been the standard moaning and groaning?"

"Yes, that very first night he said *not my fault* several times, and the message on the mirror was just *sorry* over and over. I thought he was saying it wasn't his fault he fell down the stairs, and maybe he was sorry that he'd hurt Lucy."

"Well, now we know it wasn't his fault that he went down the stairs, so what else might he want you to know he didn't do? And yes, he might be sorry for causing his wife grief, but maybe it was *you* he was apologising to, not Lucy."

For Rosie, this had been a whole new take on events – a very personal one. Was all this because Tony wanted her to know he was innocent of the hospital fire, and sorry for the grief it caused? And if that were the case then, "Tony was the accomplice, not the firebug" she'd said, finishing her thoughts aloud.

"Right" her aunt responded triumphantly.

"But then, if Tony didn't set the hospital fire, then he wouldn't have set the gym fire either, and he'd have no reason to kill Martin Robertson. Did someone else do that, too?"

Margaret had continued to rock thoughtfully. "I think we need to know more about those other fires. Marilyn said her dad thought the arsons at old St. Judes, the hospital and the high school were all linked. Was there anywhere else?"

"Yes. The first one was at the public school, in the early fifties."

"I remember that; Alastair Street Elementary in 1954, the year before we moved to Goderich. Patsy was at Holy Angels, and some of the public school kids transferred there, while the repairs were being done. Miss Patsy got all bent out of shape because she had to share a desk for a month or so." Margaret grinned at the memory. "Lord, she was a real little madam, then! I remember I had to sit her down and give her a good talking-to."

Well it didn't stick, Rosie had thought unkindly. Patricia (*please don't call me Patsy!*) was now the family diva, to be avoided whenever possible. The little madam had grown up to be her least favourite cousin, a fact she'd always carefully hidden from her aunt. How such a dear person could have raised such an obnoxious child had always eluded her. She realised her aunt was still speaking, and looked up guiltily.

"......... really don't see how Tony Wesley could have been responsible for all those fires. In 1953, what was he? About ten years old?"

"More like nine, I'd think."

"Well, he was at Holy Angels, and Alastair Street is clear the other side of town. I can't see him biking over there to set a fire, when he was only nine years old. And why would he go all that way? If he wanted to burn down a school, why not his own? "

Rosie shook her head. She was starting to feel they were going round in circles. "Maybe it wasn't the same person that set all the fires. Perhaps some of them were just accidents."

"Well, maybe. But if it was a firebug, surely it was someone connected to all those places – and someone older than Tony, I'd think."

Their conversation had continued in the same vein for a while and, slowly, Rosie had come to the conclusion that knowing *why* the Robertsons believed Tony Wesley had killed Martin might be pivotal to sorting everything out. But, how to get that information? She certainly couldn't quiz Marilyn again, or any of the Robertsons for that matter. Perhaps she'd have to ask Mr. Carscadden, after all.

As she sat trying to get her thoughts in order, her aunt said suddenly; "Who was Marilyn Robertson's dad?"

"Jack Coker; he made it to Fire Chief before he retired. That was about ten years ago, I think."

Her aunt clapped her hands. "Well, we don't need to worry about getting info on the fires. I know Jack, we both golf at Harbour Lights, and there's nothing he likes better than spouting Fire Department stories. In fact, he likes it so much he can't keep a golf partner." She had given a mock sigh. "Ah well, another sacrifice being demanded of me, I guess, in pursuit of the truth. I'll arrange a round with him next week, when I get home."

They both laughed, and then had to put their speculations aside to deal with yet another canine calamity. Moira had returned with Gussie who, on this outing, had contrived to pull them both into a burr patch; "He spotted a rabbit, Auntie Ro and I couldn't hold him back." The next hour was spent picking burrs off Moira's clothes and combing through Gussie's coat. "I swear, sometimes this dog's more trouble than he's worth," Rosie grumbled to her aunt. Margaret shrugged and nodded. "Well, he is a beagle, and I have to admit anyone of my acquaintance who's owned one has never repeated the experience."

Rosie couldn't resist grinning to herself now, recalling Gussie's hang-dog expression as she tugged the last of the burrs out of his tail. This last adventure had finally worn him out and, in contrast to yesterday afternoon, their return drive was blissfully quiet. Both occupants of the back seat were fast asleep.

Tomorrow morning, when she took Moira home, she'd ask John to make some discreet enquiries at the hospital mortuary. Then she could follow up with Lucy, and encourage her to apply for an exhumation order; there shouldn't be any trouble getting Doctor Caduggan to authorise it, thanks to Auntie Marg. And once the autopsy had proved Tony was dead before he went down the stairs, the police would have to get involved. Maybe she was getting ahead with the investigation, after all.

"Are we nearly home?" Moira's voice rose plaintively behind her.

"Only about ten more minutes, hon. You've had quite a sleep back there – what's Gussie doing?"

"Nothing. Just snoring."

"That's good – don't do anything to wake him, now." Rosie knew he'd be in full cry, once he got the scent of home. "Are you looking forward to seeing your mom and dad, and Bobbie?"

"Oh yeah, but I wish we could have stayed at Gams one more night. We could've had a fire, and roasted marshmallows and everything." A glance in the rear-view mirror confirmed what Rosie already heard in Moira's voice – her niece was indulging in a giant pout.

Both her aunt and Moira had tried to persuade her to stay over on Sunday night, but she knew only too well what the traffic would be like tomorrow on Highway 21. And there was all Moira's stuff to organise, before she went home. Elspeth would have mountains of Bobbie's laundry and camping gear to deal with, so Rosie felt obliged to return Moira's clothes in good order.

The thought of late night laundry made her irritable, and she answered with uncharacteristic tartness. "Gam told me that Uncle Steve lit the fire pit every night, so I don't think you missed much by leaving today..." She spotted her niece's expression in the mirror. "And don't be sulking at me. You're going back with Bobbie in August, so there'll be lots more opportunities to roast marshmallows." They drove the rest of the way in silence.

The sun was almost down as Rosie pulled into her driveway. Gussie had woken the instant the Buick turned off the highway, and Rosie was grateful that it was only a few blocks to home, so his excited yipping and whining was short-lived.

*   *   *   *

Back at the cottage Margaret was sitting by the window, watching the last of the sun's rays disappear into the lake. After Moira and Rosie had left, she had gone down to the dock and gazed quietly at the water for a while, hoping to slip into a trance state and gain some insights into the dangerous matter at hand.

She was very afraid for her niece; mere words couldn't convey the depth of evil she felt, whenever impressions of the killer came into her mind. This was no simple matter of revenge, and she was relieved that Rosie had come to the same conclusion and dismissed Gord Robertson as her chief suspect.

However, she did agree with Rosie that the fires and death of Martin Robertson were elements crucial to solving the crime. Once resolved, she had no doubt that the identity of the murderer would become clear.

But trance states, like ghostly visitations, cannot be summoned at will and after an hour Margaret gave up and went back inside. She was chilled from sitting by the water, and picked up a shawl from the back of the rocking chair. Draping it round her shoulders, she sat down and began to rock slowly. Far from being lonely at the end of a family cottage week, she always enjoyed the brief calm before the next group arrived.

As eldest surviving sibling, the cottage was her responsibility and would remain so for as long as she could handle it. Then it would pass to Peter, if he outlived her and stayed fit enough to take it on. And after that, to Michael (though how he'd manage from the West Coast she had no idea) and then to Rosie – Doctor William's eldest grandchild. Under the terms of his will the cottage was held in trust, for the benefit of the entire Cornish clan, with the eldest member of the direct family appointed mandatory caretaker for their lifetime. The only person to escape their turn was Sebastian – and he'd had to become a monk to do so!

Tomorrow evening, Peter would arrive for a week. He preferred to spend most of his time at the cottage alone, "recharging the batteries," as he said. He was pastor of a large and busy parish, which in its heyday had accommodated three priests. Now, except for a very elderly deacon and the occasional seminarian, he handled everything on his own, so his quiet week at the cottage was eagerly anticipated. She would come back next Saturday, and they'd have a high old time together, talking over their various family and parish problems.

Margaret felt something brush by her feet and, looking down, saw a familiar misty outline. "Well, Henry, I think I'm for bed. Lots to do tomorrow before I head home – can't leave the place untidy for your Uncle Peter now, can I?" She stood up to draw the curtains and heard the echo of a ghostly *woof*, drifting through the empty room.

Chapter 14 – Down Among the Dead Men

"More lemonade?" Elspeth picked up the frosty jug and held it in the air, questioningly.

"Thanks, El." Ice clinked refreshingly as Rosie took the jug and refilled her glass. She leant back in her chair, enjoying the welcome coolness of the damp glass in her hand. It was very hot and, far from clearing the air, the previous night's heavy rain had only increased the humidity.

Elspeth fanned herself with a section of the newspaper. "At least I won't have to drag the hose round here to water the garden." She sighed. "You should see the pile of towels and clothes Bobbie brought home. And his sleeping bag is past saving – they must have camped out in a swamp!"

Rosie chuckled. "But apart from that - you enjoyed your trip?"

"Oh Rosie, it was wonderful. Just to have some time to ourselves, without that phone ringing endlessly." Elspeth moved her chair back further under the patio umbrella – the red hair and white skin of her Scottish forebears made her a prime candidate for sunburn.

Looking at her elegant sister-in-law, Rosie reflected on the unfairness of genetics. Moira had inherited her mother's colouring, but had missed out on Elspeth's tall, willowy figure; that, of course, had gone to Bobbie. And Moira? Well, her red hair and green eyes may have been Scottish, but her body type was Norfolk fens through and through. Seen from behind Rosie, John and Moira were as alike as peas in a pod; short and sturdy, with the Cornish family's four-square build. An adolescent girl's worst nightmare!

"......three floors of shoes!"

"Sorry El, what was that?"

"Macy's! I couldn't believe it had three floors of shoes. I bought this stunning pair of evening shoes for the Conference banquet – really bad of me, because I'll probably never wear them again, but they were so *perfect* with my gown......."

Rosie's concentration drifted. Yes, I'd probably enjoy clothes shopping too, if I had a figure like yours, she thought spitefully. Then she administered a mental slap – her sister-in-law was a wonderful person, it wasn't her fault she was gorgeous – and answered; "Yes, I always loved wandering around Macy's, too. 'Course, I was a starving music student at the time, so I never bought much, but it was fun, all the same." She felt her heart lurch unexpectedly at the memory. Her future had seemed so bright back then; the road to fame and fortune stretching smoothly ahead, neatly signposted by academic success.

Their conversation was interrupted by the sound of car doors slamming on the driveway. "Mom, Auntie Ro, we're back," Moira's shout echoed through the hall and, almost immediately, she appeared at the patio door, followed closely by her father and brother.

"Moira, there's no need to be shouting at the top of your lungs." John spoke sternly but his admonition was tempered with a smile. Like everyone else, he found it hard to be cross with his ebullient daughter.

"Sorry, Dad." The response was automatic and, unconcerned, Moira bounced around the patio table to give Elspeth a kiss.

"Did you have a good lunch?" her mother asked.

This time it was Bobbie's turn to sound enthusiastic. "Yes, we went to Burger...."

Elspeth put her hand up. "No, don't tell me. I'd rather not know. Although I'm sure fruit and vegetables didn't figure much in the meal."

Moira looked at her mother innocently. "French fries and onion rings are vegetables."

Bobbie chimed in; "And there were strawberries in the milkshakes."

"And I had my burger on a whole-grain bun….."

John laughed. "Alright you two, that's enough. Stop teasing your mother - you know how she feels about healthy eating."

As she listened to their good-natured banter, Rosie appreciated how tired her sister-in-law must have been, to raise so little protest when John suggested taking the kids out to eat. She and Elspeth had shared a light (*very* light) lunch of mixed salad greens with a dusting of low cal. mozzarella, and now Rosie's mouth was watering at the thought of french fries and onion rings.

The two kids soon drifted away; Bobbie to his piano, to catch up on two weeks missed practice, and Moira to call Chelsea, and crow about the clothes her mother had bought for her in New York.

Rosie finished the last of her lemonade and stood up reluctantly. "Well, I should be getting home – let you make a start on all that laundry."

Her sister-in-law smiled across the table. "Hey, it's a holiday. The laundry can wait until tomorrow. But are you sure you won't stay for supper? I won't be cooking – it's too hot and they've all eaten that huge lunch – but there's loads of salad and I could boil you a couple of eggs. I think there's tofu in the fridge, as well…"

Any lingering thoughts of staying for the evening evaporated. Rosie was in serious need of something far more substantial than salad and a boiled egg. And as for tofu – well, given the choice, she'd rather eat the packaging it came in, than those slimy white cubes. Ugh! The very thought made her shudder!

"No, I should get out in the yard and pull weeds, while the ground's good and soft. But I did want a quick word with John before I go. Did he go into the study?"

Elspeth cocked her head to one side, and listened. "No, he's washing the car, I can hear the hose running."

Getting up, she came round the table to give Rosie a quick hug. "Thanks again for keeping Moira. She always loves coming over to your place – and visiting Gussie takes some of the pressure off her endless pleas for a dog."

"My pleasure, El, you know that. She's a real breath of fresh air in the house; makes me realise how *spinsterish* I'm getting, living all alone."

Her sister-in-law gave a look of mock-horror. "Rosie, don't say that! You couldn't be spinsterish, if you tried."

"I hope you're right. And, on the bright side, I think Gussie's finally lost some weight, thanks to Moira. When we have our next weigh-in, I'll be able to look Dr. Katz in the eye at last." She picked up her purse and rummaged through it for sunglasses. "I'll call you later in the week, El. Don't work too hard."

Elspeth was already crossing the patio toward the swing seat. She waved a languid hand. "You too. Speak soon."

Rosie crossed the spacious hall, opened the front door, then paused to savour the strains of Debussy's sad melody, *Des pas sur la neige*. Such a difficult piece and Bobbie was playing it almost faultlessly. Lord, he was talented!

She spotted her brother at the far end of the driveway, hose in hand.

"You heading home?" he called.

"Yes, but have you got a minute? I want to ask you something."

John turned off the hose and strolled down the driveway toward her. "Before you get started, Rose. No, I haven't spoken to Elspeth about Moira's experience, and I don't intend to. I'm not going to discuss it with Moira either. If it happens again, then I'll re-visit my decision, but until such time I prefer to let sleeping dogs lie." He gave her a challenging look. "I know you don't agree with me, but I'm her father and it's my decision to make."

It was on the tip of Rosie's tongue to ask what century her brother thought he was living in, with his paternalistic approach to family decision-making. But with an effort, she bit back the sarcastic retort. Right now, she needed John's co-operation, not his antagonism. So, taking a deep breath, she tried to look suitably chastened.

"Well, I guess you know best." Cringing inwardly at the apparent capitulation she thought savagely – *yes, let's all break out our twin sets and pearls, father knows best.* She glanced at her brother and gave him a sweet smile. Expecting a verbal tussle with his sister, John was taken off guard and smiled back. Good, she thought - advantage, Rosie. What was it mom always said? *You can catch more flies with honey than vinegar.* She took a step closer and put her arm through his. Walking down the driveway beside him she said; "But as I'm here, maybe you could help me with another little problem. I need to find out why there was no autopsy on Tony Wesley."

*   *   *   *

It was several days before John could follow-up on Rosie's request. Office hours were double-booked, as the staff tried to clear the back-log created by his two-week absence. So it was Thursday before he finally got out of the office, and drove the short distance to Memorial Hospital to visit one of his patients.

Everything was on schedule. Marianne Holder was in some discomfort, but was looking forward to the promised relief of her laparoscopic cholecystectomy. After discussing the procedure, John gave her a last reassuring smile and headed for the elevator. As he descended, he recalled the misogynistic description of a typical gall-bladder sufferer that he'd memorised in medical school; fair, fat and forty. Marianne was certainly textbook - interesting how often those old-style formulas held true.

The elevator doors opened and he stepped out into a gloomy passage-way. Despite Admins. determination to improve the basement (this year's paint job was bright yellow, with cheery prints hung along the walls) nothing could dent its dreary institutionalism. The basement was, in every sense, a dead space. He hoped Rosie never had occasion to come down here. Despite his professional attitude of scientific scepticism, it was easy to imagine a whole slew of unhappy spirits wandering these shadowy corridors, just waiting to encounter a receptive psyche.

Several departments were housed in the basement, but there was rarely anyone about. Uncomfortably aware of his solitary footsteps, John was relieved to see the path. lab. lights ahead, their brightness a stark contrast to the adjacent mortuary's black rubber doors. These were unmarked, on the premise that anyone who had business in the morgue knew where it was, and everyone else should stay well clear.

The lab's reeded glass door swung open smoothly. Two white-coated techs were seated at a central counter, both peering into microscopes. John spoke more heartily than he intended. "Hi Ahmed, Connie. Is he in?"

Without looking up, Connie Black gestured in the direction of a rear office. "Hi Doc. Yup, go on back. Just follow your nose – he's got a new machine."

John laughed. "Nothing like a strong brew to cover the smell of formaldehyde, I guess." This witticism was received in silence and, feeling mildly embarrassed, he hurried toward the office at the back of the lab. A large, printed sign instructed visitors to *Knock and Enter,* and he obliged.

Dr. Andrew McGillivray looked up from a dog-eared copy of "Pathology Today" and greeted his visitor with a gruff "What's up, doc?" His bewhiskered face was almost hidden behind the stacks of reports, periodicals and files which mounded untidily across the front of his desk.

"How're you doing, Andy?" John dumped a battered box file off the seat of the only other chair in the office and sat down. "Still working on your filing, I see."

The pathologist grunted. "Easy for you to say. You have the estimable Ms. DeGroot and her dedicated helpers to keep your paperwork in order. How is everything at the practice, anyway?"

"Busy. We're thinking about another partner – the work's getting too much for just two of us."

"Well, good luck with that. Haven't you heard? There's a shortage of family docs." He looked at his watch. "Good timing. Just gonna make a brew." Without waiting for a reply, he got up and headed for the only uncluttered surface in the room - an old fashioned walnut credenza pushed hard against the back wall. In pride of place squatted an enormous espresso machine, its black and chrome bulk emitting puffs of steam and hisses worthy of a Faustian imp.

McGillivray measured beans into the hopper, pressed a button and stepped back as sounds reminiscent of a wood chipper filled the room. "The key to great coffee is grinding fresh beans every time" he shouted. John nodded dumbly and curbed his impatience. He knew from past experience that he'd get nothing from his colleague until the ritual was complete.

The pathologist picked up a chipped mug and wiped it out with piece of paper towel. He waved toward the black monster. "What do you think, then? It's a Grande Maestro – just got it. Amazing machine." He tamped beans and jiggled the container into the machine, positioned his mug carefully, then watched in reverential silence as a double stream of black liquid gurgled into it. "You haven't tasted coffee until you've tasted this. Here, try it." He held the mug out to John.

"Thanks all the same, but I'll pass." Andy McGillivrays's coffee was notoriously strong – on the one occasion John had accepted a cup, he'd driven through a red light on the way home and finished his evening office hours in record time.

"Suit yourself." The pathologist poured milk into a metal jug and more hissing ensued as the steamer did its work. He sipped slowly then pronounced; "Nectar of life, John, nectar of life." Sitting down again, he leant back and regarded his visitor benignly. "So, if you don't want a coffee, what brings you down to the depths this fine afternoon?"

John leant back in his chair. "Just tying up a few loose ends, Andy. Broken neck, about three weeks ago, name of Wesley." He made a quick calculation. "It would have been Friday, June sixteenth. Ambulance call, probably around eleven at night."

McGillivray was already tapping on his computer keyboard. "One of yours, was he?"

"No, don't think he was on anyone's list. Rosie knows the widow and she's got a few concerns."

"Okay, let's see what we can find." He scrolled down lists of names. "Mmm, can't see him – no wait, here he is." A chart opened up on the screen. "Contusions, mild concussion, broken ankle….how old did you say he was?"

"Dunno, about fifty-five, I think."

"Well, this can't be right. Says here age is seventy-nine." He continued scrolling. "Sorry, John. Wrong day, wrong Wesley – this is Clodagh's chart." He grimaced. "She was only on three main for two days, and we almost had a mutiny." Closing the screen he re-opened the admissions list.

John smiled ruefully. "Par for the course, I guess. What happened to the old girl?"

"Oh, that's right; you were at the AMA and missed all the excitement. Traffic accident. Ran the lights at King and the bakery van hit her." After several more minutes of peering at the computer screen he looked up; "That's it. All that's under Wesley is the queen bee. Are you sure he was brought in here?"

"Positive. And Mason's picked him up from here."

"Well, I can't find him anywhere in the system." McGillivray grabbed a stack of file folders and passed half across the desk to John. "Take a look. Nothing like doing things the old-fashioned way."

The room was quiet for a few minutes as they both skimmed through folders. Then; "Here he is." McGillivray riffled quickly through the contents of a green mortuary file. "*Anthony Michael Wesley. D.O.B 22/5/44. Emergency admission, 22:55, June 16, 2000. Expired 23:15, June 16, 2000.*" He passed a page across the desk and pointed to the signature beside *Attending Physician.* "Christ! This explains why there's nothing in the data base."

To the untutored eye, the scrawl was indecipherable, but John recognized the name instantly. *Aubrey Niven, M.D.* "Shit! Medical advisory has got to do something about Aubrey – he can't go on ignoring procedure like this, I don't care who he is." Dr. Niven was a perpetual source of exasperated annoyance to John and most of the medical staff.

McGillivray nodded. "I agree. But that's easier said than done. He knows everyone on the Board, doctored most of them at one time or another – hell, he probably delivered half of 'em." He drained his coffee mug. "Not easy to fire the hospital's *pater familias*. And he's a handy fill-in when we're short in emerg."

John's expression darkened. "I know all that. But he's almost deaf, refuses to wear a hearing aid and won't learn the computer system. As a result, he can't access or update patient files. There's going to be a major screw-up one of these days, Andy. It's just not good enough."

"Save it, John." The pathologist spoke abruptly, his attention focused on a yellow post-it note stuck inside the file folder's cover. "You and I both know the *dear boy* (he said the words in an exaggerated English accent) is a fixture until he either decides to retire or drops dead." He peeled off the note and fingered it absently.

"What's that?"

"A note I wrote myself." He passed the scrap of paper across the desk.

John read: *Origin neck hematoma? Accident site photos? Call family re: autopsy?*

McGillivray watched him reading, finally saying quietly;"I remember the guy now." He glanced longingly at the espresso machine, but didn't succumb. "I got called in Saturday morning. There'd been a bad accident on the highway in the early hours, and we were expecting at least two to come down from emerg. While I was waiting, I had a quick look at the overnight intake." He leant forward and began shuffling through the papers in Tony Wesley's file. "According to the E.M guys, Wesley was still breathing when they picked him up, but he either died in the ambulance or in emerg. Aubrey took one look and pronounced him."

"So what's bothering you? Technically, the guy died under the hospital's care, so there's no problem with Aubrey signing him off."

"I know. But something didn't gel. I found a straight line hematoma across the back of his neck, around C3. I couldn't see how that happened if he pitched head first down a flight of stairs."

"Maybe he hit a post or something on the way down?"

McGillivray shrugged. "Anything's possible but, without photos, or a look at the scene, I can't say for sure."

"Do the police have photos?"

"No idea. I wrote myself that note, meaning to follow-up later in the day. But all hell broke loose down here – we ended up with four from the pile-up and I forgot all about Tony Wesley. Until today." He looked despondent. "Might have dropped the ball on this one, John."

"Only in your own mind." John tried to sound up beat. "He'd been certified accidental – not your call."

"Yeah, but look who certified him." The pathologist shook his head. "What's the widow asking about, anyway?"

John didn't want to be the bearer of bad news, but he had no option. "She wants to know why there wasn't an autopsy."

McGillivray's face was a thundercloud. Without speaking, he got up and went back to the espresso machine and turned on the grinder. "Why the hell didn't she say something at the time?" he shouted over the racket.

John understood his friend's reaction. There was nothing worse than failing to meet personal standards of care, and both men held themselves to very high standards indeed.

"She was in shock - barely knew what was going on until after the funeral. Now she's worried he'll be remembered as a drunk. There was a bottle found at the scene."

Neither spoke while McGillivray brought his coffee back to the desk, opened a drawer and pulled out a wrinkled paper bag. "Have a cookie" he said, pushing the bag toward John. "Meet Ferguson's new, healthy alternative."

John took one and bit into it. A shower of crumbs scattered onto the desk and, without thinking, he swept them into his hand and dropped them into the overflowing waste paper basket. Fourteen years with Elspeth had taught him a thing or two. "Not bad" he said, coughing as a crumb caught in his throat. "Bit on the dry side, though."

"Yes. Well, you can't get the right results without the right ingredients" came the answer, and they both knew the pathologist wasn't talking about cookies.

"Look Andy, if you're really not happy about this Wesley business, why not get in touch with the widow? She'd probably be glad to request exhumation and autopsy – a chance to set her mind at rest."

McGillivray chewed thoughtfully for a second. "That's not a bad idea. But I'd rather see the police photos first – could resolve a few issues and save the family some grief." He brightened. "You say Rosie knows her? How is she, by the way? Still on her own?"

John grinned. "One of these days you're going to get up your nerve and ask my sister out. That torch must be getting pretty heavy by now."

"Give it a rest, for God's sake." He cleared his throat. "I simply thought if Rosie knows the widow, she could ask if the police took photos at the scene. Less upsetting than coming from me."

John was still smiling. "To answer your questions, Rosie's very well, and yes, she is still on her own." His friend's face was bright red now - time to put him out of his misery. "I'll give her a call later; ask her to find out what she can from Wesley's widow." A thought struck him. "Wonder if it's worth having a word with Aubrey? You never know, he might have noticed something."

"Did you see many airborne pigs, when you came in today?" McGillivray growled. He swallowed the last of his cookie, then swept the crumbs off his desk and onto the floor, definitive proof that there was no woman in his life. "If you're determined to waste your time, you'll find him in the Chairman's Lounge. Today's the first Thursday, so there's a Board meeting this afternoon. Our esteemed Dr. Niven always shows up to mingle with the great and the good, before they begin their deliberations."

John stood up. "Well, I'll give it a shot; the police could have come into emerg. For all we know, Aubrey may have spoken to them."

"Don't hold your breath." The pathologist gave a little cough and began shuffling through the pages in Tony Wesley's file. "Umm –mm....."

"Something else, Andy?" John tried not to smile at his friend's discomfiture. Whatever was coming must be about Rosie.

"Yes, well, I was wondering how things stand – you know, about Rosie's husband?"

"No change there. Unofficially, he's dead. Not a trace of him for seven years...," John paused, as a sudden realisation hit him, "...almost to the day, as it happens." Tomorrow would be the seventh anniversary of David Rowe's mysterious disappearance while out boating. Seven years of Rosie waiting for news that never came. Maybe now she'd accept his death and get on with her life.

"Well, that's good news... no, I mean, that's not *good news* exactly, but..."

"I know what you mean, Andy. We all wish Rosie would put the past behind her, and make a fresh start." He glanced at McGillivray, busily rearranging pens in his desk tray. "I think she's tired of being on her own."

The pathologist didn't look up, but said; "Do you think I should give her a call?"

"She can only say no. Go for it, Andy – you might be surprised." He waited for an answer, but when McGillivray didn't speak he went to the door and opened it, saying briskly; "Enough of the lonely hearts club, I've got to go. I'll let you know what we get from Wesley's widow and Aubrey too, if he's got anything useful to say."

The pathologist looked up, all business now. "Thanks, John. I'd like to get this one tidied away, for sure."

John pulled the door closed, only to see it re-open immediately as McGillivray lumbered through. "I'll walk up with you – just remembered I need to see Mike Walters before the meeting."

For one brief shining moment, John thought his friend had decided to report the latest Niven debacle to the Chief of Staff. But McGillivray started droning on about insufficient parking for the medical staff - his favourite hobby-horse.

"…….. absolutely no space. Last time we spoke, Walters assured me that the Board had a plan in place to resolve the issue. *Just keep it to yourself until the official announcement* he said, and that was back in February…."

Just keep it to yourself. The phrase jogged John's memory. "Sorry Andy, that reminds me. Rosie said Tony Wesley's family want their concerns about the autopsy kept quiet until everything's resolved."

"No problem there. I'm never keen to have my shortcomings open to public scrutiny." He opened the lab. door, and the two headed toward the elevator that would carry them upward, into more exalted circles.

Chapter 15 – Puzzle Pieces

"John, dear boy. How good to see you - take a seat, take a seat." Dr. Aubrey Niven waved expansively toward a Sheraton style chair, placed opposite the leather wing back in which he was comfortably ensconced. "I haven't seen you in an age. Are you presenting to the Board this afternoon?"

John sat down carefully, balancing the cup of tea pressed on him by a Ladies Hospital Auxiliary volunteer (*Darjeeling, English Breakfast or Earl Grey, Dr. Cornish?*). He'd only narrowly escaped the plate of petit fours and lady fingers she'd waved under his nose – as usual, the Chairman's Lounge on Board meeting day had the curious ambience of a Gentleman's Club hosting a Victorian tea party.

"Hi Aubrey. Good to see you looking so well." He cast around vainly for somewhere safe to place the delicate cup and saucer, and finally put them down on the floor by his feet. "No, I was in the path. lab. with Andy when he remembered he wanted a word with Mike before the meeting. Still trying to get some answers on the parking issue, I think." And he glanced over to the far side of the room, where McGillivray had his quarry trapped in a corner.

"Ah yes, the parking. I agree, it just gets worse and worse," Dr. Niven nodded sagely. "Memorial has grown so rapidly and, of course, staff parking was never properly addressed in the first place." He refilled his glass from a decanter placed strategically on the small wine table beside him. "Would you care for a scotch, dear boy? They always lay on excellent single malt for Board meetings."

"No thanks, Aubrey. I've got evening office hours, today." The silence lengthened between them, as Aubrey applied himself to his scotch and John sipped tea, all the while racking his brains for a discreet segue into the Wesley death. Finally, his elderly colleague saved him the trouble.

"I gave up evening hours last year. Too many requests to fill in at emerg, don't you know. Found I couldn't handle both." Niven drained his glass and reached again for the decanter, catching John's look of disapproval as he did so. "Don't worry; I shan't be driving myself home. No, my ride is all arranged," and he raised his glass in mock salute toward the Ladies Auxiliary volunteer. She blushed, and gave a little wave in reply.

John was hard pressed not to smile. Aubrey's ability to charm the fairer sex was undiminished by his advancing years, and there were still some lonely widows in town hoping to snare the debonair bachelor.

Whether it was the scotch, or merely the proximity of a willing listener, Dr. Niven was soon chatting volubly. "Yes, I decided a while back to let the practice wind down - not take on any new patients. Of course, I still see my regulars, but their numbers are dwindling fast. We're all getting older – some of my list have been with me since I came to town. Can you believe, that's forty-five years ago now!" He brightened. "I know I complain about emerg. but, surprisingly, I find it quite energising. Bit more challenging than the endless round of arthritis, bunions and diabetes, if you know what I mean." He reached for the decanter and topped up his half empty glass. "In fact, I've been thinking of taking a regular shift – move some of the load from you chaps in the busier practices."

There's a bit of bad news for Medical Advisory, thought John. He smiled weakly and said; "Very generous of you, Aubrey. Matter of fact, I think you filled in for me a few weeks back. Mid-June – I'd registered for the A.M.A Conference and had to switch my shift." Across the top of his glass, Dr. Niven looked vague. John hurried on, trying to sound disinterested; "Andy mentioned I'd missed a rough night; nasty smash-up on the highway, and there was a local death as well…"

With studied care, Aubrey set the decanter back on the wine table. Then, steepling his perfectly manicured fingers beneath his chin, he replied; "Yes, I remember now. That was a bad night, right enough." His words were becoming slightly slurred. "First thing, E.M.S brought in a broken neck; gave me quite a shock when I saw the name, I can tell you. Fellow got drunk as a lord and fell down his back stairs – probably never knew what hit him. Bad business." His gaze dropped, and he seemed to lose himself in his own thoughts.

You don't know how right you are, John agreed mentally. "Oh, was he one of yours, then?"

Dr. Niven didn't answer, just went on speaking in a slightly aggrieved tone. "I missed the r.t.a., though. Already home before it happened. Surprised they didn't beep me, actually. Thing like that, it's usually all hands to the pump."

"Well, the day staff were probably on by then, and Andy said several victims were d.o.a." John knew why Dr. Niven's beeper had stayed silent. In a crisis, the last thing E.R. staff needed underfoot was a senior physician with impaired hearing and a very limited grasp of technology. Raising his voice slightly, he asked again. "The broken neck. Was he one of yours?"

"No – well, not for years. But his mother's a patient, Clodagh Wesley. It was her boy, Tony." Niven smiled smugly. "The whole family signed on just after I hung out the old shingle. Quite a coup - leading family, new doc in town and all that. Huge boost to the practice, don't you know." He paused, then drank deeply. "I delivered Carmel; saw young Tony through rheumatic fever, measles, all kinds of broken bones. That boy was unbelievably accident prone." He leant back in his chair, yawned and closed his eyes.

Oh God, don't go to sleep now, John thought seeing his chance for information slipping away. He got up and went across to the wine table, deliberately bumping Niven's leg as he passed. "Think I'll join you in that drink, after all," he said heartily and, picking up a crystal tumbler, poured in a small measure of whisky. "You were saying, Aubrey? About Tony Wesley? Expect it took quite a while to get finished with the police."

Dr. Niven pulled himself up in the chair and looked blearily at John. "Police – no. There were no police, just his mother-in-law, and the wife carrying on alarmingly in the waiting-room. And Mr. Anderson, of course."

"Peter Anderson?"

"Yes, Mrs. Wesley's lawyer."

John made his way back to his chair. "Sorry, I don't see the connection."

Niven reached for his drink, swallowed a mouthful then spoke with the concentrated effort of someone trying to sound sober. "E.M. boys had been keeping him going in the ambulance, but there were no vitals by the time he got to me. Once I knew who he was, I asked one of the staff to call his mother." He waved a dismissive hand, "Not a clue who she was, by the way. Could've been anyone, nurse, cook, cleaner - they all wear the same wrinkly outfits these days. Scrubbs, they call 'em. More like scruffs, if you ask me." He chortled and leant back in his chair again.

Reflecting on the truism that alcohol frees the tongue but locks the brain, John took a deep breath and prompted: "So someone called Clodagh Wesley, and Pete Anderson came?"

Niven looked at him indignantly. "Well, she could hardly come, could she?"

Trying to curb his irritation, John tried again. "She was out of town?"

"No – where'd you get that idea?" Niven had raised his voice and several people turned to look in their direction. "It was past eleven and Mrs. Wesley suffers from night blindness. She never drives after dark. So she sent Anderson down with instructions, simple as that." He slumped back in his seat again.

With instructions. The phrase was so in keeping with Clodagh Wesley's reputation that, for a moment, it didn't strike John as odd. Then reality took hold. Here was a woman receiving a call to say her only son was on the brink of death, and her reaction was to send her lawyer to the hospital *with instructions.* John was amazed. Night blindness or not, no mother he'd ever met would have let anything, short of her own deathbed, keep her from her child *in extremis.* He struggled to summon a polite response.

Sensing John's disapproval, Aubrey began trotting out platitudes. "No doubt realised it was pointless to come rushing down – didn't want to see him like that – much better to remember him the way he was." He cleared his throat nervously; "It was pointless for her to be here, anyway. There were no vitals at all – brain dead for sure. EMS weren't entirely convinced he was breathing when they picked him up, but the wife insisted." He looked away.

Despite evening office hours, John downed his whisky in one. He was sorely tempted to remark that it was impossible for Clodagh to remember her son "the way he was" because she hadn't seen him in thirty-six years, but swallowed the words and tried to look sympathetic. If he wanted to get a clear picture of what happened in the E.R that night, he needed to keep Aubrey Niven on side. Gritting his teeth, he muttered; "Yes, probably better all round. But why send Pete Anderson along?"

Aubrey leant forward and spoke in hushed tones. "Wanted to make sure he wasn't autopsied. Just the same when her husband died – couldn't bear the thought of him being cut about. Finds it all very distressing."

John couldn't restrain himself any longer. "Where the hell did she get off, making that kind of decision?" he said loudly. Heads turned again, but he went on regardless. "It was up to Wesley's wife to make that call."

"I know, I know, but there it is. And I've always found it more helpful in the long run to be accepting of my patients' more..." he cast about for a diplomatic description, " *eccentric* views." Chuckling, he drained his glass. "I remember one dear lady who brought her cat into the office for treatment of an abscess. Insisted that Mackintosh was the reincarnation of her late husband, and as such, couldn't be doctored by a mere vet."

Although he already knew the answer, John asked; "So what were the family's views on autopsy?"

"I didn't ask, dear boy. I'm sure they were in agreement with Mrs. Wesley; she was his mother after all. And frankly, I couldn't get any sense out of the wife once she knew he was dead." He waved, acknowledging several Board members filing past into the meeting room.

"You don't think..." John began, but Aubrey cut him off.

"I don't know why this of such interest to you, John. There was absolutely no need to investigate further – accident, pure and simple. Body positively reeked of alcohol. All very sad of course, but poor chap had a long history of drinking and getting in trouble. I should know. Doctored him all through high school. Even got an underage girl pregnant, if I recall."

They were interrupted by the L.H.A volunteer, come to pick up John's china and their glasses. As she added the decanter to her tray, she blushed and said hesitantly; "The board meeting is starting now, doctors, so we'll be closing the lounge shortly."

Dr. Niven beamed at her; "I'm ready anytime you are, Rosemary, my sweet."

Blushing ever more deeply, she replied: "Then I'll meet you at the front entrance in ten minutes, Dr. Niven," and bustled away.

Watching this little exchange, John recalled the afternoon he'd sat as a small boy, listening to his mother's bridge group breathlessly sharing the tale of Dr. Niven's arrival in Little Yarmouth. The doctor's finely tailored suits and cut-glass accent had caused quite a stir in their rural backwater, and many a longing glance had been cast his way.

Alas, he'd spoken often of an adored fiancée back in London, busily organising her trousseau. But weeks had turned to months, and the elusive Daphne had never materialised. It was whispered about town that she was reluctant to leave England for the wilds of Huron County, and there was much unspoken sympathy for the jilted doctor.

As the years passed, and many hopeful candidates for the position of Doctor's Wife were kept charmingly at arm's length, the accepted wisdom became that poor Dr. Niven's heart had been so shattered that he could never love again.

John had long ago come to the conclusion that the elegant Aubrey's romantic inclinations lay in an entirely different direction, and the ladies of Little Yarmouth had been doomed to disappointment from the start. Now, glancing across the room at Rosemary, dreamily folding tablecloths with a little smile on her lips, he hoped her expectations didn't extend beyond a peck on the cheek and a courtly wave goodbye.

Dr. Niven rose unsteadily; "Well, we've got our marching orders, dear chap. All good things must come to an end."

John stood up in turn. "Yes, I'd better be on my way. I promised Elspeth I'd get home for an early supper, before office hours."

"Ah yes, the ladies do like to keep us on a short leash, don't they?" Aubrey reached for John's hand and shook it warmly. "So enjoyed our chat, dear boy. Must do it again soon," and, swaying slightly, he started toward the door leading to the elevator bank. John made for the stairs, then changed his mind and joined his inebriated colleague as the elevator doors opened. It might be a kindness to see Dr. Niven safely out of the hospital.

*   *   *   *

Rosie unplugged her vacuum cleaner, re-wound the cord and wheeled it into the hall closet. She looked up to the first landing where Gussie sat, poised for flight.

"It's alright – I'm not coming up there with it. The monster's back in its den." The beagle twitched his ears, but didn't move. "Come on, Gus – don't be silly. I promise the vacuum won't eat you." Still no movement; just two reproachful eyes gazing down at her.

She sighed in frustration; Gus really was a master at piling on the guilts. It was her own fault, she should have known better than to get the vacuum out. Not after all the drama of their trip to the vet this morning. For heaven's sake, Dr. Katz only wanted to weigh him; the way Gussie carried on you'd think he was in for an amputation, at least!

She lost patience. "Alright, please yourself. But I'm going into the kitchen and I'll be opening the fridge…," the rest of her bribe was lost to the phone's insistent ring.

Rosie ran into the front parlour and grabbed the phone off the piano. She had taken Sister Mary's admonition to heart and gone back to her daily vocal practices, but today these had been cut short by the veterinary expedition. "Hello?" she gasped out. The niggling thought that it wasn't just her vocal chords needing exercise was resolutely pushed away.

"Rosie, are you alright?" Her aunt's voice was full of concern.

"Yes, fine thanks, Auntie Marg. Just ran for the phone, that's all." She plunked herself down on the piano stool. "And I've just finished vacuuming all through so, between that, and the dog having a nervous breakdown, I'm done in."

Her aunt laughed. "Weigh-in day, was it?"

"Yes. But the good news is he's lost a pound this month, so Dr. Katz was really pleased. All thanks to Moira, of course. Maybe I could get her to live here permanently, until I've got Gussie down to twenty five pounds."

More laughter from the other end of the line. Then; "I'm just checking in to see how the investigation's going."

"No progress at all, I'm afraid."

"Did you speak to John?"

"Yes, I saw him on Monday and he said he'd help. But I haven't heard anything since."

"Well, he's probably playing catch-up at the practice." Margaret sneezed twice in quick succession. "Hang on, Rose, I need more tissues; my allergies are hell today."

A moment later, she picked up the phone again. "There, that's better. Its ragweed everywhere on the golf course this year; that new groundskeeper's not a patch on Vic Watson. If you ask me, a weed free fairway is well worth the occasional homicidal melt-down."

Rosie felt a stab of excitement. "You played golf with Jack Coker!"

"I certainly did. We only made it to the ninth (pled my advancing years and heat exhaustion), but he was a mine of information, both useful and otherwise." She sneezed again.

"Well, don't keep me in suspense, Auntie Marg. What did he say?"

"First off, it's no wonder he golfs alone; talk about a one track mind. His only topic of conversation is the fire department. Response times, equipment, training, discipline; according to him, it's all gone to hell in a hand cart since he retired. I got the complete history of his forty years at the fire hall, and a more Machiavellian den of intrigue you couldn't imagine. Do you know, when he was up for Chief...?"

Rosie could stand it no longer. "Auntie Marg! The fire bug?"

"Oh, right. Well, it was still a volunteer outfit when he joined in 1949. He wasn't called out much in his first few years; just grass fires, bonfires, people burning trash, that sort of thing. But the Alastair Street school fire was different. He remembers it particularly, because it was his first *real* fire."

"Why did he think it was arson?"

"Apparently, it was obvious to everyone. Gasoline soaked rags had been piled in an office supply cupboard and set alight. All that paper, solvent and stuff went up like a roman candle. Could have levelled the building if the janitor hadn't come back unexpectedly and seen the smoke."

Rosie gave a little shudder. "Looked like an inside job, then?"

"Oh, no question. Someone had to know the janitor's schedule to be sure there'd be no-one in the building to raise the alarm. Definitely a staff member or student. Most of the damage was confined to the Principal and secretary's offices, so the general consensus was a disgruntled student, or ex-student."

"But it was an elementary school. The oldest kids there couldn't have been more than eleven. I'd think someone would notice an eleven year old carrying a gas can into school, wouldn't you?"

Margaret didn't answer immediately. An image had flashed across her consciousness of a boy, crouching in semi-darkness, dropping rags into a bucket. She struggled to sharpen her focus. Something circular – black – a shiny disc – wheels! She could see wheels. He was in a garage.

"Auntie Marg? Are you still there?"

"Yes. Just need a minute or two – hang on." She closed her eyes and took a few deep breaths. "Sorry, things got a bit hazy there for a while." Rosie understood, and waited. After a short pause, her aunt went on; "Looks like he didn't need to take the gas can to school; he soaked the rags in gas in a garage somewhere. Probably at his own house." She felt suddenly nauseous. "He's full of rage, Rosie. He's just a child, but so full of hate."

Unaccountably, Rosie felt a lump rise in her throat. There was something heart-breaking in the image of an angry, vicious child soaking rags in a bucket of gas. For a brief moment neither of them spoke, then Rosie cleared her throat and asked; "What did Jack say about the other fires?"

"All set exactly the same way. St. Judes, the high school, the hospital; all started with gas soaked rags in some type of storage closet. The only exception was the hospital, where there was an explosion as well. That's because the fire burned really fast and reached the area where medical gas cylinders were stored."

"And there was no investigation into any of this?"

"Oh yes, police reports were filed, but nothing ever came of them. Jack said all the firefighters knew they had an arsonist in town but, as long as it was just property damage, the police didn't seem to care. Not even when old St. Judes burned to the ground." Margaret's voice cracked. "Not until the hospital fire."

Rosie knew what she was thinking. If the police had put more effort into finding the fire-bug early on, then their family tragedy might have been averted. "I guess they paid attention after that" she said, surprised at the bitterness in her voice.

"Yes, that police investigation was very thorough, but still came up empty. The fire department even called in an arson expert; by then it was a municipal service, so they had access to more technical resources."

"When you saw the boy just now, did you get any sense of who he was?"

"No, nothing. He was crouching down. I couldn't tell if he was fat, thin, short or tall. Just a sense that he was very, very disturbed."

"Could it have been Tony Wesley?"

"Well, it could have been, I suppose. But as we said before, why would he go clear across town, and how would he know what hours the janitor worked? No, I think it was a kid from the school, someone who lived close by. And there's another reason to think that, too. Jack said the following year there were two other fires at that end of town. Knox Presbyterian, also on Alastair Street and the Boy Scout hall, a block south on Burns. Very little damage in both cases, but the same gas soaked rags were used."

"And the police couldn't figure out who was doing it? That's unbelievable! It had to be someone with a connection to all those places; how many people could that be, for crying out loud!"

"Well, in their defence, the 1955 fires were never reported. Neither the minister nor the scout leader wanted to file official complaints."

"And that begs the question of why. They probably knew who it was."

"Whoa, slow down Rosie. I think you're jumping to conclusions here."

"No, I don't think so. I'd bet anything our little arsonist belonged to the Boy Scouts and went to Knox with his parents every week, all gussied up in his Sunday best."

Margaret was starting to feel very tired. All joking aside, it had been hot as Hades on the golf course, and she'd been glad to finish at the ninth. And that unexpected psychic jolt had drained her even more. Trying to keep the exhaustion from her voice she replied; "You could be right, I suppose. But I think I'm about ready to take a break from our nasty little friend. It's been a long day, and I could really do with a nice cup of tea."

Rosie was instantly contrite. "I'm sorry, Auntie. You know what I'm like when I get the bit between my teeth; I just go on and on. Almost as bad as Jack Coker." She was relieved to hear her aunt chuckle.

"No, not quite that bad, Rosie." She sneezed again. "Damn allergies! Now, be sure and let me know what John digs up at the hospital, and if the Wesley family need an exhumation order I'll snag old Caduggun next bridge night."

"Thanks Aunt Marg. Don't know what I'd do without you."

"Nor I, you, my dear. Bye for now. God bless."

"Bye, Auntie Marg."

Rosie made her way into the kitchen, glancing up the stairs as she passed. No sign of Gussie. That meant he was either on her bed, or under it, depending on how ill-used he felt.

She made herself a vegetarian ham sandwich, set it with a strawberry yogurt and glass of mineral water on a tray and carried everything through into the living room. Her mind was whirling with the details of those long-ago fires but, try as she might, she couldn't pull everything together.

The more information she got, the more questions she had. Now she knew the fire-bug's history, but where did Martin Robertson fit in? It was only Marilyn's comment that linked Tony to the high school fire and Martin's death. Suppose the Robertson's were wrong, and there was no connection. No, Tony had gone to great lengths to highlight the gymnasium fire and the tragedy on the CPR track, so both must be important.

She heard the click-click of claws crossing the floor, and then Gussie was up on the couch beside her. Breaking off a piece of her sandwich, she held it out to him. He wolfed it down and licked her hand. "I guess we're friends again, eh boy?" The dog nudged closer and licked her arm.

They finished the sandwich together, (she did have the yogurt to herself) and, while Gussie scoured the floor for crumbs, she sat quietly trying to sort through the puzzle.

She was almost certain that the solution hinged on the Robertson's belief that Tony was responsible for Martin's death. Marilyn had said; "I

t was all about that fire at the high school", and she would have said more if Gord hadn't given her the evil eye. There was no way around it; she'd have to find an excuse to talk to Marilyn again.

"Now, what do I know about Tony Wesley?" she said to herself. Gussie looked up questioningly, then resumed his crumb hunt. She went to the end table, pulled open the drawer and rummaged for pen and paper. It took several minutes, and by the time she sat down again she'd resolved to de-clutter all the drawers in the living room.

She wrote: *Wealthy family. Controlling mother, possibly abusive father. Ordinary little boy. Good student at high school in first year. Major behaviour issues by third year and after.* She shuddered, remembering his grade eleven Year Book picture. *Recovered alcoholic. Good husband and father. Serious health problems later in life. Adamant in refusing to come back to town, until almost destitute.*

And what did she know about the arsonist? On another sheet, she wrote: *Possibilities: Lived near Alastair Street school and Presbyterian church. Attended both, and the scout troop on Burns Street. Male, possibly around eleven at time of elementary school fire. Known to have set four fires in the north end of town between 1954 and 1956. Very disturbed.*

She set the two pages side by side and gazed down at them. Two boys, close in age, attending different schools at different ends of town. One Catholic, one Protestant, unlikely to meet casually. So what was the connection?

Then, as if a light switched on, she had the answer. "High school! They met at John Galt." That's when Tony changed, when he came under the influence of a powerful and twisted personality. Tony didn't set the north end fires, but he could have been an accomplice to the ones at the high school and hospital. Remember, two people were seen running away from that. At a stroke, his motive for killing Martin Robertson was re-established.

The arsons stopped after the hospital tragedy. Why? Too much police interest? Or maybe, the deaths had shocked the two of them into abandoning their destructive hobby. They'd never caused fatalities before.

Tony's Year Books were still piled on the coffee table, and Rosie's hand trembled as she reached for the topmost. *1955-1956,* his first year. The firebug was one of these classmates; someone he'd been so afraid of that he'd stayed away from Little Yarmouth until he had no choice but to come back. And had those fears been realised, the night an old friend came calling with a bottle of rye?

She found the Grade seven class photo; Tony and twenty five other bright young faces smiled out at her. All of them were familiar, and Rosie struggled to believe what she intuitively knew. That one of them was already an arsonist, and well on track to becoming a cold-hearted killer as well.

Chapter 16 – Full Circle

A bakery had stood at the corner of Murdoch and King for ninety-seven years, and the Ferguson family had owned it for most of that time. Like the *Clarion* one block east, Fergusons was a Little Yarmouth institution. But mere longevity hadn't been enough of a buttress when Tim Hortons and Dunkin' Donuts came to town, and in the nineties the shop had started a slow slide toward bankruptcy.

So, like the Clarion, Fergusons re-invented itself. Renamed *The Wee Scottish Bakery,* it built new success on a canny combination of Hibernian nostalgia and unbeatable quality. Now it was once again secure in its status as Little Yarmouth's go-to place for fine cakes, pastries and savouries.

Connie Black pushed open the door and stepped inside. As usual, the shop was full of customers. She joined the line and let her eyes wander over the tempting array of scones, shortbread, muffins, and cream cakes invitingly displayed in a glass fronted case under the counter.

Since transferring from Haematology to Pathology the previous year, she had got into the habit of stopping in at the bakery most mornings, on her way to work. It was all McGillivray's fault. The permanent aroma of fresh coffee in the lab. triggered her sugary cravings relentlessly, and now a thickening waistline stood testament to her daily indulgences. She knew she would have to get serious about cutting down, but this wasn't the time. Not right now, not with the weekend coming up. Maybe she'd start dieting on Monday; Monday was always a good day to begin a new project.

Yesterday she bought a bag of "Healthy Alternative Cookies" but they were just *too* healthy - not enough fat and sugar to qualify for the description of "cookie" in her opinion. She'd passed them on to the boss; he'd eat anything, as long as it came with a mug of coffee. Now there was a real addiction!

"Hi there, stranger."

Connie turned round to see Amanda Price, a past colleague from Haematology, standing close behind her.

"Hi, 'manda, how are you? Haven't seen you for a while. How's everything in the department?"

"Just the same; too much work, not enough staff. They never did hire your replacement, you know. Some days I don't even get a lunch break – that's why I'm here. Just love their sausage rolls." They moved closer to the head of the line. "What about you? Do you like Pathology?"

"It's not bad. Work's more challenging and its better money, so I guess it was a good move. I'd been in haematology too long, anyway. Only down side is that McGillivray's a bit of a slave-driver."

"Wouldn't suit me – down in the basement, right next to the morgue. Too creepy by half," and Amanda shuddered theatrically.

They shuffled forward as two more customers squeezed in through the door.

"How's Alan making out this term?"

"Bit discouraged. Not much talent in the football team again this year; he reckons there's no chance of making the championships. Poor guy still dreams of getting the Eagles back on top one day – lost cause, if you ask me." The crowd at the counter was thinning out, and Connie was surprised to see three people serving; usually it was just Dougie and his mother, filling bags and working the till.

"Look at that" she said. "He's finally hired some help. About time, too; his mom looks really frail. You'd think he'd have more consideration, making her work at her age."

Amanda laughed. "Frail? You haven't seen her in action, have you?"

"What do you mean?"

As if on cue, Mrs. Ferguson snatched at the paper bag their new recruit was holding and hissed; "I *told you* – cream horns go in a *box* stupid, not a paper bag." The girl's eyes filled with tears and she fled into the back kitchen. Mrs. Ferguson rounded on her son. "Douglas, for God's sake, why do you insist on hiring retards? But I suppose I shouldn't expect any better – you always were a fool for a pretty face."

The unfortunate Dougie hung his head in silence, and the lack of a response seemed to further infuriate his mother. With an exasperated snort she threw a pastry box toward him. "You know what you are? You're just a waste of space. Here, finish this order and be quick about it." She turned on her heel and demanded: "Right. Who's next?"

Connie looked round, expecting to see embarrassed faces everywhere. But no one seemed surprised; they were all just looking ahead, still edging dutifully toward the counter. She glanced questioningly at Amanda.

"They can't keep any help," Amanda whispered. "His mother's impossible to work with; nobody stays more than a week. I think they've been through every high school student and senior in town."

"Well, what d'ya know? I'd have thought she'd want to retire, at her age."

"No such luck. No, poor old Dougie's stuck with her until she croaks."

By now they were almost at the counter, and Connie thought it wiser to stop discussing Dougie and his harridan of a mother.

"We had a visit from one of your favourite people yesterday. John Cornish dropped in." Amanda's crush on her chubby family doctor had been an ongoing joke in Haematology.

Despite herself, Amanda blushed. "I wish everyone would stop saying things like that. I just appreciated his counselling when Al and I went through that bad patch, last year." She began rummaging through her purse. "You'd better decide what you want – the old gal doesn't like to be kept waiting." She pulled out a five dollar bill. "What did you mean anyway, about McGillivray being a slave-driver?"

Connie recognized a change of subject when she heard it, but couldn't be bothered to keep up her teasing. "He's okay, but everything has to be done so fast. Guess it's 'cos he's hopped up on caffeine all day. Someone needs a report in twenty-four hours? McGillivray wants it done in twelve, and it had better be fully complete. He's always breathing down our necks. And it's not like he's so perfect, either."

"How so?" Amanda always enjoyed a good gossip about the senior medical staff.

"Doc Cornish told him yesterday that some family thinks he screwed up an autopsy on their nearest and dearest."

Amanda's eyes opened wide behind her glasses, and she gave a little gasp. "No, I don't believe it!"

Pleased to be the bearer of such impressive news, Connie went on enthusiastically; "Well, believe it! I heard him say the family have serious concerns they want resolved, but McGillivray said he wants to keep it all quiet."

"Shit – that sounds bad. Who was the patient?" Then a thought struck her. "God, please don't say there was any blood work involved."

"Sorry, 'manda, I don't know." Surprised by the note of panic in her friend's voice, she said quickly; "But it can't be anything to do with you. What's the problem, anyway?"

"You know Al and I split up for a while last year?" Connie nodded. "Well, I kind'a lost interest in everything. Nothing seemed important anymore, and I guess I got sloppy." Amanda looked embarrassed. "I made some bad mistakes, okay?" Seeing Connie's expression she went on hurriedly; "Nobody died or anything, but let's just say I've had all the warnings I'm going to get, and I really need this job."

"Jeez, I'm sorry 'manda."

"Look, can you remember a name, or when it was? I could have a quick check; make sure I didn't miss anything."

Connie closed her eyes, trying to recreate the brief snatch of conversation she'd overheard the day before. "The first name was definitely Tony. Tony something – Tony West, Westney… Tony Wesley. The patient was Tony Wesley."

Amanda breathed a sigh of relief. "Thanks, Connie, I owe you one." She pushed the five back into her purse and turned to go. "I'm not going to wait. I've gotta check this out, put my mind at rest. You don't have any idea when this Wesley guy died, do you?"

"No, but I can ask Ahmed - see what he knows. I'll give you a call."

Amanda was already at the door. "Thanks, Connie" she called. "Appreciate it," and then she was gone.

"Do you know what you want?"

"What?" With a start, Connie turned back to the counter where Mrs. Ferguson was irritably rustling a paper bag.

"There are people waiting, you know."

"Yes, sorry. I'll take a jelly doughnut, two shortbread cookies and a sausage roll, please." Amanda's lunch suggestion had sounded delicious.

*   *   *   *

Pete Anderson, Errol Fryer, Bill Gifford, Jackson Haynes, Dave Mason and Vic Watson. There they all were; her final short-list of suspects, the end result of a long and sleepless night.

Rosie sat at her desk, gazing at the list and nursing the oversized mug of coffee she had poured in the vain hope it might wake her up. She had barely slept the previous night. The bedroom was stifling and, when she eventually drifted into sleep, her dreams were vivid and disturbing. Bathed in sweat, she'd finally woken at 3 a.m. and had gone downstairs to the relative coolness of the living room.

Her mind had been a jumble of bizarre images. David, sailing his boat down the railroad tracks, a small boy crouching in a corner, two figures running pell-mell into darkness, a train whistle. She'd sat on the couch, trying to connect up the wisps of ideas that kept drifting through her head, but none of them made any sense.

Accepting the futility of going back to bed, she had picked up pen and paper and finished her review of Tony's grade seven classmates. There were twenty six students that freshman year, twelve girls and fourteen boys. Relying on Aunt Marg's insight she eliminated all the girls, plus Tony and Martin Robertson. For a brief moment, she had considered the possibility that Martin was the arsonist, (the Robertson's lived in the north end and likely attended the Presbyterian church) but as he couldn't have been involved in the hospital fire, she discounted him. That reduced her suspect list to twelve.

On the assumption that the arsonist and killer were the same person, she'd crossed off Winston Arnott (killed in a motorbike accident) and Ross Metcalfe (died of leukaemia). Now she was down to ten names.

Finally, she'd eliminated Pete Ross, Tyler Carroll and Garnet Brent. They had all completed university and gone on to successful careers away from Little Yarmouth.

Of course, there was always the chance that one of them had come back on June sixteenth specifically to kill Tony Wesley but, if that were the case, why wait until now? Sault Ste. Marie was just as accessible for murder. No, she was comfortable crossing them off the suspect list.

When she read over the seven remaining names, four of them stood out; Bill Gifford, Jackson Haynes, Dave Mason and Vic Watson - all four had been on her original suspect list. The other three were Joe Mackie, (the *Clarion's* delivery man), Errol Fryer and Rob Murdoch. Rob Murdoch? Why was that name so familiar? Wait; he's dead too. The farmer who'd enlisted Auntie Marg to prove he'd died accidentally, not by suicide. She crossed him off the list.

And Joe Mackie? Poor soul was so asthmatic he could barely lift a bundle of Bulletins, let alone throw a body downstairs. Another name crossed off.

Errol Fryer? Local hog farmer. Yes, certainly big enough to do the deed. She made a mental note to do some checking on their local purveyor of sausages and ham.

By this time the sky had been pink, the dawn chorus in full warble and she was desperate for sleep. But today was Friday, and a working day. So she had dragged herself off to the shower, thrown on the first clothes that came to hand and choked down some burnt toast and coffee. To Gussie's disgust, there was no early morning jaunt around the block. Just a quick run round the garden, and the promise of a long walk at lunchtime. Now it was 10 a.m., and she was rapidly losing the struggle to keep her eyes open.

"Lord girl, ya look like death warmed over." Liz thumped a plate down on the desk in front of her. "Here, have a couple of cookies – fresh out the oven."

"Thanks Liz, I could do with something to get me going." Rosie took one gratefully and bit into it. It was delicious; Liz was justifiably renowned for her cookies.

And because the recipe was her grandmother's, she was content to leave it without any "healthy" modifications (a fact for which Father Matthews was deeply grateful.)

Now the housekeeper collapsed into the spare office chair, and groaned "Sweet Jesus, I'll be glad when Saturday's over. All this cleanin' and dustin'. I hope his bishopship appreciates it."

"I know." Rosie looked at the stacks of program sheets strewn across her desk, waiting to be collated and adorned with neatly tied red ribbons. "But the Confirmation Mass is always a big deal for the kids and their families, even without a new Bishop officiating." A few months earlier their diocesan Bishop had retired, and this Saturday was his successor's first visit to St. Judes.

"Well, I can't see the point, meself. He's just a man like any other – puts his pants on one leg at a time. All this bowing and scraping. And why Father thinks he'll notice if the organ pipes are dusted or not, I can't think." Liz wasn't a "cradle" Catholic; she'd converted when she married Steve, in the vain hope of pleasing his excessively devout mother. Her United Church upbringing routinely kicked in when faced with Catholicism's more hierarchical traditions.

Rosie finished off the second cookie. "Those are really good Liz; you could make a fortune with that recipe."

Liz sniffed. "Don't know 'bout that, but my old granny did know her way round a kitchen, that's for sure. At home, I make 'em in batches of four dozen at a time, and the whole lot are gone over a weekend. Steve and the boys like to eat hearty."

No cholesterol worries there, thought Rosie. As if reading her mind, Liz went on; "Can't be doing that here, of course. No, I only make Father the occasional dozen, and I freeze half of those for the next week. He'd eat the whole lot in one go, otherwise."

Rosie started to get up. "I'd better go wash my hands; don't want to get grease stains on these programs."

"Oh, sit yourself down for a minute and keep me company. I'm not goin' back in the church until the League ladies are gone, can't be doin' with them underfoot. All this fussin' and primpin'. Every darn statue's got a floral wreath stuck on its head."

Rosie couldn't suppress a giggle. "Well, the C.W.L takes these events very seriously, you know. And the church always looks lovely when they do the decorating."

But Liz wasn't about to be mollified. "And the Hall kitchen's no better. Wall to wall doilies, napkins, silver trays; never seen anythin' like it."

"Father's keen to have the Tea extra nice this year. After all, it's really a dual celebration; the Confirmation Mass and Bishop Doyle's first visit to the parish."

Liz gave another sniff of disapproval. "Just wants to score brownie points with his new boss, more like."

Rosie couldn't let that pass. "Now, you know that's not fair, Liz. And even if Father does want to make a good impression, what's wrong with that?"

Liz didn't answer. Instead, she gestured toward the coffee maker; "That coffee fresh?" When Rosie nodded, she crossed the room and poured herself a mugful. "Oh, don't mind me; I'm just fed up with all the extra work. I've been hours polishin' them pews." A wicked gleam came into her eyes. "With a bit of luck, Mrs. Hargitay will slide right off her front row seat, and give us all a good laugh."

A mental image of the hefty C.W.L President tumbling into a heap at Bishop Doyle's feet leapt unbidden into Rosie's head. She dismissed it hastily. Joanne Hargitay was a very worthy person; it was just unfortunate that she couldn't express her opinions more graciously. She smiled to herself at the thought of Liz and Mrs. Hargitay; the irresistible force meeting the immoveable object. No wonder they were so often at loggerheads.

Liz glanced down at Rosie's desk and spotted her list of names. "Them the confirmation names?"

"Oh, no," Rosie covered her list of murder suspects quickly. "Just reunion committee stuff." She pulled a sheet of paper out of the typewriter. "Just finished typing it up. Want a look?" She passed it across the desk.

"Always like to see what names the kids choose for their confirmation." She scanned the list. "Oh, Star Bright's picked *Rose*. That's nice; she must think a lot of you."

"Well, she and her brother do sing with me at the Folk Mass once a month. But I don't know if that's why she chose it. Maybe she's got a devotion to St. Rose of Lima; you know, crowns of roses and trailing white robes. Very appealing to teenage girls." She swept the suspect list into her open desk drawer, then had an unexpected flash of inspiration. "Liz, you went to Alistair Street school, didn't you?"

"Yeah. Nowhere else to go in them days, 'cept Holy Angels for the cath'lics."

"Do you remember Errol Fryer?"

"Errol Fryer?"

"Yes. He's got a hog farm out on one of the concessions."

"Oh, I know who ya mean. Best place around for chops and sausages. No, can't say that I remember him; he was in a different grade to me. Why d'ya want to know?"

"Just a disagreement on the reunion committee." Rosie crossed her fingers under the desk. Stretching the truth again, but hey, all in a good cause. "We've been going through old Year Books" she added, hoping the irrelevant comment would somehow deflect more questions.

"No, never really knew him. But his brother, Jimmy was in my class. We all rode the bus together."

"They were bussed in?"

"Yeah, we all were. Fryer's is on the sixth concession and we was on the third."

"So, Errol's dad had the farm before him?"

"Fryer's have been on their place for four generations. It was Errol that took it to hogs, though; his dad always had beef cattle. So, what was the disagreement?"

Rosie was saved from further dissembling by Father Matthews' sudden and dishevelled appearance at the door. "There you are, Liz" he said sharply. They both looked up in surprise. The usually dapper priest was in his shirtsleeves, with smudges of dust on his rabat, trouser legs and face. "I can't find the silver gilt thurible anywhere. We didn't use it at Christmas, so it's bound to need cleaning. Do you have any ideas?"

Liz got to her feet. "No worries, Father. I think we put it in the basement lock-up. Remember, we took all the good stuff out of the sacristy and put it down there after the break-in."

Father Matthews pulled out a handkerchief and wiped his brow. "Yes, yes, I think you're right. Now, Rosie what about incense?"

"Two boxes in the cupboard here, Father. We've got more than enough."

"Thank goodness for that. Well, I'd better get to the basement and bring up everything that needs cleaning. Liz, you'll have time for that this morning, I expect?"

Liz gave a tight little smile. "Yes, Father. Of course, lunch will have to be rather basic. Tuna salad okay?"

The priest's shoulders sagged slightly and Rosie caught an almost inaudible sigh. "Thank you Liz, that will be…just fine."

As she followed him out, Liz looked over her shoulder at Rosie and winked.

Rosie took the suspect list out again and crossed through Errol Fryer's name. No way he'd be carrying gas soaked rags to school on a bus. And no way could he get into town by himself to set the fires at the church and scout hall. No, Errol was definitely off the hook.

"Well, those programs won't assemble themselves" she said aloud, and headed down the hall to wash her hands. As she passed the kitchen, Liz called out; "I forgot why I came into the office in the first place. What'ya doing Tuesday night?"

Rosie hesitated. As usual, she was doing nothing on Tuesday night but, having no interest in any of Liz's leisure activities, was reluctant to admit it.

"Not sure, really. I may have to pop over to John and El's," (not exactly a lie, she *might* have to go, if John didn't get back to her soon).

"Just thought ya might like to come over to Stella's." She saw Rosie's puzzled expression. "My sister-in-law? Ya know Mike's wife? Marilyn's doin' a Colour Party at their place; clothes and make-up and stuff. Could pick ya up a bit, get a new look goin'."

Rosie was just about to offer her usual non-committal, "Well, I'll try," when she realised Liz had said *Marilyn*. "Who did you say's doing the party?"

"Marilyn, Marilyn Robertson. She's a rep for *Colour Me Beautiful.*"

Rosie could hardly believe her luck; the perfect opportunity to grill Marilyn had just dropped into her lap. She went into the kitchen. "You know, I think I would like to come. I could do with a bit of a make-over. What time's she starting?"

If Liz was surprised by Rosie's about-face, she didn't show it. "Seven-thirty. Stella lives just round the corner - ninety-seven Duke Street. I've been to Marilyn's shows before; the stuff's nice and not too pricey."

"Right, that's a date then." Rosie turned to go. "Always assuming we survive tomorrow, of course."

"Ya got that right, girl!"

The morning sped by in a blur of phone calls, deliveries and minor crises, until finally the clock reached noon, and Rosie could lock the office and head home for lunch.

For heavens' sake she thought, walking briskly along Victoria Street. The way everyone is carrying on you'd think it was the Archangel Gabriel coming tomorrow, not just a new Bishop.

She had Gussie's lead ready in her purse, and snagged him neatly as he hurled himself through the front door. "Yes, good to see you too, boy" she said, rubbing his ears affectionately before they set off around the block.

It was so hot that neither of them was inclined to dawdle, and just fifteen minutes later Rosie was in her kitchen serving up lunch; diet kibble for Gussie and a vegetarian hotdog for herself. Unfortunately this smelt so much like the real thing, she only managed to eat half of it before having to share the fake dog with the real one. Well, it won't do him any harm, she thought, and saves me a bunch of calories.

She looked up at the kitchen clock; 12.35 p.m. If she drove, rather than walked back to work, she'd have time for a little rest. It had been such a crazy morning and the living room looked cool and inviting. She sat down on the couch and closed her eyes.

The phone woke her. She sat up with a start and looked at her watch. Oh God, she'd fallen asleep! It was nearly one! She leapt up, grabbed the phone and shot into the hall. "Hello? Sorry, just on my way out, can't talk."

"It's El, Rosie."

"Hi, El. I'm late for work, and the place is a madhouse today. I've got to go; call you tonight."

"No, wait Rosie. That's why I'm calling. Do you want to come over for barbeque tonight? John said to tell you he's got something to report, whatever that means."

Well, and about time too, thought Rosie. "Love to," she answered. Then memories of the tofu lurking in Elspeth's fridge leapt to mind. "But don't bother making me anything. I'll bring veggie patties. What time?"

"John's promised to be home by six, so any time after that."

"Great. Gotta go."

"And bring Gussie. Moira's in dog withdrawal."

"Will do. See you tonight."

Elspeth's "bye" was cut short by Rosie clicking *off*, and tossing the phone onto a hall chair. She was out the door and into the car before Gussie realised she was gone.

Chapter 17 – Revelations

"Mrs. O'Halloran? Can I do this bit again, please?" Josh Andrews peered anxiously at the music stand in front of him. "I still can't get this entrance right." He gestured at the music with his trumpet.

Loretta O'Halloran took a deep breath and counted to ten. She'd said all along that a *Te Deum* with trumpet was way over the top, but if Father had his heart set on turning the Confirmation Mass into a musical extravaganza, who was she to complain?

"Okay Josh, but this'll have to be the last time. You're doing really well, you know. A bit of extra practice at home tonight and it'll be perfect tomorrow." She called out; "Sorry Rose, shouldn't be too long now. Just Mireille's violin solo after this, then we can get to the *Veni Creator*."

From the depths of the choir cupboard, Rosie shouted back; "No problem. I'm not in a hurry," and continued foraging for sheet music and the choir's battered concert folders. She felt for young Josh. This was the eleventh grader's first solo performance, and it sounded like he had a bad case of stage fright.

In short order she found all the music, and sorted the sheets into performance order. Unlike the organist, Rosie thought tomorrow's ceremony was going to be splendid. St. Jude's little choir was well prepared, and everyone seemed pleased with her choice of mixed traditional and contemporary music. Of course there were still a few rough spots, but nothing she couldn't fix at their final run-through tomorrow

She was laying folders side by side along the length of the front choir pew when Liz came toiling up the loft stairs, feather duster in hand. "You don't need to get at these pews, do you Liz?" she said, raising her voice to be heard over Josh's umpteenth run at the *Te Deum*.

"Nah, I'm done with pew polishin'." Liz came toward her stiffly, stopped and leant back, stretching slightly. "Rosie, have ya met my brother Mike's wife?" She waved her duster in the direction of the stairs. "My back's startin' to go, so Stel's come over to help me finish up."

Rosie glanced down the stairwell. A tiny woman with a beehive of improbably black hair was struggling upwards, hauling St. Jude's ancient vacuum cleaner behind her.

"Hi Mrs. Johnson" she called; "nice to meet you. Can I give you a hand with that?"

Stella Johnson grunted. "No need, and it's just Stella, by the way" and, with one last heave, she dragged the machine over the topmost step and into the loft. It was almost as big as she was.

As the *Te Deum* slowed to its final chords, Loretta began shuffling through her music, getting ready for the next soloist. "Just watch the timing there, Josh," she said absently. "Everything else is spot on. See you tomorrow." Josh looked unconvinced, but began packing up obediently.

The organist turned apologetically to Liz; "I'm sorry Liz; everyone's been late this afternoon, so I'm running well behind. Can you give me another half an hour?"

Liz eased herself down onto a pew. "Whatdy'a think, Stel?"

"I think if you don't get home and into a hot bath, you're gonna seize right up." Stella gave the old vacuum a vicious shove across the loft. "And if those cheapskates on your parish council would cough up for a new vacuum, you wouldn't have half the back trouble you do. Bet they'd change their tune if they had to do the vacuuming."

The machine in question keeled over and fell backwards, sending a reverberating crash through the empty church.

'Almost as if it knew we were talking about it,' Rosie thought fancifully, sliding another completed stack of music into a folder. Aloud, she said; "You know Stella's right, Liz. Last time your back went out, you couldn't stand upright for a week."

Liz stood up gingerly. "Yep, you're right; that's me done." She made her way carefully toward the stairs, calling back over her shoulder "Just give that balcony rail a quick once-over, Stel. then run the vacuum round when Mrs. O'Halloran's finished." Her voice floated up from the stair well. "I left the feathery there on the front pew. See you tomorrow Rosie, God and the Epsom salts willin'."

Rosie and Stella turned energetically to their appointed tasks, while Loretta waited impatiently for her next soloist to arrive. Ten minutes passed as she sorted music and riffed brief snatches of various hymns and anthems from Saturday's program. Rosie was just about to suggest a run through of her solo, when Mireille Aucoin came scurrying up the stairs. "Sorry, Mrs. O'Halloran; my mom was late picking me up."

"Well, I just hope you know your piece; we don't have much time left," Loretta said tartly, as the youngster lifted a violin from its case and began arranging her music on the stand. After a few false starts, the beautiful notes of Schubert's *Ave Maria* filled the air, and it was soon apparent that, yes, Mireille did know her piece. It was almost perfect.

By now, Rosie and Stella had finished their work and were sitting side by side on the front choir pew.

"Liz says you're coming to my colour party."

Rosie, lost in the music, jumped. She had completely forgotten Stella was there.

"Yes, I'm looking forward to it. I've never been to one of Marilyn's shows."

"I've been to three; she says I'm a Cool Winter." Unzipping her overall, Stella proudly revealed a neon pink tee. "Got this last time. She says it's one of the best colours for a Cool Winter."

Rosie's heart sunk. If Stella's black hair, pink top and blue eye-shadow were an example of Marilyn's expertise, then whatever she purchased on Tuesday night was destined for the nearest charity bin. Then she reminded herself that fashion wasn't the reason for her unexpected night out. With a bit of luck, Marilyn might provide the key to the Tony Wesley mystery; and that was worth far more than the price of whatever she felt obliged to buy.

"Yes, it'll be fun to find out what I am," she said lamely.

Stella smiled and nodded, then looked pointedly at her watch. "How much longer d'you think they'll be? I've got Mike's supper to get started."

Mireille had finished playing and had gone to stand next to the organist, watching intently as Loretta pencilled notations on the music.

"Not long, now" Rosie replied. As the silence between them grew, the thought occurred to her that here was a great opportunity to get some background on Tony's estranged family.

"Liz said you're working up at Mill House," she said brightly. "How's Mrs. Wesley holding up? It must have been difficult for her recently, what with losing her son and then the accident."

Stella grimaced, and said in flinty tones. "Don't know about her, but it's sure been hard on the staff. The old witch's a pain in the butt at the best of times, but these last few weeks... Well, I've come close to handing in my notice more than once, and she's had Mona Norris in tears almost every day."

Rosie spared a regretful thought for her old school friend. Mona must have been truly desperate for a job to apply for the housekeeper's position at Mill House last year. But work was hard to come by in Little Yarmouth, and if you could say one good thing about Clodagh Wesley, it was that she paid well.

"I guess grief takes people in different ways," she offered non-committally.

"She didn't seem very grief-stricken to me. Although..." Stella paused, as if uncertain how much more to say, then continued in a rush; "I guess she did try to make it up with her son. Told your reverend there," she jerked her head in the general direction of the rectory, "that she went round to his house that night."

"What night?"

"The night he died, of course."

Rosie's jaw dropped. She stared at Stella open-mouthed, literally left speechless by this astounding revelation.

Stella took her silence for criticism. "Don't look at me like that, I couldn't help hearing, I was right outside the door, scrubbing the hall tiles." She shifted uncomfortably in her seat, then went on defensively; "She shouldn't talk so loud if she don't want people to overhear."

At a stroke, everything became crystal clear. Clodagh, summoning Father Matthews to Mill House the day she was discharged from hospital, then Liz's comments about the old lady's lengthy confessions; *Goes on and on she does. Don't make her any better person though, does it?*

She said quickly, in the most soothing voice she could muster. "Oh no, Stella, I do agree with you. Mrs. Wesley has a very penetrating voice." As she'd hoped, Stella's expression softened. "So did she put things right with her son before he died?"

Confident now, Stella leaned toward Rosie and said under her breath; "Well no, that's the thing, you see. They had a big row. She says to your reverend, *'our last words were spoken in anger.'*

Rosie listened intently. Small wonder Father Matthews had looked uneasy, when she enquired after Mrs. Wesley. Clodagh probably thought her actions had led to her son getting drunk and falling to his death. And if she confessed that, then Father Matthews must believe the same thing. Or, even more staggering, perhaps she had confessed to pushing him down the stairs! Were the arsons unrelated to Tony's death, after all?

She dismissed that idea immediately. No, Tony had been leading her in the direction of the fires from the very start. And it wasn't a female figure she'd seen throwing his body down the basement stairs. Just another blind alley.

Stella was still going on, her voice pitched to carry above the organ; ".... 'course, in the United Church we don't hold with telling our sins to a minister. We just go directly to the Lord." This last statement was pronounced with a self-righteous smirk.

Her tone irritated Rosie, who almost pointed out that the United Church didn't hold with eavesdropping or repeating private conversations, either. But she held her tongue. For certain, the fleeting pleasure of delivering a

sarcastic zinger would pale beside the resultant frostiness of her reception at the Johnson house next Tuesday night. Better keep everything light. And to be honest, she'd encouraged Stella to repeat what she'd heard, so 'I'm not exactly occupying the moral high ground, either' she reminded herself sternly.

So with a weak smile, she resorted to the time-honoured catch-all for difficult situations; "Well, you know, *different strokes* and all that."

The last haunting notes of the *Ave Maria* drifted through the church.

"Lovely work, Mireille. I think we can leave it there." Loretta gave the girl an encouraging smile, and began switching music around, looking for Rosie's piece.

"How are you getting home? I can give you a ride if you like, after I've finished with Mrs. Rowe."

"No thanks, Mrs. O'Halloran; my mom will be outside. She just ran to the store while I did my rehearsal."

"Well, off you go, then. No late night tonight, mind. You need to rest those fingers."

As Mireille clattered happily down the stairs, Rosie came to a decision. "Lorrie, it's getting on for six, and Mrs. Johnson still has to vacuum up here. Why don't I just come in a bit earlier tomorrow, and we can run through my solo then. I know it fairly well, so it won't take long." And anyway, she added mentally, there's no way I can concentrate now; not after Stella's bombshell!

Loretta didn't take much convincing. With a sigh of relief, she said; "That would be a huge help, Rosie" closing and locking the organ in one fluid movement as she spoke. "The boys have got softball tonight, and I don't like them to go out without eating," now she was stacking music, "and Sean won't think to feed them." She grabbed up her music case and swept across the loft, looking back from the top of the stairs. "Nine forty-five suit you?"

Rosie nodded. "That'll be great."

"Right then." Loretta glanced across to the far side of the loft, where Stella was searching moodily for an electrical outlet. "Sorry to have held you up, Mrs. Johnson. Maybe see you again soon" and, in an instant she had disappeared down the stairs.

Rosie was right behind her. "I'll leave you to it then, Stella" she called, over the roar of the vacuum cleaner. "See you Tuesday night." Whether she heard or not, Stella didn't pause to reply.

*   *   *   *

It was very pleasant, lolling on the swing seat, idly pushing herself to and fro, to and fro, with the tip of her sandal. Across the patio she could see John scraping off the barbeque, (Gussie drooling at his feet), and from the kitchen she could hear Elspeth clattering dishes, as she stacked them in the dishwasher.

For some reason, they had absolutely refused to let her do anything this evening. So finally she gave up offering to help, and taken full advantage of their unexpected solicitude.

The hot and humid weather of the past few days was cooling down at last, and now the sky was beginning its transition from the soft pink of evening to the indigo of night. Rosie lounged back, enjoying a pleasant, wine-induced drowsiness that was spreading through her limbs.

"Rosie, can I get you another glass of wine, or maybe a liqueur?" She opened her eyes to see Elspeth standing beside her, a bottle in each hand.

"No thanks, El. You know I'd love a liqueur, but I'd better give it a miss. I am driving, after all."

"John'll take you home."

"I know, but tomorrow's a really big day at the church. Practice in the morning and then all the hoo-ha of the Confirmation Mass, and the Bishop and the Tea. Plus alcohol always dries out my vocal chords." Rosie drained her wine glass, and set it down on the table. "So I'll leave the liqueurs 'til tomorrow night; by then I'll be needing a few drinks."

John strolled over and sat down beside his wife, leaving Gussie snuffling hopefully under the barbeque. "He looks as if he's lost some weight" he said, nodding in the dog's direction.

"Yes, indeed. A whole pound this past month; Dr. Katz actually cracked a smile at his weigh-in. All down to Moira, of course. Where is she, by the way?"

Elspeth gave an exasperated roll of her eyes, then said with weary resignation. "Gone upstairs to change, for the second time. I told her white wasn't a good colour choice for an evening with Gussie."

"Oh, right." Moira's white capris hadn't survived past the first ten minutes of the girl/dog reunion, and now it seemed that her pretty pin-tucked shirt had suffered the same fate. "He's a bit of a handful, I'm afraid."

Her sister-in-law gazed into her wine glass and murmured a non-committal, "mmm-m." No chance there'll ever be a resident dog in this house, Rosie thought.

Taking advantage of the opening, John looked across his wife's head at Rosie and raised his eyebrows questioningly. She met his gaze and nodded a signal of understanding.

"So, I did get the chance to have a word with Andy McGillivray, Rose." John's tone was a study in nonchalance.

"Oh, that's good. What did he say?"

Elspeth looked from one to the other. "The pathologist? The one that's got a bit of a thing for you, Rose? Has John been setting you up on a date?"

Rosie's face flushed with embarrassment. "Hardly." The single word was uttered rather more forcefully than she had intended.

John gave a dry chuckle "No, it's not that; although maybe not such a bad idea." Rosie glared at him and he grinned back. "No, the night before we left on our trip, the husband of one of Rosie's friends died under… unusual circumstances. She asked me to make a few enquiries on the widow's behalf, that's all."

"Oh." Elspeth lost interest. After fourteen years as a doctor's wife, her antennae automatically withdrew the instant any conversation veered into medical realms.

"He cleared up the mystery of the missing autopsy, right enough." John paused for effect.

"And?" Rosie was hard pressed to keep the impatience from her voice. For heavens' sake, why must people hoard information to themselves, until the last possible minute? Don't they know how annoying that is?

"Five little words. *Dr. Aubrey Niven* and *Clodagh Wesley*." John sat back, looking very pleased with himself.

"I'm sorry, John; I don't understand."

Elspeth got to her feet and began clearing glasses from the table. "If you're going to start complaining about poor Dr. Niven again, I'm going in. I ought to check on Bobbie anyway; it's gone awfully quiet up there." And, without another word, she headed inside.

"El…" but it was too late. John's appeal was lost in the *swish* and thump of the sliding patio door closing behind his wife. "Oh, Lord. What is it about Aubrey Niven that makes every woman feel sorry for him?" He looked at Rosie, but she just widened her eyes and gave a tiny shrug.

"Not a clue, John. Whatever pixie dust he scatters doesn't work on me, but I do remember mom getting all flustered when he came to see dad at the house, one time."

John wasn't amused by her flippant tone. He snapped; "Well, his social aspirations are the main reason a suspicious death got signed off as accidental." Seeing Rosie's hurt expression, he immediately regretted his bad temper. "I'm sorry Bud, but that pompous brownnoser really gets under my skin."

When Rosie said nothing, he proceeded to tell her everything he had learned about Tony Wesley's E.R. admission, on the night of June sixteenth.

It was impossible for Rosie to stay mad at her brother for long, especially when he used her childhood pet name, so she relented and said; "Looks like it all came down to keeping Clodagh happy then, right?"

"Got it in one," said John. "But the really interesting part is that Andy took an unofficial look at the body next morning, and didn't like what he saw. So he'd planned to call the widow, (Lucy is it?) and see about an autopsy, but there was a rush in the morgue and….well, it got overlooked."

"What the hell constitutes a *rush* in a mortuary?" Rosie asked hotly. Although that wasn't really the question she wanted answered, or why her temper was rising. It was the injustice of circumstance that was getting to her; how all the events of that night had neatly conspired to favour the actions of a cold-blooded killer.

If anyone but Dr. Niven had been on duty in the E.R., then Tony's death would have been flagged as suspicious right from the start. There would have been blood tests, an autopsy, and police involvement. Who knows, maybe even an arrest by now. It's almost as if the Devil's taking care of his own she thought, and shuddered involuntarily.

John spread his hands apologetically. "I know how you feel, Rose. Andy's sick about it, but sometimes these things just happen. The department was swamped. There'd been a bad traffic accident, and multiple victims all came down at once. And, don't forget, Mason's picked your guy up really fast."

"Yes, and that was down to Clodagh, too" Rosie retorted. "Well, now I've got something to tell you about our town's *grande dame*." And without naming any names, she recounted what she knew about Clodagh's visit to Tony, and her belief that she was responsible for his death.

John looked shocked. "Oh God, this keeps getting worse and worse," he said. "So, now it looks like the old girl had an ulterior motive for yanking Aubrey's chain."

With sudden insight, Rosie realised that she'd been so immersed in Tony Wesley's life and death over the past weeks that she'd forgotten it was only she, and Aunt Marg, who knew all the background to the crime. She'd never got around to telling her brother about her vision in the Veteran's Avenue basement, or the arsons for that matter.

With this is mind, she leant forward and said reassuringly; "Well, that may be the case, but I don't believe for one minute she was responsible. She may *think* she is, but Aunt Marg and I've been investigating a whole different angle to this story, and Clodagh doesn't figure in that at all. But the one thing we're both certain of is that Tony Wesley was killed in cold blood."

John's face drained of colour and he was about to speak, when they were interrupted by Moira and Bobbie, both carrying trays with cups, saucers and the various other accoutrements of after-dinner coffee. A moment later, Elspeth followed them out with a large carafe and dish of chocolate mints.

The sound of their voices also brought Gussie from under the barbeque where he was still lurking, clinging to the vain hope that something meaty might drop into his jaws.

"C'mon Gus," Moira and Bobbie called one after the other, and Rosie spotted they each held something in their hands.

"You haven't got bones there, have you kids?" she asked anxiously. "The only ones I let him have are the big knuckle bones from the butcher. Cooked bones can splinter and hurt his insides."

Moira opened her fingers. "No, Auntie Ro, just jerky chews from the pet shop..." she giggled as the beagle started pushing his nose into her hand; "Stop it, Gus... sit, there's a good boy, sit." But the dog had easily prised his treat from her hand and, having demolished it in one gulp, was busy repeating the process with Bobbie. After this second successful assault, the beagle disappeared up the garden to digest his reward in peace.

Still laughing, Moira reached across for an after dinner mint, only to have her mother move the plate aside. "Not with those hands, you don't. Both of you go on inside and wash up again; who knows where that dog's mouth has been."

Rosie, who did know where the dog's mouth had been, nodded in agreement. "Yes, guys, you really don't want your hands near your mouths after being round Gussie's. He had June bugs for dessert, you know."

"Eeeww..." the patio door opened and closed behind Moira's rapidly retreating back.

"You too, Bobbie."

"Ma! I'm not eating anything."

John had recovered himself sufficiently to weigh in on the hygiene debate. "Robert; don't argue with your mother. Get washed up now!"

Elspeth smiled at her husband and started handing the coffee cups around. She had just picked up the carafe when a yell came from inside; "Mom, Auntie Megan's on the phone."

"Moira, there's no need to shout" Elspeth called back. "Sorry, Rose" she said, getting up. "Family crisis; I'll have to take it."

"That's okay, El. No problem."

John seemed to think an explanation was in order. "Megan and Joe've hit a matrimonial curve. I think he's moved out."

"Oh, I'm sorry." Rosie had only met El's sister a few times, but had liked her instantly. Joe, not so much.

"Good riddance to bad rubbish, if you ask me. I never liked him." John dropped his voice and looked over his shoulder. "But don't tell El that."

Rosie nodded, and mimed zipping her lips.

"So, are you going to fill me in on why the two of you think this Wesley was murdered?"

"It's a long story, John and," Rosie glanced into the kitchen where Elspeth was walking back and forth, phone in hand, "I don't think I've got time to go through it all. But, in a nutshell, we've found out that Tony got mixed up with a really bad guy in high school, and that was why he left town. Also, why he wouldn't come back for years."

"And you and Margaret think that when he did come back, this charmer killed him?"

"Basically, yes."

"And you've taken it upon yourselves to bring him or her to justice?"

"It's a him. And yes, that's why Tony can't rest. That's why he contacted me....and Moira. If I can't sort it out, he won't move on. Look," she fished in her pocket for the list of murder suspects, and laid it in front of her brother; "We know it's someone from his high school class. I've been able to eliminate a lot of people, and now I'm down to these five."

John looked doubtful. "How do you know it was someone in his class? Why are you so sure of all this?"

Rosie sighed. "John...."

But her brother interrupted. "Alright, no need to take that resigned tone. You've got inside information, right? The dead guy's been whispering in your ear, but unfortunately can't tell you the most important fact; who broke his neck for him!"

Rosie was too tired to be cross. "Check, check and check again" she said, sketching imaginary tick marks in the air. "Look, you're not being very helpful. I didn't *ask* Tony Wesley to haunt me, but now that he is, I've got to see it through." She pushed the list of suspects toward him. "One of these five people is a killer, take my word for it."

Frowning, John studied the crumpled piece of paper. Almost immediately he burst out; "For Christ's sake, Rose! *Dave Mason?* You've got to be kidding! And Pete Anderson? If he were a psycho killer, that wife of his would be long dead!"

Rosie gave a rueful smile. "You're not saying anything I haven't said to myself a hundred times, John. But there it is. It's got to be one of these five."

"Now, Bill Gifford I can understand. But Jackson Haynes? Sorry, you'll have to give up on that one, I'm afraid."

Rosie shook her head. "No, he's my best bet. I really want it to be him; he's such a nasty piece of work, and he carries a grudge for ever."

"I'm not disagreeing with you, Rose. I wouldn't want to meet Haynes on a dark night, either. But fact is, he couldn't have killed Tony Wesley. On the sixteenth of June, he was in Memorial recovering from back surgery he'd had the previous day. I should know; he's my patient and I booked the op. Saw him on the sixteenth as it happens; one of my last stops, before going home to pack." Seeing his sister's crestfallen expression he said regretfully. "Sorry Bud, but he couldn't have done it."

"Oh, rats" Rosie wailed. "I'd set my heart on it being him. Going to the Post Office would be so much nicer, if he was serving life for murder."

John laughed, then picked up the list again. After thinking a moment he said; "And I think you'll find Vic Watson's a no-go, too."

"Why? He's definitely got form." Rosie's love of British crime procedurals slipped out.

"That may be but, if I remember right, he's still at the half-way house in Goderich, so he'll be under curfew. Plus, he's got no wheels; his wife took the car when she left him." He passed the paper back to Rosie. "Who says I'm not helpful. I've got you down to three suspects."

"Thanks, I think."

John leant forward and touched her hand. "Seriously Rose, I'm worried about you. What are you going to do when you get this list down to one name? Confront whoever it is and tell him to turn himself in? Appeal to his better nature? Pray his conscience will be his guide? You can't go to the police, you've got no evidence."

"But that's why knowing about the missed autopsy was so important,"Rosie said eagerly. "Once I tell Lucy why it wasn't done, I'm sure she'll request an exhumation. Then an autopsy will prove Tony wasn't drunk, and didn't break his neck pitching down the stairs. It'll go to the police, I'll tell them about the arsons and it'll be out of my hands." She smiled triumphantly. "No need for me to ever go near the perp." She liked North American crime procedurals, too.

"Well, at least you won't have any trouble getting an autopsy. Andy as good as said he'd authorise it; although first he would like to see any photos the police took at the scene. Can you ask Lucy about the police report?"

Rosie wanted to hug him; all the pieces were falling wonderfully into place. "For sure" she said happily. "I'll call her first thing tomorrow. It's so great that Andy's on side like this."

But now her brother was looking at her with his head to one side, as if trying to remember something. Then, with a hard stare, he said; "Did I hear you say something about *arson*, just now?"

"Mmm…yes." Rosie averted her eyes. "Auntie Marg and I think there may be a connection to some old arson cases, that's all."

"That's all? Arson *and* murder?" John repeated incredulously.

"John, I know it's hard to believe…."

"What's hard to believe?"

Elspeth's voice, coming unexpectedly from behind her, made Rosie start. She scoured her brain for an innocuous answer but, in the end, could only stammer an inarticulate; "Er….."

John took a stab at deflecting his wife's question. "How're Megan and the kids?"

But El wasn't to be put off. "Everyone's fine. Now, you two have been sitting here with your heads together all evening. So come on, tell me. What's going on and why is it hard to believe?"

Rosie looked at John, raised her eyebrows and shrugged.

Finally, in tones that were decidedly snippy, he said: "Well, if you must know….Andy thinks it's possible that Tony Wesley didn't die accidentally. That he was murdered."

Seeing her sister-in-law's puzzled expression, Rosie added helpfully; "Tony Wesley was my friend Lucy's husband."

Elspeth looked more excited than shocked. "Murdered? Oh, wow." She gave them both a searching look. "But that's not all, is it?"

John pursed his lips together, and finally said reluctantly; "No, but I don't want any of this spread around, El. And I particularly don't want the kids to know."

She looked miffed. "John, I could write a best-seller with what I hear about people in this town. But I'm the perfect doctor's wife, when it comes to what goes on inside these four walls; deaf, dumb and blind. So please, give me credit for a little discretion."

"Alright then," her husband acknowledged grudgingly. Taking another deep breath he said; "If it is murder, then the killer is probably local. Someone who knew Wesley in school." He paused. "Someone we all know."

Now Elspeth was shocked. "Not still living here?"

"More than likely."

His wife paled, and her eyes widened with fright.

Oh God, we've scared her half to death, Rosie thought. She'll be looking at everyone sideways from now on. Summoning her calmest tone she said; "But there's no need for you to worry, El. We think it's all about Tony's past. It wasn't a random murder; no-one else is in danger."

"But… someone we know?" Elspeth stammered, looking back and forth from one to the other. "What're the police doing about it?"

"It's all hanging on getting an autopsy right now. Once that's done, the police will take over."

John decided the conversation had gone far enough. He went to Elspeth and put an arm round her shoulders. "Look, El, just put it out of your mind. It's nothing to do with us; Rosie only got involved because Lucy was distraught and asked her to help."

Elspeth blinked at him. "You're right," she said hesitantly. "It just took me by surprise, that's all. The thought that someone in our little town might be a murderer; a wolf in the fold, so to speak."

Rosie nodded. "Yes, that's it exactly. You somehow expect violence in a big city, but not in places like Little Yarmouth." She reached for an after-dinner mint and slid it slowly out of its neat little envelope. "But we're deluding ourselves if we think we know our friends and neighbours through and through. The sad fact is, you can never really know someone; we all keep secrets from each other." Unnoticed by Rosie, her brother and his wife exchanged a knowing glance.

Something, maybe the taste of the chocolate mint in her mouth, or the feel of its crinkly brown wrapper in her hand, opened the floodgates of Rosie's memory. Odd how food holds such power to unlock the past she thought, her mind drifting back to the last dinner party she and David had hosted in their home.

That had been a summer evening, too; the french doors open wide, moths and June bugs batting at the screens. Good friends, candlelight, laughter around their enormous antique dining table. Red and white flowers, and little flags; of course, it had been Canada Day. That year they had decided to do something different and have a dinner party, instead of their usual holiday barbeque.

And less than a week later, her world came crashing down. July seventh, 1993. David took the *Dewey Rose* out, and never came back.

Suddenly Rosie understood why John and Elspeth were giving her the kid glove treatment tonight. Today was the seventh anniversary of David's disappearance.

It also explained why he'd been creeping into her thoughts and dreams recently. And then came another, less welcome, realisation. 'Seven years without a trace. He's officially dead.' How could she have forgotten such an all-important date? Did that mean she was finally over him?

Some of this must have shown on her face, because, when she looked up, she caught John and Elspeth watching her sympathetically. She glanced away. No, I'm not talking about that stuff tonight, she said to herself.

Instead, she looked pointedly at her watch. "Lord, is that the time? Thanks guys, for such a great evening, but I'd better get going. Early start tomorrow."

She stood up, all brisk resolve, and looked around. "Where's that dog? Gussie, Gussie…" As she expected, there was no response. "John, give me a hand flushing him out; he's probably back there digging up your shrubbery."

Her brother and his wife got up quickly, relief evident on their faces. Apparently none of them wanted to tackle the elephant in the room.

El spoke eagerly; "I'll get a flashlight." She opened the patio door, calling as she went inside; "Kids, your aunt's leaving. Come and say goodnight."

*   *   *   *   *

Not far from the patio where the Cornish family were enjoying their pleasant summer evening together, someone else was contentedly strolling through his garden.

He was in a self-congratulatory mood. 'Finally got the upper hand with those slugs' he thought, bending down to refill a saucer of beer in the Hosta border.

It had been a bad summer for pests; slugs, snails and, he giggled, the biggest pest of all. But, as usual, he'd got the upper hand. He smiled broadly; booze had always served him well in getting rid of unwanted crawlers.

That was an interesting conversation he'd overheard today in the bakery. Dear Tony's family were finally asking questions; well, good luck with that! Even if someone figured out how the moron was finished off, there was nothing to connect him to it. He'd been too clever, covered his tracks too well.

Still annoying though; trust that nosey doctor to put his oar in. That's the Cornish's for you, always thinking they were better than anyone else. His sister must have put him up to it. The perfect Miss Rose, dear little Lucy's friend. What a pair of sweethearts! He spat viciously into the dirt.

Walking along the path his eye fell on a snail, and he watched it briefly as it made a slow, silvery progress across the concrete.

In one swift movement, he picked up a white painted rock from the flowerbed edging, and smashed it down on the unsuspecting little animal. The resultant *crunch* was deeply satisfying. He waited, delaying the moment of gratification, then slowly lifted the rock and took a long, pleasurable look at his handiwork.

He had never flinched from dealing with unpleasant necessities, learning early in life that pests must be ruthlessly eliminated before they got out of hand. With the tip of his shoe, he pushed aside the broken, gelatinous mess that had been a living creature just moments before, then placed the rock carefully back into its appointed space. Humming softly to himself, he took a pair of secateurs from his trouser pocket and began to methodically dead head the roses.

After a few minutes he heard her voice, calling his name, and he moved further down the garden to avoid answering. But it came again, more insistent this time; she must have come outside, looking for him. Blind rage began to boil up, and the neat *snip, snips* of his secateurs became rough and brutal. She called again. A voice inside his skull began screaming obscenities, until finally the noise became unbearable and he hissed under his breath; "Fuck off, you fat old bitch! For fuck's sake, can't you ever leave me alone?"

It took him a few moments to control the anger and modulate his voice back to its usual tone. Then he called levelly; "I'll be right in. Just dead-heading a few roses."

Shortly afterwards, Little Yarmouth's wolf turned and walked back through his garden, up toward the house. He'd come to a decision. He'd been more than patient with her for a very long time, but now she was becoming a real pest. It was time he took matters in hand; time to deal with her permanently. As he opened the back door, he was smiling.

Chapter 18 - Memories

It was getting late. The "snooze" button had taken care of two earlier wake up calls, but now a four legged alarm clock had decided it was time for Rosie to get up, and he was impossible to ignore.

Keeping her eyes closed, she dragged herself into a sitting position, and muttered; "Alright boy, I'm coming, I'm coming." Swinging her legs down onto the floor she moved her feet tentatively back and forth across the rug, searching for slippers. No luck; well, she'd just go barefoot. No way she was bending down.

Her head was pounding, and her mouth felt as if she'd spent the night chewing feathers. She opened her eyes slowly. Thank God there was no bright sunlight streaming in through the window. Then she saw the streaks of rain and wondered idly why it always seemed to rain on Mondays.

Gussie bounced across the bed and whined in her ear. "Alright Gus, I know you're hungry. I'm coming". He jumped off the bed with a thud and disappeared onto the landing.

After a moment, she stood up slowly and reached for her robe. Better let him out first, she thought. Then a cup of coffee – that'll help. Her eyes turned to the clock radio and, instantly, her slow motion morning leapt into top gear. The clock's digital face was glowing 8:55 a.m.!

Rosie beat her personal record for showering and dressing, and made it to work only five minutes late. She skipped breakfast; no time and no appetite, thanks to last night's bottle of wine. No walk for Gussie either, and his eyes had followed her reproachfully as she raced out the front door.

At nine-forty Rosie was sitting behind her desk, struggling to focus her thoughts on the day ahead. Father

Matthews had left a draft thank-you letter and list of recipients in front of the Remington, so she guessed this was the first order of business. So many names! Who'd have thought it took that many people to get Saturday's celebrations off the ground?

The phone shrilled and, closing her eyes, she picked it up quickly. "St. Judes' parish office" she said softly – even her own voice aggravated the headache. It came as a surprise to hear Liz's familiar drawl.

"Mornin', Rosie. Just lettin' ya know, I'm not comin' in today. My back's just terrible."

"Gosh, I'm sorry to hear that Liz. But I can't say I'm surprised; you shouldn't have been on your feet all day Saturday, you know."

"Couldn't let Father down, now could I? And it did all go off amazin', even if I say so myself."

"Yes, it was a wonderful day. And Bishop Doyle seems very nice – I think he's going to be well liked." After the Mass, their new shepherd had mingled enthusiastically with his flock, and St. Jude's parishioners were easily pleased.

"Did I tell ya he came over and thanked me for all my hard work, Rose? Said I kept the church *sparklin'*. His very words, *sparklin'*."

"Yes, you mentioned it on Saturday, Liz." Rosie couldn't help grinning. The bishop's got himself a real fan, she thought irreverently, even if he does "put his pants on, one leg at a time."

"Well, gotta go, Rose. I'm seeing Doc Drucker at ten. Tell Father I'm not sure when I'll be back in – best if he don't expect me for a couple of days. Bye now."

Looks like Burger Burger's all set for an up-tick in sales, Rosie thought wickedly. "Okay, Liz. Take care of yourself, and don't be rushing back too soon. We'll rub along fine for a while."

She turned back to the thank you letters, but Father Matthews' repetitious phrases of appreciation couldn't hold her attention, and she soon slipped into a mental rewind of the weekend's events.

Saturday had been a lovely day, and she had been kept busy enough to avoid thinking of David the whole time. Before leaving for choir practice she called Lucy, planning to invite her over for Sunday evening. She was eager to share John's information, and also figured she would need quite some time to gently broach the idea of an exhumation. But nobody had picked up at the Curtis house, so she reluctantly left a message asking Lucy to get in touch.

The Confirmation Tea had fizzled out with the bishop's departure, (promptly at six as per his itinerary) and Rosie was home by six thirty, facing the prospect of an evening alone with her thoughts. That had propelled her to load Gussie into the car, and head down to the lake. They walked miles along the shore, with the dog exuberantly retrieving every piece of driftwood she threw into the water. Exhaustion ensured a good night's rest for both of them on Saturday night.

It was Sunday before David finally caught up with her. After Mass, she spent the afternoon working in the garden, but evening found her at a definite loose end. She had been surprised not to hear back from Lucy on Saturday, and quite disappointed when there was still no response on Sunday. Rosie began to realise how anxious she was to prove Tony had been murdered, and then safely hand everything over to the police. Unfortunately, the first steps in that process depended on Lucy's co-operation.

Not to be discouraged, she had picked up the phone and called her aunt. For sure, Margaret would be keen to hear all the details of John's visit to the mortuary, and a good brainstorming session would cheer her right up.

But there was no reply there, either. Was no-one at home this weekend? Auntie Marg must have gone back to the cottage - out in the woods where there was no land line. And like her niece, she had no interest in having a cell phone.

So, in desperation, she had turned on the T.V. But, after a boring hour of flicking idly from one channel to the next, her mind everywhere but on the screen, she capitulated at last. It was time to lay some personal ghosts.

She had gone upstairs to the guest room, opened the wardrobe, and pulled out the tattered cardboard box holding her wedding album. Sitting on the bed, she had slowly turned the pages.

It had been a beautiful wedding. She lingered over the photo of David, her mother and herself; he was holding her hand and she had her arm around her mom. Mary had counselled that at thirty-seven, Rosie was a bit past the age of princess gowns and voluminous tulle veils, and she had agreed. Together they chose an A-line wedding gown of ivory lace with a chapel train, and a rose-strewn, wide-brimmed hat. "I looked quite glamorous" she said to Gussie, busily nosing around the album box on the bed.

The memories had begun crowding in and this time, instead of pushing them away, she let them come. Those first years in Vancouver had been filled with happiness; David joined the Yacht Club, she joined the Bach Choir. Their lives had been filled with friends and travel.

David was an excellent dentist and his practice had expanded steadily. Strange that she had married a dentist, having such a fear of them. But he was so gentle, so kind; all his patients loved him. And she'd loved him, and believed in his love for her. He'd kept up that pretence right to the bitter end; until the very day he disappeared.

Then came the scandal, the debts, the police. She was interviewed again and again. For the longest time, they suspected her. Followed her, because they were sure

David wasn't dead and she knew where he was. Certain that she also knew where he'd taken all the money from his investment scam.

Everything she owned was sold to pay back the people he had cheated, but most of his victims were still left with virtually nothing. She got hate mail and threatening phone calls; her tires were slashed, windows broken. Eventually the police gave up on her and said she could leave British Columbia. She slunk home to her mother and stayed out of sight, existing on Prozac and sleeping pills for a whole miserable year.

By now the tears were flowing fast and she was having trouble keeping her emotions in check. Gussie had whined and looked at her anxiously, his ears drooping. "It's all right, boy" she gasped out, before hurrying into the bathroom. Then she closed the door and howled.

When she had finally cried herself to exhaustion, she went downstairs and pulled a bottle of wine from the fridge. Waving it high in the air, she choked out; "That's it, David! I'm celebrating! I don't care if you're alive or dead. I don't care if you're rotting at the bottom of a lake, or off somewhere living the high life. Seven years, and I'm done." She had opened the bottle and taken a few gulps. "So, here's to me. TO ME, you bastard!" Taking another long swig she twirled around, tears streaming down her face. "Hey everybody, look at me, I'm a widow! The law says he's dead. David's DEAD and I don't care!"

Then she had caught sight of Gussie, watching her from the kitchen doorway, one paw raised pathetically. Even from across the room, she could see he was trembling. Filled with remorse, she got down on the floor and called him to her. "C'mon boy, it's all right. I'm sorry, I'm sorry for carrying on like this; I'm such a bitch." She had hugged him and, easily comforted, his tail was soon wagging as he licked her face over and over.

After a while she had stood up, taken a glass from the kitchen cabinet and, bottle in hand, had gone into the living room. With Gussie beside her on the couch, Rosie had steadily worked her way through the wine, finally closing the door on her life with David.

Now, despite being alone in the office, her face flushed with embarrassment over her behaviour of the previous night. She cringed at the thought of all that raw emotion, that total loss of self-control, even as a less conventional part of her psyche whispered that the melt-down was a necessary catharsis.

Immersed in these thoughts, she failed to notice a large black and white shape padding in from the hallway, until it levitated and landed with a *thump* on her desk. Purring loudly, Donny bumbled his way across the stacks of paper and envelopes, intent on getting her attention with his usual strategy of affectionate head butts.

Rosie gave the cat a quick hug, then firmly deposited him back on the floor. He re-appeared instantly on the desk, this time to begin kneading his paws up and down on her pile of finished letters.

She stroked him absently. "Yes, Donny. I know you're hungry. You'll just have to wait a little while longer . I want to finish a few more of these letters first."

She went back to her work, but Donny was persistent. He continued purring and butting her face and, when she still ignored him, he took to swatting the paper in her typewriter. Finally, after he made several abortive attempts to lay across the keyboard, Rosie capitulated. "Alright, you win, let's get to the kitchen." Then she leant forward and whispered into his ear; "And it's probably lucky for me that Liz's isn't in there to spot my giant hang-over." Donny opened his big blue eyes as wide as he could, and winked up at her slowly.

Chapter 19 – The Committee meets Again

Rosie's session with Donny was the highpoint of her morning. Apart from his sister, she didn't see another living creature the whole time. The rain continued to pour down, proving an effective deterrent to anyone who might have otherwise dropped in for coffee and a chat.

There was no sign of Father Matthews. When Rosie and Donny went along the corridor to the rectory kitchen she called out to announce her presence, then tapped on his office door. But silence prevailed, and when she peeked inside she saw a vacant chair and tidy desk.

'This is getting more like the *Marie Celeste* every minute' she said to herself, wandering into the kitchen to feed an increasingly vocal Donny. Seel had not deigned to accompany her brother on his morning rounds, but materialised instantly the can opener went into action. Typically, she then ignored the plate of food Rosie placed in front of her, opting instead to sit on the countertop and stare haughtily at her benefactor. Her disdainful glances indicated precisely where a church secretary ranked, in her feline view of the rectory hierarchy.

Having fed the cats and been put well in her place, Rosie went back to the office and concentrated on finishing Father Matthew's letters. Around eleven the phone rang, for only the second time that morning. She snatched it up. Her headache was slowly improving, but sudden, high pitched noises still felt like red-hot pins being pushed into her skull.

"St. Judes' parish office" she announced in subdued tones.

"Hello Rose." Father's sounding very chipper today, she thought. "It's Father Matthews here. How are you, today? Recovered from all our excitement, I hope?"

"Yes, Father, pretty much. Everything certainly went off well, don't you think?"

"It did indeed. I believe we all played our parts to perfection." There was a pause, then the priest cleared his throat. "Is Mrs. Curtis about? I need a quick word."

Rosie couldn't resist a little smile; she was about to make his day. "No, I'm afraid not, Father. She called in first thing to say her back was really bad, and she was off to the doctor. Probably won't be in for a few days." She visualised the gleam creeping into his eyes, as he realised he had a few days reprieve from "healthy" eating. "Is there anything I can help with?"

"No, thank you Rose. I was just calling to say that I won't be back in time for lunch. But I'm sorry to hear she's under the weather. I'll phone her later; we must make sure she doesn't hurry back before she's fully recovered."

Rosie was grinning broadly now; she was enjoying this immensely. "Yes, of course. But what about your meals, Father?"

"No problem at all," he replied airily. "Don't you worry about me. I can boil an egg and make a sandwich or two. And, as it happens, today's already taken care of. That's why I was calling. Pastor Davis has kindly invited me to lunch at his home; his wife's famous for her fried chicken, you know."

Ah yes, thought Rosie, all is made plain. Today's the second Monday of the month; Ecumenical Group meeting in Goderich. I'm really losing track of things.

"In fact...." the priest was continuing in an increasingly jocular manner; ".....the last time I lunched with Caleb and Ruth, I was too full to eat any supper. They believe the Lord's bounty is meant to be enjoyed."

'Translation; very big servings.' Rosie was instantly ashamed of the ungenerous thought the moment it leapt into her head. In a small voice she said; "That's a real bit of luck, Father. Will you be back this afternoon?"

"Probably not before you leave, Rose. I've got some hospital visits lined up, and then I'm going to call on the Murcheson's."

"Oh, right. I hope they're doing better." Twenty year old Pete Murcheson had crashed his motorcycle on the holiday weekend, and his parents had taken him off life support two days later. The funeral had been last Thursday. That was Rosie's next task; tackling the mammoth pile of Murcheson memorial donations, swept aside on Friday in favour of Confirmation preparations.

"Yes, we can only pray for that. But it's a terrible thing to lose a child, Rose. Life is never the same….." his voice faded away, seemingly at a loss for words.

He's such a caring man, Rosie thought, waiting for him to continue. But when he stayed silent, she said gently; "Well, I'll see you on Wednesday then, Father. I've fed the cats. Is there anything else you'd like me to do, today?"

"No, thank you. Mrs. Curtis has everything in such apple-pie order that I'm sure we'll manage until her return. God bless now, have a good day."

"You too, Father. Thanks, bye for now."

The rest of the morning passed slowly, uninterrupted by phone calls, visitors or cats. By noon, all the letters were on Father Matthew's desk awaiting his signature and Rosie was scurrying, head down, across the church parking lot.

It was still teeming, and now the wind had picked up making it difficult to keep her umbrella from blowing inside out. And to make matters worse, in her rush that morning she had left her rain jacket hanging in the hall, and the short dash to the car resulted in a soaking. 'Déjà vu' she thought, slamming the car door shut in a shower of raindrops. 'Just like the day I went into Lucy's basement; that was a wet Monday, too.'

To make up for her neglect that morning, she had planned to take Gussie for a long lunchtime walk, but he wasn't impressed by the weather and was soon pulling towards home. Unusually for a hound, he had an odd aversion to getting his paws wet. So it was just once around the block, then back for a leisurely lunch together.

Rosie was not looking forward to the afternoon and, ignoring her conscience, made little effort to get back on time. After all, nothing much was happening and the office was really dreary today. So she was mortified when, ten minutes late, she pulled into the parking lot and spotted a burly figure huddled close to the office door, rain streaming off the sides of an oversized black umbrella.

She drew in close to the church, wound down her window and shouted; "Hang on, I'll be right there." The figure lifted the umbrella slightly and, with a frisson of fear, she saw Dave Mason's bald head and long black raincoat. She looked intently at his outline; was this figure she had seen throwing Tony's body down the basement stairs? The odds were one in three that she was staring at a killer.

A cold sensation in the pit of her stomach made Rosie want to keep going; to just drive straight home and lock all her doors. The last thing she should do was be alone in an empty building with a suspected murderer. Then, the rain beating in through her open window brought her to her senses. Dave couldn't know the rectory was empty, and why should he want to harm her anyway? He didn't know of her investigations into Tony Wesley's life and death. Plus, if her suspicions were unfounded, how would she ever explain herself next time they met? She'd be so embarrassed. Social convention trumped fear, and she pulled reluctantly into the nearest parking spot.

As she gathered up her purse and umbrella, she saw him heading across the lot toward her. She was suddenly afraid again, and had to fight the urge to turn on the ignition and drive away fast. Dave reached for her door, and tugged it open. "Here Rose, duck under" he shouted over the wind blustering about. "This umbrella's built for four" and, with a firm grip, he held it over them both as she scrambled out. He grasped her arm tightly and, side by side, they half ran back up the path.

At the door her wet fingers fumbled with the keys, and she struggled to speak calmly "Dave, I'm so sorry I'm late. Were you waiting long?" The office door finally swung back and she hurried inside, relieved to put some space between them.

He stood at the door, shaking the worst of the water off his umbrella. "No, I'd only been here a few minutes. Figured you wouldn't be long." Was it her imagination, or did his voice sound threatening?

She propped her unopened umbrella in the boot tray, and hung her rain jacket up behind the door. Turning, she forced a smile. "Well, take that wet coat off and sit down. I'll pour us both a coffee." 'Must keep everything light' she said to herself.

But he didn't move. "No thanks, Rose. I can't stop. Mom took a bad turn on Saturday and I can't be gone too long."

"Oh Dave; nothing serious, I hope?" Fear took a back seat to concern. Rosie was fond of Dave's mom, who had been a special friend of her own mother. It was hard to imagine the feisty Luella Mason being laid low by anything less than the bubonic plague.

"I don't know but, as usual, she's refusing to see anyone. I tried to get her to go to Urgent Care today but she wouldn't have it."

How could a murderer be so concerned about his mom? She began to relax; this was just the same old Dave. John was right, no way was Dave Mason a psychotic arsonist. "There's been a nasty summer flu going round. Do you think that's it?"

"Well, she's been throwing up a lot and… you know…" he blushed, "the other as well."

Rosie found his embarrassment rather endearing; the result, she supposed of being a life-long bachelor. And how much of that situation was down to the formidable Luella, she wondered. Then thinking again of her own mother, who had been anything but formidable, she asked; "Your mom hasn't had any chest pains, has she?"

Dave looked miserable. "She hasn't said. I tell you Rose, I don't know whether I'm coming or going. It's impossible to make her do anything, you know that."

Rosie did know. Dave's mother was another of Little Yarmouth's business matriarchs; cut from a similar, if more kindly, cloth as Clodagh Wesley. She had handled the office side of the Funeral Home all her married life, and was still a force to be reckoned with.

"You could go down to the Drug Mart and have a word with the pharmacist," she suggested. "They'd be able to recommend something for the vomiting and diarrhoea. That might be all she needs."

Her words had an immediate effect. Dave seized enthusiastically on the opportunity for practical action. "What a great idea, Rosie. You're a genius; yes, maybe that's all she needs. And the pharmacist will know about this flu that's going round." He picked up his umbrella. "I'll head down there right now. Thanks, Rosie." He opened the door and started to leave. "See you later."

All fear forgotten now, Rosie called after him; "Dave? Why did you come by, anyway?"

He paused on the step for a minute, then came back inside. "God, I'm so worried about mom that it went right out of my head." He pulled a fat envelope from his inside pocket. "Memorial gifts from Pete Murcheson's visitation" he said, laying the envelope in front of her and topping it with a receipt book. "A lot of those donations are in cash, I guess his motorcycle buddies aren't into cheques, so I'll need you to sign for it." He shrugged apologetically. "Sorry about that, but anything over a hundred dollars, you know…"

Rosie picked up a pen and scribbled her signature. "No problem, Dave." She handed the book back to him. "Can't be too careful with cash around."

"No, but I always feel bad asking when it's people I've known forever." He glanced down at the signature. "I think your pen's run out, Rosie. Here, use this." He took a pen out of his pocket and passed it to her with the book.

Rosie smiled and signed for the second time. "That's a nice pen" she said, rolling the elegant blue cylinder over in her hand.

"Yes, it's one of those Astoria's we ordered for the loot bags." He pointed to one side. "Look, the printing shows up really well."

Rosie peered at the gilt lettering. *John Galt High School. 1950 – 2000. A half century of excellence.* "Yes, you can see every word; and it writes beautifully." She leant over to hand it back. "That reminds me; there's a committee meeting tonight. Are you going?"

"No, not with mom so sick. Dougie can give our report. He's got the posters and all the promotional stuff, anyway. It'll just be show'n'tell this time, so he doesn't need me."

Rosie gestured again with the pen; "Don't forget your pen, Dave."

"You keep it, Rosie. It's just a sample; they sent us a whole bunch." He went to the door and retrieved his umbrella. "Thanks again for the advice. I'd better get going, don't want to leave mom too long. Bye now."

"Bye, Dave. Hope your mom's better soon."

"Me, too." He gave her a quick smile and stepped outside, opening the umbrella as he went.

"Oh, and don't forget to call Ellen Fish with your regrets. We don't want *Chair* Anderson getting all bent out of shape, now do we?"

As he headed down the path the umbrella moved up and down in a gesture she hoped was a farewell salute, not a comment on Dave's opinion of Pete Anderson.

She poured herself a coffee and stood at the window, watching the rain. How silly to be afraid of Dave Mason, it was ludicrous to think he'd spent his youth burning down buildings. No, she was crossing him off her list; the killer had to be either Pete Anderson or Bill Gifford. Her money was on Bill Gifford, everyone in town knew he'd tried to drown his wife in their pool last year.

Having run out of reasons to procrastinate, Rosie went back to her desk and opened Mason's envelope. She counted the cash; five hundred and twenty seven dollars! Better leave that in the safe until Wednesday, when she could check it over with Father Matthews.

The wall safe in Rosie's office was the direct result of a burglary on the night of the previous year's Christmas Bazaar. Although only four hundred dollars and a few pieces of church plate had been taken, it had been a frightening wake-up call for everyone. "A sign of the times," Father Matthews had said, watching sadly as one beefy electrician installed a building-wide alarm system, and a second fitted the wall safe.

When the Finance Committee Chair was asked to suggest a picture for security camouflage, Patrick Myles had chosen a brightly coloured print of Moses holding up the Ten Commandment tablets. On the day he hung it in her office, Rosie had wondered aloud if this choice represented a last-ditch effort at dissuading any would-be safe cracker. Her comment had been met with stony silence; Clodagh Wesley's son-in-law was not known for his sense of humour.

Now she lifted the technicolour art-work off the wall, opened the safe and locked Mason's envelope securely inside. Replacing the picture (why did it always remind her of a hockey player hoisting the Stanley Cup?) she went over to the filing cabinet and pulled out a bulging folder. She sighed; for heaven's sake, it looked like *hundreds* of Mass cards and memorial donations needing receipts. The continuous roll receipts were in a box under her desk so, puffing, she dragged that around to the front, and threaded the topmost receipt into the Remington's platen. It was going to be a very long, dull afternoon.

And so it was. The hours crawled by, with not even phone call to relieve Rosie's ennui. The all-pervading silence was broken only by her typewriter's industrious clatter, and the rattle of rain beating against the window. By four o'clock she had finished typing all the receipts and torn them off the roll. Too late to start on the memorial schedule now, she thought. I'll just do the receipt signing, then finish everything up on Wednesday.

No matter how you cut it, signing fifty-seven receipts (thankfully, not *hundreds*) is a chore, and Rosie's hand was quite cramped when she finally laid down her pen. She looked up longingly at the clock; 4.24 p.m.

I've been so bored today, she thought, I'm almost looking forward to the reunion meeting. Everywhere had been deathly quiet following Friday and Saturday's excitement; rather like the let-down after Christmas. And then, David's anniversary….. No, stop right there; she gave herself a mental slap. You've finished with all that, stop picking at the scab.

She stood up, covered the typewriter and began tidying her desk. As she did so, her eye fell again on Dave Mason's pen. She picked it up; let's hope all the loot bag stuff is as nice as this, she mused. But what was nagging at the back of her mind? She turned the pen over in her hand. The colour? The printing? Maybe it was just that she'd seen it at the last meeting? No; if memory served, she'd been a little out of things, when the samples were passed around. So what was it? It was like having a phrase on the tip of your tongue but being unable to find the words.

Unexpectedly, she started to shiver. The temperature was plummeting, and all thoughts of the pen disappeared as she watched the window glass begin slowly frosting over.

Well, I'm not surprised, she thought. I've been so wrapped up in myself this weekend that I've barely given Tony a thought. "I suppose you want to remind me of my priorities," she said aloud, her breath hanging in the air like white smoke.

She turned and looked all round the room, but couldn't see any manifestation of a ghostly visitor. So she addressed the empty space; "I'm sorry Tony, I've been a bit distracted these last few days. But, I've made some real progress; I think we're almost there."

In response it got even colder. Numbed, she gasped for breath but there was none; the room had been sucked dry of air. Summoning the last of her strength she stumbled toward the door but, as she reached for her jacket, it leapt off the hook, flew across the room and landed in a heap by the sacristy door.

As soon as it hit the floor the room began to warm, and she was able to catch her breath again. 'I guess he's made his point' she said to herself, between gasps. She glanced up at the clock; it still read 4:24 p.m.

As normality re-asserted itself, she began to feel annoyed. "Well, wasn't that the perfect end to a perfect day?" she grumbled, snatching up her bag, umbrella and jacket. Her sympathy for Tony was fast evaporating and, as she left, she slammed the office door behind her angrily.

Without bothering to put up her umbrella, she ran pell-mell through the rain toward the Buick. Dragging the car door open, she threw everything onto the front passenger seat, and spat out furiously; "For heaven's sake! As if I don't have enough on my plate without a ghost throwing temper tantrums!"

*   *   *   *

Although it did not start well, the reunion meeting ended on an uncharacteristically lively note.

There were not enough members present to make a quorum, and Peter Anderson was so annoyed by the poor attendance that he was even more of an officious bully than usual. Ellen Fish took the brunt of his temper; as committee secretary it was her unenviable task to read the list of regrets, and also to try and explain why Sharon Lewis and Carol Hunter were A.W.O.L.

"That's two meetings now that Mrs. Lewis has missed without notification, Ms. Fish." The Chair fixed a gimlet eye on the unfortunate secretary, as if Sharon Lewis's absence was somehow a dereliction of duty on Ellen's part. "I think we may safely assume she has reneged on her commitment. Please advise her that her participation is at an end."

Ellen whispered "Yes, Chair."

"And…. Mrs. Hunter?" A faint flush of colour spread across Anderson's face. Rosie made a mental note to pass his discomfiture on to Carol; she'd get a kick out of it, for sure.

The secretary squirmed in her seat. "I don't know, Chair."

"Well, this just isn't good enough Ms. Fish. As secretary, you should be in contact with all our members immediately prior to every meeting."

For one awful moment it looked as if Ellen might burst into tears, but she recovered herself. "I'll do that next time, Chair."

"A bit late in the day, if I may say so. There are now only two meetings remaining on our calendar, before the Reunion is upon us."

Rosie glanced around the table at the three other members present. They all looked as if that day couldn't come soon enough.

Harvey Schnurr had sent his regrets; Rosie had heard on the grapevine that he wouldn't be attending any further meetings. 'Guess the peasants didn't appreciate his *expertise* enough,' she said to herself. His condescending attitude to the town wasn't going down well in John Galt's staff room, either. And Carol? Although Rosie had phoned twice about their room project, she hadn't responded. Not a peep since their unfortunate heart-to-heart in the Creamery. Oh well, I've done most of the work by myself, she thought, so finishing it solo won't be a problem.

Their esteemed leader was expounding again. "As this will be a very short meeting due to the many absences," he again fixed a steely glare on Ellen, "I propose that we dispense with a break and just work straight through. Any objections?"

A murmured "no" rippled round the table, and Dougie Ferguson reached across it for a doughnut. As usual, the table was heaped with his largesse.

"Good. Ms. Fish; Correspondence and, in the absence of Mr. Scott, the Financial Report, please."

Head down, Ellen whispered her way through both reports, casting frequent looks sideways as if to make sure she was performing to the Chair's satisfaction.

"Thank you, Ms. Fish. As we are two members short of a quorum, we can't move to accept the Financial Reports, until the next meeting. Hopefully by then, our numbers will once again be up to strength." Another baleful glance at the unfortunate Secretary. "So, moving on to the Activity Reports. Ms. DeGroot? Updates on the dance, please."

The willowy Elaine stood up and handed round a stack of neatly printed sheets. Expenses to date were clearly itemised, as was projected income from ticket sales. Rosie was surprised to see that thirty-four tickets had already been sold. It looked like the dance was on track to be a highly successful fund-raiser.

While Elaine was reviewing the minutiae of her report, Rosie was trying to think why she looked so familiar. It was the Chair's accolade; "Excellent report Ms. Degroot, very efficient," that finally jogged her memory. Elaine DeGroot was John's office manager at the practice;

the person he always referred to as "our frighteningly efficient Ms. DeGroot."

Dougie was up next. As Dave had predicted, their report was just show'n'tell. Posters, pens and coasters were handed round to general approval, and other items for the loot bags discussed. No accolade for the dishevelled Dougie, however. Just a withering glance at the jelly stain on his golf shirt and a taciturn; "Thank you, Mr. Ferguson. And now, will you enlighten us as to your plans for the effective distribution of these exceedingly vivid posters?" The poster design had not been Pete Anderson's choice.

Dougie remained standing, his ears starting to glow red. He mumbled something to the effect that he and Dave were working on that, then sat down abruptly.

God! That Pete Anderson is real piece of work, Rosie thought angrily. Spiteful, too. Yes, I can see him skulking round in the dark, setting fires in revenge for imagined slights or insults. She glared at him, and he dropped his gaze. That's right, look away you creep. You and Gifford are neck and neck on my list, now.

But the Chair had not finished with Dougie. "Really? I should have thought your plans would be well in hand by now. You are the publicity and promotion coordinators after all, and it is your responsibility….."

"Oh, for God's sake Anderson, get off that damn high horse before I push you off!"

Rosie's head swivelled round so fast she nearly cricked her neck. Alan Price had pushed his chair back, got to his feet and was standing with a sheet of paper in his hand.

"Before you call on me, *Chair,* here's my report on the sports events. Everything is organised, and I'm perfectly capable of making sure it stays that way. And you'll have to trust me on that one, because I won't be attending any more of your damn meetings." And with that, he walked over to Ellen, handed her his report and left.

There was total silence in the room. Several slow minutes ticked by while Anderson collected himself. Then he cleared his throat and managed to squeak out; "Mrs. Rowe's report on her room project is the last on the Agenda, so after that I think we'll call it a night." He looked down at the table and gestured that Rosie should rise. "Mrs. Rowe?"

Rose got up obediently, and gave a brief rundown on the items most recently lent to the fifties/sixties room project. Her report was soon finished but, as she sat down, she was overcome by an irresistible urge to poke the bear. She stood again.

"Just an idea for distributing posters, *Pete*"…Anderson looked up in annoyance at the familiarity and Rosie responded by smiling sweetly, "…..I think if all the members each take fifteen and commit to putting them all up, that'll take care of our distribution problem." She smiled at Dougie. "Okay, Dougie? If you think that's workable, I'll take mine and Carol's now. I can drop hers off to her anytime."

Elaine DeGroot chimed in; "That's a great idea. Rosie. Doug, give me fifteen as well, will you?"

Dougie was already counting posters into piles. He smirked at Anderson. "How about you, *Pete*? Fifteen, or do you think the Chair should take thirty?"

Seeing that his control of the meeting had slipped away Anderson reddened, then said stiffly; "Motion to adjourn?" Four hands shot up. "Well, that takes care of everything for tonight, so I'll see you all back here on the twenty-fourth. Hopefully, with a better attendance." He glanced meaningfully at Ellen Fish, but she ignored him and looked down the table.

"I'll take my posters tonight as well, Dougie" she said. "I think they're just lovely."

Chair Anderson gathered up the papers scattered on the table in front of him, shoved them into his briefcase and, without a word to anyone, stalked from the room.

Elaine sniggered; "Oh dear, I think we've upset him," and Rosie, Dougie and Ellen all joined in the general laughter.

"Ladies, please, give me a hand with these." Dougie waved at the piles of goodies heaped on plates in the middle of the table. "Come on, you can't all be dieting. Help me out; here, take some home." And he started putting doughnuts, muffins and cookies into empty pastry boxes.

"Well alright, just to help you out" Ellen said hesitantly, taking a box of doughnuts as she passed him on her way to the door. "Mom's really fond of your doughnuts, Dougie. Thanks; see you in two weeks."

"Not for me" Elaine said, "I'm not into all that sugary stuff." Dougie's face fell; Rosie had long suspected he had a bit of a crush on Elaine.

"You could take some into the practice tomorrow," Rosie piped up. "John likes a muffin with his coffee." She turned to Dougie. "They'd stay fresh until tomorrow, wouldn't they Doug?"

"Oh yeah, for sure. These apple muffins stay moist for ages."

Elaine sighed. "Okay, okay; *waste not, want not,* my old granny used to say. Give me a couple of muffins, Dougie; who knows, I might make a few brownie points with the boss."

Now Dougie was looking at Rosie; "What about you, Rose?"

Rosie knew that whatever she took, she would eat over the next twenty-four hours. No point pretending to herself that she'd freeze anything; one sugary bite and it would be "goodbye, diet." I'll take a box and drop it in a bin on the way home, she thought. That way I won't hurt

Dougie's feelings. "Sure, Dougie I'll take a few." It wasn't hard to sound enthusiastic.

He picked up the last box, then turned to her apologetically. "Sorry Rose, the bottom's out of this box. You haven't got a bag or anything, have you?"

After a moment of feeling foolish that she'd embarked on this pointless charade, Rosie remembered the fold-up plastic shopping bag she always carried in her jacket pocket. "Yes, I do" she said brightly. "Never go anywhere without a shopping bag. Got to save the planet, you know."

She went over to the coat rack, and ran her hand around the inside of her jacket pocket. No, wrong pocket, just some tissues and a dog biscuit and……something caught between her nails and fingertips. What on earth is it? She pulled her hand out and frowned down at a thin, silvery piece of metal.

When she had picked it up in the basement at Veteran's Avenue, she hadn't been able to place what it was. But now, she recognised it instantly. It was a pen clip from an Astoria pen, just like the one Dave had given her this afternoon. Now she'd seen a whole pen, she realised the design of the clip was quite distinctive.

Automatically, she reached into her other pocket for the shopping bag, and passed it wordlessly to Dougie. Her mind was racing. There was no way that either Tony or Lucy would have had an Astoria pen; only a committee member would be carrying one around. With a shiver, she knew that it was someone from the committee that had gone down those basement stairs and, effectively, that let Bill Gifford off the hook. Here, in her hand, was the final proof that Tony's killer was Pete Anderson or…she didn't want to think about this….Dave Mason.

"Are you alright, Rosie?" Dougie had come up behind her and taken her arm. "You look as if you're about to keel over." He pulled a chair round and sat her down gently. "I'll get you some water."

But all Rosie wanted to do now was get home and organise her thoughts. "No, thanks, Doug, it's nothing, really." He looked unconvinced; I'll have to do better than that, she thought. "It's this diet I'm on. Not enough protein and I think I missed some carbs today, as well." She got up and went back to the table. "Maybe I'll eat a muffin on the way home."

Dougie had wrapped a few muffins and cookies in napkins, and was putting the neat little packages into Rosie's plastic bag. "That's a real good idea. Are you sure you're okay to drive, though?"

Rosie pulled on her jacket and said firmly; "Oh, yes, I'm just fine now, thanks anyway." Then, lifting the bag she shook it gently. "And thanks a million for these." Not wanting to linger she started across the room, but then thought her haste looked a bit dismissive. Dougie only wanted to help. So she half-turned, and called over her shoulder; "Thanks again, Dougie. Take care; see you next time," before hurrying through the door.

Within minutes she was driving slowly towards home, the bag with its mouth-watering little packages lying on the seat beside her. She concentrated hard, keeping her hands on the wheel and her eyes on the road, but her mind was not so easily controlled. Annoyingly, it kept returning to the bag and its delectable contents.

She was halfway home when her will power finally gave out. Reaching across the seat, she made a quick exploratory grab, and snagged a giant peanut butter cookie. "What the hey" she said aloud. "I've had quite a shock. And in the absence of hot, sweet tea, I think a peanut butter cookie will set me up quite nicely."

Chapter 20 – Social Encounters

By morning the rain had stopped, but the sky was still overcast and the temperature unseasonably cool. And that was just fine with Rosie, who loathed hot, sticky weather, having always preferred bundling up to stripping down.

Breakfast was over, (it didn't take long to eat a bowl of lo-cal. cereal with a half-cup of one percent) and now she was skimming through last week's Clarion.

In his report the previous night, Dougie had said the first reunion ad was in, and Rosie was curious to see what kind of deal Willie Robertson had given them. The canny old publisher was notoriously tight-fisted, and although he had promised the committee a "two-for-one" deal, she wasn't expecting much.

Her expectations were not misplaced. Listening to Dougie, she had wondered why she hadn't already spotted the ad, (Rosie always read the Clarion cover to cover). Now she knew why. It was tucked away on one side of the Classifieds, squeezed between "Help Wanted" and "Farm Equipment." The end result was that, unless you were researching employment opportunities for chicken pluckers, or stood in dire need of a disc harrow, you wouldn't be adding the upcoming John Galt Reunion Weekend to your calendar any time soon.

"I just hope we didn't pay the going rate for that ad" she said to Gussie, who looked up eagerly at the sound of her voice. Having given up begging for today's non-existent toast, he had been dozing peacefully while awaiting his morning walk. Now, after paying careful attention to Rosie's words he concluded that, as she was not talking about either food or the great outdoors, whatever she was saying was of no great importance to him. He laid his head on his paws, closed his eyes and went back to sleep.

Rosie finished her orange juice and contemplated the day ahead. She always looked forward to Tuesday. It was the one day she kept strictly for herself; no chores, just whatever took her fancy. Sometimes she went into Goderich to window shop or meet up with a girlfriend for lunch. Once in a while she'd take in a movie, or some local event. Whatever she did, Tuesday was always her day for R. and R.

But not today. The looming prospect of a dreary evening at Stella's *Colour Me Beautiful* party had sapped all her enthusiasm for a regular Tuesday expedition. After a half-hour spent vainly trying to whip up enthusiasm for the drive into Goderich, she decided to give up on leisure and just run errands this morning.

'Probably for the best, anyway' she said to herself. This plan would leave her free to spend all afternoon reviewing what she had learnt about Tony Wesley's life and death. She had to be well primed to tackle Marilyn tonight with that all-important question; why did the Robertson's believe Tony was responsible for young Martin's death?

She stood up and carried her bowl and mug over to the dish-washer. "C'mon Gus; time to get our show on the road" she said, rinsing the china before stacking it neatly inside. The beagle got lazily to his feet, stretched and followed her out into the hall.

There was no excuse to shorten their walk today. It wasn't raining, blowing or broiling hot, and Rosie knew both she and the dog needed to put a lot more effort into their daily exercise. Gussie, who hated rain, had been a total couch potato all the previous day, and Rosie was convinced she had put on at least three pounds overnight. Sadly, she had failed spectacularly in her resolve to pitch the fat-laden contents of her shopping bag into a bin on the way home.

To her shame, she had eaten three cookies and a muffin before reaching her driveway, followed by another muffin with her bed-time tisane. "It's always the same" she had groaned, brushing muffin crumbs from the front of her blouse. "I might as well just sign up for Carbaholics Anonymous. *My name's Rose and I'm a muffin addict!*"

Before going up to bed, she had taken the remaining cookies and muffins outside and set them prominently on the lid of her garbage bin in an open invitation to the neighbourhood raccoons. Maybe, after a midnight feast, those voracious little bandits would be stuffed enough they'd give her bird feeder a miss for one night.

Rose and Gussie walked for an hour, and it was mid-morning before they finally trailed back up the driveway. She was really tired, but resisted the temptation to sit down with a coffee; once sitting she wouldn't want to get up again.

She unclipped his leash and, in one movement, hung it back on the hall stand and lifted down her purse. The beagle panted toward the kitchen and his water bowl. "Won't be long, Gus," she called as she went back out through the front door. *He's so pooped he won't even notice I've gone,* she thought with a smile.

As she climbed into the Buick, Rosie ran through her mental list of errands. 'First stop the dry cleaners, then the bank, then the IGA to stock up on fruit and veg. Must get back on track with this diet.' Backing out, she spotted the pile of reunion posters on her rear seat. 'And I'll get a few of those posters up round town, while I'm at it.'

Driving along Cedar Street, she had a sudden inspiration. Carol should be at work today; she'd call round to Bronson Realty and drop off her fifteen posters. After all, she had volunteered for the committee, so putting up a few posters was the least she could do. Carol had ducked her long enough; what's the old saying? *If the*

292

mountain won't come to Mahomet, Mahomet must go to the mountain.

It was fairly quiet uptown, and she soon finished her running around. She left posters at every stop and also dropped one at the Pet Store, and the Clarion Office. So, as she pulled into the parking lot behind Bronson's Realty, she was congratulating herself on making a great start. Five down, ten to go, she thought; more than enough for today.

There was only one other car in the lot, and Rosie recognized it as Carol's old Honda. 'Good, looks like she's on her own in the office' she said to herself, as she went round to the front and pushed open the door.

The Real Estate office was in a converted two-up, two-down row house. The original front window had been replaced by a large bay, and most of its lower panes were covered by photos of properties for sale. All the interior walls had been knocked through, and there were two work stations on each side of the space. At the back was a glassed-in cubicle; private domain of Charles Bronson, broker, licensed R.E.C.O. agent and sole proprietor of Bronson's Real Estate Holdings.

Carol's desk was closest to the door, and she looked up with an expectant smile as Rosie entered. The smile faded when she saw who it was. "Oh, hi Rosie. I guess I know why you're here. Look, about last night...."

Rosie, who had no interest in listening to excuses, cut her off by laying the pile of posters on her desk. "That's okay; you weren't the only one missing, by a long shot. I just thought I'd better bring these posters by. We're all supposed to get fifteen up around town ASAP."

"No problem," Carol sounded relieved. "How'd it go, anyway?" She pushed a chair out with her foot. "Sit down and take the weight off, you look as if you've had a rough morning." Opening her desk drawer she rummaged through it, and produced a hair pick and mirror. With an approving glance at her own teased and lacquered reflection, she passed both items across the desk. "Here, you look as if you've been dragged through a hedge."

'And that's why you have so few women friends,' Rosie thought waspishly. She knew quite well what damp weather did to her unruly mop, and didn't need Miss Clairol over there criticising her frizzy coiffure. "No thanks, I'm good." She beamed across the desk. "Just the price I have to pay for natural curl. Saves a fortune on hairdressers, though."

But her barb sailed right over Carol's head. "So, anything interesting happen at the meeting?" she said casually, picking up an emery board. "Don't mind me, Rose." She began filing the nail on her index finger. "I've chipped a nail. All this pounding on a keyboard plays havoc with my manicure."

Rosie stared; surely this wasn't the real Carol? For some reason she seemed to be channelling a stereotypical dumb blonde secretary. Oh well, she thought giving a mental shrug, I guess if she wants to act like a bimbo, it's no-one's business but her own.

"As it happens, the meeting was quite interesting. For starters, there were only six of us, so Pete Anderson got in a snit right from the start. Then he took his temper out on everyone, especially poor Ellen, you know what a mouse she is, and finally Alan Price walked out." Rosie paused for effect.

"No" Carol breathed, visibly impressed. "God, I wish I'd seen that. Anderson's such a prick."

"Oh, and by the way, he couldn't mention your name without blushing. When he was quizzing Ellen about why you hadn't sent regrets, he went red as a beet." Despite being annoyed with her friend, Rosie couldn't help sharing that little gem. Anderson had treated Carol abominably and she deserved a little fun at his expense.

It had the desired result. Carol paused in her nail filing, and gave Rosie a huge smile. "Thus conscience does make cowards of us all," she quoted.

Hamlet, Rosie thought. Not such a dumb blonde, after all. With a grin, she took up the narrative again. "He was certainly a royal pain last night, that's for sure. Anyway, after Alan stormed out, we all took a bit of a stand and I think he got the message. Bit of a bloodless coup, you might say."

"Damn, trust me to miss all the fireworks." Carol laid down the emery board and picked up a small bottle of polish from the desk. Giving it a shake, she said, "I always keep a little bottle here for touch-ups. Ever thought of getting your nails done, Rose?"

Startled by her abrupt change of topic, Rosie stammered; "No, not my style; nail polish doesn't go well with gardening. I'm forever pulling weeds or pruning the shrubbery."

They were interrupted by the arrival of an unnaturally tanned man in a wrinkled beige suit. With one quick movement, Carol swept up her assorted grooming tools, and dropped them into a desk drawer. Sliding it shut, she said; "Hi, Charlie."

Any similarity between Charles Bronson and his famous tough-guy namesake was purely coincidental. The realtor was tall, thin and sported a wispy Fu Manchu goatee that definitely did not inspire confidence.

Now, he stuck out his hand, smiled and advanced on Rosie with all the focus of a rattler going after a baby chick. "Hi, there. Charlie Bronson. And what can we help you with today?"

"Sorry, Charlie. Rose isn't a client. She's on the high school reunion committee with me, and came in to leave these posters. I missed the meeting last night, because we had to work late."

Rosie caught the knowing look that passed between them. Oh dear, she thought, no lessons learned, then? She stood up, and shook Bronson's proffered hand. "Nice to meet you, Mr. Bronson." Picking up her purse she turned to Carol; "I'd better let you get back to work, Carol.

We can get together before the next meeting. I'll give you a call."

But as she started toward the door, Carol jumped up and dragged her purse out from under the desk.

"Hang on a minute, Rose." Bronson was already halfway to his cubicle and she called after him; "Charlie, I'm going for a break. There were a couple of messages; I sent the names and numbers to your e-mail." And without waiting for a reply, she fell in step behind Rosie and followed her outside.

The door closed behind them, and Carol gestured to a wrought iron bench under the bay window. Two large pots of geraniums stood on each side, Bronson's contribution to the Little Yarmouth Downtown Beautification program.

Lighting a cigarette, Carol took a long drag. "God, I've been gasping for a smoke" she said. "Alice, the other agent, is off today, so I've been stuck waiting for Charlie to come back, and it's strictly no-smoking in there." She gave Rosie a sharp look. "And before you get the wrong idea, we *were* working late last night." She inhaled again deeply.

Rosie had the feeling that Carol wanted to talk, so she leant back, stretched her legs out in front of her and prepared to lend a sympathetic ear. "How's the job going, then?" she asked. "It's been about a year, right?"

Carol leant back as well. "Ten months" she said. "It's alright, I guess. Charlie's okay, but Alice can be a bit of a bitch sometimes. Between you and me, I think she's got the hots for him."

Rosie screwed up her face. "Really? Well, no accounting for taste, I suppose. Maybe she sees you as competition."

"Could be. She isn't much in the looks department, I can tell you that." For a minute or two, neither of them spoke, until Carol finished her cigarette and stubbed it out in a geranium pot. "Listen Rose, I'm not an idiot. I know I was lucky to get this job, after all the upset at Anderson's law firm. But you know what men are like around me; at least Charlie hasn't got a wife at home to be giving him grief."

Rosie felt the same rush of sympathy that she felt at the meeting two weeks earlier. In her pragmatic way, she knew that Carol was her own worst enemy; stuck in a time-warp where she was perpetually eighteen years old. She still harboured the illusion that she only had to bat her eyelashes at a man and he'd come running; the hair, make-up, clothes all shouted "come and get me." Unfortunately, the only men that came running these days were unfaithful husbands and middle-aged roués.

So, she just murmured a non-committal; "Mm-mmm," then asked; "Divorced, or widowed?"

Carol paused in lighting her second cigarette. "What?"

"Charlie Bronson, You said he didn't have a wife. I wondered if he was divorced or widowed."

"Oh. Divorced three years ago. Just before he moved here from Waterloo." Carol picked a fragment of tobacco from her tongue. She hesitated, then said; "Look Rose, I think I owe you a bit of an apology."

Rosie sat up and gave her friend a searching look. "Why, what have you done?"

"That night in the Creamery; I was way out of line. Sorry, I behaved like a stupid kid."

"Is that all? Don't worry about it, we've all got sore spots. I didn't think any more of it." Blatantly untrue, of course. She'd spent half the night trying to figure out what lay behind Carol's melt-down. Oh well, she thought crossing her fingers, only a white lie and it's all in a good cause.

"I'd had such a crappy day; messed up some paperwork and Alice had really enjoyed giving me shit about it. And then that god-awful meeting." Carol threw her half-smoked cigarette down and ground it out with the toe of her shoe. "You know, if I could get off these frigging things I'd have enough money to lease a new car."

Rosie didn't answer. Even the most well-intentioned comment about smoking, made by a non-smoker, always came across as patronising. So she settled for; "Maybe...I don't really know."

"I'm going through a carton a week, even tried buying them on the rez. But that's such a hike, and then you've got to buy gas." She looked down at the ground. "And that's another reason I didn't go to the meeting."

Now Rosie was really surprised. Was Carol so short of money she couldn't afford to put gas in her car? "If gas was a problem, I could've given you a ride. Anytime, anywhere, you know that."

Carol laughed. "Thanks, Rosie. You're always so charmingly literal. No, it wasn't the gas. If you want the truth, I was just too embarrassed to go. Everyone knows about me and Pete Anderson, I've heard the sniggering going on. And, of course, I only joined to embarrass him, but that just backfired on me. Then there was that thing with Dougie, I can barely look him in the eye now, and to top it all off I made a real fool of myself with you."

"Dougie?" Rosie was incredulous. Surely Carol hadn't had a fling with Dougie?

Carol caught her expression. "Oh no, nothing like that," she said with a chuckle. "I'm not that desperate, yet. No, it's a bit of a long story; bottom line, I was trying to get back at Tony Wesley."

Now Rosie was all attention; what on earth had Carol done to Tony? She tried to sound disinterested. "Yes, you mentioned Tony that night in the Creamery. What actually happened between you? You said he ruined your life."

Carol opened her pack of cigarettes again, but thought better of it and closed the pack up. "He did ruin my life. He was like that, careless; no interest in what he did to other people. Just breezing along; ignoring all the wreckage he left behind." She opened her purse and took out a pack of tissues.

Rosie was surprised to see her wipe her eyes. Despite the intervening years, Tony's betrayal obviously still hurt. Well, she could relate to that.

Carol blew her nose and dropped the soggy tissue back in her purse. "I must say I'm surprised he stuck with Lucy," she went on. "I suppose getting her pregnant brought him to his senses a bit."

"But why did all that ruin your life?"

"Because I was so much in love with him I couldn't see straight. We went together for two years in high school. I used to spend hours writing *Mrs. Carol Wesley* over and over in my notebook. I convinced myself we were going to be married, and live in a huge house with a big fancy car. Everything was going to be wonderful, and then suddenly Lucy came along and he ditched me. Just like that. A few weeks before his Graduation Prom." She fished in her purse for tissues again.

"I couldn't let anyone see that I cared, so when Chris Hunter asked me to be his date, I went. Got drunk, had sex in the back of his car, and the next thing I knew I was pregnant. And he was such a loser; took off before Ian was a year old and left me to cope on my own."

Rosie found herself thinking that the more she knew about Tony Wesley, the less she liked him. Carol's description of him as "careless" sounded spot on; he'd always done just as he wanted, regardless of the consequences to anyone else. Her family could attest to that. No wonder Carol wanted revenge; she almost felt that way herself.

Carol had given in to her cravings and was trying to light a third cigarette, her hand shaking as she held the match. Finally, it caught and she inhaled gratefully. After a few minutes when she still hadn't spoken, Rosie tried a prompt.

"So, where does Dougie fit into all this?"

Carol heaved a sigh. "If only Tony and Lucy hadn't come back here," she said. "I saw them just before Christmas, walking down King like two love birds. It made me so mad, all I could think about was hurting them like they'd hurt me. Then, one evening round the end of May, I drove out to the rez. for cigarettes. And guess what? There was the bakery van, parked behind Three Eagles gas bar, and there was Tony, loading up boxes of smokes and booze. He was smuggling, Rose. Can you imagine? Dougie gives him a job out of the goodness of his heart, and that's how the bastard repaid him."

Oh dear, thought Rosie, so that's what he was doing at night, when Lucy thought he was working. Her mother's phrase, *once a toe-rag, always a toe-rag,* came back to mind. Aloud, she said; "You're right, Carol. That was a rotten thing to do. So I guess you told Doug what you'd seen."

"Damn right I did, the very next day. I wish I could say it was out of concern for him, but it was revenge, pure and simple. I wanted him to tell the police, or at the very least, fire the bastard. After all, if the police caught Tony with that stuff in the van, they'd think Dougie was involved."

And that was unimaginable. The Fergusons had been pillars of the community for three generations. Dougie's father, Fergal, had been a town councillor and elder at the Presbyterian church for years, until his early death from diabetes. And the shame of a police investigation would just about kill Dougie's mother.

When Carol didn't say any more, Rosie ventured; "So, what happened when you told him?"

"Well, he didn't say anything at first, and his face got so red that I thought he was having a heart attack. Then he wanted to know what time it was, when I saw Tony at Three Eagles; trying to figure out how come he still had the van, I suppose. Honestly Rose, I've never seen

Dougie in such a state. He started going on about how upset his mother would be if the police got involved; pacing back and forth like a caged animal."

Rosie shook her head in disbelief, wondering at how easily people like Tony (and David!) could betray the trust of others. Carol had called him "careless" and, Rosie thought, that word in its fullest meaning described him perfectly.

"Poor Dougie. He could have ended up in jail, even lost his business, just for trying to help a friend. Who knows what might have happened?" she said, still shaking her head. "What did he do?"

"I don't know. His biggest worry was that the police would come after him. He kept saying, 'Please don't go the police, don't tell anyone.' I said it was up to him what he did, but at the very least he ought to fire Tony. And that was how we left it."

"But I don't understand why that makes you uncomfortable round Dougie? You did him a real favour, letting him know what was going on."

Carol gave a little shrug. "That stuff about revenge being a dish best served cold is all crap, you know. When you get your own back, it doesn't make you feel any better. And I'm pretty sure Dougie blames me for Tony's death. I think he fired him, Tony got drunk and fell down the stairs." She bent her head. "I can't look Doug in the eye anymore. We both know that if I hadn't been so eager to stick it to Tony, he'd still be alive."

Rosie wanted to reassure Carol that she was completely blameless in the whole sorry mess, but knew that was impossible. She'd never believe her, anyway. The word "Karma" crossed her mind. Unless Rosie successfully solved the mystery and the guilty party confessed, Carol would always be remorseful over her imagined part in Tony's death. And, although her guilt was undeserved, it was probably the karmic price she had to pay for letting revenge consume her so completely.

But now, all Rosie could offer was; "You can't know that. Tony brought most of what happened on himself, and there could have been any number of reasons why he died the way he did. If you hadn't said anything, he might still have ended up the same way, and Dougie could have gone to jail."

Carol gave her a wistful smile. "Good old Rose, everything's so black and white to you, isn't it?" She got up and rubbed her hand over the back of her thigh. "I'd better go in. God, that seat's hard, I think I'm marked for life." She turned as she reached for the door. "Listen, don't say anything to anyone about that smuggling business. I promised Doug I'd keep it to myself."

Rosie nodded. "No problem." Time to change the subject, she thought. "By the way, I've got loads more stuff for the fifties/sixties room. Do you want to get together next week sometime?"

"Yes, just give me a call. No worries about the posters either, I'll get them all up by Friday, but I'm done with the meetings. I think they're harder on me than on that jerk-off Anderson."

"Yes, probably a smart move. Don't forget to let Ellen know, though. Otherwise he'll take it out on her, just for fun."

"Right." As she went inside, Carol's voice carried back to Rosie. "What the hell did I ever see in him?"

That's the question every betrayed woman has asked herself since time began, Rosie thought, as she walked towards her car.

*　　　　*　　　　*　　　　*

Since grade one, the kitchen table had been her favourite spot for homework, and today Rosie sat there the whole afternoon, focusing as diligently on the life and death of Tony Wesley as she ever had on fractions and French verbs.

Immediately after lunch, she began review every little snippet of information gathered over the pa weeks, and now it looked as if there were a glimmer o light at the end of this convoluted tunnel.

After a brief hunt she had found her initial profiles of Tony and the arsonist, stuffed in a drawer in the living room. Being a great believer in getting things down on paper, she was soon scribbling away, expanding on these initial thoughts. As she wrote, the jumble of facts and impressions she'd been mentally accumulating for weeks began to slowly coalesce.

It was a while before she reached the final, and most important, paragraphs;

Fact: Everything had changed in Tony's second year at high school. Before that, he was a model student.

Reason: He'd come under the influence of a clever and manipulative arsonist.

Fact: Sister Mary B. said Mike Wesley gave his son a major thrashing over "some scrape" at school before Christmas. Possibly 1959?

Reason: Tony's involvement in the gymnasium fire and Martin Robertson's subsequent death? The time line was right for both.

Fact: Thanks to Carol, Tony's use of the bakery van for smuggling had been exposed.

Reason: Money. It explained why Lucy thought her husband was earning "a really good wage", when Dougie had said the job was "only minimum wage." It was probably smuggling proceeds that were going to fund the promised move out of Veterans Avenue, and into "a nicer place."

Reading over her notes, it occurred to Rosie that a more orthodox sleuth would now be considering Tony's illegal activities as a prime motive for his murder. Certainly the most logical conclusion.

But her investigations were never orthodox or logical. She was always guided in one particular direction;

the arsons. And most illogical of all, her
ys dead.

ny triggering her visions of fire, Tony
her to the pen clip in his basement and
's Principal's Address in the 59/60 Year
And, she thought guiltily, it wasn't a temper
tantrum that caused her jacket to fly across the office
yesterday – just Tony, trying to draw her attention to the
pen-clip in her pocket. Then an uncomfortable thought
struck her. Maybe it wasn't just the pen clip; maybe he'd
also been pointing a spectral finger at Dave Mason.

The hall clock chimed six and she heard the
familiar *click-click* of Gussie's nails as he wandered into the
kitchen. Moments later, his empty food bowl rattled. "Yes
Gus, I know it's supper time," she muttered irritably. "For
heaven's sake, you're more work than a toddler
sometimes." But, demanding habits aside, he did have a
point; time was getting on and they both needed to be fed.

Reluctantly she closed her notebook, went over to
the sink and dragged his kibble container from the
cupboard beneath. She measured out Dr. Katz's approved
half cup serving and set it down in front of the excited
beagle, now whimpering with expectation. "There you go,
soon sorted" she said, as she crossed to the fridge.
Opening the door, she gazed inside and waited for
inspiration. "What's tasty, filling and zero calories, Gus?"
she asked. The only reply was a sound of contented
crunching.

*   *   *   *

"Thanks so much for your attention, ladies. Order
forms are in the back of the catalogues, and I'll be in the
kitchen when you're ready." Marilyn circled around
Stella's tiny lounge, passing out catalogues and pens, then
disappeared through a narrow archway into the hall.
Stella followed, saying as she went; "Tea and coffee in the

kitchen, girls, and treats on the table. Help yourselves. I'm going for a smoke. "

Rosie looked around at her fellow party-goers. There was Liz sitting opposite, very upright on a straight back chair, with the slightly dazed look of someone taking strong painkillers. Her sister Dora was next to her and Steve's two sisters, Maria and Judy, had commandeered the loveseat. The sixth guest had been introduced by Stella as her next-door neighbour, Tia.

Tia looked about twenty-five, and she had smiled and given a little wave of greeting before sitting down quickly at the back of the room. Judging from her elfin build, spiky yellow hair and nose ring, Rosie suspected she was feeling rather out of place in this roomful of polyester pants and sensible shoes.

Dora and Maria got up and made for the coffee table, where a row of Ferguson's white pastry boxes were lined up, disposable plates and paper napkins stacked beside them. Rosie thought it a fair bet that Stella wasn't into fancy entertaining.

The thought of "fancy entertaining" brought a nostalgic twinge, as she recalled her mother's meticulous preparations for her afternoon bridge parties. Silver coffee spoons were polished, linen napkins ironed and dainties prepared. Every minor social occasion had been an event in her childhood.

When did that all disappear, she wondered. Social niceties had somehow melted away when nobody was looking. Now everything had to be fast and convenient; silver spoons and linen napkins were as out-dated as Sunday hats.

Well, time to pay the piper, she thought with a sigh. She began flipping through the catalogue, looking for items priced low enough for her budget, but high enough that Marilyn and Stella wouldn't think her a complete dead loss as a customer. Apparently, how much everyone spent determined what Stella received as free product, and

Marilyn had also announced that if she achieved five hundred dollars in sales, she'd be the lucky recipient of "tonight's amazing bonus item." No pressure, then, on the assembled family and friends!

After her personal colour analysis, Marilyn had pronounced Rosie a "Warm Autumn" and directed that she stay clear of anything pastel, and concentrate on earth tones. Keeping this in mind, she eventually selected a camel shirt and moss green scarf. She had just finished adding up the damage, (seventy-eight dollars with tax and shipping!) when a little voice at her elbow made her look up.

"Hi, you're Rosie. You sing at the church, don't you?" The waif-like figure indicated an adjacent chair. "I'm Tia. Is anyone sitting here?"

"No, I don't think so. Nice to meet you, Tia. So, you're a parishioner at St. Jude's?"

Balancing a coffee, Tia sat down, her thin top bunching up to reveal a navel impaled by several silver rings. Now she was closer, Rosie could also see a row of studs piercing the outer shell of each ear. Ooo, that must have hurt, she thought, wincing inwardly. She'd barely been able to endure a basic piercing in each lobe.

"Yes, I suppose you could say that. When I was at home, I went regularly with mom and dad, but I don't get there every Sunday, now." Tia hesitated, apparently torn between an untruth and the possibility of giving offence. To her credit, honesty won out. "Well, actually, I don't go at all, these days. Kurt likes to sleep in on Sunday mornings."

She sipped her coffee, then reached over to put it on the table, giving Rosie a glimpse of her tattooed back as she did so. Wow, thought Rosie, I wonder if Kurt's a biker, and she's his moll?

Tia smiled shyly. "You probably don't remember, but you sang at our wedding three years ago. And we always go to Midnight Mass, we couldn't miss hearing you sing at Christmas. Your voice is just wonderful; Kurt calls you his Christmas angel."

Rosie was dumbstruck. Compliments were few and far between in her life, and Tia's unexpected comments threatened to bring tears to her eyes.

Blinking fast, she said; "It's so kind of you to say that. Do you like music?"

"Yes, just to listen to, I can't play or anything." Tia opened her catalogue. "But Kurt's a musician. He plays cello in a string quartet, *Musica Amabile*, maybe you've heard of them?"

Rosie almost laughed out loud, as the wild inaccuracy of her pre-conceived notions hit home. "Sorry, no. Does he perform locally?"

"Only for weddings and funerals and things like that. They tour a bit, though. Last year, they got a gig on a cruise ship; great money, but he was gone for months." She closed her catalogue and leaned toward Rosie. "I don't like any of this stuff, do you?" she whispered. "I only came because Stel's so good about looking after Charlie when I'm late getting home."

"No, I'm not very keen, either. Is Charlie your little boy?"

Tia laughed; "I 'spose you could say that. No, Charlie's our collie. I'm a pharma rep. for Bio-Tek, and I've got this really ginormous district. If I'm back in the boonies, I don't get home until all hours, so Stel lets him out and feeds him."

She reached over to one of the pastry boxes, and lifted out a cream slice. "M-mmm," she murmured, slowly licking off some cream filling that was oozing around the edges. "It's been worth coming just for this, though. I haven't been into the bakery for years; said I'd never go back after that old cow fired me."

In a twinkling, Tia finished off her first pastry and was reaching for a second, then remembered her manners and held out the box. "Sorry, would you like one?"

Involuntarily Rosie recoiled, as if Tia were proffering a box of worms, not pastries, in her direction. "No, thanks all the same, but absolutely not." She chuckled. "I made a pig of myself last night, thanks to Dougie, so today is definitely *new leaf* time."

"How is poor old Doug, these days?"

"He's fine. I'm on the high school reunion committee with him. Did you work in the bakery for long?"

"No. No-one works with the dreaded Mrs. Ferguson for long. I tried it the summer before I went to university, but she drove me nuts. Nothing was ever right. And it was awful the way she treated Dougie. Spoke to him like he was three years old. Anyway, one day she got me so rattled that I dropped a batch of shortbread, and got fired on the spot. So, I called her a few choice names and vowed never to darken the bakery door again."

She licked around the edge of her second cream slice. "Course, that's what my mom calls *cutting off your nose to spite your face.* Old Ma Ferguson doesn't miss my custom, but boy, do I miss her cream slices." And she finished the second one with relish.

"Rosie." Liz called out from the doorway, where she was standing ram-rod straight. "I've done my order so I'm off home. Could ya tell Father I'll be back to the rectory on Thursday?"

That'll come as a blow, Rosie thought. "Well, yes, but are you sure you're ready?"

"Doc Drucker thinks it's better for me to keep movin', and I'm not gettin' any rest at home, anyways." She turned stiffly. "I'll see ya Friday."

"Okay, I'll tell him. Take care, now."

Moments later, Stella reappeared in the doorway. "Marilyn's free, if anyone else is ready to order."

Rosie got to her feet quickly. "Yes I'm all set, Stella." She turned to Tia. "It's been lovely meeting you, Tia. I'll look for you and Kurt on Christmas Eve." Then, as an afterthought, she said; "There are some really pretty scarves on page fifteen. If you can't find anything you like, maybe you could get one of those for your mom. Put it away for Christmas."

Tia smiled conspiratorially. "Great idea, Rosie. I'll get a couple. See you at Christmas."

Rosie followed Stella along the hall and into a red and white kitchen. Everything matched so aggressively that the checkerboard effect was dizzying.

Marilyn was perched precariously on a stool at the breakfast bar, and gave her a welcoming smile. "Hi Rosie. Glad you could make it tonight. Did you enjoy the presentation?"

"Yes, it was really interesting." Rosie handed over her catalogue and order form, then climbed onto the opposite stool. As Marilyn reviewed item numbers and prices, she occupied herself by trying to come up with a verbal ploy to bring Martin Robertson into their conversation.

"You've spent over fifty dollars, so you can get a lipstick for half-price, if you want. That's a great deal; our lipsticks are really long-lasting." Marilyn was every inch the sales professional.

Rosie hesitated. She didn't want a lipstick, but she needed to keep Marilyn happy. "Oh, okay. What colour do you think?"

Marilyn cast her eyes over Rosie's Colour Profile card. "You're a Warm Autumn, so I think Cinnamon Spice would be the best," and she pulled out a tester from the kit in front of her.

Rosie glanced at it. "Looks lovely, I'll take one."

"Now, what about the specials? Our Rotunda bag is only $49.99 this month." She reached down and lifted a large, purple sac bag from beneath her stool.

Dear Lord, that looks like a huge egg-plant, Rosie thought. "No thanks, Marilyn. I think I'll leave it at that."

"Well, for real leather that's a steal, you know. And it does come in two other colours."

Rosie shook her head. "No, it's really not my style. But thanks, anyway."

"Okay, then." Marilyn dropped the bag down on the floor, and flashed another expansive smile. "So, with shipping and tax, that'll be eighty four dollars and ninety cents. Cash, cheque or credit card?"

Rosie gulped. She better get some good information out of Marilyn for this price. "Cheque please, Marilyn."

"Right then. Make it payable to me, please Rose. The order'll be shipped to me, and I'll deliver to you."

Rosie handed over her cheque. Time's up, she thought, it's now or never. "Marilyn, could I ask you something? It's a bit delicate, actually."

Marilyn looked up from her paperwork, her curiosity piqued. "Sure, Rose. What is it?"

"It's about that conversation we had when I picked up the bulletins a week or so back. You know I'm on the reunion committee?"

Marilyn nodded.

"Well, as I mentioned, we've been researching the school's Year Books, and we've come across a few um…. unhappy events." Rosie hesitated and looked over at Marilyn. Her expression was unreadable. "We're not quite sure what to do for the best. These things are all a part of the school's history, but we don't want to cause anyone distress."

"You're talking about Martin, right, and the fire?"

"Not so much about Martin, but the fire for sure. You see, it prevented the football team from defending their championship that year and, as they've never won again, there was a really long-lasting effect on the school."

"Well, that's all very fine. But that fire had a much worse effect on the Robertson's, you know. I should think that needs to be considered ahead of anything else."

Rosie saw her opportunity. "Yes, I really agree. I remembered what you said about Willie still having such a hard time with it all, and I'm inclined to recommend that we just ignore the whole episode."

Marilyn looked mollified. "That would be the best choice, if you ask me. I'm sure Gord and his dad would appreciate the consideration."

Getting to the nitty-gritty now, Rosie thought. She contrived to look confused but disinterested. "I don't quite understand the connection between Martin's death and the fire, though."

Marilyn gave a sigh. "Well, the way old Carscadden told it at the inquest, Marty was cut from the football team and set the fire in the equipment room out of spite. Some of the boys saw him, and a few days later he got beaten up. The kids said he took off towards the tracks, and the next anyone knew, he'd been hit by a train."

Finally, the $64,000 Dollar Question! Rosie took a deep breath. "But why did the Robertsons's blame Tony Wesley?"

"Another boy saw him chase after Marty. He followed, found Tony with Marty's bike, and the little shit told him he'd pushed Marty onto the tracks. This other kid was afraid to say anything, but some time later he told his mother, and she told Doris Robertson." Marilyn looked up at the kitchen clock. "Stella, give the other ladies a reminder, would you? I'm nearly ready for the next order."

Rosie felt like tearing her hair out; who was it, she wanted to scream. But she just said. "Really? Well, that must have been a hard thing to tell a friend."

"Yes, but that's the odd thing, she wasn't a friend. Far from it, actually. I remember Gord's dad saying, the two women couldn't stand each other; they were both members of the Women's Missionary Society at Knox and were always at odds over something or other." Marilyn closed her eyes in concentration. "Now, what was her name? It's that woman who's got the bakery. Ferguson, that's it. Mrs. Ferguson. It was her boy, Douglas, who said Tony did it."

Rosie almost fell off her stool. Wow, she thought, two major surprises today, and they both involve Dougie, of all people. But if he knew something that bad about Tony, why give him a job? I know Doug's kind-hearted but...."

"Rosie, your receipt!" Marilyn was waving a piece of paper at her.

"Sorry, Marilyn. I didn't hear you." She took the receipt and slid inelegantly off her stool. "Thanks, see you soon." By now, Stella had come in with Maria and Judy and they were standing by the door, catalogues in hand. "And don't worry about the reunion business. I'm sure I can persuade the committee to forget all about that..... thing, you know."

"Thanks Rose. I'll give you a call when the order's in; it's usually just a few days," and Marilyn turned her attention to her next customers.

Stella walked with Rosie down the hall. "Have you got a jacket, Rose?"

"No, I took a chance that the rain was finished. What've you done with Mike tonight?"

Her hostess laughed. "He's in the basement with a few beer and a family sized bag of chips." She opened the front door. "Well, thanks so much for coming; did you enjoy it?"

Rosie nodded enthusiastically. "Yes, it was great. Marilyn really knows what goes with what." Reaching the door, her eye was caught by a large, framed portrait of two cats sitting on a chair together. "Are those two yours?"

"Yes, Fluffy and Snowball. They're upstairs under the bed right now; you know cats, don't like their routine disturbed." She smiled fondly. "But we love 'em." She opened a drawer in the hall table and took out a little pack of business cards. "Young Tia did it. Got a nice little business going on the side; real talented, she is. And a sweetheart, too. Gave it to me last Christmas as a thank-you for looking after her dog." She handed Rosie one of the cards. "Here, I always keep a few of these handy to give out when someone admires my picture." Rosie peered at the card in her hand. *Henrietta Tillson – Professional Pet Artist.*

All thoughts of spirits, arson and murder vanished magically away, to be replaced by that greatest of all shopping thrills; the unexpected discovery of a perfect Christmas gift for that hard-to-buy-for person.

She never knew what to get for Auntie Marg but, this year, she'd have it nailed. A posthumous, pastel portrait of the late (and in her case, unlamented) corgi, Henry!

Her excitement lasted all the way home.

Chapter 21 – The Ties that Bind

On Wednesday, when Rosie arrived home from work, she was relieved to find a message from Lucy waiting on the phone. Although surprised not to have heard back sooner, she'd been hesitant to call again and had begun to wonder if Lucy and her parents had gone away for a short break.

The voice-mail was terse and to the point. "Hi, Rosie." Lucy sounded tired and strained. "Sorry not to have called you before this, but dad took a bad turn last week-end, and we've been at the hospital almost full time ever since. I'll be home tonight, so I'll try and catch you later. Thanks, and sorry again."

Oh dear, as if she hasn't got enough to deal with right now, Rosie thought, idly sorting through the stack of mail and flyers she had brought in from the mailbox. Hydro bill, not too bad. Water bill – oh God! You'd think water would be cheap, living right next to Lake Huron. 'Well, that's it. No more lawn sprinkler going all evening,' she vowed, setting the offending bill aside.

The only items of interest in the whole bundle were the Clarion and the latest Sears catalogue so, taking lemonade from the fridge, she gathered them together and headed for the terrace. She could see Gussie down at the bottom of the garden, lapping water from the lily pond, but decided it was too much effort to chase him off. That cast iron stomach could easily handle a bit of algae.

It was a lovely afternoon. The sky was a perfect eggshell blue and Tuesday's brisk winds had blown away all the humidity. Rosie settled back in her chair, and picked up the paper. A warm breeze rustled the pages and carried the scent of her mother's rose bushes across the garden.

Nothing much happened in Little Yarmouth between June and September, so it didn't take long to go through the Clarion. Even the obituaries diminished; people didn't seem to die as often in the summer. She found the second Reunion Weekend ad easily this time, located prominently on page three opposite *Letters to the Editor* and Willie's editorial on the evils of skateboarding in the cemetery.

Sitting there in the sun was wonderfully comfortable, idly watching the swallows swoop back and forth across the lawn. Her mother had loved them. She called them her little Spitfires, shooting down every enemy mosquito and gnat in the garden.

After a while the gentle background noises of the garden began to weave their drowsy spell and Rosie leant back in her chair, letting the paper slip from her fingers. Soon her eyes were drooping as she drifted into that strange place between wakefulness and sleep. The sounds of the garden receded and she heard muffled footsteps, coming closer, then moving away....

She was standing in a high, open space with lines or patterns painted on the ground. It was dark, but ahead she could see a rectangle of light. Walking away from her and towards the light was a hazy figure. Now it stopped and was standing to one side. "Why are you doing that?" It was a boy's voice, high and uncertain. "Why are you doing that?" The rectangle of light was blocked, as larger, darker shadows grew out of it and moved toward the single figure. She could smell smoke now, and something sharper, more acrid. There was danger here, and she reached toward the figure to warn him – she knew it was a boy..."

The sound of excited barking jolted her awake and, opening her eyes, she saw Gussie scrabbling wildly up the trunk of an old apple tree. With a sigh she heaved herself up out of her chair, letting the Sears catalogue slide from her lap to splay untidily on the flagstones.

"Gus!" she called, walking across the lawn toward him. "Leave it. Come here!" The barking continued, accompanied now by wild leaps. If he's chased Maybelle up that tree again I'll never hear the end of it, she thought. Maybelle was her next door neighbour's cat, and Bonnie Walsh was convinced that Gussie spent his entire waking life plotting assaults on her little darling.

But to her relief, there were no heart-rending *meows* issuing from above, just the indignant chatter of an angry squirrel squatting on a gnarled branch a few inches out of Gussie's reach. "He's got your number, Gus" she said laughingly to the beagle. Panting, his tongue lolling, the dog looked back at her then resumed his ineffectual gymnastics.

"At least that squirrel's giving you a good work-out" she chuckled, walking back towards the house. "I'm going in now, Gus" she called, using one of the few useful tips picked up from his many obedience classes. Their instructor had told them never to chase a dog, just call and walk away.

But, this time, the sight of her retreating back had no effect, and the barking continued. Oh well, if all else fails, there's always bribery, she thought. "Kibble, Gus!" She was rewarded by instant silence, followed by the sight of a brown shape streaking past, as Gussie raced her to the kitchen door.

After they both had eaten, Rosie went back to the terrace, careful to take the phone with her. Not wanting to miss speaking with Lucy, she had already decided that if her friend hadn't rung by eight-thirty, she would take the initiative and make the call herself.

Back in her chair, she tried to sort out what she had seen in her trance state. The boy asking questions was undoubtedly Martin Robertson; she couldn't explain how she knew, but she was certain of it. He'd seen Tony and the arsonist setting the gym fire, although why he'd kept that to himself she could only guess. Maybe they'd threatened him. It was just his word against theirs, and Tony was from the most prominent family in town. Perhaps later he'd threatened to tell, so they'd spread the word that he'd set the fire. And when that didn't work, Tony killed him.

Of the two shadows she'd seen coming towards Martin, one had to be Tony and the other either Pete Anderson or Dave Mason. Unthinkable, but true. Her mind went round and round the facts. It had to be Pete Anderson, Dave was on the football team. He'd never destroy the team's equipment and wreck their chance to defend the SWOHSFL title. Not unless, a little voice niggled, he was a crazy fire-bug; logic doesn't play into psychotic obsessions.

Last night, she'd finally discovered why the Robertson's believed Tony had killed Martin. But, far from solving the puzzle, that answer had only raised another question. If Dougie Ferguson knew Tony was a murderer, why did he give him the job that brought him back to Little Yarmouth? It didn't make any sense.

"Well, I can't wait two weeks for the next meeting to come round," she said aloud. There was nothing for it, but to go directly to the horse's mouth. She'd make up some committee reason for calling him, then use Marilyn's concern for her father-in-law as a ploy to bring the conversation round to Martin's death.

Forgetting her resolve to wait for Lucy's call, she picked up the phone, went back into the house and rummaged through her reunion folder, looking for Dougie's number. Two minutes later she was listening to it ring.

"Hello?" A thin, reedy voice answered, irritably.

Oh Lord, it's Mrs. Ferguson. "Hi, Mrs. Ferguson, it's Rosie Rowe. Could I have a quick word with Doug, please?"

"Who did you say? If you're one of those marketers, you can save your breath. I'm not buying anything."

Well, she's certainly living up to her nasty reputation. "No, Mrs. Ferguson; it's Rosie Rowe. Maybe you remember me as Rose Cornish?" No answer. She tried again; "I'm on the reunion committee, with Doug."

"Complete waste of time, if I ever heard of one. He's got more than enough to do round here, without traipsing off to meetings all the time."

Rosie took a deep breath. "Would Doug be at home, Mrs. Ferguson?"

Mrs. Ferguson's voice took on a harder edge. "No, Douglas is not at home."

"Oh. Then I'd really appreciate it if you could ask him to call me when he gets in." Rosie struggled to swallow her temper.

"I am not in the habit of taking messages for my son. Particularly not from people who've been investigated by the police."

Before she could recover her wits, Rosie heard a *click* and realised Mrs. Ferguson had hung up on her. For a moment, she stood with the phone in her hand, gazing at it in disbelief. "You old bitch!" she finally managed to spit out. "You're not getting away with that! I'll just come down there and speak to him in the shop."

But the lump in her throat told her she wouldn't be venturing into the bakery anytime soon. Beryl Ferguson's unkind words reminded her that long memories were one of the less attractive features of small town life.

The phone was still in her hand and, when it rang suddenly, she was so startled that she almost dropped it. "Hello?" Her voice came out as a croak.

"Hello? Rosie?"

"Oh, hi Lucy. I got your message. I'm so sorry to hear about your dad. How's he making out?"

"He's doing better, thanks. Still in I.C.U, though. But what about you? You don't sound too good."

Rosie gave a nervous laugh. "No, I'm fine. Just a few summer allergies, that's all." Yes, I'm highly allergic to spiteful old besoms, she thought. Why can't people just make an effort to be pleasant to each other, life's too short to waste being nasty …?

"…..bad of me not to call."

Rosie realised she'd missed most of what Lucy was saying, but took a stab at the general gist. "Don't worry about it. I expect you and your mom have had your hands full at the hospital."

"We've been there all day, every day since he went in." Lucy's voice wavered and she gulped back tears. "I had no idea he was so sick, Rosie. And all my troubles must have made everything worse."

"Was it his heart? I think you said something about a heart problem when you came over that night." Rosie could hear Lucy sniffling, then blowing her nose.

"Yes, his heart's really bad. His doctor says he might have to have surgery; it's all so scary, Rose." There was a silence, as Lucy made another attempt to stem the threatened flood of tears. After a minute she asked; "But what was it you wanted to tell me? In your message you said your brother found something out at the hospital."

Rosie had no intention of relaying what she knew over the phone. It would take a relaxed atmosphere to ease Lucy into accepting that Tony's body had to be exhumed. Plus, the timing was all wrong. Understandably, Lucy was totally focused on her father's illness, so there'd be little chance she'd want to jump on the bureaucratic merry-go-round of autopsy and exhumation orders. Swallowing her disappointment, she decided it would be best to downplay everything for a while.

"Yes, he did. But it's a bit complicated and John said….."

"Hang on a minute, Rosie."

Rosie heard a muffled conversation going on in the background, then Lucy came back on the line.

"Sorry about that. Mom's just come in from the hospital and she's had some news about dad's surgery."

That gave Rosie the out she needed. "Oh, I expect you've got lots to talk over, so I'll call back another time. All this stuff about the autopsy can wait. Your mom probably wants to sit down and go over things with you."

But Lucy surprised her. "No, it was really kind of you to follow up for me, and I do want to know what John found out." Her voice trembled again, and she hesitated briefly before going on. "It's a funny thing, but dad going into hospital like that put Tone right out of my mind. Isn't that awful?"

"No, it's not awful, at all," Rosie answered firmly. "Tony's gone, and there's nothing you can do for him, but your mom and dad need all the help and support they can get. It *would* be awful if you were sitting on the couch, crying over Tony, and leaving your mom to cope on her own." Shades of the past she thought guiltily, remembering her own lack-lustre reaction to her mother's diagnosis of heart disease.

For a minute there was silence, and Rosie worried that her plain-speaking had overstepped the mark. Lucy was in a highly emotional state and perhaps a gentler approach would have been better all round.

She caught another snatch of background conversation, before Lucy spoke again. "You're right, Rosie. The living must come first, and I know Tone wouldn't want me crying all the time. He couldn't stand what he called *wallowing*." She gave a little laugh. "Tony was never one to be sentimental, that's for sure. Forgot birthdays and anniversaries every year, regular as clockwork."

Why am I not surprised, thought Rosie, recalling the teenage Carol's broken heart. More and more, Tony's personality was displaying all the textbook traits of a self-involved narcissist.

Lucy was still speaking. "Like I said, I'd really like to know what happened about the autopsy. Are you working tomorrow?"

"No, I only go in three days a week, so I'm home Tuesday and Thursday's."

"Oh, that's good. How about coming for coffee tomorrow morning, then? I.C.U. visiting doesn't start till eleven-thirty so, if you come for ten, we'll have lots of time."

Rosie still hesitated, uncertain how Lucy's battered emotions would react to the news that her husband's death wasn't accidental. Initially, she'd probably be relieved to have her instincts proved right, but then the thought of disinterring his body might be too unsettling to contemplate.

On the other hand, Roy Curtis wasn't going to improve anytime soon. He might even get a whole lot worse, and Lucy's emotional state wouldn't be any better after another trip to the cemetery.

Her mind flew round and round the options until she finally opted to forge ahead. Who knows, maybe everything will turn out the way she hoped; Lucy had already surprised her once today. And if things didn't go her way, she'd just have to live with Tony's ghostly presence for a while longer.

She made an effort to sound enthusiastic. "That sounds really great, if you're sure I won't be imposing on your mom?"

"No, she won't be here. I booked her a ten o'clock appointment at Clipper Snippers up town. Thought she could do with a little pampering."

"Take my word for it, she'll feel loads better after that" Rosie answered, her mind filled with memories of her mother's last days in the hospital.

All through that long, sad week, it had taken every ounce of Rosie's energy just to get up, clean her teeth and take a shower. It wasn't until Elspeth unexpectedly booked her a hair appointment, then picked her up and drove her to the salon, that she realised how desperate she'd become for someone to take an interest in *her* needs. Afterwards, her spirits had soared, and the happier mood must have shown on her face. When she went into her mother's room, Mary had smiled up from her hospital bed and said; 'That looks more like my girl."

"God, I hope so. Trouble is, mom never really bounced back after Babs died, so dad being sick has hit really hard." Lucy's voice thickened and Rosie heard her gulp back tears. "Well, I'd better go; can't put off hearing the bad news for ever. See you tomorrow around ten."

"Yes, see you tomorrow, Lucy. Give my best to your mom. And hang in there, your dad's surgery may not be all bad news. Bye for now."

*   *   *   *

Beryl Ferguson heard the sound of the front door opening, and looked up from her handiwork. The half-finished sleeping mat she was weaving from plastic bags lay across her lap, and she was glad to finish with its sticky bulk for today.

The ladies of the Knox Missionary Society prided themselves on their good works, and this particular endeavour had been taken up with great enthusiasm. The mat-making project had been embraced unanimously by the membership, seen as a perfect fit with the Society's goals and aspirations. At a stroke they could tackle two vexing problems; how to recycle plastic bags, and how to improve the sleeping arrangements of those unfortunate enough to live in the third world.

In Beryl's limited world view, the third world meant Africa; and Africa was still the Dark Continent, still the savage place described in the fervent missionary sagas she had read as a child. While she worked, her mind had been happily conjuring images of the awed and joyous reception her mat would receive from the denizens of those far-flung mission stations and benighted *kraals*.

This beneficent glow faded on hearing her son's step in the hall, and she called out peevishly: "Is that you at last, Douglas? Where on earth have you been? It doesn't take ninety minutes to cash up."

The living room door swung slowly open. "I'm sorry, ma. I was just closing when Gord Robertson came in with the bag order. And then he wanted some doughnuts, so one thing led to another, and time just got away from us."

His mother looked at him coldly. "You're worse than an old woman for gossiping," she snapped. "You know supper is at seven sharp, another time I'll just put it on the table and let it get cold." She made a great show of struggling to get out of her chair. "Well, don't just stand there gawping, come and help me up."

"Sorry ma." Dougie hurried across the room and took her arm. "Don't you think that chair's a bit too low for you?" he suggested hesitantly.

"Nonsense – it's perfect. It was your father's chair. Saw him out and it'll see me out, too. Nothing wrong with it." She pulled her arm away from him impatiently. "I'm just stiff from standing around in the shop all day. Now, if you'd get your act together and find some proper help, I wouldn't have to be working at my age." She started down the hall toward the kitchen. "Well, don't stand there like a bump on a log, come and get the tray."

Dougie followed her into the kitchen obediently, and stood watching as she ladled stew onto two plates. "Gordie was saying his dad's taken a bit of a turn. Hasn't been at the paper all week." He began loading a large tray with the plates, cutlery and two glasses.

"He's another one that should've been long retired. But Gordon's just like you - can't be trusted to run a business on his own." The old lady picked up the bread basket, and pushed through a swinging door leading into the cavernous dining room. "Oh, for God's sake, Douglas, pick up your feet. At this rate, the food'll be stone cold before we ever get to it."

Dougie lumbered in behind her. He carried the tray to the far end of an enormous mahogany table, where two places were laid with mats, folded napkins and an old fashioned silver cruet. With shaking hands, he unloaded plates, cutlery and glasses.

His mother glared at him. "And the water jug? I swear you'd forget your head if it wasn't fixed to your shoulders."

"Sorry, ma."

Her complaints followed him as he disappeared back into the kitchen. "I don't know what's wrong with your generation – although I do know you waste far too much time on those committees and clubs you're so wrapped up in." Mrs. Ferguson dragged out her chair and sat down heavily.

Wordlessly, Dougie set the water jug in front of his mother, took his place opposite her and began to eat.

"Out nearly every night of the week. Never a thought for me, left here all alone." She laid down her knife and fork. "What do you think your father would say if he knew how you neglect me?"

Her son looked up, stopped chewing and swallowed. "Now ma, you know it's good for business to be active in the community. Dad was always involved in town projects."

"He was a Mason and a church elder!" Beryl waved her fork for emphasis. "He had some dignity, some respect in this town. But, oh no, you didn't want to do what *he* did – you had to go your own way." Her voice took on a whiny tone. "*I'm a member of the Rotary Club and the Merchants Association.*" She sawed at a piece of meat. "Pah! Just like any Tom, Dick or Harry. There's no social standing in those outfits, I can tell you."

Dougie shrugged his shoulders. "Times have changed a bit, since dad's day. I don't think that kind of thing matters much anymore."

"Maybe not to you, but it does to me and the people I choose to know. I'm always being asked why you don't stand for the church board."

Again, there was no reply. For several minutes the only sounds were the scrape of cutlery on china, and the loud ticking of an ugly ormolu clock on the mantelpiece.

"Could I have the rolls, ma?"

His request broke the silence, and revived Mrs. Ferguson's recital of grievances.

"And the phone calls! I'm sick and tired of taking messages for you when you're out. Time was, no-one would phone during the supper hour. People had some consideration in those days. But now, no-one's got any idea of good manners. Phoning at all hours of the day or night, and expecting me to take messages." She poured water into a glass and drank noisily. "I'm not your servant, you know!"

Her son broke his bread roll apart, and began to butter each piece with studied care. "Did someone call before I got home?"

Too late, his mother realised her mistake. When she didn't reply, Dougie said quietly; "I'm sorry you were disturbed mother, but if there's a message, please tell me. It might be important."

"What could Rose Cornish have to say that's important, I'd like to know." She shot him a spiteful look. "All smiles, and singing up at that roman church! I don't believe for one minute she didn't know what her husband was up to." She reached for a roll and cut it delicately in four quarters. "It was a disgrace, the way he cheated all those people out of their savings. Mark my words, she was in on it, and that money's nicely stashed away somewhere. He's no more dead than I am."

Momentarily distracted, she looked up and down the table. "Where's the butter?" Spying it at her son's elbow, she snapped. "Are you listening to me, Douglas? Pass the butter, and be quick about it."

Keeping his eyes on his plate, he pushed the butter dish toward her and muttered; "They've waited a very long time, then."

"Speak up. What are you talking about?"

"Rose and her supposedly dead husband. All that happened years ago; I'd have thought they'd have cashed in and disappeared long since."

Beryl gave a snort of derision. "You really have no clue, do you? The police have been watching her so she's got to wait. A few years is nothing when there's millions at stake."

Dougie took a deep breath and silently counted to ten. He knew from experience that his mother's prejudices were deep-rooted, and nothing he could say would make any difference to her unkind judgments. After a moment, he went on; "It may be as you say ma, but I still need to know why she called. It's probably to do with the high school reunion. We're on the committee together."

"There was no message." Beryl enunciated each word with exaggerated emphasis. "I was just to ask you to call her. Quite abrupt she was, too." Raising her napkin to her lips she dabbed delicately, then announced; "I'm ready for dessert. You may take the plates out now." She laid her knife and fork neatly across the centre of the plate.

As Dougie rose obediently, she couldn't resist a parting shot. "And of all your time-wasting activities, that high school reunion has got to be the worst. I can't imagine any of *my* old school friends wanting to sit all evening in a drafty gymnasium listening to a third rate band."

Her son gritted his teeth, and backed grimly through the swinging door into the kitchen.

Undeterred by his expression, his mother called after him; "The Goderich Ladies College always held their reunions at the Empire Hotel." She waited for an answer, but none came. "Did you hear me, Douglas?"

"Yes, ma."

"I looked forward to the Reunion Ball all year. It was wonderful; flowers, evening dress, a real orchestra. Now that's the way to organise things. I've always said, if something's worth doing, it's worth doing well."

Dougie came back into the dining room; "Well, that was a very long time ago." He laid a dish of ice-cream in front of her. "I seem to recall that the Empire Hotel burned down in the seventies. And, by then, the Ladies College had been closed for years, so didn't they have to move the dance to the Legion Hall?"

Briefly discomfited, Beryl shifted in her seat. "You know full well that I've never attended any function held in a Legion Hall." Then, fixing him with her basilisk stare, she deftly regained the upper hand; "And you've forgotten the coffee."

*   *   *   *

Rosie was at the sink washing her supper dishes, when the phone rang. She grabbed a tea towel and made a dash across the kitchen to the phone, drying her hands as she went.

The sound of Dougie's breezy, "Hi, Rose. What's up?" threw her briefly. When she didn't immediately reply, he was quick to misinterpret her silence. "Look, I'm sorry if ma was ....difficult when you phoned. She can be a bit testy sometimes, but I did get your message. Hope it's not too late to call."

"No, of course it's not too late." Here comes another white lie, she thought. "Your mom didn't give me a hard time. I hope I didn't interrupt anything, though. I know how annoying that can be, especially if you're trying to get supper on."

"That's fine then. So what can I do for you?"

All through this brief exchange, Rosie had been mentally scrambling to remember how she'd planned to tap him for information.

"It's not really important, Doug. I just wanted to let you know that I've made a good start distributing the posters, and everyone seems to really like them." Catholic guilt in full flood now, she crossed her fingers. "I dropped Carol's off, and she's promised to get them up by the end of this week."

"That's really great. I'm glad people like them." He waited expectantly.

What to say? What to say? She rushed on; "Wow, that was quite a meeting last Monday. Carol was sorry she missed the Chair finally getting his comeuppance."

Dougie's answer was a low chuckle. "Yeah, right. Pete Anderson's always been a pri.., hard to get on with, even back in high school."

An opening at last! She breathed a sigh of relief. "Yes. All this reunion stuff certainly stirs up old memories." Time to get the show on the road. She cleared her throat nervously. "Speaking of old memories. I ran into Marilyn Robertson the other night, and she started on about that bad fire up at the school, the one that ruined all the football equipment. It was before my time, so I don't remember it, but you probably do."

She heard his sharp intake of breath, then silence.

"Dougie? You still there?"

"Yes, Rosie. Look….." his voice wavered. "Thanks for all your help with getting the posters out, but I've got the shop accounts to finish tonight, so I'd better go."

"Hang on a minute, Doug." Rosie realised if she wanted answers, she'd have to be more direct. "As committee members, I think we have an obligation to respond to people's concerns." Crossing her fingers again, she hurried on; "Marilyn's worried about Willie. He's not been well lately, and she thinks he's getting upset because all the reunion hoopla will drag up the fire and that sad business about his oldest boy. What was the name she said…Mark, Michael….?.

"Martin. He was called Martin." Another long pause, then; "I don't understand why Willie's getting bent out of shape. No-one wants to dredge all that up again."

"That's what I told her. But she reckons he's afraid it'll be tied into the Screaming Eagles losing the Championship that year, and never winning again. And then, of course, Tony Wesley coming back to town and dying like that, just made everything worse." She waited for a response, but none came. "Did you know the Robertson's blame him for Martin's death?"

Doug's answer was terse. "I can't think where they got that from. The inquest ruled it an accident."

Before she could stop herself, Rosie blurted out; "But it was you that said he did it!" She heard him inhale, and then breathe out slowly, as if he were playing for time.

"Look Rose, I know you're Lucy's friend, and maybe that's why you're so interested in all this ancient history. But it wasn't true. Yes, Tony did tell me he'd pushed the kid onto the tracks, but I knew he was bragging; just showing off. We were teenagers, for God's sake. We spent half our lives trying to impress each other."

"So why tell your mother what he'd said?"

"I told you he made it up, just leave it at that." Rosie could hear the anger in his voice, sense his struggle to keep a veneer of courtesy in their conversation.

"I'm sorry, Doug. You're right; part of my concern is for Lucy. She's been devastated by his death, and the thought that someone might tell her Tony killed a boy in high school really bothers me."

"No, it's me that should apologise, Rose. I didn't mean to be rude, but you have to understand, that was a terrible time for all of us in Martin's class." Doug's voice was muffled and, astounded, Rosie thought he was crying.

When he spoke again, he sounded calmer. "I guess I owe someone an explanation, so it may as well be you. You asked why I told my mother about... about that day. It was just typical teenage crap. Tony and I had a falling out over some stupid thing; can't even remember what it was. Anyway, I wanted to get back at him so, like a fool, I told ma that he'd killed Martin. She must have told someone else, and it got back to the Robertsons." His voice cracked. "In the end, he had to leave town. Nothing to do with getting Lucy pregnant. He told me years later that the whispering finally got to him." He gave an unsteady laugh. "So there you have it; my guilty secret."

Rosie didn't know what to say. She tried to speak but Dougie interrupted.

"You said it yourself, Rosie. Reunions stir up memories; that's what they're meant to do. Unfortunately they can't all be happy memories, but we can't change the past, no matter how much we want to."

"No, I guess not. Thanks for....."

He interrupted again. "No problem. Look, I really have to go. See you at the next meeting."

"Yes, see you...," but to Rosie's surprise there was an abrupt click, followed by the dial tone. Most uncharacteristically, Dougie had hung up on her.

Chapter 22 – A Twist in the Tale

"Gus, get your nose out of the way!" Rosie gave the beagle a gentle shove, as she pushed her trowel into a mass of chickweed that was invading the tomato patch. Lord, what a mess! Ever since Tony Wesley had floated into her life she'd been ignoring the garden, and now she was paying for her negligence.

The garden at 64 Cedar Street had been laid out in an era when it was a simple matter to find a reliable and affordable gardener. Steps led down from the flagstone terrace to a wide lawn surrounded by herbaceous borders. A circular bed filled with rose bushes was cut into the centre of the lawn, with an Edwardian cast-iron bird bath towering imposingly above the blooms. From here, a crazy paving path led to Gussie's favourite haunt, the lily pond, and it was just a few more steps to the three old apple trees which made a haphazard boundary between formal and kitchen gardens.

It was in the kitchen garden that Rosie was concentrating her efforts to bring order out of chaos. Weeks of alternate heat and heavy rain had brought her flowers and vegetables on beautifully but, unfortunately, the weeds were doing even better.

She had slept fitfully after last night's unexpected phone call, and got up at first light. With breakfast over and the dog walked by seven-thirty, she decided to take advantage of the early morning coolness and make a stab at the weeding, before her coffee date with Lucy.

While she worked, she re-visited her surprising conversation of the previous evening. Questions asked and definitely answered, she thought. Dougie had offered Tony a job because he felt guilty; plain and simple. He'd unwittingly spread a lie that changed his old friend's life forever. Yes, most people would be ashamed of that.

But what had he thought when Carol told him that the old friend was abusing his kindness? That Tony was using the bakery van to run a smuggling operation, carelessly putting Dougie's reputation and livelihood at risk. Those were questions she couldn't ask, without betraying Carol's confidence. And for all his assurances to the contrary, was Dougie right in his belief that Tony's confession was mere braggadocio? It was quite possible that he was deluding himself, and Tony really had killed Martin Robertson.

It was getting hot. Rosie wiped her brow with her sleeve and sat back on her heels to survey her work. Gussie pounced on the spot she'd been weeding, and began to dig exuberantly in the turned earth.

"Right, so now you're going to dig? Some of that enthusiasm would have been appreciated when I was struggling with the weeds." The beagle turned his face to hers, tongue hanging out, nose covered in dirt. He looked so pleased with himself that she had to give him a hug.

"Oh Gus, I'm going round and round in circles," she said into his fur. "The sooner I get Lucy's okay to dig up that troublemaker, the better." With a groan she stood up, stretched and looked at her watch. "C'mon, I've got to go in for a quick shower." But the dog ignored her, his attention distracted by the swarm of angry ants he'd disturbed with his energetic digging.

It was well past ten when Rosie finally pulled into Agnes and Roy Curtis' driveway. Her shower had been quick enough, but enticing Gussie away from his excavations, and then cleaning him up, had taken quite a while.

She got out of the car and glanced around. Everything about 17 Albion Way was immaculate. Windows shone, paintwork gleamed, the front lawn was bowling green smooth. Rosie suspected that even the birds' nests overhead were constructed of twigs set in at neat right angles.

She pressed the doorbell, and heard Westminster Chimes herald her arrival. Moments later, the door swung back and Lucy was giving her a bear hug.

Rosie's first thought was how much better her friend looked. Despite the worry of her dad's illness and the scant four weeks that had passed since Tony's death, Lucy seemed brighter somehow; for all the world as if a heavy weight had been lifted from her shoulders. She had left Veterans Avenue behind in more ways than one.

"Come on in, Rosie; coffee's brewing." Turning, she led the way into a sun-drenched living room. "It's so good to see you. I can't believe it's only been two weeks since we got together. So much has happened, it seems like ages ago."

Rosie could certainly agree with that. She sat down gingerly on a spotless beige sofa, careful to keep her dusty purse away from the upholstery. "Yes, you've got that right. So, what's the news on your dad? How's he doing?"

Lucy smiled happily. "They finished all the tests and decided he doesn't need surgery, after all. Seems the problem was with his meds, more than anything else. So, lots more monitoring at the doctor's office until they get things right, but it looks like he's dodged the bullet for now."

"That's wonderful; your mom must be so relieved. When's he coming home?"

"A few more days. Doc Drucker wants to make sure he's completely stabilized, so probably Sunday or Monday." An aroma of freshly brewed coffee drifted into the room. "I'll get the coffee. How do you like it?"

"Black, with sweetener" Rosie said, and watched Lucy go toward the kitchen. After sitting a moment or two she got up, crossed to the window and gazed out enviously. If only her borders looked that good!

The rattle of spoons on china announced Lucy's return and Rosie went back to her seat. "I just love your garden; those colour combinations are stunning. Who's the gardener in the family?"

Lucy handed across a china mug and sat down opposite her on an equally beige loveseat. "That's dad. He's always loved his garden. I think that's been the worst part of his being sick; not being able to work out there all day, every day." A shadow passed across her face. "But Carl's been wonderful. He's been coming twice a week to mow, and weed, and trim, and all the million other things dad wants doing."

Although Rosie knew she'd heard the name before, she couldn't place who "Carl" was.

Lucy spotted her puzzled expression. "Carl Wheelan. My sister's husband, remember?"

"Oh, yes. You told me he's getting married again, right?"

Her friend sighed. "Yes. Mom and dad have been really upset about it, but what can you do? Babs has been gone for two years, and he deserves to be happy again. Life must go on." She spooned sugar into her mug, and stirred thoughtfully.

Rosie glanced at her friend, expecting to see tears glistening. But, to her surprise, Lucy was dry-eyed.

"Try one of my brownies, Rosie." She gestured toward a plate heaped with chocolaty temptation.

Rosie took one and bit into its moist sweetness. And yet another diet falls by the wayside, she thought regretfully. Can't be helped, though; definitely impolite to refuse.

Between mouthfuls, she said; "I'm sorry I was so late, but Gus was helping me with the weeding, and it took ages to clean him up."

Lucy laughed. "I know you don't want to hear this, but he really is adorable."

Rosie grinned back. "Say that after you've tried hauling him into a laundry tub."

Their conversation slipped into generalities. The high school reunion, the weather, Rosie's foray into the world of Colour Me Beautiful parties; it was as if neither of them wanted to confront the darker reason for their cosy coffee klatch.

It was not until they had finished a second round of coffees, and Rosie had polished off another brownie, that Lucy finally said; "So, I guess your brother found out why no-one thought Tone's death was worth investigating."

At last. The moment Rosie had been anticipating for weeks. She had so much to explain, but where was the best place to start?

"Yes, he did. And most of the reason was quite simple." She went on to describe Dr. Niven's history with Tony, and how that had cemented his assumption of a drunken accident. How the mortuary had been overloaded by victims of the highway pile-up, and how Clodagh Wesley had imposed her wish that Tony not be "cut about." She was just about to start on Andy McGillivray's suspicions, when Lucy interrupted.

"That old bitch! I might have known everything was down to her." Her composure dissolved, and she fumbled in her sleeve for a handkerchief. Rosie made to get up, but was waved back. "No, I'm alright. I'm more angry than anything else." Wiping her eyes she said vehemently. "She took it all over, you know. Everything to do with the funeral, even decided what charity was to get the donations. Bibles for Lepers! Tony didn't care about that sort of thing. He'd have wanted the money to go to Sick Kids, or to some outfit that helps people with bad lungs."

Rosie nodded. "I must say I wondered when I was doing the memorial cards." She stole a glance at her friend, expecting to see more tears, but Lucy appeared calm again. Her fears that Lucy could not cope with an exhumation evaporated, and she prepared to launch into the most important part of her story. "You remember telling me you thought there was something funny about the accident?" Lucy looked blank. "Because Tony was on the wagon? Because there was no liquor in the house? Well…"

"Yes, I remember saying that. But it turns out I was a bit of a fool."

Rosie was taken aback by Lucy's sudden change of tone. "Whatever do you mean?"

"I mean some chickens finally came home to roost."

Rosie held her breath, wondering which of Tony's many secrets had come to light.

Lucy drained her coffee mug, and said; "The rent's running out on Veterans Avenue, so Carl and his son-in-law Todd went over to move my furniture to a storage locker. Dad went too." She cleared her throat. "That was the day before he got sick. I guess the hauling around was just too much for him." Tears began to well up, and she brushed her hand across her eyes.

After a moment she started again. "We've got this old trunk in the basement…"

Remembering her clandestine efforts to open that same trunk, Rosie cheeks reddened and she dropped her eyes guiltily.

But Lucy didn't notice her discomfiture. "Tony'd bought it at an auction years ago, and he used to keep tools and stuff in it. It was locked, and he said he'd lost the key when we moved." Her voice trailed off and she gazed down into her empty mug. "Can I get you another coffee, Rose?"

"No thanks, two's my limit. I'll be in the bathroom all afternoon if I have any more." She smiled at her friend, but the weak attempt at humour missed its mark.

Lucy was studying the patterned carpet, apparently lost in thought. "I always took everything he said as chapter and verse," she said softly, almost to herself. "Never questioned him, just assumed he was always telling God's truth." Then, in an abrupt about-face, she said suddenly; "You know what people say the word *assume* means, don't you Rose?"

Rosie shook her head, nervous about what was coming next.

"When you *assume* something, it makes an *ass* of *u* and *me,* that's what they say. I sure wish I'd kept that in mind, over the years me and Tone were together." She looked around the room wistfully. "My mom and dad have been married fifty-five years. How many lies do you think they've told each other in all that time?"

Now distinctly uncomfortable at the direction of their conversation, Rosie stammered; "I don't know. I should think it's near impossible to live with someone for years and not tell at least the occasional white lie."

"Well, I have quite a claim to fame then," Lucy said, twisting her handkerchief into a tight little ball. "I never told Tony so much as a white lie, in all the years we were together. And now I find out he was lying to me, and for who knows how long." Now her voice was shaking with the effort to stay in control, and tears were starting to run down her cheeks.

'Oh God, whatever has she found out?' Rosie thought as she went around the coffee table and sat down by her friend. "Luce, what's all this about? What makes you think Tony was lying to you?"

Lucy blew her nose and coughed. "Sorry, Rose; It seems I always start bawling when we get together." She tried to smile.

Ignoring the sudden jolting memory of her own experience with betrayal, Rosie forced herself to sound cheerful. "That's okay; I have that effect on people sometimes." She took her friend's hand. "Lucy, this past month has been a terrible ordeal for you. First Tony's death, the funeral, and everything that went with it. And now your dad being so ill. There'd be something wrong with you, if you weren't in an emotional state."

"I guess you're right. Rosie."

"Believe me, I am right. You can't keep these things bottled up; a good cry is nature's way of releasing the pressure." She reached over and picked up the plate of brownies. "And here's a better one; chocolate."

Determined to lighten the mood, she began regaling Lucy with details of the Great Committee Rebellion. The cookie plate was soon empty and they were giggling together like schoolgirls.

"I'm almost scared to go to the next meeting, but I promised Carol I'd keep her up to date," she finally managed to gasp out.

Lucy was brushing crumbs off her hands and onto the empty plate. "Looks like Carol's choice in men is almost as bad as mine," she said, with a wry smile. After a minute she cleared her throat. "You asked me why I know Tony was lying?" Rosie nodded. "That trunk in the basement. Carl and Todd tried to get it up the stairs, but it was incredibly heavy. So dad called me and said would I mind if they broke the lock, to get some of the stuff out. I didn't care; I certainly didn't want anyone getting hurt trying to shift that old thing." She paused.

"So what was in it?" Rosie prompted.

"When dad came home, I could see there was something wrong. He didn't want to tell me, but I got it out of him. There were tools in it alright; a pair of old work boots, and a pile of other junk. But down the side, wrapped up in newspaper, they found ten cartons of cigarettes."

Rosie's temper started to rise; that stupid ass had brought his work home with him! But why should smoking be such a crime in Lucy's eyes? Then she remembered Tony's bad lungs. He must have promised never to smoke again. She said soothingly; "Well, I know he shouldn't have been smoking…," but then the second shoe dropped.

"That was nothing; I could have dealt with him smoking, no problem. Although I can't think where he got the money to buy that many cigarettes. No, it was much worse than that. Right at the bottom, dad found two bottles of rye rolled up in bubble wrap. He was drinking again Rosie, after he vowed he'd never touch another drop."

I can't believe I've got to make excuses for this numbskull, Rosie thought with a surge of anger. It was obvious to her that none of the contraband was for Tony's own use; he just hadn't got round to selling it on. Maybe it would be better to tell Lucy about the smuggling, but which was worse? Thinking your husband had fallen off the wagon, or knowing he was a criminal? And telling what she knew meant she'd have to break her word to Carol. In desperation, she tried sweet reason. "But you'd have known if he was drinking, you'd have smelled it on his breath. He couldn't keep a secret like that for long."

Lucy gave her a long, hard look. "It's no good making excuses Rose, he was out all hours. Sometimes I gave up waiting and went to bed before he came home. I felt sorry for him, thinking he was working overtime with Dougie, but he was just off somewhere with a bottle."

Rosie tried another tack. "You're making assumptions, again. Remember when we first talked about his accident? You thought someone *gave* him that smashed bottle and he was taking it down to the basement to put it out of temptation? Well, maybe that did happen, and the same person gave him the other bottles, too." But even as she suggested it, Rosie knew this explanation had more holes in it than a colander.

"And for what possible reason would someone give Tony bottles of whiskey? It doesn't make any sense." Lucy shook her head. "I know you mean well, but I'm not fooling myself anymore. I think coming back here was just too much for him; or maybe he was drinking all along, I don't know. And, to be honest, I don't want to beat myself up over it anymore."

She dabbed at her eyes, and then gave a wan little smile. "He was my world Rosie and I loved him, but in my heart I always knew he didn't love me the same way. And he was never easy to live with. It was like he had something locked away inside that I couldn't reach. No," she drew herself up and squared her shoulders. "I've had lots of time to think since I came back home, and I've come to terms with the truth. Tony got drunk and fell down the stairs, and there's an end to it. Mom always warned me that drinking would be the end of him."

Rosie felt panic setting in. If Lucy stayed convinced that her husband's death was a drunken accident, there'd be no way to persuade her to have him exhumed. There was nothing for it; she'd have to tell her about Tony's illegal activities. After all, he was only trying to make extra money for them both; hadn't he said something about moving to a nicer place just before he died?

"Lucy, I think you should know…"

But her friend cut her short. "No. No more about Tony for a while. Let's take a break from all this depressing talk. How about some really good news? You won't believe it, but I've got a job!"

"Wow! That's fantastic. Where is it?"

"Well, it's only part-time for starters, but I'm going to be the new Administrative Assistant at…" she paused for effect, "Mason's Funeral Home!"

Rosie's mouth gaped open, and it took a moment of struggle to compose her features into a smile.

"And it's so close I can bike there until I've saved enough to get the car fixed. 'Course, it's mainly evenings and weekends, but what else am I going to be doing? Dave says his mom hasn't been well and can't manage the office by herself anymore and….."

Rosie barely heard the rest of Lucy's excited explanation. *Looks like Dave's not going to miss his opportunity a second time,* she thought and smiled to herself. *Well, good luck to him.*

With an effort, she stifled the niggling thought that, if Dave were a serial arsonist and murderer, he might have an ulterior motive for hiring Lucy - one that had more to do with surveillance than romance. *Not to worry,* her mental dialogue continued, *once that autopsy is complete the police will step in and Tony's murderer will be safely behind bars.*

"…really excited, and I'm starting on Monday."

"I'm so pleased for you, Lucy. Dave's such a nice guy *(no, I don't believe he's the killer!)* and his mom's a real sweetheart. I'm sure you'll do really well there."

"Yes, he was so kind to me after Tone…" she gulped, "you know, with the funeral and everything. I don't know what I'd have done if he hadn't offered to help me out like that. It was a real comfort to know Tony and I will be together again, one day." She stopped in sudden confusion, and her hand flew to her mouth. "Oh, shit. I shouldn't have said that. I promised Dave I wouldn't say anything." She gazed at Rosie uneasily. "It was just that old Mrs. Wesley was so determined to have her own way and…" her voice drifted into silence.

This sounds interesting, Rosie thought. *What's Dave Mason been up to now?*

Over the years, she had discovered that the easiest way to get someone to share a secret was to feign disinterest. So she said lightly; "Don't worry, I didn't hear anything," and mimed zipping her lips. "But I do know what you mean about Mrs. Wesley. It's always been her way or the highway."

Lucy nodded eagerly, relieved to have found a kindred spirit. "Everything had to be how she said. I know she was paying, but Tony was my husband and we'd always planned to be buried together."

Rosie concentrated on maintaining a bland expression.

Predictably, her friend rushed on. "It wasn't illegal or anything. Dave said it was my decision, because I'm next-of-kin, no matter who was paying." She was twisting her handkerchief back into a ball again. "If they'd put Tone in the Wesley plot like she wanted, I could never be buried alongside him."

The hairs on the back of Rosie's neck began to stand up, a sure sign that she was about to hear bad news. She gave a little shiver and then, despite herself, couldn't keep from saying urgently; "You mean, he *wasn't* buried in the family plot?"

"Do you promise not to tell anyone?"

Rosie nodded, her palms sweaty with apprehension.

"It's just that if Mrs. Wesley found out..." Lucy hesitated.

Unable to bear the suspense any longer, Rosie interrupted brusquely; "I understand, Lucy. Don't worry; I'll never breathe a word to anyone."

Lucy took a deep breath and said in a rush; "Tony wasn't buried anywhere. I had him cremated."

There was complete silence. Rosie was too shocked to speak. For a moment it seemed that the simple process of moving her lips to produce intelligible sound had passed beyond her capabilities. The phrase "struck dumb" bounced around her brain. She'd read it in books and heard it in movies, but had always taken it for poetic licence, not literal truth. Now she knew differently.

Then she felt the room getting colder, and waves of sadness and despair began to wash over her. Looking across Lucy's head she saw a familiar smoky outline undulating in the far corner of the room. Long, thin appendages reached out toward them, and she began to struggle for every breath. Soon the room was in total darkness, and from its black depths came a rasping whisper; "It wasn't me. Not me ..."

She became aware that Lucy was leaning over her, her face filled with worry. "Rose? Rosie? Are you alright?" An arm went round her shoulders and the cold edge of a glass was pressed to her lips. "It's all right. Just try to drink some water."

She sipped obediently, her mind racing. Whatever can I say, she thought. The truth's not an option. I can't tell Lucy that her dead husband's rattling around the room, having a phantom snit because my best chance of solving his murder's just been scuttled.

After a moment, she pushed the glass away and murmured, "I'm fine now. Really. It's just that my sugar levels go out of whack sometimes." This was as good an explanation as any. Given the number of brownies she'd eaten it wasn't entirely untrue.

"Well, you sure scared me. You went as white as a ghost. Don't you worry that might happen while you're driving?"

"No, I'm usually more careful with my sugar intake." Not a lie, either.

But Lucy was persistent in her concern; "Well have you been to the doctor? Is there medication you can take?"

Rosie barely heard her. Her mind was still reeling from the realisation that her scheme to catch Little Yarmouth's murderous arsonist had just collapsed in ruins. How was she ever going to sort things out, now that there wouldn't be any autopsy results to show the police? There was no Plan B.

Her disappointment was so keen that all she wanted to do was make her goodbyes and leave. But that wasn't on. It wasn't just rude, it was illogical. In Lucy's view, her decision to cremate Tony should be of only passing interest to Rosie, except for the Clodagh Wesley angle.

So ignoring the army of butterflies that had taken up residence in her stomach, she said airily. "Oh, John knows all about it. It's a hereditary condition, actually. Quite a few women in my family have had it. We all learn to cope."

She sat up and reached again for the glass. "And don't you worry about the cremation. Dave knows his business, and if he says it was alright, then I'm sure it was." She sipped casually. "Plus, most people in town would be happy to see Clodagh taken down a peg or two."

Lucy sighed. "I know, but we still mustn't let it get out. She's so vindictive, and Dave said she'd make his life a misery if she knew. I told him that if it came to that, I'd say it was all my idea."

Rosie felt the stirrings of suspicion. "So you didn't suggest it, then?"

"No. I thought everything was done and dusted. But, the day before the funeral, he took me aside and said he could see I was very upset about the burial, and he'd arrange for cremation if I wanted. But we'd have to keep it to ourselves."

Rosie couldn't help but be intrigued. "So, what was in the coffin?"

"It wasn't empty, if that's what you're thinking", Lucy said defensively. "I put a lock of Tone's hair in, and his class ring and…" she looked embarrassed. " Oh dear, it sounds a bit silly, now."

"I'm sure it wasn't. What else did you put in?"

"His dental plate."

Despite Rosie's determination to keep a straight face, the mental image of a dental plate being ceremoniously borne away to the Wesley family plot was too much to bear. She felt her lip twitch, and was relieved to see a similar expression cross Lucy's face. Then they caught sight of each other, and burst into simultaneous gales of laughter.

Rosie recovered first. "Oh God Lucy, I'm sorry. I don't know what came over me. That was unforgivable."

But Lucy was still chuckling. "No, it wasn't Rosie. It's very funny," and she started laughing again. After a minute she managed to say; "It seemed sensible at the time. Dave said dental plates don't burn, so I thought it was a good idea to put it in the coffin." She wiped her eyes.

Questions came crowding into Rosie's head, pushing out her feelings of disappointment. Why had Lucy asked her to find out about the autopsy, if Tony was already ash in an urn? And what really lay behind Dave Mason's readiness to breach his professional standards?

For breach them he had, she had no doubt of that. Although his duplicitous action might not have been illegal, it was certainly unethical. Was this just affectionate concern for his high school sweetheart, or was he making doubly sure that Tony's murder could never be proved?

"I don't understand though, Luce. Why did you ask me to follow up about the missing autopsy, if Tony was already cremated?"

"Because he wasn't, then. The crematorium has a schedule, and Dave had to wait to go on that day. I think Mason's is on a Thursday." Lucy hung her head, avoiding Rosie's eyes. "And then I moved back home, and every day just ran into the next, and I forgot what I'd said about Tone's accident." She looked up, shame-faced. "I feel like a complete idiot, sending John on that wild goose chase."

For crying out loud, Rosie thought. Now Lucy's feeling guilty over this miserable business. How many more people have to have sleepless nights because they imagine they've wronged that s.o.b? Carol, Dougie and now Lucy. Even that old harpy Clodagh Wesley thinks she contributed to his death, while the only guilty ones are the murderer and his victim. And although Tony's certainly suffering, it looks like his killer will get away scot-free.

She patted her friend's hand. "No, don't think that for a minute. He was happy to help, and he did get the answer to your question." 'And to mine', she added mentally. Then, another thought struck her. "How did you explain the…er," she floundered for a delicate term. "box, you know.. container, to your mom and dad?"

"Well, that's the thing, you see. I couldn't bring the urn here so I took it to…"

She was interrupted by the sound of the front door opening and Agnes Curtis' cheerful voice in the hall. "It's only me, pet."

"Hi, mom. We're in here."

The living room door opened, and a heady scent of perfumed hair spray announced Agnes' return from the beauty parlour. "Hi there, Rosie; it's nice to see you. I was hoping to get home before you left."

"Hello Agnes. How are you?" Although Agnes was one of Rosie's favourite parishioners, she wished Clippers had been a bit slower with their ministrations this morning; she had a feeling there were more revelations to come. "Lucy told me the good news about her dad. It's wonderful news that he'll be home soon."

Agnes beamed. "Yes. Sunday or Monday, for sure. And he's feeling so much better." She glanced down at the empty mugs on the coffee table. "Can I get you girls some more coffee?"

"No thanks, mom."

Rosie chimed in "No, not for me either, thanks Agnes."

Agnes cast a surreptitious glance at her watch. "Well, how about a bowl of soup and a sandwich? The food's so expensive in the hospital cafeteria that we generally eat before we go."

Rosie wasn't in the mood for a jolly luncheon, and the prospect of social chit-chat was distinctly unappealing. All she wanted to do now was get somewhere quiet and re-think her next move. "That sounds tempting, but I should be going. I've got some errands to run, and then a dog to walk." She stood up and started across the room. "Be sure to give Roy my best wishes," she said as she passed Agnes, "And your hair looks great."

Agnes blushed. "Yes, Chips always does a nice job." She patted a stray curl back into place self-consciously. "I'll let Roy know you were asking after him."

Lucy followed Rosie out into the hall and opened the front door. Glancing behind her, she said softly; "Thanks for everything, Rosie. Will you tell John how much I appreciate his help?"

"Sure, Lucy. By the way, good luck on Monday." A thought struck her. "Why don't we get together for lunch sometime next week? My treat. You can tell me all about the new job."

Lucy looked over her shoulder again. "Actually, Rose, now that you know about..." her voice dropped to a whisper, "... the cremation, maybe you could help me with something."

"Of course I will, if I can. What do you need?"

"You know I said I couldn't bring the urn back here?" Rosie nodded. "Well, I took it to Veterans Avenue, and hid it in an old air vent down in the basement. But obviously I couldn't tell Carl about it when they went to move my stuff, and I haven't been able to face going back into that house on my own." She shuddered. "I keep seeing him, lying at the bottom of those stairs..." her voice faded away completely.

Rosie touched her briefly on the shoulder. "No problem. When do you want to go?"

"The tenancy's up next Monday, so it's got to be before then. How about Saturday morning, around eleven?"

"That'll be fine; shall I pick you up?"

Lucy shook her head. "No, it'll be easier to meet you there. I can make some excuse, and borrow mom's car." She gave Rosie a quick hug. "And..." she hesitated, "...there's something else."

I can guess what's next, Rosie thought. It's not only Tony's ghost that I'm going to be hosting for a while. She looked questioningly at her friend.

"Could you hold onto the urn for a few days? I'm planning to ask Dave if I can keep it at the Funeral Home, but it doesn't seem right to start asking for favours right off the bat." Lucy smiled apologetically.

Rosie smiled back. "Don't you worry about a thing, Luce. Tony can sit in my guest room as long as he likes," adding to herself 'he's already quite familiar with the wallpaper.'

Agnes' voice came from the kitchen; "Lucy; lunch is on the table."

"Coming, mom". Lucy stepped back into the hall. "I keep saying *thankyou*, but it seems so inadequate somehow."

"What are friends for?" Rosie started down the path, then half-turned and called; "See you Saturday."

Lucy smiled, gave a wave and disappeared inside.

Rosie waved in return, unlocked the car and got in slowly. For a few minutes she sat collecting her thoughts and battling the frustrated tears that were building up behind her eyes. Moments later she pulled away from the curb with a feeling of glum relief. At least now she could relax and dispense with the cheerful façade.

Less than two hours ago, she had been happily confident that Tony's murder would soon be solved, and he'd be free to move on to his next appointed destination. But, without a body, she knew that goal had slipped from her grasp. She had nothing to take to the police that would convince them to open a murder investigation. Unless the killer suddenly suffered a crisis of conscience, (and how likely was that?), Tony's death would be forever remembered as a drunken accident.

Beside her, on the front passenger seat, lay her bundle of reunion posters. Before leaving for Albion Way this morning, she had put them there as a reminder to get some up around town. So, telling herself sternly to 'get a grip,' she turned the car toward the town centre.

But, despite her resolve, her eyes were soon clouded with tears. Looking around, she spotted the only public place where a person could sit and cry without fear of interruption.

Brushing the back of her hand across her eyes, she drove through the cemetery's wrought-iron gates and parked under a canopy of trees. For the next little while, the squirrels and birds busying themselves overhead were to have their daily round disturbed by sobbing, hiccupping and some very unladylike language.

Chapter 23 – More Surprises

After a while Rosie stopped crying. She lay back and closed her eyes, worn out by the maelstrom of emotions unleashed by Lucy's confession. She was shaking with disappointment and frustration, and there was a furious anger curling around in the pit of her stomach. It was so unfair! After everything she'd done, her one chance at success had been snatched away. Damn Tony Wesley! And damn Dave Mason as well; the cremation was all his fault!

Even worse, it was yet another sign that he might be the killer. Angry tears started flowing again, and she dug through her purse for more tissues.

She was still wiping her eyes when a sharp tap came on the window. For a moment, Rosie gazed uncomprehendingly at the face peering in. Was that really Dave Mason or an apparition conjured by her fevered imagination?

"Rosie? All you all right?" The car door swung open and he looked in anxiously.

She gave her nose a vigorous blow, swallowed and tried to sound calm. "Yes," she choked out. "I'm fine, thanks." Her mind was racing. What the hell is he doing here? Did he follow me? No, I'm getting paranoid; he's a mortician and this is a cemetery. He probably spends a lot of his time here.

"Well, you don't look fine to me." A hand was extended into the car. "I think you could do with a coffee. C'mon, I won't take no for an answer."

"No, I have to get home. I'm okay now, really." She reached to pull the door closed.

But he held on to it firmly. "Rosie, I won't pry, I promise. But you're in no shape to be driving." His tone lightened; "And I could do with some company; it's been a rough morning."

Short of being deliberately unpleasant, Rosie couldn't think of any way to decline this unnerving invitation from a murder suspect. She looked around uneasily; the cemetery was deserted.

Unfortunately she had never mastered the trick of saying "no" firmly but graciously. So she took Dave's proffered hand reluctantly and let him help her out of the car. All the while, a little vignette was playing in her head; her family gathered around a headstone, shaking their heads over the inscription; *Rosie Cornish Rowe. She didn't want to be rude.*

It was very hot but Dave set a brisk pace along the path, making for a rustic bench next to the cemetery's public water tap. Trailing along behind him Rosie noticed he was carrying a small gym bag, and slowed her pace even further. Oh God, what did he have in the bag? A knife, a gun? Gloves and a rope? And what better place to hide a body, than in a cemetery? There were probably any number of deep holes already dug, just waiting for an occupant. She'd disappear without trace....

He reached the seat, turned and watched her progress intently. "I know, this seems like an odd place for a coffee break. But I usually stop here around this time on Thursday morning." He began to unzip the bag. "I don't want to introduce a gloomy note but ..," he reached into the bag and Rosie came to a full stop; "...Thursday's our day for cremations and it's always chaos in there." He nodded toward a low building visible in the distance. "The town really needs to spend some money updating those ovens. It takes forever to get the job done. I can be in there all day if I've got several clients."

Rosie stayed where she was, her eyes on the gym bag.

Dave sat down and waited. When she didn't move he patted the bench and said; "The seat's quite dry, you know." Then, sensing her reluctance, he went on apologetically; "I'm sorry Rose. I always forget people don't like hearing details of the business."

He reached into the gym bag and pulled out a flat tupperware container. "Actually, I'm kinda glad to get a chance to ask you about something." Prising off the container's lid he looked inside and grimaced; "Mmm... raw carrot sticks. Thanks mom." He dropped the container down on the bench, rummaged around in the bag and pulled out an oversized Thermos.

A wave of relief washed over Rosie. Having half expected to see a meat cleaver materialise in his big paw, she gave herself a mental slap and marched resolutely toward him. I'm getting paranoid she thought, as she reached the bench and sat down. This is ridiculous; I've got to get a hold of myself. In as normal a voice as she could muster she asked; "So how's your mom doing?"

"Much better, thanks. I got some stuff from the pharmacy like you suggested and it picked her right up." He poured steaming liquid into the thermos cup and passed it to her. "It's unsweetened. Mom wants me to limit my sugar intake, but I can't drink it like that." He dug around in his pocket; "I always carry a few packets with me; want one?"

Rosie sipped at her coffee. "No, thanks. I'm trying to lose weight."

"Good idea. That is...I don't mean to say you *need* to lose weight." He floundered, blushing to the roots of his hair. "It's not that you're fat...Oh God, I always say the wrong thing..."

Rosie couldn't stop herself from leaning across to pat his hand. "Not to worry, Dave, I know what you mean." And how bizarre is this, she thought. I'm in the cemetery, having a merry little picnic with my best pick for town psychopath. Maybe Tony Wesley will drift on by and complete the picture.

Dave began intertwining his fingers and flexing them back and forth. He cleared his throat. "All joking aside, Rose. I'm glad I ran into you like this, because I've been wanting to get you alone."

Panic began tying her stomach in knots again. With her mind racing she tensed, gripped the thermos cup tightly and glanced around. The car's not far away and it's not locked. If he lunges at me, I'll throw the coffee in his face and make a run for it. Luckily he's not looking right at me; God, I wish I'd worked out more... She began to inch along the bench, out of his reach.

"Seems like there's always someone listening in on private conversations in town." His voice was pitched low and he was studying his hands. "But not here; nice quiet places, cemeteries."

Rosie took a deep breath, turned towards him and got ready to fling the hot coffee in his face. "I guess so." She was surprised by the steadiness of her voice.

"You've been talking to Lucy." He spoke softly, but his tone was accusatory.

"Yes, I saw her this morning, actually."

He still didn't look at her, just started slowly cracking his knuckles, one by one. The sound grated on Rosie's overstretched nerves. After a moment's thought, he said slowly; "I think it's time I made a bit of a confession."

Rosie didn't reply. Matters were taking a very unexpected turn, and she knew the outcome would either be very good or extremely bad. "Sorry, Dave. Not sure what you mean."

He shot her a penetrating look. "Yes, you do."

She leant forward and prepared to run. "Well, Lucy did mention that you'd offered her a job. She can't wait to get started on Monday."

To her surprise, Dave's face creased into a wide smile. "Really? She said that?"

Something in his expression made Rosie relax. Hang on a minute, she thought. I think this confession's got more to do with high school romance than high school arson. She said gently; "Of course she did. But what's that got to do with a confession?"

Now he was looking at his feet. Finally he muttered; "You know how I felt about her in high school, Rose."

She smiled and nodded for him to go on.

"Well, when they came back to town and I saw her again, I knew nothing had changed. All I wanted to do was meet up with Wesley some dark night and knock all his teeth out. Then I got the call to pick up a body from the hospital, and it was him. That sonnofabitch." His face flushed again. "Sorry about the language; he always did bring out the worst in me."

"I'm beginning to think he brought out the worst in a lot of people."

"Damn right." He hung his head; "I'm ashamed to admit it now, but I was glad to see him flat out on that gurney. I never got the chance to beat him up, but I did enjoy pumping him full of embalming fluid."

Rosie shuddered. "Dave, I get the point. Could you leave off with the gory details, please?"

Strangely, Dave's "confession" had made Rosie less certain that he was Tony's killer. Which was odd, because he certainly hated him enough. Or maybe Dave, the psychopath, was just a skilful manipulator trying to cover his tracks. What better way to divert suspicion than to admit hating the victim?

"Sorry, I keep forgetting." He took a carrot stick and chewed it absently.

Rosie decided to change the subject. "How does your mom feel about Lucy working at Mason's?"

"It was her idea; well, not hiring Lucy particularly, but getting in some help. Since she got sick, the office work's been piling up. I think she's finally accepted that flying solo's too much for her. Of course, I thought of Lucy right away." He spotted Rosie's half-smile and added hastily; "No. It wasn't like that. Her mom told me at the visitation that Tony'd left her penniless, so I knew she could do with a pay check." His expression softened; "And she's such a kind person; she'll be wonderful with the clients."

"You're right. She'll be perfect, particularly after what she's just been through."

"Carrot stick?" Dave waved the container in her direction. "Until I had my check-up, Mom always made carrot cake for me to bring to the crematorium. Then Doc Drucker said I had to lose weight, so now I just get the carrots."

Rosie took one without enthusiasm. "My sympathies" she said, and for a few minutes they munched together in a morose silence.

While she was eating, Rosie reviewed her situation. She soon reached the conclusion that this scary run-in with one of her prime suspects could be quite useful. Here was a golden opportunity to get Dave's version of the school fire and Martin Robertson's death. Maybe even shed some light on whether he'd been involved or not. Yes, it was definitely time to trot out her "worried Willie Robertson" story.

She shook the dregs of her coffee from the cup. "Thanks for the coffee and carrot stick Dave, but I'd better be going. I want to finish getting my reunion posters up." She handed him the cup. "Speaking of the reunion, did you hear what happened at the last committee meeting?"

Dave grinned; "Yeah, Dougie dropped by and told me. Sorry I missed all the fireworks."

"I don't know about you, but I'll be glad when it's all over. We seem to be stirring up some bad feelings."

He gave her a puzzled look. "Whadya mean?"

"Oh, mainly ancient history. Stuff from before my time." Smothering her conscience, she crossed her fingers and ploughed ahead. "There've been complaints." A bald faced lie, but necessary in the circumstances. At least now she had his full attention.

"Who's been complaining? I haven't heard anything."

She feigned surprise. "Really? Maybe I was mistaken. But I thought from the way Marilyn Robertson spoke that Willie had made his feelings known to the committee."

Dave looked annoyed. "Not to me, he hasn't. What's his beef, anyway?"

Rosie sighed loudly and tried to sound reluctant. "Well, she thinks he's worried that all this focus on the past will get people talking about his son's death again." She paused, and looked at him meaningfully. "You know? Martin? The accident on the CN tracks?"

He looked blank.

She tried again. "The fire in the gym when all the football equipment got ruined?" Dave shook his head.

I can't believe this, she thought. "The year the team couldn't defend their High School Championship title? You were on the football team, weren't you?"

At last he seemed to understand. "Oh, yeah, I remember something about that."

Trying not to let her exasperation show through, she said testily; "I'm surprised you don't remember. To hear some people talk, losing the football equipment was the single worst thing that ever happened to John Galt High."

Dave was wiping out the thermos cup with a paper napkin. "Well, I guess it was pretty bad. The Eagles never won the championship again after that, so I can see why it's a sore point with some folks." He poured himself a coffee. "But what's the connection with Martin Robertson?"

Taken aback by Dave's apparent lack of interest, Rosie considered her answer carefully. Perhaps this was just another example of psychopathic cunning. "The story goes that Martin set the fire, because he was cut from the team. A few days after that, he fell in front of a train. It was never determined if he died accidentally or if he... killed himself." She barely stopped herself from saying "was murdered."

"What year was this?"

"1959. In November."

"Well, I remember that year, for sure. But I can't figure why anyone would say Martin was cut from the team; that makes no sense. There were a lot of injuries that fall, and the Eagles were short manned. I was out practically the whole semester. Smashed my leg up in October; two breaks and a complicated fracture. Now *that's* something I won't forget." He gazed out pensively at the gravestone studded vista. "Never much use to the team after that."

Taking a gulp of his coffee he swung round to face her. "That's why I don't recall much about the fire and Martin Robertson. The leg was a real mess and needed several surgeries, special physio. the works. Couldn't get it round here then, so I went up to Toronto and stayed with my uncle Phil." He chuckled. "Missed a couple of month's school, too. Not that I cared much about that, of course."

Rosie stared at him incredulously, barely able to believe her ears. He had the perfect alibi! "So you weren't in town when the fire happened?"

"No, I was in hospital most of October in traction. When I finally got the plaster off I still couldn't come home, what with all the out-patient and physio treatments. So I just stayed in Toronto, feeling sorry for myself." He drained his cup and began to wipe it out again. "Kinda lost interest in everything going on back here; you know how self-centred kids get."

Dave, you gorgeous man, I could kiss you, Rosie thought excitedly. Then caution set in. She tried to sound casual; "Oh. I guess all the excitement had died down by the time you came home?"

"Yup, it must've been December when I got back because the Christmas lights were up on King. I remember that 'cos when Dad picked me up at the station, he joked that the town was all lit up for me."

Rosie was elated. She'd cracked it! Dave couldn't have set the school fire which meant he wasn't the serial arsonist or the killer. By default, the culprit had to be Pete Anderson. Not that I can do anything about it, she reminded herself. But just knowing Dave's out of the frame makes everything better somehow.

".....don't know how we can stop people remembering the past. I thought that's the point of having a reunion." Dave was still speaking.

She'd lost the thread, but jumped in anyway. "That's right. But I did tell Marilyn I was sure the committee would take Willie's concerns to heart."

"I don't know about that, but it sure looks like a case of *least said, soonest mended* to me." He sounded disinterested. "And who'd want to draw attention to something like that, anyway?"

Rosie's eyebrows lifted. "Really? I should've thought in your business you'd have lots of first-hand experience with tragedy vultures." She stood up and looked at her watch. "Darn. If I don't get home soon, there'll be a puddle in the hall. Thanks again for the coffee and company, Dave." She bent down and gave him a peck on the cheek. "You can't imagine how much difference you've made to my day."

Dave's face reddened, and he smiled sheepishly. "Well, now you've made my day, too." She turned to leave but he caught her arm. "Before you go though, I still have to ask you something." He hesitated, then said in a rush; "A bit of feminine advice."

Rosie tried not to smile, because she had a good idea of what he wanted to ask. "Is this about Lucy?"

"Yup. Well... I just wondered how I should handle things....you know, when I should mention how I feel..." His voice tailed off as he pulled a handkerchief from his breast pocket and wiped his brow.

Rosie sat down next to him. "I know this is really important to you, Dave. But you've got to be patient. Despite what everyone says about Tony, Lucy loved him and they were together for a very long time. She has to come to terms with her loss, and that won't happen overnight."

Dave looked at her miserably. "But I don't want to lose her again."

"I'm afraid that's a risk you'll have to take." His shoulders sagged with disappointment, and Rosie felt a rush of sympathy for him as she went on; "Look, there's zero chance she'll leave town. Her parents need her right now, and she's really excited about the job with you and your mom." She gave him a quick smile and stood up. "Just be a kind friend for a while and I'm willing to bet the rest will follow. You were high school sweethearts, after all."

He nodded his understanding. "Okay. It's just that I'm not very good at this kind of stuff, and I don't want to get it wrong. I don't even know if she likes me."

Rosie silently counted to ten. For crying out loud, are we back in eleventh grade? "Of course she likes you, Dave. You're an old friend. But she's got more important things on her mind and you've got to give her space." She glanced at her watch again. "I hope that helps. Sorry, but I've really got to run."

"Oh, right. Guess I should be getting back to work, too." He stood, picked up the tupperware and tipped a heap of carrot sticks out onto the grass. Giving her a conspiratorial smile he said; "At least the rabbits and squirrels appreciate mom's chopping skills." Then, with a little wave he started down the path; "Thanks for the words of wisdom, Rosie. I'll play it cool, don't worry."

Hurrying in the opposite direction, Rosie could hear him whistling cheerfully as he strolled toward the crematorium. She smiled to herself. Now she knew Dave wasn't a murderous arsonist, she was more than happy to wish him the best of luck with Lucy.

Her warm and fuzzy feelings evaporated the instant she opened the car door. She had forgotten to crack the windows so, despite being in the shade, the Buick was hotter than an oven.

After several minutes of fumbling to wind down the front windows she realised her hands were shaking. She had no idea if this was due to Dave's ultra-strong coffee, or to her emotional roller-coaster of a morning. But the end result was the same; she was all thumbs. Eventually she got the windows open, turned the key in the ignition and drove off through the cemetery at a far from sedate pace.

Her eye fell on the posters, sliding around on the front seat. "Not a snowball's chance in hell," she said aloud. She'd had more than enough for one day; all she wanted to do now was get home and relax. Tony Wesley and his guilty secrets would have to wait.

*   *   *   *

"St. Jude's parish office." Cradling the phone against her ear with her shoulder, Rosie continued pulling at her typing, lodged firmly under Donny's recumbent bulk.

"Hi, Rose. It's Marilyn. How's…."

Rosie's chin lost its grip, and the phone clattered to the floor. "Now look what you've made me do," she said to Donny, as she scrambled to retrieve the hand set. The cat looked at her and yawned.

"Sorry, Marilyn, I dropped the phone. How's everything with you?"

"Oh, pretty good." Marilyn's tone belied her answer. "Just wanted to tell you your order's in. I could drop it off this evening, if you like."

Recalling her reluctance to go to Stella's "party,, Rosie was surprised at how eager she was to see her purchases. Guess that tells me something about the state of my wardrobe she thought, glancing down at her limp top and too-tight pants.

"Yes, sure. I'll be home all evening," adding silently 'same as usual.' "Any idea what time you'll be over?" Silence. "Marilyn? Are you still there?" She thought she could hear angry voices in the background.

"Sorry, Rose." Marilyn sounded flustered. "I'm at the paper and Gord's shouting something." Another muffled conversation, then; "Sometime between seven and nine, I guess. Is that okay?"

"That'll be fine." Marilyn's presence at the Clarion could mean only one thing. Concerned, Rosie asked; "Is Mr. Robertson still sick?"

"Not sick, but this heat really gets to him." She gave an exasperated sigh; "Have to go, Rose, I've got customers lining up. See you tonight."

"Yes, thanks Marilyn. See you later."

Now with both hands free, Rosie leaned over and gently pushed Donny to the far side of her desk. Why he found napping on her paperwork so irresistible was a mystery, but he certainly never missed any opportunity to do so. Of course, it was her own fault for leaving the interior office door open. 'New rule,' she told herself. 'Always close that door before going to lunch.'

She retrieved her stack of typing and gave it a brisk shake, watching as a cascade of black and white hair fell to the floor. "I can see why Liz isn't your biggest fan," she said to the cat. Donny ignored her and closed his eyes.

The afternoon wore on. It was very stuffy in the office, and Rosie had just decided to go to the rectory kitchen for a cold drink when the outer door opened. A wave of heat preceded Dave Mason into the room.

"Hi, Rose. We've got to stop meeting this way." He chuckled rather too heartily and dropped an envelope onto the desk in front of her. "Think that's the last of the Murcheson donations. Had a lot of out-of-town family drop by this week." He shook his head. "Doesn't matter how long I'm in the funeral business, it's still tough to see a young guy go like that."

Rosie looked at him sympathetically. "I can well imagine," she said quietly.

Unusually for him, Dave seemed at a loss for words. He shifted from foot to foot and an awkward silence soon filled the room. Rosie wondered if he was feeling embarrassed by yesterday's confidences, and was just about to mention the weather (the only safe topic she could think of) when Donny decided it was time he had some attention. In one sinuous movement, he stood up and began rubbing the side of his face along the edge of Dave's black jacket.

"Hey there, big fella" Dave said, clearly relieved by the distraction. He began scratching the cat's neck to the accompaniment of a loud and ecstatic purring.

Rosie scurried round the desk. "Donny, stop. I'm sorry Dave, you'll be covered in cat hair."

"Not to worry, Rose; it'll brush off," and he continued petting his new found friend until Donny, sated, jumped down and ambled toward the door into the rectory. "What a great cat" he said, brushing hair off his hands and then off his jacket.

"Yes, he's very affectionate," she replied. "Can be a bit much at times, though." But not today, she thought. Today, he was actually useful.

"Well, I'd best be on my way." Dave headed toward the door, then pulled up suddenly and turned around. "Nearly forgot. I knew I meant to tell you something. Do you remember that John Doe we buried a coupla' weeks back?"

"The guy who fell off the railway bridge?"

"Yup, the very same. Wouldn't you know? Now we've buried him, someone's come looking."

"No! After all this time? You're joking."

"I'm not." Gratified by her response to his news, Dave went on cheerily; "Had two cops in the office today. O.P.P. finally got a DNA match for a guy called Rick Edwards. His brother's been looking for him and followed the trail here."

"Here? Little Yarmouth, you mean?"

"Yup. Apparently, last the family heard from him, Edwards was working in Little Yarmouth. Driving a truck, or some such thing."

"So, he wasn't a homeless wino?"

Dave shrugged. "Don't know about that. He'd been arrested as a teenager for joy-riding and drug possession, but being under-age, those records were sealed. That's why his fingerprints never showed up when the cops first checked him out."

Rosie wondered how Dave knew so much about Rick Edwards. She'd always found the police very tight-lipped when it came to their "enquiries."

"It was good of the O.P.P. to fill you in on all the details." She gave him a quizzical smile.

"Alright; guilty as charged." Dave put his hands up in mock surrender. "The cops didn't tell me anything except John Doe's real name. They're just trying to find out where he was working last fall. I got the rest from my cousin, Althea."

Rosie was none the wiser. "Althea?"

"She's a civilian clerk at the Goderich detachment. Does up all the reports. Likes to chat." In a stage whisper he murmured; "I can trust you to keep that to yourself, eh Rosie?"

"Cross my heart and hope to die," she said, surprised by the little shiver of apprehension that went sliding down her spine. "So does this mean the police will be opening up an investigation?"

"Althea says the family are pushing for it." Dave leant forward and dropped his voice again. "But between you and me, I don't think the cops'll have much luck. When we picked him up last year, no-one could tell how he'd died." When Rosie didn't respond, he added; "He'd been lying on the track. Trains do a lot of damage, y'know."

She sat down abruptly. "Thanks, Dave. I got the picture the first time."

"That's okay, then." Dave was always blithely unaware of the normal reaction to his detailed descriptions of violent death. With a shrug he turned back towards the door; "Oh, and another thing. The cops said they'll be canvassing the town for a few days; trying to find out where the guy worked, where he was staying and all that. Don't be surprised if you get a visit. They're going to check all the churches just in case Mr. Edwards had found Jesus."

"Right. I'll mention it to Father Matthews. Thanks for letting me know, Dave." He was stepping through the door. "Say hi to your mom for me."

"Will do. See you, Rosie." The door swung shut and he was gone.

In the spirit of "advice to the lovelorn," Rosie made a mental note to suggest to Dave that he avoid regaling Lucy with the more gruesome aspects of his profession. She'd be willing to bet that hearing those details would cast quite a chill on the progress of his romantic hopes.

She glanced at the clock; 4:15 p.m. Thank goodness the afternoon was nearly done. There was just time to find Father Matthews and pass on Dave's 'heads-up' about the impending police visit, before she could close up the office and head home.

*   *   *   *

Across town, Sister Mary Bernadette was also watching the clock, but not with eager anticipation for the end of her work day. She was using the second hand as a stand-in for her metronome, which had disappeared from the school's Music Room at the end of term.

"One, two, three; one, two, three...slow down, Peter. This is Handel's Largo, not Handel's presto." Eleven year old Peter Marcellus grinned at his teacher. He was a hard working but reluctant pianist, and they both knew he would rather be playing baseball than Handel. "Sorry, Sister." His playing slowed briefly but soon picked up speed again, jollying the piece along to its conclusion.

His teacher sighed and gave him an appraising stare. "Note-perfect Peter, as usual. But you must get the timing right, and much more expression is needed, if you want a good mark in your exam."

"Yes, Sister." He glanced at the clock.

"Alright. Off you go. I'll see you on Tuesday, and remember *molto espressivo*."

In an instant, the youngster had grabbed up his music bag and bolted to the door. "Bye, Sister."

"Bye, Peter." Thankfully, Sister Mary eased herself down onto the piano stool and closed her eyes. Much as she enjoyed her young students, she had to admit it was getting harder to carry a full teaching load. Her fingers strayed to the piano keys, and the strains of Handel's poignant composition were soon filling the room again.

As she played, her mind drifted to her pupils. Dear Peter; he'd never be more than a competent pianist. Fortunately, that wouldn't cause him any grief. Music wasn't his dream, it was his mother's and she couldn't grasp that no amount of drill or practice will ignite an ambition you don't want for yourself.

Now Bobbie Cornish was a whole different story; music was life to him. Talented and driven, he'll scale the heights and forge a glittering career, of that she had no doubt. Then thoughts of another star pupil, Bobbie's aunt Rosie, came to mind and she remembered how that career had died before it ever started. She cautioned herself aloud; "Remember, nothing in life is ever guaranteed."

Without warning she was hit by a stab of anxiety so sharp and unexpected, that at she first mistook it for another angina attack. But even as she reached into her pocket for nitro-glycerine, she realised this was not a physical pain; it was a warning.

Laying both her hands in her lap, she slowed and deepened her breathing and concentrated her mind. The silence in the room became palpable, bringing with it the aura of a malevolent personality. With chilling clarity, her mind's ear heard him giggle and say; "Nosey little Rosie. Now, what do you know?"

The old nun closed her eyes and murmured the prayer invoked for centuries against the Devil and his servants. "Holy Michael Archangel; defend us in the day of battle. Be our safeguard against the wickedness and snares of the Devil...." Sister Mary knew this was all she could do to help to help her beloved student but, for the first time in her life, wondered if it would be enough. She felt a terrible evil gathering its strength, surrounding Rosie with menace and drawing her onto a path that led to mortal danger.

*   *   *   *

Rosie hurried to the front door, grateful that Marilyn's arrival had coincided with one of Gussie's garden forays. For once, she could welcome a guest into her home without having to shout over his ear-splitting yaps. She swung the door wide. "Hi, Marilyn; come on in. It's good to see you."

Her beauty consultant looked decidedly frazzled. "Sorry I'm a bit late, Rosie. I've been delivering all round town." She handed over a vivid pink carrier bag. "Here's your order."

"Oh, great." Rosie peeked into the bag. "Have you got a minute to come in for a cold drink? I've made lemonade, or there's wine chilling if you prefer?"

Marilyn sighed heavily and fanned her face with her hand. "Oh God, yes, please. Lemonade sounds wonderful. It's so humid tonight and, wouldn't you know it, the a/c's dying in the car."

Rosie waved towards the living room. "Go on through, Marilyn. It's nice and cool in there. I'll get the lemonade."

When she came back a few moments later, Marilyn was standing by the window air-conditioner, still fanning at herself ineffectually.

"There you go." Rosie passed across an icy glass, damp with condensation. In the summer, she always kept a few tall glasses in the fridge, unconsciously following her mother's oft-repeated dictum; *a cold drink is always more refreshing served in a chilled glass.*

Marilyn sat down on the couch. "You're a life saver, Rosie." She took a long draught, then pressed the glass to the side of her face. "You know, I love doing the colour parties, but the deliveries can be a real pain. Particularly after a long day at the paper."

Rosie nodded her agreement. "Yes, I can imagine. So, will Mr. Robertson be out for long?"

"Not sure. But the good news is that him and Gordie have finally agreed to hire someone in full time." She took another deep swallow and set the glass down on the coffee table. "I've told them both, over and over, I'm not working at the paper permanent."

A thin trail of moisture beads started trickling down the side of the glass and she retrieved it quickly. "Sorry Rosie. This lemonade'll leave a ring for sure. Have you got a coaster?"

"Yes, somewhere here." Rosie sighed as she pushed aside a stack of magazines. "Someday I'll get all this stuff sorted out." A pair of coasters peeked out from beneath one of Lucy's year books. "There you go."

"Well, lookee here." Marilyn picked up the book and started idly turning its pages. "What made you dig all these out?"

"The reunion. I'm on the committee."

"Oh, right." She took a second book. "You've got quite a collection here."

"Well, they're not really mine; they were Tony Wesley's. Lucy lent them to me. He was years ahead of us, so she knew I wouldn't have those editions. She thought I could use them."

Marilyn was checking dates. "These begin at fifty-five. I started in fifty-four, so I've got that one, if that's of any help."

Please, no more year books, Rosie thought. That's the last thing I need. She smiled and tried to sound enthusiastic; "Thanks Marilyn, but I'm pretty certain we've got all the earlier ones by now."

"Well, just so you know, the offer's there." Marilyn handed an open book across the coffee table. "Look at that. Do you believe those hair-styles?"

Rosie glanced at the picture in front of her and chuckled. Yes, everyone did look ready for the sock-hop. She recognized a few faces: Lionel Barrymore, the super in Carol's building; Loretta O'Halloran's husband, Sean; a moonfaced Dougie Ferguson and finally Marilyn, her head crowned by a mane of back-combed black hair. "Interesting how some people don't change much at all, and others look entirely different after a few years," she said, closing the book and passing it back.

"Right." Marilyn was still shuffling through the books, checking dates. "Here's the next one." She flicked through the pages. "Yes, that's my grade nine picture. I'd got my hair cut, by then." She turned the book around and pointed.

Rosie sighed and stretched out her hand. Was anything more mind-numbingly boring than admiring Marilyn's high school photos?

Without warning, the book slipped from her grasp and fell face down on the carpet. "Oops, these are heavier than they look," she said, picking it up and skimming through to grade nine. She soon spotted Dougie smiling out from a photo array. "Here you are." She looked carefully at the picture. "No wait, this can't be right. You're not in this group." She turned another page. "This is it. Wow, you did have all your hair cut off." But even as she spoke, her mind was wandering from Marilyn's changing hairstyle. What had she just seen that wasn't quite right?

For some reason, Marilyn was prattling on about Elizabeth Taylor. "I just *loved* her hairstyle in that movie…what was it called? Something about the summer…" She thought a moment, then pronounced triumphantly; "*Suddenly Last Summer*, that's what it was. Anyway, I wanted my hair to look the same as hers in that movie."

"Mmm-mm." Rosie wasn't listening. She looked down at the cover of the book in her hand; *1956-1957*. After a moment, she began thumbing through it again.

"What're you looking for, Rosie?"

"You started grade nine in nineteen fifty-six, right?"

Marilyn nodded.

"And Doug Ferguson was in your grade?"

Marilyn nodded again.

Rosie found what she was looking for. "Well, it looks like the class photos got mixed up that year." She held the book open and pointed. "His picture's in with the grade eights."

"That's weird." Marilyn took the book from her, and peered at the grade eight class picture. Frowning, she searched her memory and then her face cleared. "No, that's right. I'd forgotten. Mr. Ferguson got really sick in our grade eight year, and Doug had to work all hours in the bakery. He missed so much school time his grades were terrible, and old Carscadden held him back a year."

She turned the page and passed the book back across the coffee table. "There I am. That style really suited me; very soft round the face. Maybe I should go with something like it again; I bet it would take years off. What do you think?"

Rosie barely heard the question. Marilyn's self-absorption had set her pondering an intriguing chicken-or-egg scenario. Did her narcissism stem from *being* a beauty consultant, or was it the reason she became one? Either way, she found it unfathomable that someone of Marilyn's age could still be so fascinated by their own appearance.

"Rosie? If I took my old year book into Clips, do you think they could copy that style?"

Sending up a silent plea for patience, she answered; "Probably. I've always heard good things about them, although I can't speak from experience."

"Yes. You're one of those lucky people with naturally curly hair, aren't you?"

Ignoring the rising hackles that always followed this irritating comment, Rosie stretched her lips into a smile. She didn't trust herself to speak. Fortunately, the hall clock spared her any further annoyance.

As a final loud *bong* reverberated through the hall, Marilyn exclaimed; "God! Is it ten already? I'd better get going. Gord'll think I've been stolen by white slavers."

Standing, she drained her glass, set it down carefully on a coaster and turned toward the hall. "Thanks so much for the lemonade and little chat, Rosie."

"My pleasure, Marilyn. And thanks for delivering the order."

"Any problems with it, just give me a call." Marilyn pressed her business card into Rosie's hand. "And I've left a catalogue in the bag, so if there's anything else you'd like I can order it anytime."

By now they were standing at the front door. Rosie swung it back just as the first fat drops of a cloudburst came splashing onto the dusty path.

"Here comes a storm. Maybe things'll get cooler now," Marilyn called as she ran heavily down the porch steps to her car.

"Bye. Drive carefully." Rosie waved her goodbyes, then turned back inside and hurried across the hall. Gussie was barking loudly at the kitchen door, voicing his indignation at twin insults; missing a visitor and being shut out in the rain.

"Alright Gus, I'm coming," she called. Any minute now the phone would ring, and Bonnie Walsh's aggrieved tones would be asking her to *please keep that animal quiet.*

Chapter 24 – Another One Bites the Dust

She was in the school gym with a crowd of people, all milling about aimlessly, wandering off in different directions. She knew she had to stand in a particular spot, but couldn't remember where to go. Then she saw the risers. That was it! Her place was on a riser. She tried to struggle through the crowd, but no-one would let her pass. Peter Anderson was waving at her from the topmost level. "Do you want your picture taken, or not?" he shouted. Instantaneously she was standing between him and Dougie Ferguson. But that was all wrong. "You can't be here, Dougie" she said. "You're not in this picture." Dougie just smiled and reached out towards her. He had very long teeth. She tried to back away and felt herself falling, down…down…down.

Rosie sat bolt upright in bed. Her heart was pounding and her nightdress was sticking to her, damp with sweat. "What a crazy dream," she said aloud, trying to calm her rattled nerves.

She reached up and switched on the light. Yes, as expected, the bedside clock read 3:00 a.m. Anytime she had a nightmare, she always woke from it at 3:00 a.m.

Gussie raised his head languidly, and gave her an inquiring look. "No, it's not time to get up yet. Go back to sleep, boy." Reassured by her voice, his tail thumped the counterpane just once before he laid his head down with a sigh.

Rosie watched him enviously. I bet he's already doggo she thought, fearing that her night's rest was probably over. She resisted the temptation to get up and go downstairs; such late night excursions invariably resulted in a raided cookie jar, followed by guilt and a sugar hangover in the morning.

She switched out the light and resolved to make a serious effort at slumber. What was Elspeth's latest relaxation technique? Her sister-in-law was always trying the latest fad, then recommending it to Rosie as the definitive solution to her stubborn weight problem. Qigong, mantras, yoga, transcendental meditation; El had enthusiastically embraced them all at one time or another Now she was into Visualised Repose. How did that one go? Something about the ocean.... Oh, right; *visualise a beach at sunset; hear the rhythmic sound of waves breaking on the shore....*

Rosie closed her eyes and tried wriggling her toes through imaginary sand. She focused on the cries of seagulls flying overhead and the gentle *shush* of a wave-washed shingle. She concentrated very hard; sleep didn't come.

'I'm useless at this New Age stuff,' she said to herself, acknowledging defeat. More to the point, all the mental gymnastics had increased her wakefulness, rather than lulling her to sleep. And to add to her annoyance, the only image she had successfully visualised was of the living room and the coffee table, standing four-square with Tony Wesley's Year Books stacked neatly on top. Somehow that had sneaked into her consciousness, and now adamantly refused to be dismissed.

Out of the blue, her heart resumed its acrobatics; what was it about those books? She opened her eyes and stared into the darkness. It took several minutes, then inspiration struck.

Her list of suspects! Last evening, Marilyn said that Dougie Ferguson had to repeat grade eight. That meant he'd spent four years in the same class as Tony Wesley; but because she'd used the class photo of Tony's freshman year as her starting point, Dougie hadn't been included on the list of suspects.

She shook her head. No; that was too ridiculous. Dougie Ferguson? She couldn't imagine a more harmless individual. He spent his life baking and decorating cakes; his biggest thrill was creating a sugar-free cookie, for heaven's sake. No; her killer had to be Pete Anderson. All this about Dougie was mere coincidence.

But even as she mentally dismissed him, uncomfortable facts about Little Yarmouth's genial baker began nibbling away at her denial.

She knew the Ferguson family lived in the old Scottish part of town, and that both of Dougie's parents had been very involved at Knox Presbyterian. This meant he would have gone regularly to services there. He also lived close to Alistair Street school and to the Boy Scout Hall on Burns. Even old St. Judes had been in the north end of town. The juvenile arsonist who targeted all those places had to have lived locally; no way could he have walked any distance carrying a bunch of gas-soaked rags.

Also problematic was Tony Wesley's personality change. That had started in grade eight, coincidentally the same year Dougie joined his class. And perhaps most troubling; Dougie had abruptly left school and joined the military just six weeks after the hospital fire, and there had been no more arsons in town after he left.

Then another, more chilling thought came to mind. Army training would surely include techniques to kill silently and efficiently with a swift blow to the neck.

As she lay evaluating Dougie as potential killer material, another uncomfortable fact popped into her head. By his own admission, he was responsible for spreading the tale that Tony pushed Martin Robertson in front of a train. She only had *his* word that Tony had confessed to that crime. Suppose he'd killed Martin; what better way to cover his tracks than to spread rumours about someone else?

Questions buzzed around her head like angry bees. Why did he invite Tony back to Little Yarmouth? A guilty conscience? The desire to make amends? Or had Tony become a threat in some way? She shook her head again. No, it was all circumstantial; her bets were firmly on Pete Anderson. Then, as if to convince herself of his guilt, she gave up on sleep and began an inventory of the lawyer's credentials for the post of psychopathic arsonist and killer.

It seemed only a moment before she was poking her head out from beneath the sheet, surprised to see the faint light of dawn creeping through her window. Despite all her tossing and turning, she had finally fallen asleep. I've discovered a new relaxation technique, she thought; reviewing murder clues. Definitely not one to share with Elspeth, though.

She looked across at the clock. 5:38 a.m. Did she really want to get up this early? She had woken with two thoughts uppermost in her mind; a thorough review of all Tony's class photos (in case she'd missed any other suspects) and a long chat with her aunt.

Thank goodness she had Aunt Marg to help with her 'cases.' John was a dear, but he couldn't be expected to understand the challenges of living with their family peculiarity. Sometimes she wondered if he believed in the Gift at all, or was merely humouring his aunt and sister. Perhaps his medical mind had written off their experiences as nothing more than inherited mental quirks. If so, that didn't bode well for Moira. No matter, she reassured herself. I'll always be there for her, just as Aunt Marg's always been there for me.

She gave a little shiver. Despite July's daytime heat, early mornings could still strike cold this close to Lake Huron. She plumped her pillow and straightened the sheet. The disturbed night had made her sluggish, and now all she wanted to do was close her eyes and go back to sleep.

But that was not to be. Her movements had woken Gussie, and he was more than ready to eat breakfast at the crack of dawn. After a brief interlude of tail thumping, pawing and whining, the desired result was achieved and a bleary-eyed Rosie was following his eager progress downstairs to the kitchen.

By 6:00 a.m. she was sitting in the living room, her mug of coffee forgotten and cooling on the end table. The collection of year books were lying open before her, scattered across the coffee table.

As soon as she had fed Gussie and let him out into the garden, she started checking Tony's class photos, year by year. Other than Dougie Ferguson, no new faces had smiled out at her, proof that no additional students (or potential suspects) had joined Tony's class in grades eight through eleven. No, it wasn't someone who'd *joined* his class that had piqued her interest, but someone who was unaccountably *missing*.

To her astonishment, Pete Anderson's picture disappeared after grade nine. Despite her best efforts, she had not been able to come up with any logical explanation for his absence from two consecutive photo sessions, other than he had left John Galt High. And if he left the school in 1958, he couldn't have been there to help Tony Wesley set the gymnasium fire in 1959. She had to know the answer; unfortunately, the only person she could ask was the pedantic nitwit himself. Plus, she'd have to come up with some plausible reason for asking....

After a moment's thought she reached for the phone, then pulled her hand back; it really was far too early to be calling anyone. With a frustrated sigh, she headed for the front door and her morning paper, in the vain hope that its predictable litany of woe could distract her from a disturbing possibility. A possibility that was threatening to become an unavoidable conclusion; Dougie Ferguson, Little Yarmouth's affable, roly-poly baker was also a ruthless killer.

*   *   *   *

"Bye, Gammie, bye..." Little hands waved from the mini-van's windows as it bumped along the gravelled track leading up to the road.

Margaret gave a sigh of relief. Much as she loved her grandchildren and their offspring, she had found the past week oddly stressful. No doubt part of that was down to Gerry and Ainsley's inability to control their two pre-schoolers, but in her heart she knew that most of her unease stemmed from a very different cause.

It was more than a week since she had spoken to Rosie, and with every passing day she had become more apprehensive. Her return to the cottage the previous Sunday had given her just enough time to prepare it for this most recent family onslaught, and there had been little time to dwell on her niece's sleuthing activities.

However, as the week wore on, her intuition began working overtime and soon worry was intruding on every quiet moment. Something bad was brewing, she was sure of it; but, try as she might, the details eluded her.

By Friday, she had been so desperate to hear Rosie's voice that she asked Gerry if she could borrow his cell phone. But, typical of their disorganized lives, he had left his phone at home and Ainsley's battery had died. So all she could do was promise herself that, immediately after their departure on Saturday morning, she'd close up and drive straight to Little Yarmouth.

For the first time in her life, Margaret felt cut off at the cottage. With nothing to be done, she'd had to content herself by vowing to buy a cell phone as soon as she got back in town, and never coming again to Heron Lake without it.

Now having seen her dear, but annoying, grandson and his family on their way she bustled about the cottage, hurrying through all the routine chores necessary to leave it safely unoccupied. All morning a terrible feeling of dread had been growing, and she knew she had to reach Rosie and warn her.

At last she was done and, picking up her bag, she locked the door and walked briskly to the car. She paused before getting in, breathing slowly to steady herself before getting behind the wheel.

She reached out for the car door then shivered, as a shadow passed across the sun. All around was silence. No rustling came from the undergrowth, the birds were still; even the gentle lapping of water against the shore had ceased. Without warning she was enveloped in darkness, and felt herself slipping away into its bottomless depths.

In the blackness she could hear far-off voices in conversation; no, just one voice, harsh and bitter. "Little Miss Perfect, you think you're so clever. I know your game, I've been watching you. Want to know the truth? Don't worry, you'll know it soon enough….." She could see Rosie getting into her car, driving, driving... where is she going? He's waiting like a giant spider in its web….

Margaret came round with no idea of how long she had been lying on the ground. It took several minutes to gather enough strength to stand, check herself over for broken bones and climb into the car. Panic began to overtake her, as her consciousness flooded with images of Rosie moving ever closer to an implacable evil.

She fumbled with the ignition key – did she turn it left or right to start the car? Everything was jumbled and confused…. she couldn't think straight... Her hand was shaking and she almost dropped the keys….

"No. Stop it." she said, aloud. "This isn't helping anyone." Calmed by the self-admonishment she closed her eyes, placed both hands squarely on the wheel and focused her mind.

Her concentration paid off. Primos! The little gas station cum general store was an hour down the road, nearly half-way to Kincardine. But they had a pay-phone, and she'd be able to call Rosie from there. 'Right, that's a plan' she said to herself; 'time to get this show on the road.' Then calling up every scrap of self-control, she put the car in gear and drove carefully up the winding track toward the road.

᛬   *   *   *

"It's no trouble at all, I assure you." Peter Anderson's clipped tone belied his words; he obviously considered committee calls at nine-thirty on a Saturday morning to be a great deal of trouble. Rosie envisaged his expression as he resigned himself, yet again, to the heavy burden of *noblesse oblige*. "How may I be of assistance, Mrs. Rowe?"

The phone was sweaty in Rosie's hand. "Thanks so much, Pe...Chair." She corrected herself just in time; no need to put his back up, even if his pretentions are a pain in the neck. "It's just that we're (no, don't mention Carol!) um...I'd planned to put a montage of class photos on the wall in our Fifties/Sixties room, but when I was going through the relevant year books I noticed several instances of missing students. Probably just people out sick when the photographer came in, that kind of thing you know..." She let her voice trail off expectantly.

"Really, Mrs. Rowe! I don't understand what you expect me to do about that."

Clearly, the chatty approach wasn't going to work. On to flattery, then; always a reliable tactic when dealing with pocket Napoleons. "Sorry, Chair, I'm not explaining myself very well." She softened her voice to a more honeyed tone. "No, I just wanted to run the idea past you; you have such a *feel* for what's appropriate in any given situation. Do you think I should give up on the idea? I'd hate to be the cause of offending anyone who'd missed getting their pictures done." She paused, then added meaningfully; "I've heard it was a financial issue for some students back then." (God, this is so lame! I sound like a complete idiot).

But she hadn't misjudged her mark. Anderson's voice reflected the self-satisfied smirk that she knew was spreading across his face. "Your sensitivity does you credit, Mrs. Rowe." His overly modulated tone oozed superiority, and Rosie felt her hackles rising. "But I don't think you need concern yourself too much. There could be many excellent reasons that photos were missed, and I'm sure no *intelligent* person would take offence over such a minor issue. No, you have my permission to go right ahead with your little project. I'm sure it will be very....effective."

As she was still without the answer she needed, Rosie restrained herself from telling the lawyer where he could take his "permission," and what he could do with it once he got there. Instead, she took a deep breath and said sweetly; "Thank you *so* much, Chair. It's always really helpful to get your perspective." (Careful, don't overdo it.) "And as you say, there could be so many reasons for photographic gaps. I think even you missed a year, on one occasion. Isn't that right?"

As she hoped, Anderson could not resist rising to the bait of her inaccurate statement. He gave a short bark of laughter. "Ha! You're quite wrong there, Mrs. Rowe. I was never absent from anything. But you won't find me in any class photos after grade nine. No, we moved to Montreal in the summer of fifty-eight; father got a major promotion to the bank's head office." She heard the pride in his voice, and wondered at the persistence of such snobbery in this day and age. "And that was quite an improvement on Little Yarmouth, I can tell you."

So there it was - the answer at last. All her questioning, theories, suppositions; everything had led to this moment on the phone with "Chair" Anderson. It wasn't the answer she'd wanted to hear. After John had given Jackson Haynes his alibi, she'd hoped fervently that the killer would prove to be Peter Anderson. He was certainly nasty enough. But therein lay the danger of letting personal feelings intrude on a factual exercise.

Now she was faced with the dilemma of what to do about Dougie Ferguson. She wouldn't be shopping at the *Wee Scottish Bakery* ever again, that was for sure. Of greater urgency, how was she going to use what she knew to release Tony Wesley's spirit? The only person who might have some clue how to solve that problem was her aunt. Definitely time to ditch the stuffed-shirt.

Anderson was still droning on. ".....most convenient to live at home while studying at McGill, of course." Lost in her own thoughts, Rosie gave no answer and he, obviously expecting some admiring comment, said sharply; "Mrs. Rowe? Are you still there?"

To cover her inattention, she gave a little cough. "Yes. Sorry, Chair; I'd dropped my handkerchief. Allergies, you know." She blew her nose ostentatiously. "Well, I mustn't intrude further on your weekend. Thank you so much for the advice. I'll be sure to report on my er... little project at the next committee meeting. Thanks again." Rosie hung up quickly. Not being blessed with x-ray vision, she was denied the pleasure of witnessing Anderson's irritation at this arbitrary dismissal.

Within minutes, she had dialled her aunt's number and was listening in frustration as its ring pealed on unanswered. "Drat; gone back to the cottage, I guess" she muttered, replacing the handset rather more forcefully than it deserved. Maybe it was time for them both to invest in cell-phones. After all, how complicated could the things be? Moira and all her school friends seemed to handle them with ease.

These technological musings were interrupted by the phone springing back to life. Rosie's spirits lifted. Aunt Marg *was* at home and had just missed her call. She snatched up the receiver; "Hello? Auntie Marg?"

"No, Rose. It's Lucy. Are you waiting for a call? I can ring back in a few minutes, if you like."

"No; it's nothing pressing." Rosie swallowed her disappointment. "How's everything going? Are we still on for eleven this morning?"

Lucy dropped her voice; "Actually, that's why I'm calling." She hesitated, and Rosie heard Agnes' voice in the background, followed by the muffled response; "Just coming, mom."

"Lucy? What's up?"

"Dad's improved so much they've decided to release him today, instead of Monday. We've got to go pick him up at the hospital, so I can't make it to the house for eleven."

"Wow! What great news; I bet your mom's over the moon. No problem going to Veterans, though. We can go after lunch, if you like."

"That's just it. It may be tricky for me to get away later, what with getting him settled and everything. And mom will probably want the car to run for prescriptions, and who knows what else."

"Well, how about Sunday afternoon? I'm singing at Mass in the morning, but I'm free after that."

For a minute, Lucy said nothing, then; "Maybe. Trouble is, mom wants to have a family lunch on Sunday. You know; Amber and Todd, maybe Carl as well. Just a bit of a celebration for dad's homecoming. I might not get a chance to disappear."

Rosie began to lose patience. For heaven's sake, now what was going on? Only forty-eight hours earlier Lucy's top priority had been retrieving Tony's cremains, but today that little expedition seemed to have dropped off her to-do list entirely.

Caught unawares by her feelings of annoyance, she said more abruptly than intended; "I thought your lease was up on Sunday...," then caught herself mid-sentence, as the real reason for Lucy's reluctance clicked into place. Even with back-up, she was afraid to go into the basement at 26 Veterans Avenue. And who could blame her? Rosie, of all people, knew that it was more than Tony's ashes that lay silently waiting in that cold, dark house.

"It is." Lucy was apologetic. "Look..., I hate to ask...." She hesitated, hoping her friend would fill in the blanks. But Rosie deliberately let the silence lengthen between them, until Lucy finally blurted out; "I don't suppose you'd go over there without me, would you?"

Suppressing the ungenerous thought that this might have been Lucy's hope all along, Rosie answered grudgingly; "I could, I s'pose. But how will I get in? I'm guessing the place is all locked up."

"No problem," came the eager reply. "I'll stop by your place on our way to the hospital and leave my house key in your mailbox."

Rosie rolled her eyes and sighed in resignation. Perhaps it would be better to go alone. Tony could well put in an appearance and, by now, he was probably annoyed by her lack of results. If he was really ticked off, who knows what he might pull out of his paranormal bag of tricks, and some of that stuff was difficult to explain away.

"Alright; I'll watch out for you. Now, tell me again; where exactly did you hide the urn?"

Chapter 25 – Truth Will Out

It was close to noon when Rosie pulled into the driveway at 26 Veterans Avenue. Having been relieved of her obligation to be at the house by eleven, she had taken the time to enjoy a leisurely breakfast, followed by Gussie's equally leisurely constitutional.

Their stroll was uneventful, and they had almost reached home when the morning had taken a very strange turn.

All had been well until they passed the mailbox at the end of the pathway. As usual, the beagle was pulling ahead of her, eager for his water bowl and post-exercise snooze. She had given the leash a little jerk. "Hold on, boy. Let me pick up this key before I forget," she said, opening the box and peering inside.

Inexplicably, the moment she put her hand on Lucy's neat white envelope, the dog had given a series of ear-splitting howls, yanked the leash from her grasp and fled to the porch. With visions of bleeding paws or swellings from multiple wasp stings filling her head, she had rushed up the steps, only to find him pressed, trembling but unharmed, against the front door.

Once inside he had quickly calmed down. But the instant she draped his leash over the newel post and turned to leave, Gussie had flung himself against the front door, and no amount of calling or cajoling could induce him to move.

Now seriously worried, she sat down on the floor next to him and checked more thoroughly for any sign of injury. Yet again, she found nothing. Finally she convinced herself that his behaviour must be due to an approaching storm; his hearing was sensitive and the sound of thunder always made him crazy.

Grunting with effort, she had heaved the protesting beagle up from the floor and carried him, wriggling and squirming, into the kitchen. It took several knobs of cheese and some fancy footwork, but she finally got him successfully corralled.

As she picked up her purse, the sound of his whimpering caught at her heart and almost made her turn back. But hard reason prevailed. How long would she be gone? An hour at most and, if a storm was brewing, it was best to get Lucy's gloomy errand over and done with now. Then she could be back home to comfort Gussie when the worst of the weather blew through.

*　　　　*　　　　*　　　　*

Margaret chewed at her lower lip and tried to curb her impatience. The trip from Heron Lake had been an exercise in frustration. Within minutes of leaving the cottage, she was trailing behind an interminable parade of slow moving vehicles. On this particular morning, it seemed that every rusty farm truck and swaying camper from miles around had opted to take a leisurely jaunt along the Eleventh Concession. Consequently, her hour long run to the general store had slowly expanded into a ninety minute crawl.

She had just reached the point of wondering if an actual scream might reduce her tension level, when the store's rusted red and white gas sign came into view. With a sigh of relief, she flipped her indicator light and turned into the weedy parking lot. Despite her age she flung back the car door, took the veranda stairs two at a time and gave Primo's weather beaten door a hearty shove. As usual it resisted, so she shoved it again. Some things never change.

Although it was well over a year since she was last in the store, the elderly proprietor greeted her warmly. "Buon giorno, Signora 'opkins" he called from behind the counter. "You need-a gaz?" "Ciao, Signor Primo. Yes, fill it please," she replied, glad that the gas tank was almost empty. If she hadn't needed fuel, she'd have felt obliged to purchase something from the store's eclectic inventory. After a year's absence, coming in just to use the pay-phone would have been deemed discourteous.

"I need to use the phone, Signor Primo."

"Si, the phone, she is at the back." He waved toward the rear of the store, then bellowed; "Marco, gaz. Pronto."

Margaret picked her way carefully along a narrow aisle cluttered by racks of clothing and overflowing cardboard boxes. The wall racks groaned with an astonishing variety of goods; everything from plaster Madonnas to cast-iron skillets were piled high, heaped cheek-by-jowl in dusty stacks.

Reaching the phone she fumbled in her purse for change. Despite her determination to stay calm her heart was thumping with apprehension, and she murmured firmly to herself; 'Everything will be alright once I've spoken to her. I know everything will be alright.' She inserted coins and shakily dialled Rosie's number, all the while repeating, 'Everything will be alright' over and over again, like a mantra.

After several rings she heard her niece's cheerful; "Hello…"

"Rosie; thank God I caught you. Look, I'm on my way over to…" and then she fell silent. Rosie's disembodied voice was still speaking; "Sorry I'm not available to come to the phone right now but……"

There was nobody home at 64 Cedar Street except Gussie, huddled miserably against the closed kitchen door. At the sound of Rosie's voice coming from the answer phone, he lifted his head and howled inconsolably.

*   *   *   *

The door swung back with an ominous creak. Despite her nervousness, Rosie stepped into the dingy hall with a smile. "Welcome to the haunted house" she said under her breath, half expecting to see Tony Wesley drifting towards her.

On the drive over, she rehearsed what she would say to him when he materialised. Because he would show up; of that she was certain. On the plus side, she could assure him that she had identified Dougie Ferguson as his murderer. Unfortunately, on the minus side, she'd have to acknowledge that she couldn't prove it, and had no idea how to see justice served. He wasn't going to be pleased.

And then, just as she turned onto Veterans Avenue, she was struck by the thought that Tony had never asked her to bring his killer to justice. She'd jumped to that conclusion all by herself. No; the only message he'd ever given her were the words *not my fault* repeated over and over again.

With sudden insight, she realised that Tony Wesley wanted forgiveness, not revenge. He desperately needed her to know he was not guilty of something, as if his release depended on her acknowledgement of his innocence. This whole thing was personal, after all.

Now, standing so close to where he had met his violent end, she recalled her aunt's cryptic warning; 'This business with Tony Wesley is just the tip of the iceberg, and part of it comes very close to you.' Her words at last made sense. The "iceberg" was Dougie Ferguson's career of arson and murder, and the part which came very close to Rosie were the deaths of her father and grandparents. Logically, it must be the hospital fire that was weighing on Tony's spirit. But two figures had been seen running away that night, so he *was* there. Was he really innocent of that terrible crime?

With these thoughts uppermost in her mind she walked slowly along the passageway, expecting at any moment to encounter the bone-chilling cold that always heralded her "client's" approach. But, although damp and musty, the temperature was normal for a house that had stood empty for weeks. She reached the basement door and, after a moment's hesitation, opened it and switched on the light.

An unpleasant aroma of earth and mould wafted up the stairs towards her. It was sadly familiar; she'd smelt it in her own basement, just before the diagnosis of a damaged watercourse had drained her piggy bank. "Bad luck for whoever owns this place," she said aloud.

Carl Wheelan and his helpers had done a thorough removal job, and the small space was completely empty. Ducking her head, Rosie grabbed the hand rail and, with more bravado than confidence, stepped firmly onto the rickety stairs. As she descended she scanned the far wall for the grill covering Tony's makeshift resting place. Lucy had given her very clear instructions, and she spotted it right away. At the bottom of the stairs she skirted around the ominous stain on the floor, trying to banish the melodramatic thought that here was local folk-lore in the making. "Roll up, roll up," she muttered in sepulchral tones. "See the terrible bloodstain that never fades."

The air vent was set close to the ceiling, and Rosie had to reach up to hook her fingers through the slatted grill. She gave a quick tug, but nothing moved. "Oh, wonderful!" she said crossly. "Don't tell me I need a screwdriver." Lucy hadn't said anything about bringing tools. Blowing out her cheeks in exasperation, she stretched her five foot four height to its maximum. Now standing on tip-toe, she had just enough height to see that the grill wasn't screwed in place, only pushed in unevenly.

It took several minutes of rattling and pulling (and two cut fingers) before the grill finally clattered to the floor. Assuring herself that Lucy was far too good a housekeeper to let giant spiders nest in Tony's niche, Rosie thrust her hand into the dusty space and was instantly rewarded by the feel of something solid. She dragged it out and, seconds later, was examining her prize; a small, unadorned grey pot.

Well, Dave certainly hadn't let his feelings for Lucy get in the way of business. Or perhaps he was just "sticking it" to his rival, one last time. Judging by its appearance, the container (it hardly qualified to be called an urn) had come from the lowest end of Mason's budget line of funeral accessories.

As if on cue, Rosie heard footsteps overhead. Oh Lord, she thought, he must be really wound up. Looks like I'm in for a full-blown corporeal manifestation this time. With Tony's mortal remains in hand, she made her way across the basement and headed up the stairs to her ghostly rendezvous.

To her surprise, she saw that the doorway at the top was obscured by a dark shape. For a moment, she was confused; was this reality or illusion? The last time she'd been in this basement she'd seen the same figure, but that had been a vision of the past. Why was she seeing it again?

"Who's down there?" Rosie's blood ran cold; this was no vision. She recognized the voice immediately, even without its usual chummy tone. For the second time today, her aunt's words came back to her; 'It's the living you should fear, not the dead.' Well, she didn't need warning about Douglas Ferguson, arsonist and murderer. She reassured herself that he knew nothing of her investigations, so could have no reason to harm her. Just brazen it out, then. But the question remained; what was he doing here?

Her feet were like lead, but she kept climbing the stairs. One foot in front of the other; up, up by sheer force of will. She should say something. But her throat was so dry, she was afraid there'd be no sound. She swallowed hard and forced herself to sound pleased. "Is that you Dougie? It's just me, Rosie." She was almost at the top and could see him planted there, immovable, blocking her way. She licked her lips; must speak normally. "What are you doing here?"

He smiled back at her, genial persona fixed well in place. "Ma sent me home to get her arthritis pills, and I saw your car from her bedroom window. Thought I'd better check up since the place's empty."

Rosie was flummoxed. "Sorry? Do you live next door, or something?"

For a minute he didn't reply, just kept smiling down at her. Then; "No; we live on Alistair. Our garden backs onto the yard here. Mind telling me how you got in?"

She was almost level with him now. "Lucy lent me her key; she asked me to have a last look round. Make sure everything's cleaned up for the next tenant, you know." She swallowed again. "She was coming too, but her dad was unexpectedly discharged from hospital this morning."

Dougie still didn't budge so, taking her courage in both hands, she squeezed past him and into the hall. The front door and safety were steps away. "I suppose she asked you to keep an eye on the place for her, being as she's still technically the tenant."

"Not exactly." She was close enough to see that although his lips were smiling, his eyes were chips of black ice. "Didn't she tell you I'm the landlord?"

Her surprise was genuine. "No. She said they dealt with an agency."

"How typical of my dear old pal, Tony. Never one to give credit where credit was due. I let them live here practically rent-free, and all he did was complain."

She took a cautious step sideways. "That was really nice of you, Dougie. Lucy told me how much she appreciated your kindness to them."

"Is that right?" Rosie caught the hint of a sneer in his voice. "Well, if she did, she'd be the first of my tenants to ever appreciate anything." He took a step towards her, and she resisted the impulse to back away. "My grandfather bought into the Avenue in the thirties. Now these dumps are more trouble than they're worth." He chuckled grimly. "It was Grandpa put the gate in the wall back there," he jerked his head backwards. "He liked to drop by unannounced on rent day." He noticed the urn in her hand. "What've you got there?"

"This?" She handed it to him. "It's Lucy's; nothing that belongs to the house. She asked me to look for it. It's…," (don't let him know Tony's been cremated), "…a pet urn. Her cat died back in the Soo, and she had it cremated."

His eyes narrowed, and for a moment she thought he was going to throw it to the floor. "Well, well. Isn't that just fine and dandy?" he muttered to himself. "Writing to me, asking for money 'cos he's bankrupt, and she's spending it on a dead cat."

Rosie forced another smile and tried to keep her voice from shaking. "People do get very attached to their pets, I guess." Annoyingly, she heard her voice tremble; the effort of trying to sound nonchalant was beginning to wear. "Speaking of that, I should be getting home to let the dog out." She stretched out both hands for the urn. "Can I have it, please?"

Ignoring her request, Dougie began passing the container from one hand to the other. "Shall I tell you something about your little friend's late husband?" He shot Rosie a glance of such pure venom that it was all she could do to keep from backing away. "He was useless. The only thing reliable about good ol' Tony was that he'd always let you down when it counted. And no guts at all; first sign of trouble and he was outta there." He glared at her.

Every instinct was screaming at her to run for the door. But that would show her hand – he'd figure something was wrong. Right now he didn't know anything, so why be afraid? No; just keep chatting. Keep up the pretence that everything's okay.

She looked up at him from under her lashes. "Yes, Lucy said as much. Between you and me, it didn't sound as if she had much of a life with him." Dropping her voice, she whispered conspiratorially; "I think he was an alcoholic." Why was he looking at her so strangely? Maybe a change of subject would distract him. "That was quite some meeting last week. Do you think anyone will show up next time?"

Ferguson seemed not to hear. He took a step closer, and this time she couldn't help but shrink back against the wall. "We had a lot in common, y'know. His mother was the same as mine - never could please either of 'em. And old man Wesley was a bastard; not quite in dear old dad's league, but damn close." His voice took on a sing-song quality; "*Spare the rod and spoil the child;* that was their excuse for beating the shit out of us."

He giggled unexpectedly, and the sound sent shivers down her spine. She felt the colour drain from her face and knew he couldn't fail to notice. "What's the matter, Rose? Not feeling so good? Sorry, I can't offer you a chair or a muffin this time."

She looked at him in astonishment. He was talking about the night she found the pen-clip in her pocket! Had he recognised it, too? "That's okay, Doug. Low blood sugar, you know." She took a sideways step, but he mirrored her action and blocked her in. All she could do now was bluff. "Look, I don't know what's bothering you, but I have to go." She drew herself up and said loudly; "Give me Lucy's property and I'll be on my way."

To her surprise, he gave a laugh and stepped back. "I give you credit for nerve, Rose" he said, passing her the urn.

Hands shaking, she took it from him and started toward the front door. But he got there first and stood leaning against it, arms folded, teeth bared in a predatory grin. How right you were, El. *A wolf in the fold*, for sure.

"I've always liked you, Rose. It's a real pity you couldn't keep your nose out of my business."

She decided there was no point in taking the soft approach and decided to go on the offensive. "What the hell are you talking about?" she said hotly. "Get out of my way. I don't know anything about the bakery."

He giggled again. "Oh, good try. But you and I both know I'm talking about something else entirely. Questions, questions, questions. I didn't clue in for a while. All that chat at the committee meeting, and then raking up the past with Marilyn Robertson. You even got your brother in on the act, didn't you?" He heard her sharp intake of breath, and chuckled. "That's right, I know all about the pending autopsy. Amazing what you hear standing behind a bakery counter."

She cleared her throat. "Doug, I can't understand why any of this is of interest to you. I was just following up for Lucy; she had a few concerns about the accident, that's all…"

Ferguson took a step towards her and, desperate to keep up the pretence of ignorance, she held her ground. "Really? Yes, I tried to tell myself that, too. Even after I saw your face when you pulled that pen-clip out of your pocket the other night. Found it in the basement, I s'pose?" Another wolfish grin. "Trust Tony to make everything more difficult, thrashing about. I thought I'd picked up all the pieces, but hey; no one's perfect." Turning quickly, he reached up and slid the top door bolt into place.

With heart pounding, Rosie began to back away. There was no escape through the front door, but he'd said something about a gate in the back wall. If she made a dash for it, could she outrun him?

He turned back to face her and she froze. "Intuition's a funny thing, isn't it, Rose?" His expression put her in mind of a cat, eyeing its doomed prey. "I've always had a really strong sense of self-preservation – always known when some-one's working against me." He began walking toward her; "I wasn't really sure though, until you started asking me about Marty Robertson. Had you going for a while there, didn't I?" He slipped back into his creepy sing-song voice. *"That was a terrible time for all of us in Martin's class."* Another horrible giggle. "You've got no idea how hard it was to keep from laughing, remembering that spineless little wimp."

Flooded by a surge of rage, Rosie lost all sense of caution. She shouted at him; "How can you say that! I bet it was YOU that killed him, not Tony. YOU pushed him in front of that train because he'd seen the pair of you setting the gym fire." Oh, shit; now she'd done it! Mom always said her temper would be the death of her. She tried taking another step backwards, but her legs were like jelly and almost gave way.

He stopped in his tracks and stood looking at her, an amused smile playing round his lips. "My, my; quite the temper when you're roused. But you're wrong about that. Marty killed himself; jumped right in front of the 4:20 express before Tony could grab him."

Despite her fear, Rosie couldn't let that pass. "He killed *himself*?" she said incredulously.

"Oh, yeah. Like I said a real wimp. He was going to Arse-cadden to rat us out, but me and Tony beat him to it and said we'd seen *him* light up the gym. Well, it was no contest; two against one. Then I spread the story round school and poor ol' Marty was in deep shit. Everyone's punching bag for a week. Worked like a charm."

He chuckled at the memory and Rosie's blood ran cold. Seeing her expression, his face darkened and he hissed; "Oh, for Christ's sake! If the stupid prick was too dumb to keep his mouth shut he deserved everything he got. We didn't do anything. All that happened that day was me, and Tony, and a coupla' other guys cornered him on Station Street. He starts shouting about how he didn't want to live and took off for the tracks. Tony went after him, but he was a crap runner and couldn't catch up." He grinned at her. "All to the good, I thought. One less feeb in the gene pool."

So, Tony hadn't killed Marty, he'd tried to save him. Had he understood then just how evil his best friend was? Or did that come later, after Dougie told his mother he'd seen Tony push Marty to his death?

For a brief moment, Ferguson's revelation distracted Rosie from her dangerous predicament. Then reality set in. She was in a locked house with a murderer; if she was going to survive she had to stay focused.

Her mind worked furiously; he was going to kill her, of that she had no doubt. Her only chance was to get into the back yard, then out through the connecting gate. There was sure to be a lock, or a bolt, on the other side so she'd be able to secure it behind her. She'd have to break into the Ferguson house, but trespassing was the least of her worries. But first she had to get to the kitchen.

Her arms ached from the weight of Tony's urn and for a fleeting moment she toyed with the idea of hurling it at Ferguson. Her athletic ability was nil, but she might get lucky and hit him in the head. No, if she missed, he'd be on her in a flash and she was too far from the back door to have any hope of escape. Best save it as a last resort.

Instead, she took a deep breath and gave him an appraising stare. He stared back coolly, and she felt anger flood through her again. Damn him! He thought he was so clever; he was actually enjoying this. Hadn't she read somewhere that psychopaths have huge egos? Maybe if she could keep him talking, flatter that ego, he'd drop his guard long enough to give her the time she needed.

She knew suddenly that it was pointless to keep up a façade of ignorance any longer, and said offhandedly; "Well, here we are then. Bit of an impasse, wouldn't you say?"

"No, I wouldn't say that."

His tone sent fear curling round the pit of her stomach, but she ignored it and tried again. "You're guessing that I've discovered some secret that could hurt you. Well, even if that's true, you've been way too smart to leave any proof, and without proof it's just my word against yours." She looked at him boldly. "Look Dougie, I don't care what you and Tony got up to years ago and the last time I spoke with Lucy she'd accepted that Tony's death was a drunken accident. So that's it – end of story."

He didn't answer and, to her surprise, she saw that his eyes had taken on a distant, dreamy look. Realising he wasn't watching her, she took two cautious steps backwards.

Her movement seemed to rouse Ferguson from his reverie. He spoke abruptly. "Can you imagine what it's like to have power over life and death?" Now he was looking straight at her, fists clenching and unclenching in a way that sent fear coursing through her every vein. "Well, I know. I discovered it when I set fire to that cesspit they called a school on Alistair. I knew then I had special powers. No-one could go against me." His voice softened. "I thought Tony was the same, wanted to do the same things. But he was spineless. He got scared after the gym fire, threatened to tell if I did it again."

"So it was you and Tony set fire to the football equipment?"

"Damn right we did." He hooted with laughter and she started nervously. "Showed that sonofabitch coach he couldn't bench me. We fixed him but good." He gave her a sly look. "Of course, that wasn't my best work." When she didn't reply, he demanded; "C'mon Rosie, fess up; you've always wanted to know, haven't you?"

Rosie knew exactly what he was talking about. And yes, more than anything else she needed to know why this pathetic madman had destroyed her family. But some instinct warned her not to show any sign of weakness, not to give him the satisfaction of seeing her pain. So she lifted her chin, looked him straight in the eye and said nothing.

Her silence seemed to egg him on. "It nearly didn't happen, y'know – my Halloween bonfire. All that careful planning, and then that fucker Tony showed up out of nowhere, grabbed the gas can and took off. A real little hero; I enjoyed beating the crap outta him."

The dreamy look came back, and she snatched her opportunity to slowly put first one foot, and then the other behind her. How much further was the kitchen?

"Christ, what a show. The roar of the flames, the heat and then the explosions when those tanks blew – it was incredible." Watching her face, he added; "As I recall, you could smell roast meat clear across town."

It was all Rosie could do to keep from throwing herself at his smug, porcine face. She wanted to smash him, to beat his head in. But she knew a loss of self-control would be fatal. So she swallowed her rage and just murmured; "Burning down a hospital; what a wonderful achievement. I'm sure you were very proud of yourself."

Clearly, this wasn't the reaction Ferguson expected. His neck muscles bulged, and she flinched as he shouted; "They deserved it! Pumping that old bastard full of insulin – keeping him alive! Without them, he'd have been dead and I'd have been free of that stinking shop. But, oh no. They had to fix him up, keep him alive so he could go on making my life miserable."

The fit of temper disappeared as quickly as it came, and he continued in a softer tone. "You know what they say about absence making the heart grow fonder? Well, after I joined the army, Mother's letters were so full of how much my dear father missed me, I almost felt sorry for him." He smiled cheerfully. "Such a pity he died within weeks of the prodigal's return. I'd always heard insulin dosage was quite tricky, particularly if the patient's eyesight's not too good."   He was watching her again, gauging her reaction.

Rosie struggled to maintain a calm, detached demeanour, but the hairs on the back of her neck were standing bolt upright. He'd killed his own father! On the positive side, this admission showed she was right about Ferguson's ego; given the opportunity, he couldn't resist bragging about his murderous exploits. On the negative, she was also right that her survival depended on keeping him distracted.

Casting about for something more to keep him talking, she said the first thing that came to mind. "What made you decide to join the army?"

"Seemed like an easy out. Things were getting a bit hot round here; guess the town fathers didn't take kindly to their doctors being barbequed."   He smirked, and she fought off a wave of nausea. "And Tony was losing it. I knew he'd crack if I stayed around."

He lent sideways to rest his shoulder against the wall and she felt a flicker of hope.   He was so full of himself, so eager to impress someone, anyone, with his cleverness that he'd almost forgotten she had to be eliminated.

"But I don't understand why you stayed in town after your father er…….passed away. You said you hated the bakery."

His answer came quickly, almost eagerly. "Yes, but after he was gone I could do what I wanted. Show mother what a good job I could do…."

For a moment, Rosie heard a small boy's overwhelming desire to please his mother. Sadness washed over her; all those lives ruined or lost because one bitter woman wouldn't give her son the love and approval he craved. She wondered who would owe the greater debt when the celestial books were balanced; mother or son.

He seemed to have almost forgotten her presence; "Course, Tony high-tailed it out of town almost as soon as

I came back, so no problems there. Guess looking at me made him feel guilty all over again." Ferguson chuckled; "He didn't do so badly, though. Had little Lucy to keep him warm through all those long, cold nights up in the Soo."

Did she detect a note of envy? She reminded herself that domineering mothers often had a way of keeping their sons all to themselves. Dave Mason was another case in point.

Lost in reminiscing, Ferguson had stopped watching her and was gazing off into the middle distance. She cautiously slid her left foot back and shifted her weight. Thank God! Almost opposite the basement door now; the kitchen was just behind her. Was it time to...?

"And then, years later, I get a phone call. He starts putting the screws on. Oh, nothing too obvious just, could I help him out with some bill or other, for old times' sake. Then they'd laid him off, and he was getting behind on the mortgage. Could I cover a month or two for him? Every coupla' months it was something else." Ferguson's face flushed and his voice hardened. "He never *said* anything, of course, but we both knew where he was coming from. Finally, it comes out he's sick – only got a year or two left. So I figured, what the hell, this place was empty; maybe I'd get him back here, get him involved in my other little venture. Then he'd have to keep his mouth shut."

Rosie had tensed, getting ready to throw caution to the wind and make a run for the back door. But now he was watching her intently, almost as if he had caught on to her plan. And, despite her situation, her curiosity had been piqued. What was this other little venture?

"So you offered him a job at the bakery?" To her dismay her voice quivered, the attempt at sounding disinterested a miserable failure.

"I suppose you could say that." He took a step toward her and she tightened her grip on the metal urn. "Last fall I'd had to er.....how shall I say it? I'd had to let my driver go." He laughed. "Literally and figuratively. He'd got rather greedy, you see. Wanted a bigger share of my extra-curricular activities."

Her jaw dropped. The smuggling! That was Dougie's "little venture." Tony was on a regular pick up run when Carol spotted him at Three Eagles. And the unfortunate Rick Edwards had been his predecessor.

Ferguson saw her face, and clued in instantly. "Oh, I see. Carol couldn't keep her mouth shut, after all. She was so thrilled to tell me what a naughty boy Tony had been. After that, there was no choice – I had to get rid of him. And that reminds me; she's another loose end I'll have to tidy up."

He leant back against the wall. "All my dear mother's fault, of course. There was no way I could keep *her* in her accustomed style on the proceeds from a bake shop. Luckily, that problem's going to resolve itself very soon; I have a feeling that she's not long for this world. The elderly are so very fragile, you know; one slip and it's all over."

Rosie felt panic taking hold and, before she knew it, she'd gathered all her strength and pitched the urn at his evil, grinning face.

Sadly, even terror couldn't make her aim true. He laughed and ducked. "Rosie, Rosie, what a shame. You've been planning that all along, and now you're out of options."

She turned and ran frantically toward the back door, but she'd underestimated his agility and he was behind her in seconds. Her hand was on the knob, twisting it back and forth, back and forth; why wouldn't it open? Horrified, she felt him grab her arms from behind, twist her around until they were face to face. He slammed her back against the door, one hand pinning her arms above her head, his forearm across her throat. His distorted features were inches from her face. She could smell his bad breath and almost retched.

"As soon as I saw your car Rosie, I knew this was the day I'd put an end to your meddling. So, of course, I locked the door behind me when I came in." He pushed his forearm deeper across her throat and, wincing, she saw the gleam of satisfaction in his eyes. A slow smile spread across his face. "I'm sorry and all that, but I can't have you telling tales round town; not with the police asking questions about Rick, and poor old Tony being dug up for an autopsy."

She tried to struggle, but his grip was like iron and he was pushing his body in hard against her. She gasped out; "You can't hope to get away with this. People know I'm here. Lucy will come looking…"

In one sudden movement he moved his arm from her throat and smacked his hand across her mouth. "You don't think they'll find you here, do you? No, I'll be taking you to my house, although sadly, you'll be in no state to appreciate mother's décor." She tried to bite him, but his fingers gripped her cheeks so tightly that her eyes watered. His voice seemed to be coming from far away. "Hush now, hush. Don't worry, just relax; I won't make it last too long."

With one unexpected, violent movement he swung her round, and she screamed as he yanked her arms down, and behind her back. Instinctively she kicked out backwards, and heard him swear as her heel connected with something. For one brief instant, his grip loosened and she wrenched herself free. Staggering, she stumbled into the hall, but he grabbed her shirt and dragged her backwards. She lost her footing, and the world exploded into a million lights as her head hit the floor.

Seconds later, he was on top of her, his hands round her throat, relentlessly squeezing her life away. She thrashed out, but her arms were so heavy she could barely lift them. Just as blackness descended, his grip relaxed and she gasped down a brief second of blessed air. He lent forward and whispered in her ear; "Not so fast, Rosie. I've been wanting to try this for such a long time. Don't spoil my fun." Then his hands were round her throat again, this time with thumbs pressing hard against her windpipe. There was a roaring in her ears and, as consciousness slipped away, she knew this was the end....

She opened her eyes; all around was icy cold mist, and her first thought was that she was dead. Her second thought was, if she was dead, why was her head pounding and why was she looking at the hallway's worn linoleum floor? Then she was gripped by terror; where was he? Gone to get a sack to drag her body through his garden?

She clambered to her feet, but dizziness and nausea engulfed her and she had to lean back against the wall to regain her balance. Then in a heart-stopping moment, she saw her assailant half-standing, half-crouching against the staircase balustrade.

Strangely, even though she knew he was within an arm's reach of her, Rosie's fear began to ebb away. She could sense another presence close at hand, one whose arrival was always accompanied by an icy fog.

Now Ferguson's gaze was fixed at a point above her head and, as she watched, he moaned and threw out his arms as if to ward off an attack. She heard him cry out; "No, no. Get away! It can't be you, you're dead, get away..."

The mist was lifting now and she could see him quite clearly, face contorted in horror, eyes fixed on the shadowy figure that was advancing inexorably toward him. He started backing up, and the apparition matched him step for step. Another moment and he would be at the top of the basement stairs.

Rosie couldn't bear to look. Unwilling to witness the inevitable end of this karmic encounter, she covered her face with her hands. At that very instant, Dougie

Ferguson gave a terrible scream and toppled backwards down the stairs.

In the ensuing silence, Tony Wesley turned and looked sadly at Rosic. She stepped closer to him and croaked; "It's alright, Tony. I know you tried to help Martin. I know you did your best to prevent the hospital fire; it wasn't your fault. Now there's another place you have to be. Time to go in peace."

As she spoke, the hallway was suffused with warmth and light; she heard a gentle sigh, felt a soft breeze and he was gone. Her lips tried to form a prayer but she could only manage a broken "thank you," before her legs buckled and she slid to the floor.

After a few minutes she pulled herself upright, and crept to the top of the stairs. The light was on, and she could see Ferguson lying motionless on the basement floor. Pushing aside the thought that he might be only stunned, she walked haltingly down the stairs and touched him gently with the toe of her shoe. His eyes opened, and she recoiled in fear from the look of hatred on his face.

"Don't move. I'll call 911," she said, stepping onto the stairs. But she had no sooner turned away, than a dreadful gurgling made her swing around, and go back towards him. The man was clutching at his chest, his face blue, a thin trail of saliva running down the edge of his mouth. She recognised the signs of a massive heart attack and knew he was beyond human help.

Forcing herself to kneel down and take his hand, she leant towards him and said softly; "Dougie, you need to say you're sorry for everything you've done. Just nod your head." She watched anxiously for any sign that he had heard her. "Dougie," she whispered more urgently; "you're dying. You are sorry, aren't you? Just nod your head." For one brief instant, he seemed to relax. Then his lips formed the rictus of a grin, and she heard the faint reply; "Never sorry." His eyes stared up at her, the pupils fixed and dilated, and she knew he was dead.

Rosie stayed sitting on the bottom stair for a while, trying to gather her thoughts and decide what to do next. Finally, she got up and checked the dead man's pulse one last time, just to be sure. She had no fear that she would encounter his spirit; that had gone directly and permanently to a place from which there was no escape.

She knew she should call the police, but how could she explain what had happened? What could she say to prove that Ferguson was a serial killer and career arsonist? No one would ever believe that he had killed his father, Rick Edwards and Tony Wesley, and was planning to kill Rosie, Carol and his own mother. She would be pegged as crazy, and possibly held responsible for his death.

An idea began to take shape. Why not just go home, and feign ignorance when the inevitable police questions arose? Who was to say when he had fallen down the stairs? The row houses on either side were empty, so nobody would have heard the sounds of their desperate struggle. Mrs. Wesley was at the shop and Ferguson had come in the back way, so no one on Veterans Avenue would have seen him arrive. She made her decision; it was the only way.

She hurried up the stairs, found Tony's urn and ran to the front door. After several panicky tugs she remembered the top bolt was shot, and pulled it back. As an afterthought, she dragged her shirt off and used it to wipe the bolt clean of fingerprints. Just as she was leaving, she thought how odd the locked kitchen door might appear to a conscientious detective. Shit! The key had to be in Dougie's pocket.

Heart in mouth, she went down to the basement and, trying to ignore those staring eyes, wrapped a corner of her shirt around her fingers. His fingerprints had to stay on the key. She slipped her fingertips into his right pants pocket; first time lucky, thank God! Back to the kitchen she flew, inserted the key and turned it firmly. Now she was moving like an automaton, deliberately keeping her mind closed to the ghastly events of the past hour.

Taking a deep breath Rosie pulled her shirt back over her head, straightened it, and smoothed her hair as best she could. She picked up the urn, retrieved her purse from the hall floor and calmly opened the front door. It was important that she appear totally normal, in case anyone on the street later remembered seeing her leave. She unlocked her car, got in slowly and backed carefully out onto the Avenue.

Through sheer determination she made it all the way home, before the tears and shaking began in earnest.

Chapter 26 – Another Funeral

A-MEN. The last word of the closing hymn rang out with relieved finality, and a low murmur arose as people shuffled slowly from their pews, and down the central aisle of Knox Presbyterian Church. The only topic of conversation was the sudden and tragic passing of Douglas Ferguson; respected businessman, dedicated volunteer and devoted son. All had stood in respectful silence as Mrs. Ferguson made her stately exit, and now there was a general relaxation of tension as people felt free to express their shock and sadness.

The Cornish family contingent had taken seats in the back of the crowded church. There were four members present; John and Elspeth, (*we must go, John. I'm in and out of that bakery all the time, and he was such a lovely man*), a grim-faced Aunt Margaret holding tightly to her niece's arm, and Rosie herself, the soft silk scarf wrapped loosely around her neck a silent reminder of her final encounter with the deceased.

During the past ninety minutes, Rosie had methodically counted every light fixture, ceiling beam and pew in the austere old building. She had watched dust motes dancing in the sunlight, and pondered the length of time it might take to polish all the shining brass sanctuary fixtures and carpet rods.

In short, she had focused her attention on anything and everything that could distract her from the Memorial Service unfolding today before a packed house. Her mental distancing had been made easier by Aunt Marg's assurances that she would be nowhere in the vicinity of Ferguson's coffin. His mortal remains had been privately consigned to the family plot some days earlier.

Despite her repugnance at the thought of hearing a serial killer eulogised, Rosie had heeded her aunt's counsel that she be present. With almost the entire town in attendance, (even Lucy and her mom, she noted with a pang of irony) her absence would certainly be noted, and Rosie knew how important it was that she keep a low profile. She had the uncomfortable feeling that, despite Ferguson's death being officially attributed to cardiac arrest, the police were still suspicious of her story.

The day after Mrs. Ferguson had discovered her son's body, the police issued a routine call for information and witnesses. Good citizen Rosie responded immediately, advising them of her visit to 26 Veterans Avenue earlier on the day of the victim's death.

As expected, the entry of her name into the police data base brought up David's embezzlement and disappearance, and she was instantly flagged as a person of interest. In a heartbeat, her presence at the location of two sudden deaths went from unfortunate coincidence to suspicious activity. But, supported by Lucy's unwitting corroboration of both the purpose and time of her visit, Rosie had stuck doggedly to her version of events and, there being no evidence of foul play, the police file was soon closed.

It was now two weeks since Rosie's brush with death. Although the bruises around her throat had faded, her sleep was still tormented by nightmarish memories of her desperate struggle for life and the echoes of a murderer's gleeful laughter. Gussie had taken to sleeping at her back and, as yet, she had no inclination to banish his comforting presence to his regular spot at the end of the bed.

The first thing she did when she reached home that dreadful afternoon was pick him up and hold him tight. "I should have paid attention," she told him tearfully. "You knew something was going to happen, didn't you?" He had wagged his tail and licked her face, but her trauma was contagious, and it was an unusually subdued beagle that had curled up beside her on the living room couch.

The only bright spot that day was the unexpected arrival of Aunt Marg. Rosie had fallen asleep, too exhausted to even tend to her scratched face and bruised neck. She had forgotten to lock the front door, and was woken by her aunt's soft voice and gentle embrace.

Bit by bit, the whole ghastly tale was shared, then Margaret had covered her with a blanket and picked up the phone. Drifting in and out of sleep, Rosie had caught snatches of conversation; "So sorry, Father. Rosie's had a little accident... no, nothing too serious... just a fall in the garden. But she's very shaken, so I'm afraid she won't be singing this weekend." A pause, then; "Yes, of course I'll tell her, Father....."

"Hello Lucy? Rosie wanted me to call and let you know she found what you left at Veteran's Avenue... No, I'm sorry she can't come to the phone, she's taken a bit of a tumble in the garden... Yes, I'm sure she'll give you a call tomorrow..."

"Hello, John. It's Margaret....Could you come over right away? Rosie's had an accident. ..... No, it's not serious enough for that.... No, I really don't think a trip to the hospital's a good idea..."

Dr. Cornish made it across town in ten minutes, and one look at her brother's face had told Rosie all she needed to know about her appearance. After inspecting her arms, looking down her throat and probing the bump on her head, he sat down next to her on the couch and asked brusquely; "And where exactly in the garden did you take this header?"

She had blushed and mumbled; "The rose bed. I hit my head on the bird bath as I fell."

John sighed. "I see. Next you'll be telling me that while you were flat out among the roses, the ivy crept round your throat and tried to strangle you."

As Rosie's eyes filled with tears, Aunt Marg had said sharply; "John, stop badgering your sister. She's told you what happened. You know it's best if we just leave it at that." And that was the end of their conversation.

Now, sitting next to Rosie in the narrow pew, John reached over and took her hand. "How are you holding up, Bud?"

Rosie smiled at him gratefully. "I'm good. Every day gets easier. I'm sleeping better, too. Some nights I even manage without the pills..," her voice trailed off.

"That's good to hear. Just let me know if you need another prescription." He cleared his throat. "Ran into Andy McGillivray the other day. Apparently, Ferguson took *two* heart attacks; one that probably caused him to fall down the stairs and then a second that finished him off." He looked at her keenly. "He had absolutely no hope of survival, you know."

The Presbyterian Hymnal lay open in Rosie's lap, and she glanced down at Mrs. Ferguson's choice of closing hymn. *The day Thou gavest Lord is ended.* Today was the only occasion she had been inside a church and stayed silent the entire time. She closed the book firmly and dropped it into its place in the pew rack. "Probably just as well. I don't think Mrs. Ferguson's the nurturing type, do you?"

There were still mourners filling the centre aisle so, by unspoken agreement, the four of them stayed seated. John seemed to feel a need to talk; "Turns out he had quite the skeleton in his closet, too. Dave Mason did some research for the obituary and discovered he'd been dishonourably discharged from the military. Something about a fire and a couple of unexplained deaths on his army base."

Margaret glanced at Rosie, and said briskly; "Well, that's all finished now." She got to her feet and stepped into the aisle. "I don't know about you John, but I could do with a cup of tea. And not down in the church basement, either. I've had quite enough of funerals."

"Right, Aunt Marg." John stood up and, as Rosie moved to follow her aunt, he took her arm and said quietly; "*Is* it all finished, Bud?"

She smiled affectionately at her brother; he was far too astute not to have put most of the puzzle together. "Yes, it's over. If Elspeth ever asks, you can truthfully say the investigation into Tony Wesley's death is closed."

By the time Rosie and her family got to the church's heavy oak doors most of the crowd had dispersed. Some had gone to the basement for coffee and cookies but the rest were out on the sidewalk, shaking their heads and debating the future of The Wee Scottish Bakery.

John and Elspeth made their brief goodbyes and, as his wife embraced Aunt Marg, John gave Rosie a hug and murmured; "Andy was asking after you again." Seeing his sister roll her eyes, he chuckled. "You know, it would be a kindness to let him take you to dinner. He's a really nice guy." Moments later, he and El were hurrying back to their comfortable lives, eager to leave the morning's dreary proceedings behind them.

It was a beautiful summer day; sunny with a soft breeze and no humidity. Rosie and Margaret strolled arm in arm to the parking lot in an easy silence. Then, out of the blue, the old lady said; "So, no regrets?" Rosie understood her meaning at once.

"Absolutely not, Auntie. There was no proof of anything and, if I'd called the police, I'd probably be sitting in a jail cell right now." Instinctively, her hand went to the silk scarf around her neck. "And can you imagine what all those revelations would have done to Lucy, not to mention Mrs. Ferguson? I know she's nasty, but she doesn't deserve to have her last years blighted by that horrific tale. The shock would probably have killed her, and Dougie would have claimed another victim."

As they reached the car, she added; "And what about the town? People would've been devastated. They'd be wondering if it was safe to trust anyone, anymore."

Margaret turned and gave her niece a searching look. "You're right, of course. But knowing about that much evil is a heavy burden to carry."

With a smile, Rosie answered; "At least I'm not carrying it alone."

She unlocked the car, took her aunt's purse and helped her into the front passenger seat. Then, taking a deep breath, she said to herself firmly; 'C'mon girl; time to move on.'

"Where to, Auntie Marg? The Copper Kettle for tea, or back home for something stronger?"

Margaret winked. "I think you know the answer to that one, my dear," and, as Rosie turned the Buick toward Cedar Street she added; "Now, where have I heard that name before?"

Eyes on the road, Rosie asked; "Who are you talking about?"

Her aunt's tone was a study in innocence. "McGillivray? McGillivray? Oh right, *Doctor* McGillivray. Met him at the Country Club, you know. Dreadful golfer, but a really charming man."

Rosie laughed and said; "No match-making please, Auntie Marg."

Eyebrows almost into her hair line, Margaret huffed; "Match-making? Never crossed my mind."

Rosie looked unconvinced.

Undeterred, her aunt continued; "I was merely thinking how nice it would be to host a little dinner party. It's been far too long since I've entertained, and I owe invitations to scads of people." She glanced at her niece. "In my circle, men are in short supply, and I just thought Dr. McGillivray might make up the numbers. You'd be included, of course."

"Of course." Rosie's lips twitched. "Thank you, Auntie. I suppose I'd love to come."

Satisfied, her aunt lent back in her seat. "That's all settled then. It'll be something to look forward to. As soon as I get back to Goderich, I'll make some plans."

Oh well, look on the bright side, Rosie told herself. Aunt Margaret's dinner parties are marginally better than being trapped in a haunted house with a murderer.

57187606R10230

Made in the USA
Charleston, SC
06 June 2016